IT WAS SHELLY'S
FIRST CLERICAL COLLAR . . .

"Now, father," began Greeley as he rolled an arrest report into his typewriter, "I'll need some preliminary information before we get down to your statement."

"There's no need to write down *father,*" said the priest, a little edge creeping into his voice. "Charles Branigan will do. I'm with Saint Augustine's, near the Dairy Queen on Boston Road."

"Sister Margaret Mary Findlay of Our Lady of Regret," the nun announced to Lowenkopf. She was anxious to get on with her processing, keeping up with the priest.

Shelly made an encouraging noise. On the line under Charge he typed in *Receiving stolen merchandise. Value: $60,000?* It was his best guess—a little low, he suspected, but one that took into account wear and tear the vehicle would probably show to an experienced appraiser.

Sister Margaret, who had evidently been reading over his shoulder, tapped a finger on his estimate. "A Ferrari Testarossa? Try three times that amount. They broke all records last year and only made forty-two hundred of them."

Shelly blinked. "A hundred eighty thousand dollars? It's not even new anymore."

"They never decrease in value," she said reverentially . . .

Books by Richard Fliegel

The Art of Death
The Next to Die
The Organ-Grinder's Monkey
Time to Kill

Published by POCKET BOOKS

TIME TO KILL

RICHARD FLIEGEL

POCKET BOOKS

New York   London   Toronto   Sydney   Tokyo   Singapore

An *Original* Publication of POCKET BOOKS

 POCKET BOOKS, a division of Simon & Schuster Inc.
1230 Avenue of the Americas, New York, NY 10020

ISBN: 0-671-68850-2

First Pocket Books printing May 1990

10 9 8 7 6 5 4 3 2 1

POCKET and colophon are registered trademarks of Simon & Schuster Inc.

Printed in the U.S.A.

For Ben and Daniel

I am indebted to Detective Sergeant Tim Bauer of the Santa Monica Police Department for his generosity with time and information, as I am to John Kennedy, Eric Perez, Moira Sandrock, Nicole Castle, and Patty Sanchez.

TIME TO KILL

1

Whoever dreamed up the label "the temperate zone" for the latitudes between the tropics and the poles had never spent a summer in the Bronx, thought Detective Sergeant Shelly Lowenkopf, looking out from a double-parked Reliant at the wilting brick facades across Barker Avenue. There was nothing temperate about the density of foliage, with ailanthus sprouting through every crumbling nook, and oak, maple, sycamore and horse chestnut trees overgrowing the sidewalks, dropping twigs on the curbside cars. There was nothing temperate about the temperature, either, stuck around three digits again for the fourth day since the weekend. And nothing at all temperate about the humidity, which plastered his back to the driver's seat so that every few minutes Shelly had to sit forward, unpeeling himself with a hiss like cellophane pulled free from the roll.

The sound each time elicited a disapproving glance from his partner, Homer Greeley, whose shirt never clung to the plastic cushion or darkened beneath his armpits. Homer's neat blond head turned to face Shelly, lips pursed as if to frame a remark whose time had evidently come—though it never escaped his professional restraint. He rested a white linen elbow on the passenger door and stared past a Datsun, over a green wooden bench, through the links of a fence and into a city playground that filled most of the block in both directions below them.

The playground had been built in the thirties of rock and concrete, designed to accommodate generations of working-class neighborhood families. Its perimeter was enclosed by an eight-foot chain-link fence, gated in the middle of Barker and a parallel street on the far side of the block. In the center of the playground itself stood a brick house with green steel doors, from which basketballs and other equipment were reputedly dispensed at odd hours of the morning. South of the house were the handball courts, a single wall painted off into six courts with a stickball target in the center of each. In a rusty fence overhead, trapped Pinkies, Spauldings, and denuded tennis balls waited out the ages. North of the brick house was the basketball court, enclosed in a rectangle of black iron spears set upright in the concrete. Built into the base below the spears were sprinklers which on summer afternoons filled the court with airborne rainbows and young children squealing in their spray. The drain in the center usually clogged with leaves, flooding the court to ankle height, where the water was held by a small rise at the concrete's edge. Beyond the court were monkey bars and a seesaw, two sizes of swings and plenty of green wooden benches within earshot of the rides. Those same benches encircled the playground outside the fence, providing a place for elderly neighbors to gather, play cards, read newspapers, and enjoy the dappled shade.

Blocking the detectives' view.

"Is that him?" asked Shelly, squinting past his partner at a kid entering the basketball court.

Homer's thumb flickered toward a Hispanic male adolescent wearing an orange T-shirt over knee-length shorts. "That one? In the shorts?"

Shelly consulted the card from the gang file in the precinct house. "He's about the right age. What do you think?"

They were hoping to catch sight of Tomas Jefferson,

2

twelve years old, the last known person to have seen his cousin Felix Aguilar alive the night before. Word on the street was that Felix hustled crack for Cesar Catalan, but no one seemed to know Tomas. The two boys had stopped in a candy store on White Plains Road to buy a pack of Kools and a Three Musketeers bar around 9:15 P.M.—eight hours before Felix had been discovered, stuffed through a hoop on this basketball court with a .38 caliber bullet in his skull.

Homer shook his head. "Not unless he's grown fast."

"Teenagers do, Homer."

"A foot and a half since yesterday?"

The kid in the orange T-shirt received a bounce pass and went for a jump shot . . . missed. Shelly grunted. "Okay. So what about that one, then—on the handball court."

"With the mustache?"

Shelly tilted his eyeglasses closer to his eyes. "I thought it was the shadow of his nose."

Homer paused deliberately, trying to see the mustache as a shadow. He shook his head. "He's not going to appear, Shell, just when we want him to."

"He's not going to appear at all," said Lowenkopf, settling back behind the wheel. "We might as well paint a sign on the trunk that reads Cops Waiting. Do you think there's anybody on the block who still hasn't noticed we're here?"

"Maybe not," said Greeley agreeably, surveying the elderly bench warmers, who assiduously avoided his gaze. "But these kids spend half their lives in there. And he'll want to see the spot they found his buddy. He'll show."

Lowenkopf didn't believe that the perpetrator inevitably returned to the scene of the crime. "Only if he's not involved, Homer. And then what good will he do us?"

Greeley showed no sign of despair, returning to his window with a shrug that meant, *why don't we wait and see?* From the contentment in his crinkled brow, Shelly knew he was enjoying the stakeout—the cramped car, boring vigil, hours of unblinking watchfulness. The art of detective work, Homer liked to call it. Shelly preferred talking to people, anywhere, any time. He couldn't shake the feeling they were killing time, which made him even more restless. He sat up stiffly, stretching his back, unpeeled his shirt from the seat cushion, and looked for a reason to gun the gas.

Out of nowhere, it came: a sudden flash of red, low to the ground, crackling through the intersection at the corner of Barker like a jagged gash in the traffic, wounding the asphalt. Homer saw it too, watching with a flicker of dismay in his clear green eyes as it sliced through his plans for an afternoon of surveillance.

"What was that?"

"Our ticket out of here," said Shelly, cranking the engine. He slid the gear shift into drive with his right hand while his left clamped a bubble to the roof of the Reliant. It glared for a few seconds, doleful and silent, until the siren wailed in support. "And aw-a-a-a-ay we go!"

The Reliant kicked up a few brown leaves as it rounded the corner, tearing after the sports car. They saw it ahead, slowing but not stopping, finally running the light—a low-slung Ferrari Testarossa, its sides raked as if it had fought off a clawed beast. The patented Ferrari red paint gleamed like fresh blood in the humid air as its three-hundred-cubic-inch V-12 engine purred through the rocky gates of the park and scaled the ramp of the Bronx River Parkway.

They rumbled after it, their six cylinders chugging after its forty-eight humming valves. The blue Plymouth squealed through the intersection, siren singing, and bounced up the ramp after the smooth Italian, northbound on the parkway. The Ferrari was nowhere in sight, but a faint scent of rubber still hung in the air, in and out of the lanes. Lowenkopf and Greeley followed, their siren forcing open spaces the sports car had slipped through, leaving only a tire burn to mark its passing. The police car made its way in a cacophony of ringing horns. Shelly waved his arms at irritated motorists; Homer stared grimly through the windshield as they scattered the two o'clock traffic, tracking the new Pirellis.

At last they caught sight of it ahead, slowing to accommodate an accident in the roadway. Greeley called in the license plate as Lowenkopf closed in, cutting across two lanes coagulating upon approach to the scene of misfortune. A great misfortune it was, at that: a smart silver torpedo car lay crunched before the iron fender of a Lincoln Continental, whose grille grinned foolishly at the import. Shelly saw a marked police car, its bubble blinking silently. There were standing figures and others, reclining on blankets which were darkly stained and wrapped in forbidding shapes. To his right, an ambulance struggled through the lines of traffic tangling at the scene; to his left, the red Ferrari crept onto the greensward in the center of the parkway, crawling toward the blankets on the grass.

The frieze seemed interminable, their progress incremental. The rotating bubble atop the Reliant was not helping matters: drivers edging out of their way were complicating access for the ambulance. Shelly cut their siren, shut off their bubble, and pulled it back into the Plymouth. Then, lane by lane, he crossed to the left, one eye on the ambulance, the other on the Ferrari. The bluecoats seemed to be taking control, clearing a lane for the paramedics. But what was the sports car after?

It had, at any rate, finally come to a stop. The Reliant rolled up behind it, a few feet from the bodies in the grass. Lowenkopf cut the engine and got out, just as the passenger did from the red Ferrari, a heavy-set man in a black suit with a crisp, white collar, and a bald spot spreading through his thin crown of hair. The man did not look back but moved deliberately toward the officers in charge. Shelly watched him tap a blue shoulder and then turned his own attention to the driver of the vehicle, who reached out from behind the wheel of the Ferrari to adjust the side-view mirror. There was a glimpse of black and white which Lowenkopf did not understand until he stood beside the sleek red door and found himself looking down at a white coif beneath a black veil—the unmistakable head wear of a nun.

A pair of bright blue eyes met his, in a face that could not have been less than fifty but was animated like a leprechaun. "Can-a I help you, officer?"

It took him a moment to recover the high moral ground.

Richard Fliegel

"That was a good head of steam you worked up, Sister. You always drive like that?"

"Only when there's need," she said, lowering her eyes. He couldn't help noticing that her brogue had disappeared at the sound of his own second-generation Jewish-American dialect.

"I hope there was somebody's life at stake."

"More than that," said the nun.

Lowenkopf raised his eyebrows. "More?"

"If you'll let me open this door," she said, "I'll show you just what I mean."

A violation of normal procedure, but hardly a normal perp. Lowenkopf stepped back and swung the heavy door open for her. She climbed out nimbly, patting the fender alongside the hood as if it were the nape of a nag.

"You know what's inside there?" she said with good cheer. "A V-12 engine with double carburetor, that can do 180 miles an hour, zero to sixty in 5.6 seconds. I'll wager you don't chase one of these babies every day. Couldn't have caught us, either, if we hadn't had to stop."

Beside her head wear, she was dressed in civilian clothes—a polyester dress in a flowery print—and a cross around her neck. Her shoes were flat, serviceable; her attitude, buoyant with none of the humility speeders usually showed police officers.

"I thought you weren't allowed to wager."

"Oh, well." The sister shrugged. "No stake, of course. Just an appreciation, you might say, of the Lord's handiwork. The whole of creation is His design and this is a mighty fine piece of engineering."

"You were going to show me something?"

"You want me to do tricks, first? Walk a straight line or something?"

"I hope that isn't necessary. You haven't been nipping the sacramental wine, have you?"

"No," she said thoughtfully, "but I wouldn't want my vocation to interfere with the due process of law. We're very big on law, in my order."

"I'll take your word on the alcohol, then. You don't look

6

drunk to me. But didn't you say there was something more important than a life . . . ?"

"Of course," she said, dropping her voice, chastising him or herself. "Our unhappy responsibility here today. Follow me, please."

She led him along the grass divider, picking a path through twisted bumpers, charred parts, smoking scraps of rubber and steel, to a cluster of solemn people kneeling among woolen blankets. The ambulance had backed up to the spot and stood with its bay doors wide, while a moaning bundle in a soiled white sheath was rolled in on a gurney. One of the paramedics was already at the wheel, starting to pull away, when the second hoisted himself into the back after the patient and closed the doors behind them. As the ambulance, siren rising in volume and pitch, bounced over the divider and entered traffic on the other side, Shelly noticed the heavy-set man in the black suit squatting over a second soiled bundle the paramedics had left behind.

He seemed to be talking, gesticulating with his hands, and for a moment Shelly thought the person on the ground must be all right. Then the man rose from his crouch, turning his head as the sister's geriatric shoes trod the ground behind him. Shelly saw the square recess in the middle of his white collar and knew that the person bundled on the ground was in fact beyond the ministrations of medicine.

The priest covered the dead man's face with a corner of white sheet and sighed, wiping his hands on a soft white handkerchief which he stuffed back into his trouser pocket. In the left outside pocket of his jacket was a Bible, with red-leaf pages and a worn leather cover. When his hands were clean, he took it out and held it in his left hand as he offered his right to Lowenkopf.

"Hello, officer. Sister Margaret, I suspect, has explained our haste to you. You are, I take it, the policeman who followed us so ably down the highway?"

"She hasn't quite explained anything yet," replied Shelly, accepting the man's dry palm with some trepidation. "She did, however, insist that yours was a mission of the utmost urgency. More important, she said, than saving a life."

7

"Quite right," agreed the priest. "A life is an ephemeral thing, passing in a moment of inattention. We were concerned with a soul. Which is safe now, for eternity, thanks to the good sister's driving skills."

Sister Margaret glanced down, blushing, then looked up at Lowenkopf, vindicated.

"How's that?" asked Lowenkopf.

"The Sacrament of the Sick," the priest explained. "Essential to the salvation of a Catholic. We used to call it 'last rites' before Vatican II. Sort of a passport through the pearly gates, which has to be delivered before the actual demise. Should we have let his soul pass unsanctified to the other side?"

Lowenkopf said, "I really don't know, father . . ."

The priest offered his dry handshake yet again. "Charles. Branigan. With Saint Augustine's on Boston Road, near the Dairy Queen. Your captain knew my bishop in Vietnam."

Shelly saw no alternative but to shake the father's dry hand again. "Small world. You were, however, breaking the law, in speeding here like that."

Father Charles offered up his wrists. "If you feel the need to arrest us, by all means, officer. The law is the law—we respect that. But the sister and I also answer to a higher law, which must, I'm afraid, come first. Take us away, if you feel you should."

Shelly was tiring quickly of the agreeable, self-sacrificial outlook these people took to his duties. "I don't think we'll need handcuffs, Father Charles," he said, glancing at a uniformed officer—O'Connor—who approached then, listening to their discussion.

Father Charles turned to O'Connor. "Would you mind letting the diocese know we've been arrested? By Sergeant . . . ?"

"Lowenkopf," said Shelly.

"Lowenkopf," repeated O'Connor, jotting the name in pencil on his note pad.

"Now just a second here," said Shelly, looking from the sister's innocent expectancy, to the father's benign composure, to the grimace of unpleasantness on the features of

O'Connor. "Nobody's said anything about arrests except you, Father Charles. There are extenuating circumstances here which might have bearing on the disposition of this thing. Now—you're not planning on speeding again, are you?"

"Except in a similar case," said the priest with relentless honesty. "If another poor soul needs the Sacrament before he expires, Sister Margaret will have to bring a priest just as quickly."

"Imagine what those pistons could do on an empty roadway," she said.

"It's a holy obligation," Father Charles explained. "Like chastity, obedience, or poverty. Part of her vows."

O'Connor cleared his throat. "Can't hardly blame a sister for that, sarge," he said.

Lowenkopf was trapped—he knew what the captain would say when he entered the precinct house with a priest and nun in tow. He could hear the captain's telephone ring with calls from the diocese, from the archbishop, from the chief. There would be no happy end to this collar, no matter how it went. Indictment? Conviction? He shuddered at the idea—taking the oath, his hand on the book, while a D.A. swore him in and asked him damning questions. They'd never prosecute the case . . . would they?

And here were Father Charles and Sister Margaret, honestly promising to break the law the next time a Catholic lay dying. Lowenkopf looked up in desperation and saw the lean figure of his partner advancing over the greensward, the crease in his linen trousers miraculously sharp so late in the day. Between them they could muster the sternness to elicit a little contrition and cut these lawbreakers loose on the streets.

"Homer," he began, "I'm thinking of releasing these people with a warning. Do you have a problem with that?"

Greeley shook his head but not in answer to the verbalized question. By the steel in his partner's eyes Lowenkopf knew they did indeed have a problem.

"What is it?"

"The car," said Homer curtly. Producing cuffs from the

back of his belt, he snapped them on Father Charles and nodded for Shelly to do the same with Sister Margaret.

"The Ferrari?"

"Stolen, I'm afraid."

Lowenkopf watched as his partner stoically read the suspects their rights, confiscated the Ferrari's keys, and led them under O'Connor's baleful glare to the back seat of the waiting Reliant. They could have let the uniform take it from there, but Homer kept the collar as something to show the captain in justification for breaking their surveillance of the playground. Shelly passed a hand through his own wiry hair and rubbed the tired eyes under his wire-rimmed glasses. On the grass divider before him, the red Ferrari seemed to undulate in the heat as if its tires were still smoking. Where exactly had they gone wrong? He couldn't shake the suspicion that Tomas Jefferson was even then jumping for a rebound on the concrete basketball court where Felix Aguilar had been murdered.

2

Captain Madagascar was waiting at their desks when Lowenkopf and Greeley arrived at the squad room with Father Charles and Sister Margaret in cuffs. He sat like a stone idol on the corner of Homer's desk, his square head set on a bull neck, his small mustache twitching. His brown suit, made of stiff, thick cotton, seem to stand on its own a few inches over his neck and shoulders as if animated by a spirit that had passed from his granite limbs.

"Your wife's been calling," he said sourly, handing Shelly a crumpled message slip. "You twice, then me. Something about your son and a life of crime."

Shelly pocketed the slip without reading it. "Sorry, sir. Ruth keeps closer tabs on me now than she did when we were married."

"Keep her off my private line, at least, will you? I can't imagine how she got that number."

Lowenkopf didn't get a chance to apologize again before Sister Margaret raised an eyebrow. "Divorced?"

"For better or worse."

Madagascar dropped his foot from the chair next to Homer's desk, clearing a seat for Father Charles. Shelly

11

drew up a similar chair for Sister Margaret, then fell into his own swivel's rusty springs. The others sat without comment, the detectives and captain exchanging nods, the prisoners looking simultaneously disgraced and defiant. The nun was also curious.

"Children?"

"One. A boy."

"Any chance of a reconciliation?"

Shelly shook his head. "Till death do us part."

"That's not what that means."

"I know," he explained. "She didn't."

"Too bad," the sister said.

Madagascar scowled at the interview.

"Now, father," began Greeley as he rolled an arrest report into his typewriter, "I'll need some preliminary information before we get down to your statement."

"There's no need to write down *father,*" said the priest, a little edge creeping into his voice. "Charles Branigan will do. I'm with Saint Augustine's, near the Dairy Queen on Boston Road."

"I knew your bishop in Saigon," the captain said. "He used to bless each body bag loaded on the plane. Good man."

"We think so," said Branigan.

"Sister Margaret Mary Findlay of Our Lady of Regret," the nun announced. She was anxious to get on with her processing, keeping up with the priest.

Lowenkopf had not quite finished feeding the form into his typewriter, since the paper release would not unrelease and the carriage refused to grip. The nun watched him struggle and nearly reached over to adjust the machine. To fend her off, he said, "By the park, right? You have a hospital down there, or something."

"A hospice," she corrected. "A home for the dying. And also a school. We're mostly a teaching order, out of New Jersey. Some nursing here and there, but we usually stick close to the classroom. Father Charles is leading a class for us, as part of our court-referred after-school program. He's been very good with the boys, trying to reach children who have nowhere left to go but the reformatory."

Lowenkopf had heard of their creative child class when a judge had remanded a perfectly good collar to their benevolence instead of to the Hall where he belonged. "I hope you keep a close eye on the crosses, with that lot."

"We've never had a theft at the convent," the nun said proudly. "Nor any sort of crime—before this."

She bit her lip.

Madagascar gave the detective a dirty look. "We'll have you out of here in no time, sister—won't we, sergeant? Saving souls or whatever you good people do."

Shelly made an encouraging noise and typed in the line under Charge: *Receiving stolen merchandise. Value: $60,000?* It was his best guess—a little low, he suspected, but one that took into account the wear and tear the vehicle would probably have shown to an experienced appraiser.

Sister Margaret, who had evidently been reading over his shoulder, tapped a finger on his estimate. "A Testarossa? Try three times that amount. They broke all records last year and only made forty-two hundred of them."

Shelly blinked. "A hundred eighty thousand dollars? It's not even new anymore."

"They never decrease in value," she said reverentially. "Not to the true enthusiast, and that's most of their market. I'll bet you couldn't touch a dented one for less than a hundred fifty." Then, misinterpreting his frown, she grumbled, "I know—we're not supposed to bet."

The phone rang in Madagascar's glass-paneled office and he regarded it painfully. "Probably your wife again. Or the bishop. Wondering about the state of our souls. What should I tell His Excellency, Lowenkopf?"

"I wouldn't know, sir. I'm Jewish."

"That should make him feel a whole lot better. About cops of your faith in particular."

As the captain dragged himself toward the ringing telephone, Sister Margaret turned a shrewd eye on Shelly. "It's not your fault we're here, Sergeant Lowenkopf. That guilt is

13

mine alone. I've oftentimes heard the warning, 'Be careful what you pray for; you just might get it.' "

"You prayed for . . . a Ferrari?"

"I never would have presumed so much! I prayed for a car. Our Rambler was finally breaking down: the transmission, brakes, and front end were all slipping, but still we kept her rolling. Then the valves went. I can't really overhaul an engine myself, yet. God willing, that will come. But there was nothing I could do, you see, in a material way. So I prayed for a replacement—a car, any car, while the Rambler wheezed and shuddered."

"And you got one?"

She lowered her eyes in shame. "No. My prayers were not answered—probably because of the avarice in my heart. You have sensed it yourself. I was hoping for something like this, with Alpine stereo, seventy watts—for listening to Handel's *Messiah*. Each morning after Matins, I would check the street outside our house, hoping for a sign. It never came to me."

"Until . . ."

"We lost a ball joint. That was that—our Rambling days were done. In desperation, I asked Sister Elizabeth, the holiest of our company, to join me in prayer. She was showing some of the boys how to clean the chalk erasers, banging them against the side of the school building. She gave me such a loving smile, I knew that our prayers would be answered. The next morning was Sunday, and Father Charles came by as usual to perform the Mass. Afterwards, in the collection plate, lay a beautiful, shining key. And parked in front of the convent was the car."

Lowenkopf nodded, sharing her amazement. "A hundred eighty thousand on wheels."

"I never thought of selling it," the sister insisted, "whatever its monetary value. Forget about its advantages: its 380 horsepower at 5,750 rpm, with 1,000 rpm to spare before it hits the red line. That car was a gift from Heaven. Do you think we would sell a Gutenberg, if we had one?"

"You prayed for transportation, didn't you? You could've

bought a Porsche with a hundred thousand dollars to spare for the sick."

"If that's what He had wanted, we would have found a Porsche on our doorstep with a hundred thousand dollars on the dashboard. Besides, we didn't have the paperwork we'd need to sell a car—no registration card in the glove compartment."

Lowenkopf saw a chink in her theology.

"And that never made you doubt that the gift might not have come from . . . ?"

"It came from God," Sister Margaret repeated. "We prayed for it, and our prayers were answered. It counted as a miracle, as far as I could see, and as for doubts—you must understand, Sergeant Lowenkopf, that we are a community organized for faith. We have seen the dead rise again. Compared to that, what is a Ferrari, after all?"

It was hard to argue with a deeply held conviction, and the sister's sincerity left no doubt. He imagined the car as it must have seemed to her: an affirmation of divine love and everything she believed.

"So you felt sure you knew where it came from with no reason to wonder," he concluded, summarizing her statement for the arrest report. "No cause to suspect it might have been obtained by any illegal means."

"None," she vowed. "Our order does not look gift horses in the mouth, or donated Testarossas in the engine block. To us, innocence is an article of faith. 'Ignorance,' some may call it. We prefer to err repeatedly in believing untrustworthy souls than to err once in suspecting an honest one."

Shelly imagined how his own workday might go if he adopted a similar approach. "You must face a lot of disappointment."

"The loss is not mine alone, sergeant. Our Lord suffers for each one lost—and rejoices in each deliverance. What is my disappointment compared to His? In my vocation, one's faith is often tested. There are harder things to believe in than the Providence of a Ferrari."

Through the glass of the captain's office, Lowenkopf could

see Madagascar hang up the phone, adjust his seat cushion, and gaze out on the prisoners in his custody. When his eyes met Shelly's, he wiggled two fingers, gesturing for the detective to join him. Shelly stood, tapped his partner on the shoulder, and tilted his head toward Madagascar. Greeley cranked the report from his typewriter's carriage and set it down neatly on his blotter. The two detectives glanced at the stairs to the holding cells, at Branigan and Findlay, and exchanged a silent debate.

"Excuse us," said Shelly to the prisoners, pulling Homer by the sleeve to the captain's office.

The office inside was five degrees warmer than the outer room—Shelly never understood why. Madagascar sat writing behind a dark wooden desk that seemed to have grown right out of the floorboards. There were trays with hand-printed labels on his desk, always empty. In front of those were stacks of paper the captain piled and repiled. He couldn't bear to have the incoming sheets confuse his sorting system, though they never quite fit the neat labels. No personal items on display—family photos, paper-weights, or even an ashtray—though the wall behind him was hung with picture frames in various sizes, bearing citations, his military discharge, and a faded postcard of downtown Saigon.

Shelly fought an impulse to salute. "Captain?"

"Sit down," said Madagascar, to his desk.

The two detectives sat, in hard wooden chairs beneath the panes. Homer crossed his legs, picking a nit from the argyle ankle of his sock. From his inside jacket pocket he produced a silver pen and a note pad, which he propped on his knee.

Shelly lifted a Bic from a Styrofoam cup on the captain's desk, discovered he had no note pad, and replaced the capless pen where he found it.

The captain watched him do so with interest. When Shelly looked up, Madagascar said, "The community is of course grateful to you both for your fine work in keeping our streets safe from the clergy. The bishop expressed his opinion before you actually reached the precinct house; that was the cardinal, just now, following up, he said, on a talk with the mayor. Before I have to take a call from the pope, do you mind telling me why you busted a priest and a nun?"

Homer ran down the events of the afternoon with something like professional detachment. He could see that Madagascar was not appreciating the determination of their investigation, so he kept the story brief—a stolen car whizzing by, an embarrassing discovery.

"In other words," said the captain, "possession of a vehicle they didn't know was stolen. Cut 'em loose."

The two detectives hesitated. Lowenkopf cleared his throat. "We'd like to do that, sir. But there is a complaint."

"Who's complaining?"

"Whoever owns the Ferrari. He filed a report."

"When?"

"When the car was stolen."

"Does he know it's been recovered?"

"Not from us," Shelly said.

"Wouldn't you guess," the captain asked, "that information might please him?"

"It might," said Shelly, trying unsuccessfully to guess where this was leading.

The captain looked from one to the other.

Homer said, "It should."

"Now," said Madagascar, "we're making progress here. What we need to free Sister Bonnie and Father Clyde is the injured party's agreement not to prosecute. Do you know who the car was stolen from?"

They had learned about the theft report over the radio and hadn't thought to ask the complainant's name.

"Don't you think it's time you read the thing yourselves? Found the owner? And talked him into dropping charges on these people? So you could get them the hell out of my squad room? They make me nervous just sitting there."

Shelly glanced through the glass to the desks where they had left Branigan and Findlay meekly awaiting judgment on their transgression. His heart sank.

"Samuels has the report," Homer said.

"Bless you," said Madagascar. "Get those charges dropped. Then drive them down to their churches or

17

wherever they hang out, and give my regrets to the bishop. You think you can handle all that?"

"Yes, sir," said Homer, already on his feet. He was ready to make a break for it—that much was clear. He looked at the threshold of the office door as if gauging the running time it would take him to cross it.

"There's just one thing, captain," Shelly mumbled from his chair. If Madagascar was expecting an immediate release, his expectation would be frustrated. It had to be said; Shelly just couldn't figure out why it was always he who had to say it.

"What?" The captain glowered.

He pointed to the empty seats where Branigan and Findlay had waited out their fate.

"Our guests have been taken for pictures and prints."

3

They managed to interrupt the processing at the fingerprint desk. Sister Margaret waved a blackened hand and
Father Charles grimaced as his fingers were rolled on the ink
pad. Lowenkopf offered his own handkerchief to the priest,
mumbled regrets, and led the two to a squad car for a ride to
their separate places of residence and worship. He hoped
the case could be resolved without taking either one of them
back into custody. They were sure he could manage it. How
could they be so sure? They had faith in him, they said.

The next test followed quickly. No sooner had Homer
secured a copy of the theft report on the Ferrari from Officer
Samuels than Shelly discovered on the complainant's line
the signature of Cesar Catalan—a name that cast a pall on
their hopes for a speedy release.

Catalan was not, Lowenkopf felt sure, the man who
actually introduced crack to the Bronx, but he was certainly
one of the first to realize the market potential in converting
cocaine from an acid to a base which could be dissolved in
water or ignited by a match. Like any good businessman, he
had moved aggressively to shore up his territory, undermine
his competition, and promote a strong demand for his

merchandise. In two years he had grown from a street vendor of expensive powder to an executive with a persuasive sales force who serviced an extensive market of retail consumers. Those consumers went to considerable lengths, making extravagant demonstrations of product loyalty, in order to continue purchasing his goods. In a few short years, Cesar Catalan had realized the American dream, raising himself by his own initiative from a small-scale dealer in human despair to a major distributor of suffering and death.

They had never managed to pin on Catalan any charge more serious than possession, and that long before his business prospered. Their odds of a sturdy conviction were considerably longer now. For one thing, Catalan kept out of the retail end of his trade. His sales forces were supplied by a middle manager in whom he had reason to trust—Jimmy Twotoes—a man who understood that silent acceptance of a prison sentence would be better for him in the long run than the riskier course of talking about who had sold what to whom.

As result, Catalan was vulnerable only on the supply side, but there too he managed to keep himself at some remove. His sources were mysterious, even to the omniscient street: when the Colombians were busted, or the Haitians, or the Panamanians, his supply arrived unhindered, increased in rarity and value. It was rumored that he had his own plane, and his own team of smugglers, but no one had ever admitted a role in supplying him cocaine. The only certain truths were these: he had the source he needed; his organization thrived; no evidence had ever linked him to the industry that made him rich.

Lowenkopf and Greeley knew this much about the man who had signed a complaint reporting the theft of his Ferrari. Rather than explain this to Father Charles and Sister Margaret when the clerics were brought as prisoners to the precinct house again, Shelly and Homer decided to pay a visit to the drug profiteer and see what milk of human kindness they could squeeze out of him.

The home address on Catalan's theft report was in the

same borough, but another world—a duplex in the northern part of Riverdale, overlooking the Hudson River. A uniformed doorman under a long green awning accompanied them to a reception desk, where a woman in a gauzy dress called up on the house phone to announce the two detectives. While she dialed Catalan's extension, the doorman stationed himself between them and the elevators, ready to block access should the need arise. Lowenkopf considered the bulges under his epaulets, which hadn't grown so muscular opening doors, and wondered about the man's prior occupation. He and Greeley might have overpowered the doorman, or drawn their weapons, but could not have reached the thirteenth floor before a warning call.

The woman asked their names, which she murmured into the phone, then said, "Please go up," replacing the receiver in its plastic cradle with a crisp, impersonal smile.

Homer nodded, smiling back, while Shelly moved to the call button. The doorman reached it first, pushing Up, which lit, while the indicator showed an ascent from the seventh floor. The second car was stuck on thirteen; Shelly pushed the button again, which made no difference whatsoever. The three of them waited together until the doors on the right parted with a gentle *ding* and a whisper of rubber on steel. Homer caught the return and held the car for his partner. The doorman waited until they had both entered, and the doors had started to close, before moving back toward his post under the awning.

The thirteenth floor housed six units and a vast expanse of carpet between entrances. Catalan's was in the southwest corner, a lone door with no peephole but a fisheye mirror angled overhead and a discreet lens embedded in the wall behind them. Lowenkopf stared directly at the mirror and issued into the camera what he hoped was a stern command. "Open up, Catalan. Police."

"No need to shout, Sergeant Lowenkopf," replied a dark, slender woman, who opened the oak door between them. There was no undoing of multiple locks, no scramble to close open drawers, no sign of apprehension in her demeanor. There was no sign of Catalan, either, in the large, airy room, when the woman invited them in with a crook of her wrist.

She was about twenty-two, Spanish or Mediterranean, with delicate features and enormous, warm brown eyes, which washed over the two men like a wave. Her hair was pulled back at her temples but fell loose behind her ears, where it curled, richly black, to her shoulders. Her throat was set off by a fine gold chain and a cross with a tiny pearl. She wore a two-piece suit by Chanel, no collar but pearl buttons, and a watch marked off with coral, banded in bleached eelskin, clasped in gold. She stood shoeless in expensive hose, sinking her toes in the carpet, at once vulnerable, endearing, and smart.

"You are welcome here," she said, floating into a couch of quilted brocade.

Shelly felt welcome. The light from a bank of windows on the far wall filtered into the room, softening the corners of tables, a desk, and chairs. He would have liked to sit beside her on the overstuffed couch, but opted instead for a straight-back chair upholstered in creamy velvet. As he settled on the deep, soft nap, he glanced at his hands, suddenly aware of the black dirt at his fingernails. His shoes, too, seemed thick and crude on the intricate green swirls of the carpet. He stood, moving to the windows, which looked out over the Hudson, where a tugboat tugged a barge toward the George Washington Bridge. The sun was sinking toward the horizon; the river ran with gold. He turned his back on the shimmering scene, blinking.

"Is he home?"

She smiled. "Wouldn't you be?"

Homer had managed a better hold on his envy. "We wouldn't be in his business, ma'am. Why don't you see if he'll join us, if you don't mind?"

"There is no need for that," said Catalan, emerging from an archway that led to another vista. The crack dealer was in his late forties, shorter than Shelly but built like a bull in his upper arms and torso. He wore a white suit in some fabric that made Homer's linen sleeves look rough and creased.

TIME TO KILL

His tie was silk, pale sky blue; his cuff links, white gold crescents. His shoes looked supple and comfortable as an old pair of slippers. This was no cheap hood, Shelly observed, but a tasteful, expensive hood.

"I am with you already—isn't that so?"

"Apparently," said Homer, glancing toward Shelly, who did most of the talking for them most of the time.

Lowenkopf stepped forward into the room, edging out of the river's afternoon glow. "We are here to discuss a case with you, Mr. Catalan."

"A case?" said the crack man. "What do you want to know? Surely there's nothing I can tell you."

He was obviously expecting to be questioned about some job his people had done; Shelly decided on a direct appeal, counting on the element of surprise.

"We're here about your car," he said.

"My car?" It took him a moment to think which one they meant. When he remembered, he seemed to feel he understood the reason for their visit. "The Ferrari? It's been stolen from me . . . three days ago. I filed the relevant reports. Any crimes committed in that vehicle are no longer my responsibility."

"That's not why we're here," Shelly said, allowing a beat to elapse before explaining, "we found it."

"You found what?"

"The car—the stolen Ferrari. We recovered it. Sometimes we do things like that, you know."

Catalan laughed, a deep, rumbling gurgle. "And this is why you're here tonight? To return my Testarossa?"

"Not quite," said Shelly uneasily. "That'll happen later. You know the procedure: tagging evidence, holding it for trial, continuance after continuance. It could take some time before it's actually returned to you."

The woman released her breath with an audible sigh.

"I can wait," said Catalan. He seemed troubled by her display. "I have another car to drive. I replaced the stolen one the following morning."

"I'm glad we haven't inconvenienced you," said Lowenkopf, trying to remain polite as he worked the conversation around to Father Charles and Sister Margaret. But before he could make much of Catalan's good fortune, the drug dealer put two and two together on his own.

"You have . . . a case against someone? A suspect in the theft? I would like to know who took the auto from me."

"Not a suspect for the robbery," said Shelly with care. "All we have are some people caught, after the fact, in unfortunate possession of merchandise they didn't suspect had been stolen."

Catalan covered his mouth with his palm, thinking. "Do you mean to say that somebody accepted my Testarossa from the thieves without wondering where it had come from?"

"Yes," replied Shelly.

"Who?"

"A nun in a convent," Shelly said carefully. "She hasn't seen much of the world, and, uh . . . thought the car came from God."

"She's right," said Catalan with a dry smile. "They must. You should drive one sometime."

Lowenkopf nodded, acknowledging the humor. The effort of acting pleasant was taking its toll on him. Or it may have been the strain of watching Catalan stroke the hair of the woman who graced his couch. Something about the two of them sitting on the sofa made it hard to despise the slimeball, minute to minute. They seemed such a nice couple, posed for a family photo, side by side—though no word of affection actually passed between them. Shelly had to remind himself how the man made his living.

The woman rose to her feet, preparing to withdraw. "Can I bring you gentlemen something? Whiskey and soda?"

Homer shook his head. "We've got to be moving along. We're on duty, with other things to do."

She held up a slim palm, forestalling the need for excuses. "I perfectly understand."

"That's why," Shelly said to Catalan after the three men watched her leave the room, "the best thing all around would be for you to drop the charges against them."

"Them? Who else with the nun?"

"A priest was sitting beside her when we stopped the car on the parkway."

"So—" said Catalan slowly, "the picture is like this. You have a priest and nun in custody for this crime. If I drop my charges, you can release them. That is what you have come here to ask me to do."

"We knew you'd want the car back as quickly as possible. As for the two spirituals . . ." He let his voice trail. "What point was there in holding them?"

"You've released them already?" Catalan inquired.

"Yes."

"Well, then," he said, "perhaps you'd better pick them up again. Forgive me, but I have no intention of dropping charges against anybody. No one has ever been asked to drop charges against me. You are public servants, eh? I am a private citizen. Call me, please, when you have these criminals behind bars."

"I don't think it should come to that."

"But that is not your decision to make, Sergeant Lowenkopf. It is my decision whether to press charges, and the court's decision whether to indict. A judge can set their bail on this, and a jury can release them. For now, I want those people in your holding cell, where they can't accept anyone else's Ferrari as the bounty of their Lord."

Shelly decided it was possible to dislike the man after all, with no mental effort, and switched to a different mode of attack. "Let me put this another way for you, Catalan," he said. "My captain would like to see those charges dropped. He can be a difficult man to someone doing business in his precinct. If you refuse to drop charges, he will take it as a personal affront. Then you will have an offended police captain poking his nose in your business."

Catalan laughed. "And if I do drop the charges, what then? Will your captain allow me to go about my business unhindered? Or will he bust me just as quickly, if he gets a chance, whether or not I accuse his nun of a felony?"

"He might."

"But no promises, eh? So that is my decision. Very well. Pick up the nun, and her accomplice, too—the priest in the passenger seat. We'll see justice done in the Bronx, this once, at least."

It was the last Catalan had to say about it, his final word on the matter. The woman, too, reentering the room, seemed to have shut off like a neon sign gone cold, her warm vulnerability a memory difficult to fix on the mannequin before them. Shelly and Homer managed to find their way out of the apartment without exchanging a word until they had cleared the camera over the front door and rung for the elevator.

"The captain won't like this," Homer said.

"I don't like it much myself," agreed Shelly. But what was there to do? A complaint stood, unwithdrawn—they had caught the suspects in the act, driving the stolen vehicle. It was hard to frame an excuse to forestall the nun's arrest. The elevator came and they entered it in silence.

"We could find the ones who did it," Homer mused as the tiny silver car dropped twelve stories.

"Did what?" said Shelly, holding his stomach.

"Stole the Testarossa," Homer explained. "If we busted the thieves who actually took the car, they should be enough to cover the complaint, wouldn't you say?"

Shelly remembered Catalan's interest in the crook who took his car. "That would satisfy the asshole upstairs."

The elevator landed with a hiss.

"Fine," said Homer as they crossed the lobby, ignoring the woman at the service desk and the doorman under the awning. "I'll pick up what I can on the street. Why don't you head down to the convent grounds and see what the sisters say?"

Shelly agreed but stopped first at the precinct house, where he found another message slip: Ruth had called again. Daylight was fading; the call could cost him an hour. Greeley was in the Reliant, parked out front, waiting for a ride to a candy store under the elevated subway. Lowenkopf decided to drop off his partner, run down to the convent, and make it back before dinner. He could call Ruth when he returned to clock out. He couldn't do much about whatever was on her mind until after he finished up, anyway.

It wasn't until he was on the road to the convent that he realized he would have to face the doe-eyed sister alone.

4

When Homer stepped out of the blue Reliant underneath the elevated subway on White Plains Road, he buttoned his jacket and straightened his green silk tie. This was a time for caution: the air was growing cooler as the day pushed toward evening, and a mood of expectancy seemed to collect on the streets with the drop in the digits of the thermometer. Homer had a theory to account for it. Enervating heat discouraged sudden movements of the larcenous or violent kinds; now that the night was becoming tolerable, even comfortable, the prospects for a little restless action began to stir.

Homer was looking not for action but information. And yet how often the two coincided! Learning what was known by the denizens of the street amounted to discovering a motive for them to share what they had heard, which meant holding one hand in the cookie jar while you made a deal with the other. Shelly had explained to him the economics of the squeal: when the trouble caused by silence outweighed the trouble caused by talking, an informant spilled whatever he knew. You had to take with a grain of salt anything that came too easily—if they wanted to talk more than you wanted to listen, their information was bound to be too twisted by their motives to be of much help to anybody.

Homer remembered this lesson as he did all the others he had learned from his partner about how to deal with people. That was the only area, he felt, Shelly had to teach him. For the rest, Homer considered himself the better half of their team—at spotting details, of course, given Shelly's eyesight, but also at fitting them together to see where they pointed. Inferring the logic of the case was his bailiwick, using techniques which had made an art of police work. Homer considered himself the artist of the pair, and the scientist and technologist as well.

He loved scouring a crime scene for bits of evidence no one else had bothered to notice. Or sifting through the details that had been uncovered, turning and turning each piece in his mind until he found the glimmer of a fault line along which the case could be cracked. But, Homer admitted, there was also a time for people work, and such a time was clearly upon him. He didn't quite have Shelly's talent for helping people talk but felt sure he could learn what he needed, one way or another. Which brought him where he wanted: to Lenny's.

A small bell rang as he entered the candy store and moved along the counter on the left. It was crowded toward the front with enticing displays: Lifesavers, Sen-Sen, Turkish Taffy, Hersheys, red licorice and black licorice, Tootsie Roll lollipops and lots of chewing gum—multicolored Chicklets in boxes and a bowl; powdery oblongs of doubled pink Bazooka, rolled in a comic strip and blue-and-red wrapper; packets of Spearmint, Doublemint, Juicy Fruit, and Trident. A rack held bags of Wise potato chips, owl eyes on the lookout for the junior shoplifter's pinch. On the right were newspapers—the *Post,* out of the *Times,* with a few leftover *Racing Forms,* and a *Daily News.* The store was narrow enough for a customer in the aisle to lift a *News* with his right hand and a Jujube with his left without taking a step in either direction. Homer leafed through a paper for the weather forecast: the heat would hold another day at least.

Further back on the left, beyond the neat rows of colored

dots on long white strips of paper, the counter top cleared for a small space beside three silver swivel stools covered in red vinyl. Homer occupied one of these and twisted around, surveying the covers of magazines and comic books arranged on the wall behind him. *Playboy* and *Penthouse,* like *Hustler* and the other skin rags, were kept behind the counter—to protect their pages from teenage boys, rather than the other way around.

In the back of the store, the door of a phone booth opened and a hairy man in a flowered shirt stepped out. He had a notebook in his hand and a stubby pencil, which he stuck in the waistband of his bulging Bermuda shorts. He saw Greeley, noticed the policeman's heavy black shoes, and covered his face with a *Racing Form* as he made a beeline for the street. Homer watched him exit with a tinkle of the doorbell and twisted around, waiting for someone to come through the curtain separating the private back room of the store from the public space for customers, out front. He raised a used spoon and struck the side of a Coke glass with a chocolate smear at its bottom. It rang nicely, a clear tone despite the milky residue. Homer struck it again, for the music, once where it bulged near the lip of the glass and again down below where it curved inward toward the syrupy bottom. On the second ring, the proprietor came out from the back of his store, saw the cop, and groaned.

"I ain't got nothing for you, Homer," Lenny said loudly, glancing with evident relief at the empty phone booth in back. He was a man in his fifties, solidly built, with a cheek that screwed into a twitch every time he opened his mouth. His teeth were brown, occasionally missing. A purple bruise by his left eye had marked his face for so long, the rest of his features had rearranged themselves to accommodate it. He removed the milky glass and spoon from Greeley's reach and began rinsing them in a sink.

Homer waited until the tap squeaked shut. "What do you think I'm here for, Len? A handout? Just because you nearly had my head blown off one night? You know better than that. I've never asked for a dime from you."

"Oh, no, not a dime," the aproned man complained. "Just a little information, right? Enough to get *my* head blowed off, if anybody heard about it."

"No problem, Len. I only need to hear from you what I could hear anywhere."

"Then why don't you go anywhere else and hear it?" the man said, wiping the spoon on his apron. "Why do you always gotta hear it from me?"

"Fair enough. If I heard it someplace else first, you'll tell me what I've heard?"

"Whaddya mean, what you heard?"

"I heard that Cesar Catalan had his car stolen this week."

Len thought that over, his jaw starting to work as he looked through the plate glass of his front window. To justify its clenching, he scooped a handful of Chicklets from a basket on the counter and thrust them into his mouth.

"Jesus, you don't want nothing. Just Cesar Catalan."

"Not Catalan," said Homer, reaching over to take some gum for himself, placing a ten dollar bill on the counter in payment, "just news about his car. He didn't steal it himself, did he?"

Len rubbed his belly through his soiled T-shirt and chuckled mirthlessly. "They stole his car, too, huh? Some balls! You ever see that thing?"

"No tin can. What did you mean by 'too'?"

"Huh?"

"You said they stole his car, *too,*" Homer repeated. "What else did they steal from him?"

Len stopped chewing. "I didn't say nothing."

Homer waited patiently, eying the man as a mother might eye a lying child. When Len remained stubbornly silent, the cop spun around on his stool and lifted a copy of *Cycle World* from its place in the rack.

"Haven't seen this issue yet. Oh, wait a minute. Yes I have." His fingers released it and the magazine fell straight to the floor, where it landed in a heap of crushed pages.

"Hey, c'mon!" Len came around the counter and stooped to retrieve the magazine. "That ain't funny."

Homer didn't enjoy these things. But he knew how to do them. He reached over Len's head and lifted a copy of *Newsweek* from the rack with one hand and a *Sports Illustrated* with the other, dropping both to the floor at once.

"Hey . . . that's the swimsuit issue!"

"These are old, Len. Real old. In fact, all of them seem to be out of date. I'll help you clean out the racks."

The proprietor covered his magazines with two muscular arms to prevent the cop from lifting them wholesale. But no matter how he stretched himself, he couldn't cover them all. "I don't need no help from you."

"But you do," said Homer. "Every one of your magazines has fallen on the floor."

"They have not."

Homer stepped smartly off his stool, unbuttoning his jacket. "Not yet."

Len glared at the policeman, his jaw bulging, arms stuck to his magazines, keeping them in their racks. He shook his head, cursing the floor. "Christ Almighty! One lousy night and they nail you forever. So I set you up, one time. Does that mean you can bust my chops whenever you get a fly up your ass?"

Homer squatted beside him, too close for comfort. "Set me up? You son of a bitch . . . you handed me over to an armed felon, just to get him out of your store."

Lenny tried to pull his face away. "Nothing happened! Your partner did Cardoza before he could do you."

"Barely," hissed the cop. "No thanks to you. You called me up, invited me in, and showed us out the back. Bernie Cardoza! You know how he felt about me? Like the man with an axe in your nightmares! That's why you're going to tell me now what I need to know."

Lenny's lip trembled, tempted to talk but not permitted to do so.

From the counter, Homer lifted a disposable lighter, which he ignited.

"Aw, C'mon—" Homer snatched a *Life* from below Lenny's elbow and held it over the flame. Its lower edge crinkled, blackened, and caught. Lenny's arms sagged. Homer looked over at the magazine rack and Lenny resumed his post.

"All right, already," Len said, watching his *Life* go up. "It ain't much, but I'll tell you what I know. I can't hold all these fucking magazines anymore."

"Let's have it."

Len sat down on the floor beneath the magazine racks and let his head fall back on a copy of *Yachting*. "Somebody ripped off Catalan, Monday night. Only I don't know nothing about stealing his car. Where'd you hear that?"

"Somebody donated it to the sisters of Our Lady of Regret."

"No shit . . . to the nuns? Now that's what I call religious! But I don't know about that. What I hear is, somebody got the drop on Jimmy Twotoes in the middle of a connect and copped the coke and the cash. Left 'em high and dry with one hell of an excuse to think up for his boss."

"Somebody robbed Catalan's crew right in the middle of a drug buy?"

"You know that kid, Aguilar? They found in the playground? He was the one Catalan blamed for fucking up that night. You see what he did to repay him. Know what he's gonna do to me, if any of this gets back?"

"He won't hear your name from me," said Homer reassuringly, "so long as you keep talking."

"That's all I know," said Len.

Homer reached for a *People* magazine, but Len grabbed it faster.

"Don't you know when to quit?" he said. "I already told you that much—enough to land me in shit. Whaddya think I got to gain by holding out on you now?"

It was a point, a definite point. Homer sat back on his stool. "What happened to Jimmy Twotoes?"

"How the fuck should I know? Go find him yourself, if you really care. You know the club on Bronxdale, by the theater? Yahoo, or something? That's where he hangs out. Why don't you take your business there for a while?"

Greeley knew better than to walk into that club alone—he should taxi down to the convent and hook up with Shelly.

They had arranged to meet again at the precinct house, but Homer felt sure his partner could not have penetrated the church bureaucracy quickly enough to have left already, leading a nun in handcuffs. Shelly would have to wait for the mother superior, who would have to pray for guidance. Homer was confident he could still catch him at the convent—and the club in question was practically on the way. He'd pass it, if they went by White Plains Road. What harm could there possibly be in slowing as they drove by, just to make sure that Jimmy Twotoes hadn't fallen off the end of the earth?

Twenty minutes later, Homer sat in a cab in front of an old residential building whose medical apartments had been emptied of dividing walls, leaving a space on the ground floor which had been converted into a private music club. No liquor license, but a slick, painted sign beside the entrance read Club Wah—BYOB, and the jazz flowing out through the sheeted windows was cool—or was it hot? Homer wasn't quite sure which, but found the combo's lyrical strains pleasant, in their way. This was Shelly's taste, really, but now that he was listening, Homer hardly minded. He opened his window, leaned back into the taxi's torn seat cushion, crossed his legs, and began tapping out the rhythms with his palm on his knee.

The cabbie shoved aside the plastic shield between them. "How long we gonna sit here, Bud?"

Homer pulled out the wallet from his inside jacket pocket and held up his sergeant's badge. "This is a stakeout."

The cabbie slapped his temple, pushing his cap to one side. "Just what I needed tonight! The meter's gotta run, anyway. Company policy."

"All right," said Homer, "let it loose."

He sat back, hoping to end the exchange, but the cabbie's interest was provoked. He peered through the window at the club, watched two girls knock at the door, and turned back to Homer. "What're we looking for?"

Homer tried to discourage his questions as quickly as possible. "A guy with two toes on his right foot."

"What'd he do?"

"Nothing that we can prove."

The cabbie nodded as if he understood. "Then what do we want him for?"

"He may know something about a stolen car."

"You trying to find it?"

"Nooo," said Homer slowly. How was he going to end this? "We have the car. And we know what happened to it."

"Yeah? What happened to it?"

Homer saw he had invited that question himself. "It was given to some nuns who prayed for one."

"By who?"

"Nobody knows."

The cabbie whistled. "No kidding. There must be a lot of that going around."

He lapsed into silence, for which Homer was grateful, until he realized what the driver had just mumbled.

"Excuse me . . . a lot of what going around?"

The cabbie shrugged. "Y'know, like you said—people giving cars to each other."

Greeley leaned forward and gripped the man's arm. "Do you mean . . . you know someone else who received an anonymous gift of a car?"

"One guy—a bus driver. We used to have a standing thing, every Wednesday night. I'd meet him at six with a bunch of wood boxes, carved ceremonial things. We'd drive around picking up one or two old geezers, then I'd drive them all by the Holland Tunnel to a house in Jersey City. Only last night, when I showed up, he tells me they won't need me anymore. Somebody gave him a van of his own. But here's the strange part, see—he don't know who coulda done it. I said he's gotta have some idea. 'One of my subjects,' he says."

"His *subjects*? What is he, a scientist?"

"A king. King of the B'hantusi, he tells me, in America, elected by his countrymen in exile here. He was sent a throne by the king in the old country. Someplace in Africa."

Homer sank into his seat cushion, staring blankly out the

window. An elected tribal king who drives a bus? This was starting to sound like Shelly's sort of police work. "But the van was a gift from a subject, you say?"

"That was his *best guess.*" The cabbie leaned over the seat, lowering his voice. "To tell you the truth, it sounded to me like he didn't have a clue who it come from."

Homer suspected he could find a clue, if he could get a look at that van. "But now that he has transportation, you probably won't be seeing him again."

"Wanna meet him? I can take you there right now."

His hand grabbed the gear shift on the driving column, ready to shove it into drive. Outside, a couple loped down the block, their limbs in synchrony, disappearing into the club. The door opened with a blast of jazz and shut, redoubling the silence. The street was empty of people again. Some papers blew at the curb.

"Let's go," said Homer, surrendering his window with a brief glance at his watch: 7:10. The search for Jimmy Twotoes could wait. One anonymous auto was peculiar enough in the Bronx, but two comprised a positive phenomenon. The cabbie hummed, his meter clicking into action again. Homer closed his eyes and listened to the sounds, his professional radar alert. Something was moving on this case, an unexpected pattern. The excitement of a fresh clue stimulated him, and lent a warm fragrance to the wind at his window. Or the flowers in the park were blooming nearby in the crisp, summer air.

5

Lowenkopf was spared responsibility for handcuffing
Sister Margaret a second time, because when he arrived at
the convent near the southern end of Bronx Park, the sisters
were at Vespers. A novice setting plates and cups in the
refectory told him that their order heard the Mass and
received the Eucharist with the early evening service; Sister
Margaret could not be disturbed. But the novice had indeed
seen Father Charles, ten minutes earlier, crossing the
grounds toward the school.

Lowenkopf asked what the priest might be doing there,
after hours, during the summer.

She shrugged indifferently. "Am I the father's keeper?"
But the question disturbed her and, remembering that she
should have answered *yes,* the novice frowned. "Why don't
you go over and see for yourself?"

The convent was located on a square city block owned by
the sisters of Our Lady of Regret, which also housed their
academy, a private high school with after-school programs
for the larger community, and a smaller structure that had
once been a chapel. The chapel had been moved inside the
academy, and the small building had been converted into a

hospice for children orphaned by the AIDS epidemic. Shelly experienced an inner sigh of relief when he learned that he would not have to go into the hospice after Branigan, and made his way to the academy in fair spirits.

Inside, the school seemed deserted. Empty hallways echoed from the shuffling feet of generations of boys and girls in blue woolen jackets with the school's insignia stitched over their hearts. There was a smell of old ammonia rising from the floors, and a stuffy, dusty silence drifting down from the sliding wooden windows, sealed for the summer. The ceiling fixtures were alternately lit, dripping wan pools of yellow light on the tiles directly below them, receding into darkness in between. Shelly stood at the foot of the staircase, listening for noises, and jumped when he felt a presence behind him—Father Charles, in a sweat suit, carrying a nylon satchel.

"Hello, there, sergeant," the priest said cheerily. "What are you doing here?"

His voice rang ominously in the corridors.

Shelly was there to rearrest him, but, reluctant to break the bad news, said, "They told me I might find you here."

"I like to use their racquetball courts after school hours," Branigan said, lifting his satchel as evidence.

"I need to talk to you, father."

"Do you play? I've an extra pair of shorts in my bag, and an extra racquet in my locker. We'll talk as we go. Otherwise, I'm afraid you'll have to wait until I'm through. I'm devoted to the game—and I don't use that word lightly."

Lowenkopf knew that the time had come to cuff the man and take him back to the precinct house, from where he would be bused for the night to the local jail. Shelly imagined Father Charles sharing a cell with Tony ("the Ratchet") Constanza or Slim ("Shiv") Silverman, and decided to put that off. Branigan might tell him something useful now, but all talk would cease with his arrest. Shelly lifted his trouser cuff and shook his square brown loafer. "No sneakers."

The priest unzipped his satchel and tossed out a pair of Princes. "Use these. I'm wearing Reeboks, anyway." He raised the cuff of his own pants to confirm that his feet were indeed shod in black leather running shoes.

Shelly followed him down the stairs to a damp locker room in the basement. The smell of dirty socks, disinfectant, and a rusty water heater assaulted his nose, provoking a catalogue of twenty-five-year-old memories. Though he'd never been in the room before, Shelly knew the location of its toilets and showers, the chill of its tiles under his feet, and the clang of its aluminum doors as the locker slammed shut on his dangling pants, leaving him bare legged in oversized shorts and a snug sleeveless jersey that read The Saints.

As they headed downstairs to the courts, Shelly heard the muffled *thoom-thoom* which meant that someone else was playing on a court. "I thought we were alone," he said.

Branigan shrugged. "They won't bother us."

At the foot of the stairs the air was warm, having trapped and retained the heat of the late afternoon. Three steel doors, each with a little square of double-thick glass, confronted them like the moral choices in a parable. Branigan opened the middle door, stepping onto a waxed pine floor surrounded by whitewashed walls two stories high. Overhead and behind them, a thick mesh screen was set in the rear wall, behind which lay an observation area with wooden benches, accessible from above. Shelly hoped no one would appear there during their game, to watch him be shamed by the priest.

"So," he said to Father Charles, his voice damped down by the echoing chamber, "here we are. Now tell me about the nun. How well do you know her?"

The priest popped the lid on a fresh can of racquetballs, squeezing one near his ear. "Margaret? She's not really a *nun*, you know—that word is properly reserved for a cloistered contemplative. The sisters here all do good works."

"Like driving priests around?"

Branigan bounced the new, blue ball and tossed it over to Lowenkopf. "Serve."

Shelly crouched between the service lines, dropped the

ball, and smashed it into the front wall, where it lifted, grazing the left wall near the back. It came crashing back from Branigan's racquet, straight to the front left corner, and rolled across the floor past Shelly's ankles.

"My serve," said Father Charles.

Shelly ceded the serving line, retreating to the center of the rear wall. He was saved from the embarrassment of Branigan's devotion by a muffled rapping on the double-thick glass in the door. Through it he gratefully discerned a black and white veil and coif—a sister of mercy whom Shelly had never seen, banging her fist on the door.

As he opened it, her voice came, ". . . ranigan! You're needed in the hospice right away!"

It took the father one instant to register what had been shouted, another to drop his ball and racquet, and a third to run off the court, dragging the breathless sister behind him. Shelly started after them, but the priest called back, "You wait here. Practice. Get your serve in shape. I'll be back, by Jesus, I'll be back!"

He watched them climb the stairs, three at a leap, and turned back in silence to the court.

Though not quite in silence. As he crouched, estimating the angle of his swing to the wall, he heard again the *thwoom-thwoom* of another ball in play. Another single player on a court, he realized, since the rhythm of the volley marked regular intervals rather than the short, staccato crackling of a racquetball game. He served his ball, returned it, missed the follow-up, recovered the ball and his position at the line. He served to himself again, misjudging his swing so that the ball came back directly at his head. He stepped aside, let it strike the floor and took it off the rear wall, sending it lobbing high overhead. It hit the ceiling and the top of the front wall, dropping into a bounce that brought him back to the door to catch it on the downbeat. He swung again and missed.

Thwoom-thwoom.

Stooping to retrieve his ball, he listened for a moment to the volley nearby. It occurred to him that practice was never much fun. And then, that everyone must feel as he did about it. He considered wandering over to the next court and asking whoever was volleying whether he wouldn't prefer to play a game together. Father Charles might be a while, after all, and if he came back sooner they could all play together in a three-way competition. He was looking for a partner who might deflect the trouncing the priest was likely to hand him. He opened the door, looked out, and listened.

Thoom. Thoom. Thoom.

Shelly decided against it. For one thing, his unknown partner might be enjoying his solitude. How could he turn down the offer of a game? Not very easily, if he was reluctant to give offense. Who could be playing in this place, now, anyway? Another priest? Shelly imagined himself sandwiched between two clergymen, missing his shots but unable to holler, *shit!* He resumed his position at the service line with a new appreciation of the solitary volley. He angled his racquet, rolled his wrist, held out the ball—and heard a squeak as the door opened behind him.

He turned, expecting to see Father Charles, surprised that the interruption had been so quickly dispatched. But it was not Father Charles who entered the court.

It was a woman in a gray sweat suit with dark stains down her back and under her upper arms. A fainter stain was starting to seep through the fabric beneath the scoop of her neckline. Her face was strained and her green eyes a bit sad, perhaps from the effort of her lonely practice. She held up her racquet, twisted it, bounced a ball on its nylon strings. Would he play? He bounced his own ball, twice. She wiped her palms on the front of her thighs and took up a position in the center of the court, close to the rear wall.

Shelly was not a strong player: he had neither the power nor the speed of a true enthusiast, whose wrist and arm and body swung as one. He did not have especially fast hands, or quick feet, or a wicked eye. But he had an idea of where he was on the court and where his opponent wasn't. He won his games in his mind, with imagination and humor. When those didn't work, he lost. He looked at the woman and hoped she knew how to laugh.

He served. The ball slid along the left wall. She returned

it—faster than he had expected, a clean shot that came off the front wall spinning. He planted his feet behind it, bringing his racquet well back, raising it high behind him. She started backwards, preparing to recover his coming smash, when he pushed the ball toward the front wall, where it bounced softly, twice.

She hung her head, amazed to have let such a simple shot pass while she watched, moving in the wrong direction.

Shelly picked up the ball, dribbled it back to the line, and held it out deliberately before him. Reading the angle of his body and the arc of his swing, remembering his first serve, she edged to her left, anticipating a slider. He lobbed a bouncer over his head. It went straight back to where she had been standing—no side wall, angle, spin, or curve. She managed to stretch and scoop it up in time, but not to control it, so it came off the front wall directly into his forearm.

He looked at the front right corner. She dashed to outrace the ball . . . which again went floating gently down the left.

She sighed, resuming her place. He caught her eye as they passed, and she grinned ruefully. With dimples.

It captured him completely. Nothing excited him more than making a woman happy. He felt a tremor in his windpipe which he recognized as singing. She struck her position: loose limbed, breathing audibly, waiting for his move, ready to respond to him. If his thigh edged leftward, so did hers; if his weight shifted rightward, she did the same. Their bodies were engaged, reading one another's movements, intentions, desires.

Her face was set, determined to field the next serve. A strong face, he decided: firm jaw, clear cheeks, prominent blue eyes, all traces of mascara washed away by perspiration. Pale lipstick, if any, on big, sensuous lips, the lower of which was clasped now in her teeth. She shook her head, stretching the neck, pushing back her short blond hair with a brush of her left hand, which then plucked the nylon of her racquet.

He served. The ball came low, directly back from the front wall, skipping over the service line to her backhand.

She answered with an equally low, stinging return to the left front corner. He caught it near the side wall and spun it front and right. She scraped it off the floor and sent it back fairly fast but squarely into the center of the court. He planted his feet behind it and raised his racquet high. She started back but remembered, turned, and dove to nab the soft push at the front. The ball came off his racquet softly once again, but higher on the wall, sailing over both their heads in a slow arc that landed just behind her, ricocheted off the wall and struck the floor again right below her. And rolled between her legs.

She was trembling—with rage or sorrow he couldn't guess, until he came up behind and touched her arm. She seized his hand and looked up, directly into his eyes. Laughing. He stepped back instinctively, but she caught him by the neck and kissed his mouth.

Her breath rushed into him spicily and he realized he was panting—from fatigue, maybe, but it didn't take long to deepen in intensity. Her warm, wet kisses sent a thrill through his frame while his tightened muscles ached, adjusting to the change in their activity. She drew back to breathe. He wiped the sweat from her forehead and a glistening drop from her eyebrow. That gesture of tenderness decided something in her, and she thrust herself against him, knocking him over.

He went down hard on the waxed pine floor, with an echo that rang through the courts. The ball slipped from his grip and bounced toward the front wall, rolling to the right when it hit the line of the floor. She was climbing out of her sweat suit with a determination that stiffened his own resolve on the court.

They tangled in a snapping roll of elastic. He felt his shorts slide down over his hips and managed to extract one sneaker. Her body was cool, damp, energetic, endearingly soft, moving with an urgency that surprised him. She climbed under, around, over, and behind him, leaning against his muscles, hard, suddenly yielding, hungry to experience all directions at once, as if it were her first and only chance.

When at last she crumpled, sinking onto him, weightless, adrift, settling into the pillow of her hair, Shelly felt the cold wood floor supporting them from below, pressing against each vertebra of his spine. His eyes closed for a minute and his head dropped back, as he let the weight of his skull rest on the floor. When he opened his eyes again, pulling the lids apart, he found himself on the gleaming, empty court in a damp jersey and sneakers with his shorts around one ankle and his racquetball on his racquet near his head.

Alone.

He sat up with a start, but heard nothing moving around him. The other courts were silent; no footsteps on the stairs; the observation benches held no observers. He wriggled into his borrowed shorts, athletic supporter still in them, stood, and retrieved his racquet. For a moment, he panicked. What did he know about her? No telephone. No name. And then, he found solace in the silence of a school on the grounds of an order of contemplatives. He could do nothing more than wait and see. There was a comfort in that the sisters would have appreciated. He stuck his shirt in his waistband, and listened again for footsteps in the building overhead . . . and heard silence. If he'd ever returned, Father Charles must have fled.

Shelly was wrong about that. Twenty minutes later, after he had found his locker again, showered, and was easing untoweled back into his street clothes, the priest reappeared, propping a heavy shoe on the bench between rows of lockers. He, too, had doffed his racquetball clothes and was dressed again in a black suit with a turned-around white collar.

"Sorry I couldn't make it back. I hope you had a good round without me?"

Shelly couldn't tell if he heard sarcasm in that. He chose an answer that would play either way. "Good enough."

The priest was tired but relaxed, with a buoyancy to his voice that was hard to read. "Sister Katherine's been a little nervous lately. A heart monitor went on the fritz—she thought another soul had taken flight."

Shelly was trying to knot his tie, which fell too short in

front and too long in back. He was wondering who the woman on the racquetball court might be, where she'd come from, gone, and whom to ask. He considered Father Charles, who probably knew, but couldn't think how he might innocently describe her.

"Are you all right?"

"Sure," said Shelly. He undid his tie, recrossed it, raised the knot. Too short.

The priest brushed his hands away, knotted the tie, and buttoned Shelly's jacket over it. "Now. Ready to go? There's someone here I want you to meet."

Shelly followed Branigan up the stairs and across the lawn to the smallest of the three buildings. The hospice. He dreaded going inside, walking among the patients, but was spared that confrontation with the dying when Father Charles led him around to a small door from which escaped a roar.

Inside, a dryer was going, a single, white sheet twisting in its window. At the steel sink into which the washing machine spat its steaming water through a hose, a sister in full habit knelt, wringing out a pillowcase, once white, now stained with red.

She did not glance up or even lift her face as they entered, her concentration fixed on the soiled linen.

"Sister Elizabeth," Branigan whispered, with reverence in his hushed introduction.

Shelly watched her back. "The one Sister Margaret asked to pray for a new car?"

"The one everyone asks to pray," murmured Father Charles. "Pious as a church mouse. Charitable to a fault—if she had any, that would be it. But don't expect an answer, if you speak to her. She's taken a vow of silence, as a penance."

Shelly felt a chill climb his spine, one slow vertebra at a time. "Penance for what? What's she done?"

The priest shrugged. "No one knows. She's not saying anything, of course."

She turned and looked at the men, a scrutiny that passed over Father Charles but lingered on Lowenkopf, taking his measure. Beneath the headwear that framed her face,

45

covering all her hair, her features appeared with awful clarity, changed and yet undeniably familiar, cleansed of perspiration and transformed by the severity of her expression.

Her gaze held him fixedly, with no sign of doubt or alarm, asking nothing of him. Until her eyes suddenly broke away, glancing back at an invisible spot on the pillowcase in her hand. As she rubbed it with her thumb, the sternness faded from her mouth, softening the line of her lips.

The pout resolved all doubts about small differences—it was the face he had covered with passionate kisses on the floor of the racquetball court.

Homer was on his way to a royal audience.

The taxi drove him south and east, following Rosedale to the projects on Randall Avenue. In the buildings to either side, doors and windows were open, coaxing the evening breeze through summer apartments. They lent an atmosphere of intimacy to the neighborhood, since everyone was privy to everyone else's noises. Radios played on windowsills, voices murmured, and here and there a baby cried, or an argument ran its course. Homer felt a part of the life in the borough around him as he rarely did in his own place, on his own street, downtown.

The cabbie pulled up in front of a brick building and lifted the arm of his meter. Beyond the building, a great expanse of green lawn, edged in chain-link fence, led to the next building, then the next, in the housing authority development. Each had its own curved lane leading to the door, a glass entranceway with the address in raised numbers overhead.

Homer paid the fare with a reasonably generous tip, he thought, though the cabbie seemed disappointed, counting the bills. He reached for the key, but before cutting the engine, said, "This is police business, right? You're ordering me to leave the cab and lead you into this place?"

"It's your civic duty," Homer replied, leaving the rest unsaid. Wasn't that enough?

The cabbie hesitated. He wanted something stronger than his own responsibility. "But . . . you're *commandeering* me, aren't you? Lifting the decision out of my hands completely?"

"If you don't get out of this cab," Homer said, producing his firearm, "I'll shoot out your windshield."

"That's all I needed to hear," said the cabbie. "My boss can take it up with your boss, later."

The cabbie, at least, seemed to be enjoying his role in the investigation. He locked the four doors separately and led his passenger up the lane and into the building's lobby, where a laboring elevator hoisted them three slow stories. They rang the bell at 3B and were admitted at once, without enough delay for even a cursory check through the peephole. Inside, a silent woman in a sleeveless dress led them past a kitchen to a large living room with a sofa and a recliner, both neatly patched, two end tables, and a television set. On each table was a lamp in the shape of a carved figure, with a fringed shade. Beside the television set was a throne on which sat a man in a dashiki, deep in thought. Before him, a young couple waited side by side on folding chairs, speaking when he turned to them, each listening with rancor as the other responded.

"That is not what my father promised him!" the young woman shouted, interrupting her husband's account of their conflict. "Only if we stayed, was what he said, Your Highness. What good is a goat in the Bronx?"

"That is none of their affair," the young man insisted. "A deal is a deal, is it not? If my mother bargained badly, what is that to anyone but myself, the recipient? And she did not, the blessed lady. Be assured, Your Highness."

"I am assured of one thing only," the man on the throne said solemnly. "Neither your mother, nor her father, intended that their bargain should become a sore point between you."

"Your Highness speaks rightly about my father," said the bride. "Though his mother is another story. I wouldn't put any such idea past the old witch."

Her husband rose from his chair. "Charlene . . . !"

The king slapped his palm on the carved arm of his throne, which resounded with a wooden *thunk*. "Children! That is enough! I will speak for both your parents, being your king."

Both of them seemed to accept that proposal. An expectant silence fell. The king settled back into his seat, stretching his neck, scratching at the stubble beneath his jaw, stroking his chin. Finally he said, "If a goat was promised, it should be delivered. That is my decision."

The woman looked crestfallen, but said nothing. Her husband gloated publicly. "Thank you. Of course." He started to collect some papers into a folder at his feet, saw that neither of the other two had risen, and sat up in his chair.

The king was watching him thoughtfully. "But where will you graze your goat now? Once the debt is paid."

The young man, clearly uneasy that the interview was continuing, nonetheless managed to explain, "There is a small park near our apartment, with plenty of public grass. I can take her there in the morning, on my way to the bus."

"And who will lead her home again? And milk her udders when they are full?"

The husband looked to his wife, who shook her head. "Then I will, myself. Bring her back, then go to work."

"And where will you keep her?" the king wondered.

"In the kitchen," the young man said.

"But the kitchen is your wife's, too, is it not?"

"The whole apartment is hers as well as mine. You know that is the way of marriage among our people."

"Yes." The king nodded. "I know that. I thought you must have an agreement on that point between you. Otherwise, where would you keep her?"

The young woman, beginning to catch the drift, spoke up in a voice full of daughterly obedience. "No, Your Highness, we have no such agreement. My father would not forfeit my rights, please be sure of that."

"Oh, yes, child, of that I am certain. That is why I have been wondering what your husband intends."

The young man, unwilling to surrender his victory, said, "But you have decided in my favor. She can't be allowed to cross your wishes."

"I have decided in no one's favor," the king told them sternly. "I have decided the law. It is up to you to work out between you what it shall mean to you. As with everything else in your life together."

"But that is why we came to you," the young man stammered. "For guidance from our king."

"And you have had it," the king thundered gently. "So go now and do as I have bidden."

The young couple, looking rather perplexed, gathered their things and were shown out by the silent woman, who closed the door behind them and grinned. "They'll have to do some talking now, to figure out what you commanded. Shrewd man!"

The king sighed. "It is very difficult, to guess what my subjects have come to hear. Sometimes, they tell me in their questions what my answer should be. Sometimes I have to let them supply my answer for themselves. They will, those two, sooner or later." He stepped down from his throne, extending his hand to the cabbie. "My taxi-cab friend. You are welcome."

The two men shook hands warmly. The cabbie took Homer by the elbow and edged him forward. "I have brought someone to see you, sire. This is Detective Sergeant Homer Greeley of the New York Police Department. He needs to ask some questions about the new royal vehicle."

"My van? Has something happened to it?"

Homer said, "That's more or less what I'm hoping to learn from you. Tell me—are you really an African king?"

"No," said the king seriously. "I'm an American king. Lee Urwin is the name on my citizenship—Ur'wangli my national name. Twenty years ago, when the Hal'kaari tribe gained control of our homeland, many of my people fled here, fearing for their lives and property. Five years ago, some of us formed an association, the B'hantusi People's League, and elected our first president for a one-year term. We had the support of the African B'hantusi king, who sent us this throne and hailed the new American king. I am the fifth tribesman to be so honored. It is mostly labor, I can tell you, settling disputes between our people in which no one is ever really satisfied, attending meetings with our elders, gracing marriages, baby namings, divorces, and funerals, always fair, always reserved, the model of our dignity. Thank God this year is almost over!"

King Urwin removed his crown, setting it on the throne, and began collecting wooden boxes of various sizes, fitting the small ones into the larger ones, and some elongated carvings into the smallest. Ritual devices, apparently, or tokens of sovereignty.

"Is this . . . a living?" Homer asked.

The king shook his head. "I'm a bus driver. My predecessor delivered mail. What is important in selecting our leader each year is the individual's personal judgment and record of service to our community. And, of course, our estimate of how well one will bear the burden of responsibility."

"You have many duties?"

Urwin raised his arms in a gesture of plenitude, like Atlas holding the world before him. "Many, many responsibilities. On Wednesdays, for example, our council of elders meets at the home of a tribeswoman in New Jersey. I must attend, of course, but also bring these artifacts, and arrange whatever transportation is necessary for those of my people who cannot arrange their own. You can imagine how difficult this proved before I had a vehicle at my command."

"The van?"

"The van," agreed Urwin, dropping into the couch beside the woman, throwing an arm around her. "It appeared Tuesday night at the end of the lane leading from the entrance to this building. A note in the wiper read, For The B'hantusi King. The keys were in the ignition, dangling

51

down. I assumed it was a gift from one of my subjects, who hoped to supply what help was needed without the embarrassment of my gratitude. Do you have some reason to doubt this explanation?"

Homer told him the story of the red Ferrari, donated to the sisters of Our Lady of Regret.

"And you think," the king surmised, "the same thing happened to me? My van, a gift of a stolen vehicle?"

Greeley hesitated. "I'd like to see it, first."

"Come with me, then!" Urwin commanded, rising from his couch and heading for the apartment door without looking back to make sure they were following.

"It's the kingship," murmured the woman. "It was hard for him to adjust. Now it'll be hard to switch back."

"We'd better keep up with him," the cabbie said.

Urwin led them to a gleaming silver Vanagon parked around the corner from the cab. Its interior was carpeted, with sloping windows and armrests that raised beside the seats. In back was a length of wire connected to a UHF antenna. Homer wrote down the license plate, copied the numbers from the engine block, and inspected the body for signs of impact. He found no dents in the body, or bits of blood or paint on the bumpers.

"So far, so good," he told the king.

Urwin grunted.

Back in the apartment, Homer phoned in the numbers to his precinct house and received two answers which did not match: the van belonged to a business, the Nisei Import Company, but it had not been reported as a stolen vehicle.

"What does that mean?" Urwin demanded. "Not stolen? Has a Japanese businessman given his van to me?"

"Not necessarily," Homer explained. "A fleet of stolen vehicles go unreported every day. The odds of recovery are slight, at best. Most reports are filed to prepare for insurance claims, but most people are not covered for auto theft."

"So then—it must have been stolen. But by whom? And why was it given to me?"

"Your Highness," said Greeley uneasily, "can you think of any of your subjects who might be inclined to provide a car for his king? Out of devotion for you and national pride, perhaps? Someone with a record of these things?"

The king shook his head with certainty, thrice. "None of my people would risk the shame of involving their king in such a business. Absolutely not! Look elsewhere."

Homer nodded, unconvinced. "Well, then, can you help me look elsewhere? Can you think of anyone else who knew of your problems with transportation and might have been tempted to help? In response to some kindness of yours, let's say?"

Urwin thought long and hard, shaking his head, until suddenly his brow knitted. He seemed to think over a disturbing idea, and finally said, "One boy. An Amerasian youngster who came every night for a week to ride my bus. Sometimes, when there is one rider left, I'll strike up a conversation—about my troubles as king, or anything that comes to mind, just to lift the passenger's spirits. Especially if they seem to be low."

"Was this Amerasian kid low spirited?"

"Actually, no. But he had the photograph, you see."

"What photo?"

"Ahhh," said King Urwin, "the serviceman's photo. It was a picture of a young man, taken in front of his house, the night before he shipped out overseas. The boy showed it to me his first night on my bus, and asked if I had ever seen that house. It was a blurry photo of a nondescript white man in front of a nondescript house. I said I couldn't tell, it looked like so many. The boy said he would know it when he saw it."

"Why?" asked Homer.

"Because it was his father's house, you see," said the king. "The serviceman must have been his father."

"Did he tell you as much?"

"Of course not! Why should he? Do you tell the bus driver your business? But I drove him, night after night, up and down the streets of the Bronx. And every night he did nothing but stare out the windows, watching for that house through the glass. That's when I used to try to ease his mind, talking about my troubles with the tribe. He listened to me, nodding in sympathy, but his eyes never strayed from the window."

"Do you know his name?"

"I never ask for names," Urwin said.

"Do you think he'll show up for a ride tomorrow?"

The king shook his head. "He's gone, now. After seven nights of riding with me, he left and never returned. I guess he'd exhausted my route by then, moving on to the buses of my colleagues."

"And you think this boy could have . . . done something to secure transportation for you?"

"He might have," said Urwin after a pause. "There was a suffering that never left his eyes. Suffering makes people kind, you see. He might have taken pity on me. The Lord knows I've prayed for him—may he find his father!"

Homer nodded, confounded by a nameless Amerasian boy, who left no trace of his passing. The king had told all he knew, which provided no clue to his benefactor. What then had Homer learned that he didn't know when the evening began? One lead, he thought, only one: on the slip of paper in his palm, the name of the Nisei Import Company winked up at him.

7

By the time Lowenkopf returned to the precinct house, Greeley was already waiting for him. The blond detective sat at his desk, poring through a book entitled *Tribal Kings of Africa*. When he saw Shelly come in alone, he craned his head back toward the door. "Where's Sister Margaret?"

"She wasn't available," Shelly said, sinking into his own chair's noisy springs. It wasn't really a lie, he thought, since Homer knew him well enough to guess what might have happened.

"What happened?" asked Homer.

"Vespers," Shelly exclaimed. "Something like that—a service. I just couldn't see busting a nun right in the middle of devotions."

"You could have waited until it ended," Homer said.

"I decided to wait a bit longer than that," Shelly replied evenly. "I mean, we know where she is, don't we? We can pick her up any time we want. I was hoping we might learn something between now and then which would make that unnecessary."

"Maybe we have," Homer mumbled.

Shelly looked over sharply. "Don't tell me you found something already?"

"Maybe I did," said Homer. Nothing else.

Shelly tried to wait him out but needed a reason to stall the arrest. "All right, then . . . let's hear it already."

Homer put up his feet on the desk and recounted his evening travels, from the candy store, to the taxi cab, to the king of America. When he had heard all the details his partner chose to remember, Shelly considered what they had learned. Another donated car had been found, another anonymous gift, possibly from a teenager on a bus. Sister Margaret had said that her request to Sister Elizabeth for additional prayer power had been made in front of some boys cleaning erasers. He thought he saw a pattern in that coincidence. Teenagers doing the same thing twice: stealing cars from the rich and leaving them where they were needed. Did this represent the beginning of some strange new fad, with a public-spirited motive behind it? Or was a single party responsible for both donations? Was more than a single party involved—some new kind of gang? Shelly's head reeled with possibilities.

Homer's focus was narrower, as usual. "The first thing we need to do is to find out why the theft of the van was never reported. Maybe the thief was known to the owner, who chose not to press charges. He may not know about the stolen Ferrari."

"Wouldn't he have recovered the van before deciding not to press charges?"

"That's just what we should ask him," agreed Homer. "Or them, rather, since the van was owned as a corporate vehicle. I looked up the name in the phone book and called down to Brooklyn, just on the off chance that someone's still there. Guess what?"

"Someone is?" asked Shelly unhappily.

"Even better," Homer said, warming to their good fortune. "The whole company's out for the evening, at a function—in the Bronx. The president of their home office in Tokyo is visiting the States and spending the evening at the greenhouse of the Bronx Botanical Gardens, presenting a gift from the new emperor. Did you know Hirohito made a trip to the gardens when he visited New York in 1975? That's what the woman in their office told me. Afterwards, he sent a rare flower. Tonight they're delivering another one, building a tradition. Why don't we drive over and enjoy the pomp and ceremony?"

There were seven or eight things Shelly would have rather done than watch a Japanese businessman present a flower to the Botanical Gardens. He was hungry, for one thing—he hadn't eaten anything except a square of Sicilian pizza and a grape drink, for lunch. Neither had his partner, of course, but Homer could go for weeks gnawing on nothing but leads.

"Don't you think we can pick this up tomorrow?"

"In Brooklyn?" asked Homer. "Let's save ourselves the ride. Besides, this way we're on the trail of a clue. Instead of stumped at the starting gate."

Shelly saw he had no choice but to go; he decided to make it fast as possible. A slip on his desk reminded him that he still hadn't called Ruth back yet. "All right—the gardens. We'll ask a few questions and run. And then, Homer, we call it a night on this thing."

Homer shrugged—no problem.

Shelly picked up the car keys where he had dropped them. "I'll drive."

Fifteen minutes later they were entering the gardens through a gate across from Fordham University. Pedestrians were walking, in twos and threes and fours, around to the entrance near Moshulu Parkway—too big a crowd for a late-night stroll. Large enough for a hanging.

"Is there a concert in the park tonight?" Homer asked the guard at the gate.

"Other side," said the guard, "by the museum."

"We're not here for the concert," Shelly insisted. "We're here on police business, to see some personnel with the Nisei Import Company. Do you know anything about that party? Or are we wasting our time?"

"In the greenhouse," the guard said. "Parking ahead."

They rolled forward to a lane leading to the central glass dome of the gardens' greenhouse. As they neared, a young

57

man in white gloves waved them over, offering a parking stub as he opened Shelly's door.

"Valet parking," said Homer. "No way to discourage them. Have you a dollar?"

Shelly refused to surrender their car. "We're cops. Not guests. Leave us alone."

The young man held onto the door, waiting for him to step outside. Shelly tried to pull it shut but the leverage was against him and the door remained in the valet's white glove.

Homer opened his own door, climbing out. "Let him have it, Shell. Live a little."

The path to the entranceway ran straight from the curb, between two pools of inky water lit from below, magnifying the shadows of lily pads and streaking orange goldfish. A crowd of people congregated between the pools, silhouettes against the gleaming crystal greenhouse: women in black cocktail dresses with spaghetti straps, men in suits or here and there a tux. After the heat of the day and the cool of the evening, Homer's linen was looking downright baggy; Shelly pressed his own lapels against his chest with his palms in a vain attempt to make the cotton flat.

Inside, the domed lobby was illuminated for photographers, as small groups of businessmen and women posed below the lemon trees. About half the men were Asian, and a third of the women, talking for the most part in English, but Shelly heard a few words of Japanese float by. Directly in front of the entrance, a reception table waited, staffed by two lovely women with skin like porcelain and roses in their straight black hair. Both were slender, poised, graceful in movement—the shorter one helping a woman into a wrist corsage while the taller one stood, holding a pin in one hand and a white carnation in the other, waiting for Shelly to approach.

At a glance he could see there was no use refusing: all of the men in eyesight wore white carnations, and all the women, corsages. He would have preferred to pin the flower on himself, given the length of the pin and the thinness of his cotton lapel, but when the hostess drew near, fragrant as a summertime blossom, Shelly threw back his shoulders and offered his powerful chest—which flinched a moment later as her delicate fingers slipped on the steel and thrust the pin through his lapel and his shirt and the taut skin below his collarbone.

"Ouch!" he said before he caught himself, which touched off a chain reaction. The hostess dropped the pin, which clattered on the table. Her companion froze in sympathy, seizing the wrist of a waiting guest, who clasped her free hand to her throat with a shriek.

At the sound, a young man in a tuxedo stepped instantly forward, releasing the imprisoned wrist with the swift snap of a new corsage, restoring the woman's composure. When she returned his smile, flattered, the man looked at the hostess with a tiny shake of his head and said, "Kayoko . . ."

She gazed down in embarrassment, the sides of her page-boy hairstyle falling over her face. The man turned to Shelly with a sympathetically wrinkled brow and touched the wounded shoulder as if it might snap. He recovered the fallen carnation, freshened its petals, and slipped the pin into the lapel, through the stem, back into and out of the cloth. It was an expert move, skillful and painless. Shelly looked down to see the ragged white flower standing proudly as his rescuer bowed his head and said, "Sorry about that . . . we don't make a practice of sticking it to our customers. Let me get you a drink in compensation. Waiter—"

He spoke sharply, just loudly enough to attract a server's eye across the crowded room. In his thirties, physically fit, with the speech of a midwesterner and Japanese features—high cheekbones, no cheeks, dark brown eyes, and a pensive mouth. He wore a ruffled shirt front with black studs, black tie, and sash. Even his gestures seemed Western as his crooked finger wiggled for the waiter. In a moment they had fluted goblets sizzling in their hands, which the young man kept raising by the stem bases, trying to clink them together.

Shelly shook his head, not quite sure where to put down

the glass. The man insisted with a wave of his upturned palm and took a good swig of his own. Shelly turned to Homer, who glanced at his watch and shrugged.

Shelly drained the glass while his host watched with some satisfaction.

"Now," he said, settling both their goblets on the concrete base of a tree, "tell me how I know you."

"You don't, yet," said Shelly, moving a step toward Homer. "We're policemen . . . my partner and I. This is Sergeant Greeley. I'm Lowenkopf. We're here to investigate a robbery."

"A robbery?" said the man, aghast. "Here?" His gesture implied the greenhouse should be sacrosanct as a temple. Overhead, a glass pane glittered, reflecting the light; a lemon tree dangled fragrant boughs.

"No," Shelly said. "Not here. You are an employee of the Nisei Import Company?"

"Forgive me," replied the man, recovering his manners but not his manner. "My name is Tanagaki—Eddie Tanagaki. Yes, I am with Nisei. Has anything happened at our offices?"

"We need to speak with the man in charge," said Homer. "If you don't mind. Could you tell us who that would be?"

"It's hard to say," said Tanagaki, "if you understand the way our business is organized. I'm in charge of television sales, in the States, which accounts for most of them. Do you see that man by the flower bed?"

He pointed to a big man near a display of both red and white geraniums, waving his fists in the air as he spoke to another, half a head shorter, who listened silently, nodding.

"That's Hiro Yakura, who is officially in charge of electronic sales in this country. He is really in charge of everything here, though the smaller man beside him, Michiyo Kadomatsu, is technically vice president for all American sales. So who then is really in charge? If you walk into the next room, you'll see an elderly man with soft-soled shoes—Akira Tanagaki, the president of our company, on a visit from Japan. Also," he added, lowering his voice, "my father."

Shelly said, "Who's in charge of your truck?"

"Our truck?" repeated Eddie, struck by the question. "You mean the Vanagon? That could be any of us, really. We use it for transporting product—stereos, radios, TV sets—when there's a screw-up with the usual delivery trucks. Why?"

"When was the last time you saw it?" asked Shelly.

"The last time? Our last delivery from overseas was . . . just about two weeks ago. The trucking service picked up most of it, but we had to rush two sets to Bamm's for customer replacements, which went, I believe, in the van. It should be in the warehouse now—shouldn't it?"

"We don't know if it should," said Homer. "It isn't."

Tanagaki looked around for a telephone. "Let me call the warehouse, then. Our driver—"

Whatever he intended to say about the Nisei Company driver was cut short by a tap on his shoulder. Tanagaki turned to face a huge gray-haired Japanese man, two hundred fifty pounds or so, who murmured in his ear until the young executive nodded three times.

"I'm sorry," he said to the two detectives, "I've been summoned to my father's side. We are about to begin the ceremony and he has requested my presence before he makes his entrance."

Tanagaki followed the big gray-haired man through a portal that led from the reception area into a large domed room. Shelly glanced at Homer, whose brow furrowed in reply, and the two men trailed their only contact. As they entered the dome, the air changed, discernibly warmer and stuffier than even the monitored air in the reception room. The light, too, seemed brighter, with pinkish halogens refracting off the panes of glass that angled more steeply as they climbed toward the apex of the rotunda overhead. In the center of the floor was a three-foot-high concrete square of black earth, about twenty feet wide, in which a grove of mimosa trees had been planted, their tiny white and pink flowers stuck among prickly leaves. To either side, wooden boxes of exotic plants drooped delicate blossoms over the waxed boards of the walkway—pale orange petals streaked in white with purple stamens protruding rudely like the engorged sex organs of orangutans.

The detectives picked their way among sprawling branches and clusters of guests, while waiters in cutaways carried trays of hors d'oeuvres in and out: sizzling platters of beef teriyaki, steaming bowls of spicy shrimp, and bite-sized rolls of tuna and rice flavored with green wasabi wafted temptingly in Shelly's path. But Homer was not to be sidetracked, urging his partner on from behind. Beyond a stand of fuchsia and japonica they sidled through a glass door which opened unexpectedly on a terrace lined with dark blue spruce, green arborvitae, and an occasional holly tree in berry. Street noises suddenly replaced the party hum—less constant, more distinct than the drone indoors. They heard voices coming from further down the path, around the corner of the greenhouse, and beyond those the squeaky sounds of an orchestra tuning up.

"Here we go," said Homer.

As the cool night air struck Shelly with a fresh gust of evergreen, he felt a familiar tingling at the back of his neck. The rustling branches soothed his nerves, refreshing his appetite. After this, they could call it a night and catch a bite to eat. Shelly thought about driving down to Isabelle's for her Thursday-night special, turkey with stuffing and cranberry sauce. Was it too hot for gravy? He'd have to give that some thought—but it was the kind of deliberation his stomach was aching to begin.

He could not have anticipated how completely the next half hour would complicate his life.

8

When Shelly and Homer rounded the bend of the terrace outside the Enid A. Haupt Conservatory, they saw Eddie Tanagaki leaning toward an older man, who had to be his father, judging by the red carnation on his lapel. He was an earlier model of Eddie, with the same high cheekbones, though less gaunt below, and the same gleaming hair, less black than his son's but slicked back and longer so that behind his ears the ends stood out like the mane of a dragon. Akira Tanagaki was speaking, but not to his son; instead, he addressed his words if not his thoughts to another man, a Caucasian, six foot three with shrewd features, who stroked a white goatee as he pursed his lips profoundly in response to what he heard.

Lowenkopf tagged him as a honcho from the Bronx Botanical Gardens, their ostensible host for the evening. He wore a tailed morning coat which accentuated his height, a red tie, and a white carnation—the tip-off that his role in the coming ceremony would be less significant than his guest's. At a discreet remove, the gray-haired behemoth who had fetched Eddie watched patiently, hands clasped behind his back, as if waiting for a signal to join the three at the railing of the balcony.

The two detectives needed no such signal. As they drew near, Shelly heard Akira say, ". . . a beautiful tone to the reeds." He reached out his hand as if to touch the fragments of melody which wafted up from somewhere below the hedge. With the practiced smile of a diplomat, he shifted his head toward his son and said, "There is no need to tell me they are just warming up. That much I know about Western music. I'm not some old Jap foreigner from the movies, you know."

Everyone else grinned at the quip, grimacing appreciatively. But—had they hired an orchestra for the occasion? Shelly looked out over the hedge and saw people gathering in lawn chairs and folding chairs, on blankets and rocks, for a concert in the park, a series of performances arranged by the city for listeners in the boroughs. On the far side of some low hills below them, by a grassy slope near the museum, a full orchestra was preparing to play a recital on a makeshift bandstand. There was a festive feel in the air, like an evening block party, with a seriousness and attentiveness rare in the concert hall. The audience was interested in everything that happened: the scales of a woodwind, the tightening of a string, all of it part of the show.

On the balcony, the four men in tuxedos looked up as they heard the two detectives approach. The white goatee stepped forward, as if to block their access to his guests, but stepped back again as Shelly and Homer reached into their jackets for their shields.

"Police," said Homer.

"Sorry to disturb your evening, gentlemen," Shelly said, "but we'll only take a minute of your time. There's a nun and a priest whose liberty depends upon your information."

The tall man edged incrementally closer. "My name is Mr. Greene, with the gardens," he said. "I'm . . . responsible for what happens here tonight. If there's a problem, perhaps you should speak to me."

Shelly shook his head. "We're not here about the gardens," he said. "We need to speak to one of these gentlemen from the Nisei Import Company."

Akira Tanagaki looked for his son, who moved at once to intercept the intruders. "I can take care of this, father, if you'll allow me. Gentlemen, follow me, please."

Eddie turned briskly and walked back down the path to the domed room, evidently expecting the two detectives to follow. Shelly hesitated just long enough to see Akira Tanagaki return to the hedge, over which the noises continued, growing in volume. As a tiny crease of peevishness crossed his brow he wondered, "When are they planning to begin?"

Mr. Greene had to explain, "They . . . already have. That's Penderecki's *De Natura Sonoris*—hasn't much of a melody, has it?"

Inside the dome, guests had formed a circle around a straw mat on the floor in front of the mimosas. Eddie Tanagaki led Shelly and Homer just to the right of the mat, near the two men he had pointed out earlier—Hiro Yakura, in charge of electronic sales in America, and Michiyo Kadomatsu, his titular boss, in charge of all sales in America. Of the two, Yakura seemed the more self-assured. He was also the better dressed, in a tuxedo which showed off his powerful shoulders and the taper of his back. Kadomatsu's tux hung on his narrow frame like a suit on its way to the cleaners. Remembering Eddie's uncertainty when they asked for the man in charge, Shelly decided to suspend his assumptions about who answered to whom until he better understood the intricacies of Nisei's office politics.

Eddie addressed himself to Kadomatsu with a brief bow of his head, though he kept a careful eye on Yakura. "Kadomatsu-*san* . . . these are two police detectives who have come to ask us questions about our van."

Kadomatsu shook each of their hands with a question in his eye—evidently trying to determine the senior officer between them. As Kadomatsu turned to Homer, Shelly said, "We've located your van, sir. Did you know it was stolen?"

Kadomatsu shook his head, glanced at Yakura, who

revealed nothing, and turned to Eddie. The young man said, "I just learned about it myself, from these men. I suggested they speak to Frank, at the garage."

Kadomatsu nodded once.

Homer wrote down the name on his pad. Eddie supplied the spelling and said, "Muntz. You can reach him at our warehouse. You have the number?"

Shelly nodded in reply—the silence was infectious. He said, "Can any of you tell me how your vehicle might have come into the possession of an African tribal king?"

Kadomatsu looked alarmed; Yakura laughed. It was a throaty sound, deep and rich and confident. "An African king? This is getting better every minute. Is that really where you found our bus? In Africa?"

"Not quite," said Shelly. "It was in the possession of the elected leader of a tribal association in the Bronx. He told us it had been an anonymous gift, left at the curb near his apartment."

"Well then," Yakura said expansively, "the mystery is over! That tribe stole our bus, and you have recovered it. You have our gratitude. Now, if you will go arrest that king, we can get on with our little ritual."

He turned to dismiss them, but the two detectives held their ground. "If this was our only such case, we might do that," Shelly said.

The restraint in his voice caught Yakura's attention. "Is there something you haven't told us yet?"

"Yours is not the only vehicle left at the curb as a gift," he said. "Two days ago, a Ferrari Testarossa was also given to a convent—the keys left in the donation box, the vehicle parked at the curb."

Yakura stared at him. "A Testarossa?"

"We have the car," said Shelly. "It's hard to imagine the sisters stealing it and making up a story to cover their crime. The king, when you meet him, seems just as ethical and credible. It's hard to believe any of his subjects would have stolen the van for him."

"Do you mean to tell us," Yakura persisted, a slow smile spreading across his cheeks, "that there's a gang of car thieves loose in this borough who are robbing from the rich and leaving an occasional Ferrari to the poor?"

Lowenkopf didn't have time to answer that question, because at that moment a gong reverberated and all eyes looked up to see Akira Tanagaki led ceremoniously into the dome by the goateed Mr. Greene. They proceeded to the mat in front of the mimosas, on which the man from the gardens placed both feet, addressing the assembled crowd.

"Friends of the Bronx Botanical Gardens and associates of the Nisei Import Company—I bid you all welcome! We are gathered tonight at the Enid A. Haupt Conservatory to complete a promise made more than ten years ago, when Emperor Hirohito paid the compliment of a visit to our gardens. In the rock garden, the emperor noticed a flower growing between two stones near the edge of the walkway. He leaned over and considered the pink blossom closely. It was a local variety which suggested to his mind its more exotic Japanese cousin. 'Do you have a *shortia*?' he asked our director. 'I have some in a garden at the Imperial Palace in Tokyo. I'll send you a specimen, if you like, upon my return.'

"He meant, of course, the *shortia uniflora rosea*—rare in this country. Our director accepted at once.

"The emperor did send a specimen when he arrived in Japan, but it traveled poorly and died the first year. His son and successor recently learned of the story and decided to renew his father's offer—and so tonight we have among us a distinguished visitor and emissary from the emperor. Mr. Akira Tanagaki, president of the Nisei Import Company, has been asked by Akihito to deliver a gift his father wished us to have."

Mr. Greene then extended his arm in a genuine show-business gesture and abandoned the straw mat to Tanagaki. The businessman acknowledged a round of polite but appreciative applause with a becoming nod, which seemed intended to dissuade the audience's display but succeeded in prolonging it.

"Thank you, my friends," he said, smoothly but slowly, as if recapturing a skill that had once been automatic. "Many of you know, yes, about the emperor's visit in 1975. But how many of you know about an earlier visit to this garden, by a Japanese Red Cross mission in 1918? They were very warmly received here, for which my countrymen are grateful. I am personally grateful, further, because the leader of that mission, Prince Tokugawa, is an ancestor of mine, on my mother's side."

There was another brief round of applause. Shelly couldn't determine whether it was for the garden, whose hospitality to the Red Cross mission was being appreciated; or for the prince, whose accomplishments were being remembered; or for Tanagaki himself, whose ancestry was the object of their praise.

Tanagaki nodded as if to acknowledge all three. Then he signaled to the big gray-haired man at the terrace door, who seemed to function as a retainer as well as a business associate.

Shelly leaned over to Eddie and asked, "Who is that tackle? He seems to be everywhere your father needs a hand."

Eddie smiled coolly. "You noticed that quickly, sergeant. That is Hitoshi Shirane, my father's oldest protégé—his alter ego, really. They have worked together since my father first came to this country, in 1956. When he went back home to accept his promotion, he brought Hitoshi along— as he has every place he's been these last thirty years. They say that on my parents' wedding night, Hitoshi sat outside the door, in case my father needed any assistance."

A moment later, the light dimmed and a spotlight picked up Shirane carrying a large pot in which three small flowers listed gracefully among decorative gray rocks. All were less than six inches high, with bell-shaped blossoms and fan-shaped leaves; but the two on the ends were white and the one in the middle a pale pink. That, thought Shelly, must be what all of the fuss was about—the *rosea*, which, as if aware of its rarity, held itself a little above the other two. As the flowerpot floated toward Akira Tanagaki, the assembly clapped and murmured. With each of Shirane's steps, the blossoms seemed to nod, graciously accepting admiration, conscious of their fragile dignity.

Shelly detected no scent.

Shirane set down the pot before his boss and glanced at a waiter in the wings. At his signal, three bottles of champagne were presented and uncorked over trays of fluted goblets placed to catch the flowing effervescence. As each of the goblets was overfilled with sizzling golden liquid, the waiters whisked off, circulating among the guests, dispensing champagne. Homer lifted two flutes from a tray and handed one to Shelly; the tray then passed to Akira Tanagaki, who chose one for himself from the nine other goblets arrayed around the bottle. In a matter of minutes, everyone in the room who wanted champagne had some, and Tanagaki raised his own glass high.

"On behalf of the Emperor Akihito, as a testament to the friendship between our peoples, I deliver this *shortia uniflora rosea*—or, as we call it in my country, this *uwauchiwa*—from the Emperor's Imperial Gardens in Tokyo to the Bronx Botanical Gardens in New York City, U.S.A. In contemplating the beauty of a flower, we discover our likenesses as human beings, confronting the hand of the divine. Let the occasion remind us that each life is precious —occidental, oriental, and botanical."

With that he sniffed the flower, drained his glass—and collapsed in a black and white heap on the mat.

It took the audience an instant to realize that something was seriously wrong. For a minute, Akira Tanagaki seemed to wrestle with himself on the straw mat under the mimosa leaves. But his arm reached out spasmodically, straining toward the terrace door, and a gasp went up from the crowd. A cacophony of champagne flutes crashed to the floor. There was a moment in which no one quite understood who was supposed to respond, how. Then Akira Tanagaki gurgled, foaming at the mouth, and everyone sprang into action. Eddie started toward his father, but Shirane reached him first, kneeling over his leader, bursting his tie.

Shelly ditched his glass over his shoulder and pushed his

way to the mat, shouting "police" over the general din. No one paid him much attention but by dint of his experience and muscles he managed to reach the twitching victim before he expired.

Tanagaki lay on Shirane's arm, with his senior executives gathered around him. Kadomatsu gripped one hand, a terrible sadness in his face. Yakura seemed amused by the turn of events, although signs of concentration showed on his brow, from trying to calculate consequences. Eddie Tanagaki was clearly in shock—overwhelmed by the sight of his father's thrashing, his mind just beginning to touch the reality unfolding before him. Shirane looked impassively from the victim to each of them, reading their private emotions there, providing no clue as to how they might publicly react.

Mr. Greene was beside himself, gripping his head and wailing at the staff. "Is there a doctor? Is anyone . . . can anybody do anything?"

The waiter who had delivered Tanagaki's champagne stared at his tray in horror. It angled precipitously, and the goblets slid toward the floor. Homer stepped forward, righting the tray at the very last moment, lifting it from the waiter in a hand that was swathed in his handkerchief.

"Waiter—what is your name?"

"Fernando, sir. Flores."

"Call an ambulance," Shelly ordered.

The waiter fled toward the entrance, shoving his way through the crowd, through whom a similar impulse had rippled one minute before. Shelly looked at Tanagaki, whose twitching was subsiding but whose limbs were growing less flexible, and knew the ambulance driver could take his time.

Eddie seemed to startle from a dream and a guttural howl broke free of him. He fell over his father, gripping his arms, and the spasms seemed to flow into him. But he could not slow the older man's death, and he looked on with terror as Tanagaki's eyes bulged in their sockets, glared hard in front of him, and rolled toward the glittering dome.

Shirane's gaze moved from the father to the son, and his strong right arm left Akira to catch Eddie's trembling shoulder. The boy looked up in response and stared right into the man's stern eyes. A jumble of bewilderment, pain, and incredulity contracted his features, which softened as Shirane gripped his face with both hands and Eddie commenced weeping fiercely. The loss had penetrated the shock, Shelly knew, and his heart went out to the boy.

Easing Eddie aside, Shelly knelt over his father, listening to the cavity where the heart had pumped, reaching for the carotid artery at his throat. All silent. He tried pounding the chest, forcing air into the lungs, but nothing stirred inside. When he sat up, shaking his head, the boy was no longer watching.

Shirane lowered the head of Akira Tanagaki to the straw mat and left the corpse to his son. He stood slowly, wisps of gray hair hanging down. He looked about gravely, turning from Greene to Homer to Shelly for the face of local authority. He did not seem to be satisfied by what he saw and pivoted his weight toward the entrance, which now was choked with guests. He surveyed the scene emotionlessly, watching women weep on their escorts' lapels and men struggle to retain the blood in their colorless faces. It was a vision that made no sense according to the world as he knew it. But that world had changed irrevocably.

Shelly did not know what the man might do, and didn't care to find out. He moved beside Shirane and asked a question to distract him, tipping his head toward the corpse. "Has anything like this ever happened to him before?"

The big man stared at him, dumbfounded. "No . . . Mr. Tanagaki has never done anything at all like this. He has never died before."

"I mean," said Shelly, "has he ever had seizures? Epileptic, allergic, or catatonic? Has he ever thrown himself on the floor and screwed up his face at you?"

Shirane still could not focus. He lowered his gaze to the man on the ground and shook his head. "He has never left me this way before."

As a note of grief entered the man's voice, Shelly knew he was no longer a danger to himself or anyone else.

"I'm sorry," he said to the enormous back as Shirane's

71

bulk shifted again, retreating toward the terrace. Eddie had thrown himself over his father and was crying shamelessly, pressing his cheek to his father's. Kadomatsu squatted silently behind him, unable to say a word. Yakura stood, shaking his head and the trouser leg of his tuxedo.

Homer appeared from nowhere, at Shelly's elbow. In one hand he held the tray of champagne flutes, and in the other, a single empty glass.

"Fascinating, isn't it?"

Shelly wondered—the grief? Their timing? The spectacle of the assembly fleeing the scene? He couldn't find anything under the dome just then that he would have called *fascinating*.

Homer brought the tray around. Two flutes held champagne dregs; another six were dry, as was a seventh in his hand. "I found nine glasses from this tray still unbroken. It had twenty when it was served—at least, when it reached us. Arranged in a semicircle. The victim selected his own glass, after half had been grabbed. So how do you suppose the murderer was able to poison just the right one?"

Shelly didn't feel like thinking about it then, but Homer's question provoked his professional curiosity. "How do you know for sure that only the one was poisoned?"

Homer sniffed the brim of an empty. "All of these were full once, and nobody else is squirming. Take this one." With his free hand, he raised the empty by its stem and twirled it, reflecting the light.

"This one was mine."

Shelly Lowenkopf's dream that night began with the wrangle over the *shortia*—the lab boys trying to bag the damn thing or at least cut off a piece of petal for forensic lab analysis while Mr. Greene of the gardens protected it from their knives with his arms, at first, then his body. That part of the dream ended with Shelly in the branches of a prickly pine, munching on a sandwich of pink and white bell-shaped blossoms. But the most distressing part of his dream came later, after the vestal virgins.

The middle part of his nightmare began in that tree: under a low-lying moon, six pale girls in wispy robes danced around a coal-black lake in the center of a dark woods. Crashing through the conifers came Shelly—or a satyr, rather, with Shelly's face, and a bottomless appetite. He made quick work of three of the girls and took his time with the rest. When it was over, he sat goat legged on a broken tree stump, picking his teeth with a shard of bone while the virgins lay in every stage of undress, wailing for the goddess Diana. Suddenly, the deity rose from the ripples of moonlight on the lake; she took in the tale with a pitying glance, and turned a fierce eye on Shelly.

"Which of my priestesses have you spared, Satyr?"

"None," he said.

"None?"

"None."

For some reason, the triple exchange repeated itself in his head, picked up by the wailing girls like a hymn of violation. The words rang again in his head as he slept, gradually losing reference, until he heard them as a mantra, a repeated sound without sense: *none, none, none.* It wasn't until he heard them again as *nun, nun, nun* that a bell went off and he awoke in a sweat, his guilt plain as day.

The bell, however, had not been a dream: the telephone rang on his night table. He picked it up, blinking at the daylight streaming through the blinds, and heard his sister's sandpaper voice crackle over the line.

"It's time to call your ex," Isabelle said.

Ruth! remembered Shelly, and if it is possible to think a groan, he did so under his pillow. He had not, of course, called her back the night before—the investigation at the greenhouse had left him only enough energy and initiative to secure a greasy hamburger before retreating to his place in Washington Heights. He had not made it down to the diner for Izzy's Thursday special, with or without gravy. He listened to his sister breathing heavily on the line and felt sorry for dragging her into this. Just when she would have fallen into bed after managing the diner all night, Ruth must have called, trying to reach him. It was never fun to hear from Ruth, but he imagined how she would sound after two or three messages went unanswered, and pressed his pillow closer.

"Mmnff . . . why didn't she call me herself?"

"She tried," yawned Isabelle. "At least she claimed she did, around five minutes ago. You must've been snoozing pretty good. Who were you dreaming about—Madonna?"

Shelly remembered his dream with a warm flush. "So, uh, how is she?"

"Ruth?" Isabelle asked, as if the name had never come up. "She's all right—no worse, at least, than she used to be. It's Thom she's been trying to reach you about."

Shelly sat up at the sound of his son's name and let the pillow tumble from his head. Had he missed something important? A rush of guilt passed over him that made his strange affair with Sister Elizabeth seem a fond regret by comparison.

"Is anything wrong with Thom?"

"Not much, from what I could tell," said Isabelle, with her usual auntly tolerance. "Kid stuff, in the end. But Ruth is probably right in calling in his father."

It was difficult for Shelly to hear this speech, for two or three different reasons. In the first place, it sounded like his sister was agreeing with his ex-wife for the first time as long as he'd known them both. In the second place, it sounded as if Ruth felt some need of him or thought he should have some role to play in raising their son. Either supposition was unlikely enough, but the two coming together in the same phone call made him wonder if he was still sleeping.

He looked at the clock: 7:10.

"Gotta go, Izzy," he said. "The bad guys are up and around by now."

"I told her you would call, today. I swore it, Shell," she said. "It was the only way she'd let me hang up the phone—the only way back to my dreams. Give her a call right now, will you? Before she dials my number again."

She hung up before he could answer. The tone buzzed at his ear. He held the receiver there with his jaw, staring at the buttons, planning to push them, but stirred only when the digital flipped to 7:12. Which settled it: he had to get moving before he was late—it was now or never.

He dialed Ruth's number with a reluctance that was matched only by concern for his son. The phone rang once . . . twice . . . a third time, and Shelly's heart lightened. He had tried to call her and missed—that shifted the blame to her. The thought made him generous. He would try her again from his desk phone at the precinct house while Homer brewed his morning tea. There was even an advantage to it: he could extract himself from the phone conversation by inventing a police emergency. He didn't know why she'd respond to one after disparaging his job for

75

years, but knew he'd feel better about calling her again with a squad room of New York's finest on his end of the line.

As he reached toward the cradle, receiver in hand, he heard her pick up. "Shelly? Is that you?"

How could she tell by the ring? "Yes, Ruth," he mumbled. "It's me. How are you?"

"High time you should ask. Where the fuck have you been?"

"Nowhere special. My usual haunts."

"Like hell you have. I've tried your precinct house a dozen times already. And that shithole of an apartment. Since when do you go anywhere except back and forth between them?"

She was in feisty form this morning, he saw. He wondered if Clem was out of town. "Was there a reason you wanted to speak with me?"

She caught his tone—he was certain of it—but decided to overlook it, which made him edgier than any possible crack. She said only, "A reason? Just a tiny one. Your son has become an eleven-year-old thief. Whose influence would you guess is behind that—yours or mine?"

He was not up for another debate about his chosen profession. "What exactly is he supposed to have stolen?"

"No *supposing* about it, Shell. They caught him red-handed. If you had to teach him the seamy side of life, couldn't you at least have taught him to get away with it?"

She had not answered his question. He tried again. "What exactly did they catch him red-handed *with*?"

There was a pause in which he heard her foot tapping over the line. "You know those things on the front of cars—standing up over the grille? Like the winged girl on a Rolls?"

"Hood ornaments."

"Right. That's what he and his pals were stealing. Just for a kick, they said. They'd snap one off the hood of a Caddy, or pry one off a Beamer. Until a man down the street caught them bending back the little square on his Chrysler—can you believe it? A Chrysler? But when the police here confronted them with the evidence, they surrendered a whole collection."

Shelly imagined his eleven-year-old son being hustled into the cage. "Were they arrested?"

"You bet. I bailed him out right away, of course. But the disposition is hanging."

"So now you want me . . ."

"To spring them. Don't you cops have professional courtesy or something? I'd like to have this thing settled before Clem gets back from Houston."

It was a strong motivator for Shelly, too, though not in the same direction. "They've been booked already, haven't they?"

"Fingerprinted and photographed. Just like what his father does to people, for a living."

"Then there's not much I can do," he said. "I might've been able to talk the arresting officer out of the collar, before. Now it's up to the complainant and the court."

"Bull," said Ruth quite calmly. "There has to be something you can do. Otherwise, why the hell would anyone ever want to be a cop? It's not like I'm asking you to get him a job or anything. A salesman in a goddamn shoe store can get his kids shoes, cheap. Don't tell me you can't do as much as a lousy shoe salesman."

"Look," said Shelly, "I'll tell you what—I'll drop by after work. Maybe I can talk to the man down the street. At least I can talk to Thom."

"Oh, great," Ruth said. "Just what we need—another crappy talk. All right—so long as I don't have to listen. We'll see you when?"

"Around eight."

"I'll bet," she said and hung up without waiting to hear his reply. He couldn't blame her for that, though. After fifteen years of marriage to a cop, she'd heard the song before: eight o'clock, nine o'clock, ten o'clock—hey! What's an hour or two when there's a killer on the loose?

He entered his bathroom with a lingering sigh, which was echoed by the taps squeaking open in the tub. That old rush of adrenaline still tingled through his limbs, a sensation he rather enjoyed. It was strange to feel she could still do that to him, but comforting to see how fighting with him kept her spirits up. He lifted the little plunger on the bathtub tap and the shower streamed down, barely missing his head. It ran cold for a minute then steaming hot. To give the pipes a chance to negotiate a temperature, he shaved at the sink and brushed his teeth, combing his wiry, silvering hair, stretching the line of his neck. At forty-two, you looked either thirty or fifty—nothing in between. Shelly's best hope was to shoot for tired but young. He shaved his right cheek a second time where the bristles ran to gray and smoothed the wrinkles by his bluish grayish eyes. Some women liked men with a few years on them—experienced, they called it. He remembered his experience on the racquetball court, nicked his chin, and winced.

He tried to change the subject of his morning reverie as he stepped into the tub for his shower. How many suspects had they in the Tanagaki case? None, none, none. The water roared around his ear, drowning out the reprimand behind Sister Elizabeth's stern, sealed lips.

He chased her again from his thinking. But when he was washed and dressed in a light-gray suit he did not head for the precinct house. There was a question for Sister Margaret that kept nagging at him. She had asked Elizabeth to pray with her for a new set of wheels—in front of some boys, she said, banging erasers against the side of the school building. But what boys were around the place in the middle of the summer? It was the sort of detail that opened an avenue of inquiry: had she made the story up? If so, why? If not, the identities of those boys might be a good place to start.

If there was another reason why his heartbeat quickened and breath came more slowly as he neared the convent, Shelly didn't care to give it much thought. He tried to concentrate instead on the death in the gardens, Mr. Tanagaki and his flower from the palace. He remembered the white and pink blossoms falling to the ground, slipping from . . . a sandwich? In the hooves of a satyr. He understood the virgins already, but did he have to appear in his own dreams as an old goat? He pushed the memory from his consciousness by a deliberate act of will, parked in a red zone in front of the school, and propped the P.A.L. card in the windshield of his squareback.

The three buildings on the church grounds—a large school, a smaller convent, and an even smaller hospice—made an enclave of worn, gray stone in a neighborhood that had gone to ash and silence. Evidence of fire was apparent on many streets: buildings burned for insurance money, or simply to rid their landlords of the headaches of their management. Buses rolled through blocks on which only paper moved, blown from lots piled with garbage and deserted structures that still housed anonymous tenants. It was this, Shelly felt, that must have attracted the church-women to this site in the first place—so much unmitigated despair in need of their solace! Just standing on the sidewalk outside their residence was an act of solidarity with the poorest of the poor, an affirmation of the vow of poverty.

The door to the convent was open—unlocked, ajar. Inside was a writing desk of dark, heavy wood, positioned to serve as a reception desk. Behind it, a nun in full habit balancing a ledger told him that men could not go further and directed him to an armchair propped beside a table and lamp like a set for Alistair Cooke. Did they really think men expected a comfortable wing chair and pipe? It did look inviting, though, in a movie-set sort of way. He sat tentatively and, as the tufted leather gave, he settled back in its cracked seat. He felt like a visitor in an English club, like Sherlock Holmes's brother. He allowed himself to enjoy it until the nun returned a few minutes later from the living quarters upstairs and informed him that Sister Margaret was working at the school.

Following her directions, he made his way to the building and across the ground floor, stopping to listen at the top of the steps above the racquetball courts. No sounds arose from below. He considered running down for a quick look around, but realized that no one would be using a court at such an early hour. Later, perhaps, if the case brought him back, he might check out who was practicing and who might need a partner.

For now, his instructions led him to the north side of the building. The empty halls echoed with each of his steps as he crossed the waxed marble floor. At the far end, he found another staircase behind a door, narrower than the one that led to the courts. An aluminum sign screwed to the wall above the handrail warned that it descended to the basement.

From below, he heard the clank of hammering, metal against ringing metal. By the dim light and the suffocating air, he knew he had passed beyond the bounds permitted to students—heading for a place of darkness, heat, and endless repair.

10

As Lowenkopf made his way down the back stairs at the academy, he heard the ringing of metal beaten with a heavy instrument. The air was warm and thick, and smelled of machine oil. When he rounded the wall at the bottom of the stairs, he saw through the dimness a black shape crouched at the heels of a giant tin can, swinging a monkey wrench. As his foot stepped from the last wooden stair, the shape straightened, and Shelly saw the white band on the forehead of Sister Margaret's habit as the good woman strove mightily against the resistance of an ancient water heater.

"Sergeant Lowenkopf!" she cried out, surprised or happy to see him. "You are here with news, I trust? Have the charges against us been dropped?"

"Not quite yet," Shelly demurred. "We're still tying up a few loose ends."

"I never doubted that you would, sergeant. We may not have much around here"—with a *ding!* of the wrench on the boiler—"but one thing we have in abundance is faith." She stood, brushing dust from her skirt.

Shelly nodded encouragingly. This was going to be trickier than he thought. "You could make it easier, if you helped."

"Of course," said Sister Margaret. "We help all who ask for help here. What can we do for you?"

"It's not really for me," said Shelly, "but for yourself. Your freedom, that is. Do you remember at the precinct house, telling me that you asked Sister Elizabeth to help you pray for a new car?"

"To replace the Rambler. Yes."

"You said she was showing some boys how to clean erasers by banging them against the side of the building."

"That's right."

"The only thing is . . . we were wondering what those boys were doing here? During the summer? Isn't school out?"

The sister paused. "So it is. Then I'm sorry to say that I can't really help you, after all. I have no idea what they were doing here, banging erasers."

"But you must know who they are," Shelly insisted, trying to be reassuring. "I mean, you probably know most of the students in this school, I'll bet."

She smiled. "We're not allowed to bet—as you reminded me. But you'd lose that wager in any case. I *don't* know most of our students. I don't teach anymore, you see. Someone has to look after the boiler and screw new bulbs in the fixtures. Everyone else around here thinks a duct says 'quack!' So I was elected to the duty and discovered I rather enjoy it."

She handed him the wrench, crawled back underneath the water heater and reached out her hand for the wrench again. He pressed the handle firmly into her palm.

"Thanks," she boomed.

He crouched beside her, urgently. "The trouble is, we do need to know who heard you ask for the new car. That way, we can establish that someone other than the two of you knew how badly you needed a vehicle. Which means someone other than the two of you might have stolen the Ferrari, as a gift."

Her head appeared briefly. "You don't mean anyone still thinks we might have stolen it?"

"It's not altogether clear," he lied. "The owner has not yet decided that you didn't."

"Perhaps if you talked to him—?"

"We tried that," said Shelly.

"Perhaps if we talked to him, then," Sister Margaret said. "Most people will open their hearts when they're given half a chance. We must have faith in this person's potential, in the goodness of his soul. God will help him hear us."

"We'll need a verified, on-site miracle, at the very least," Shelly muttered under his breath. "We're dealing with Satan's minions, here."

"A procurer?" She must have pictured the car.

"Indirectly. And a murderer. He deals crack—a very nasty piece of business."

She seemed to consider that seriously, by the thinking time she gave it and the lines of consternation between her brows. Finally, she said, "Well, why don't you talk to Elizabeth, then? She must know who those boys were, cleaning erasers with her."

The suggestion took him by surprise. "She's not talking, is she? With her vow of silence and all?"

"Perhaps she will now," said Sister Margaret, "if you need her word to convince you."

"I don't need her word," Shelly said. "If you remember some boys banging erasers, that's good enough for me."

"But not good enough for everyone, it seems," the sister observed. "Not for the Ferrari's owner, whose opinion seems to count more than yours. Talk to Sister Elizabeth, please! For my own peace of mind. She'll tell you what you need to know to chase these charges away."

It was solid logic, he had to admit. But he wasn't ready to face her. He said, "She must be busy right now, I'll bet. Why don't I stop by later, or another day completely? When she's got a little more time. Maybe talking, even . . ."

"Don't be silly," said the nun, wiping the dirt from her hands. "We'll go seek her out right now. I know just where she'll be this morning, too. Today's Friday, isn't it?"

"Friday?"

"They were cleaning fish when I passed through the kitchen. It's Friday. Follow me, please."

Her tone left him little choice but to follow the sister upstairs, out of the school, and across the lawn to the hospice. Shelly quailed as they crossed the threshold. Inside, he knew, were children dying, orphans of victims of AIDS. He was never at ease in the presence of death, but this would be closer than most times. All his training, all the resources of his calling were intended to track down those who perpetrated death, and to bring them quickly to justice. Now he was in the house of his enemy, a place of inevitable suffering—by children, who of all people could least well protect themselves. Shelly shuddered at the reality with which these people lived, and admired the resolution in Sister Margaret's face as she held the door, waiting for him to enter.

They passed a small nursery, smelling of powder and diaper soap, in which two infants suckled bottles of formula. Above the cribs hung pictures on the walls, snapshots of onetime family members, and cheerful magazine photos. Across the room, a dour sister on a straight-backed wooden chair was searching for other bright pages in those same magazines. On the wall behind her, a discreet cross of some heavy metal helped her face her charges each day with a kind and loving grace.

Beyond the nursery was another small room, fitted with cots as a dormitory. There were six beds in all: two unoccupied, Shelly surmised by their tight sheets, pristine pillows, and lack of any private possessions underneath. How few and sparse were those personal things—some extra clothes, a keepsake, a toy—beneath the three beds that were claimed but momentarily empty! On the last cot reclined a boy of six or seven, with large eyes and sunken sockets in a thin, delicate face. He looked up from an oversized book when Shelly and Margaret entered.

"Heya, sister. Who's he?"

"A cop, Billy," the nun replied.

"We're not doing nothing in here," Billy said. He looked around to make sure the environment supplied no excuse for a hassle.

Shelly offered his hand to dispel the boy's suspicion. "We're looking for Sister Elizabeth."

Billy didn't accept it. "Don't tell me she's done something you ain't supposed to. She never done nothing wrong in her life."

Shelly could have challenged that, but answered instead, "You may be right. But I'm not here to arrest her. We need her help to free somebody else from charges pending against them."

"That sounds more like it," said Billy, satisfied with the results of his defense of her. "She's always helping folks. Like right now, giving Julie a bath."

"Thank you, William," said Sister Margaret, leading the way to the bath.

As they walked down the hall, Shelly asked, "That boy Billy, is he . . . sick?"

"You have to be, to earn a bed here. Orphans of mothers who died from AIDS, infected with the virus themselves."

"You keep them until—"

"As long as we can."

"Then where are the other rooms? For the older children?"

"There are no older children," Sister Margaret said.

They entered the bathroom, which was no more than that, a room with a toilet, sink, and tub. In the tub was a girl of two or three, shivering in the water. On the edge of the bath were two people: Sister Elizabeth, who was soaping the little girl's back with a sponge, and a young man of thirteen or so, who was watching, trying to help.

The sight of the sister sparked in Shelly a memory of their brief stint in one another's arms. He remembered the body beneath her habit—the tiny freckles on her upper arms, graced by short blond hairs—and an irrepressible swell of desire coursed through him. He was instantly ashamed of it, but could not deny the reaction her presence catalyzed in his blood. With an inward moan of lust and shame he said nothing, gazing at the sister on the edge of the tub, who sat blissfully unaware of his suffering.

"Hello, Robbie," said Margaret, taking a seat on the closed cover of the toilet. "This is Detective Sergeant Shelly Lowenkopf, of the New York Police Department. Shelly, this is Robert Delaud and his sister, Julie, splashing over there in the tub. I understand you met Sister Elizabeth last night."

There was a lilt in her voice when she spoke that was hard for him to read. Did she know something about what had happened between them on the racquetball court? It seemed unlikely that Sister Elizabeth would kiss and tell—but what might she confess? He looked at the nun on the edge of the tub, who looked up but gave no sign.

"Nice to meet you, Robert," he said, grabbing and shaking a soapy hand.

Robbie grunted. He was big for his age, with dark brown skin and green eyes that watched things very closely. There was also a confidence about him that Shelly sensed immediately and respected. He withdrew his hand and wiped it on his pants—to clean away the soap, Shelly hoped.

"We won't be but a minute," said Margaret. "Why don't you wash your sister? Or play with her, until we've had a word with Sister Elizabeth."

Robbie looked at Sister Elizabeth, who stood, straightening her skirt. She was dressed again in a habit though her feet on the wet tiles were bare. When they stepped outside the bathroom, into the hall, she slipped her feet back into a pair of tiny black shoes.

As the nun's hazel eyes swam up to meet his, Shelly found himself searching her face for some hint of recognition, or even a familiar expression. What had become of the smile which had so easily crossed her face? The sternness of her mouth made her seem years older. Her manner was indifferent to his presence. Didn't she wonder what he felt for her, or fear he might give her away? She could not fail to remember him, after the passionate climax of their game. So how did she stay so cool?

Sister Elizabeth looked at her hand to brush a blob of lather from her knuckle. There had to be two sides of her, of course, the nun and the seductress, but was it conceivable that she didn't know herself? From the warmth of her skin the day before, he felt the fire within—how could a woman contain that, who had vowed to remain chaste? He stared at her intently, to which she responded with a slight show of interest—or was it more than that, fiercely repressed? Had his face stirred some memory of a secret part of herself? Or was she simply wondering why on earth he was staring?

Sister Margaret saw something going on between them, but couldn't imagine what. "Do you remember, Elizabeth, about a week ago, when I told you about the Rambler? And asked for your help in my prayers?"

Sister Elizabeth nodded *yes*.

"You were out behind the school with some boys, banging erasers against the building. Do you remember who those boys were?"

A second nod *yes*.

"Would you mind telling Sergeant Lowenkopf their names?"

A third nod *yes*.

Shelly waited . . . but the sister kept her vow.

"Do you mean," he said finally, "that you *do* mind telling me their names?"

A fourth nod *yes*.

He turned to Sister Margaret. "She's still not talking."

"I can see that," said Margaret. "Elizabeth, you do realize that your information might help the sergeant arrange to drop the charges against me and Father Branigan?"

A fifth nod *yes*.

"I see, dear," said Margaret. "I quite understand. There's nothing more to discuss, then. You may go back inside to Julie. Before her brother drowns her."

With a final nod to Margaret that might have meant *see you later,* and an odd, lingering look at Shelly, Sister Elizabeth stepped out of her shoes and returned to the bath. But the door did not quite close behind her, and Shelly watched her resume her place at the edge of the tub, recovering her sponge from the water. Robbie sat with his back to the door; Julie looked from one of them to the other and splashed soapy water on herself. Some lather landed on her nose, where it clung until her brother reached forward and wiped it off.

"I don't think she'll help you," Sister Margaret sighed. "We tend to take our vows seriously, and Elizabeth is seriouser than most. But I suspect there's more to her refusal. She thinks, I would guess, that there may be some risk to the boys, if she gives you their names. Is she wrong in that?"

Not if one of them was responsible for stealing the Ferrari, Shelly thought. He shook his head.

"Then we won't be able to persuade her," Margaret declared. "She feels a powerful need to protect these kids, since no one else seems to. You can understand that, can't you?"

Yes, he understood. He watched for a minute as the two children and the nun engaged in a family scene. "What happened to their folks?"

"Their father I never knew," said Margaret. "Their mother was what is called a 'strawberry'—not a prostitute, exactly, but a woman who'll do anything for crack. When the child was born infected, she fell into despair and sought her own death with a vengeance."

From the room came a gurgle of laughter as the bar of soap slipped across the floor. Julie smiled at Elizabeth with delight in her round cheeks. Robbie turned to the nun, sharing his sister's moment of joy. Suddenly, Julie's smile crumpled in pain and she doubled forward, gripped by a cramp in her stomach. As her face hit the water, she opened her mouth to cry, but the inrush of breath sucked in mouthfuls of bath and she started to choke. The water spewed out as the girl coughed from deep in her throat, trying to clear out her windpipe. It was a horrible rasp, made worse by the pain in her stomach, still plain on her face as a grimace too old for her features. Only then did Shelly remember how she earned her place in that bathtub.

Elizabeth scooped the girl from the water and hugged her

in a towel, but the muffled eruptions continued to shake her small body. As his baby sister hacked and cried, spitting up greenish mucus, an ashen grief hooded Robbie's eyes—an old familiar ache. Julie was dying, as their mother had, of the same cause. And there was nothing he could do to help her. He turned and caught Shelly staring into his private cell in Hell.

Lowenkopf looked away only to confront Sister Margaret's unwavering gaze. "Well, Sergeant Lowenkopf, what's it going to be? Will you take me down to your precinct house with my hands cuffed behind me? Or will you let me back to my water heater, and the circuits in this place, so the sisters here can do their work with the help of 'Sesame Street'?"

Through the crack in the door, Sister Elizabeth turned to him. It was a powerful sensation for Shelly—not recognition, exactly, but a silent request for his aid. In return, her look promised nothing beyond the solace of having helped.

He said, "I'm sorry we missed each other."

Sister Margaret slapped him on the shoulder. "You're my kind of cop, Lowenkopf. An honorary Irishman."

It lent him limited comfort.

B ack at the precinct house, the real Irish cops were typing arrest reports and escorting criminals through the stations of the law. Lowenkopf arrived too late to have come directly from home, but lacked a collar in tow. It would have been easier to slip in, had not his partner and the captain and the captain's honored guest assembled earlier, awaiting his arrival. They were all in Madagascar's office, watching for him through its panes. When at last he entered the squad room, Homer pushed open the glass door with the captain's name etched on it and waited for Shelly to assume his place in a hard wooden chair near the desk.

Lowenkopf scraped the wooden floor, pulling forward his chair. The others watched him wordlessly; Madagascar squirmed in his seat. To his right, a trim man in his fifties sat sideways on a chair—his hair was white, cleanly cut, short and thick as a brush. He wore a navy-blue suit in some fine fabric with a soft sheen to it. From the sleeves of his jacket he pulled out his cuffs, which were clean with golden links.

"I think you know the bishop," said the captain, gesturing toward Lowenkopf's neighbor. "He has certainly heard enough about you, today."

For a moment, Shelly wondered if he was about to be accused of impropriety on a racquetball court—in a convent school, no less. But it seemed the bishop had arraignments on his mind.

"Have those charges been dropped yet?"

The question came from Madagascar, but the thought seemed to come from the bishop, by the intensity of his gaze as he waited for Shelly's answer.

"Not quite," said Lowenkopf wearily. "We're working on the complainant, sir. He's no fan of police—or fan of your people, either, father. We're going to have to produce some hard evidence of ignorance before he'll drop his complaint. In the meantime, we've avoided busting the nun."

"What about Father Branigan?" the bishop asked.

"Still on the loose," Shelly said, and caught the captain's glare. "If you know where he is, don't tell us, please."

The bishop rubbed the bristle on his glistening crown with a thick, ruddy palm. "I should think he'd be at Saint Augustine's. Near the Dairy Queen."

"We'll stick to Carvel for a while."

Homer was not saying much, Shelly noticed—straightening his tie and the crease in his pants, or picking nits from his sport jacket, a houndstooth pattern in another nubby fabric. Where did he buy those things?

The captain said, "What'd I tell you, Jack? You've nothing to fear from us. We know you, and the job you do, in my precinct and your diocese."

It wasn't really his diocese, Shelly couldn't help thinking. Brooklyn was its own diocese, with its own bishop in charge, who answered to the pope. But the Bronx was part of the Archdiocese of the City of Greater New York. O'Connor was the cardinal in charge of it all, who cut up his turf however he liked. If he gave the Bronx to Jack today, he might shift it to Joseph tomorrow. Jack's title was actually auxiliary bishop—but the captain liked to please his army buddy, so Lowenkopf kept to himself his thoughts on canonical purview.

There was something a little odd about Madagascar's manner, his attitude toward friendship, or this friend. It was as if he had too little practice with intimacy and approached it by what he had read in a book. Shelly realized he didn't know any other friend of the captain's—he had heard that there'd once been a wife somewhere, but nothing more definite about her. No personal photographs on his walls or complaints about visiting relatives. Madagascar did have a mother, who served, apparently, as a postal address for him to mail a card twice a year, on Mother's Day and her birthday. The bishop he called a friend of his, though they seemed to have no secrets between them—they acted like former business partners, neither quite sure what the other expected or might be prepared to offer.

"Thanks, Maddie," said Jack. "I knew I could count on you."

"Just leave your pieces of gold with the desk sergeant," said the captain.

They both laughed mirthlessly, a public display. Neither Shelly nor Homer joined in. The bishop stood, shook Maddie's hand, and bustled out the door. The captain watched as he made his way through the squad room and down the stairs.

"Good man," he declared.

The detectives said nothing.

He seemed to think about their silence for a moment, but opted to let it pass. "All right, now. What do we got?"

It was the signal to turn their attention to serious cases, which meant this morning Felix Aguilar on the basketball court and Akira Tanagaki in the Enid A. Haupt Conservatory of the Bronx Botanical Gardens.

Shelly had nothing new on the Aguilar killing: his cousin had not been found, and no one else knew anything. But Homer sat forward and said, "Lenny the Weasel told me that somebody ripped off Jimmy Twotoes on Tuesday night, during a buy. Jimmy thought that Aguilar tipped off the thieves—or maybe pretended to think so. He needed someone to blame for the theft, before Catalan blamed him. So he paid off Aguilar in a very public place, just in case anybody else gets ideas."

The captain snorted. "Anything you get from Lenny's not worth the paper he owes on it. He's probably just paying off a grudge he's got against Catalan."

"Maybe," said Shelly, "but there could be something to it. Aguilar did sell for Twotoes—we've heard that before. Maybe he was shot during the rip-off. They holed him up somewhere on Wednesday, and when he kicked, dumped his body on the court late at night."

Madagascar twitched his mustache. "Maybe. What's that? Maybe the Aces are feeling an itch for extra turf to their north. Maybe the Creeps want to move to the south. We know *why* the kid was shot: as a business move in the fast-paced trade in crack. All we need to figure out is who did it—and that you should be able to guess, if you keep your eyes open at the kid's funeral tomorrow. So tell me about the gardens."

Felix Aguilar's case was nearly closed: a gang death in the Bronx. The death of Tanagaki was another story—someone would care about him. The chief had received the first call already, from a federal trade commissioner. The chief had promised they'd put two good men on it, but all Madagascar had was Shelly and Homer. Did they think they could handle it by themselves? Or should he call in a major crimes team?

"We can handle it," said the two detectives at once. After all, what were they talking about? Tanagaki probably choked on his bubbly. If it was poisoned, they would know from the report the coroner was now dictating. It was hard to see how the case could take more than a day or two of honest-to-goodness police work. They had actually been on the scene of the crime when the dead man bit the dust. What could be more straightforward?

Madagascar eyed them uncertainly. "We'll see if you can," he muttered. "What've you learned so far?"

The answer was *nothing* as far as Shelly could see, but not when the captain was asking, who wanted proof of their thinking, if not hard evidence. He turned to Homer, who was good at these times—at making something of nothing.

Homer cleared his throat. "Well, to start with, we know the man is dead. A doctor signed the death report at 9:05 last night."

"What did he list as the cause?"

"Undetermined," Homer said briskly. "Which was the best thing to write under the circumstances. Our own investigation confirms it."

"In other words," Madagascar said, frowning, "nobody knows exactly what he died of?"

"Not yet," said Homer. "But the coroner's report should be ready any minute now."

"Why don't you get it?" the captain suggested. "To give us a place to start."

"Now that's an idea," said Shelly, rising from his chair. "Let's go, Homer. That's all we needed. And thank you, sir. Really. Thanks."

Homer was not finished with his recitation, but he followed his partner's lead. As they left Madagascar's inner sanctum, Shelly counted them lucky to have escaped with so few good ideas. Now they had a couple of hours to crack both cases before the next planning conference. As they passed the front desk on the way to the car, the sergeant handed him a message slip, from Michiyo Kadomatsu, the man in charge of American sales for Nisei. It said, "Must talk to you. Something found in Akira Tanagaki's room." It sounded more interesting than the coroner's, but first things first, thought Shelly. The captain had directed them to the morgue, so to the morgue they would go. Orders before tips—that was the sequence prescribed in the manual. Shelly was a great believer in the manual, when following it protected their autonomy.

They stopped at the coroner's for his report, then headed out to Brooklyn. Shelly drove, as usual, while Homer leafed through the autopsy. It was a soothing combination of sounds, really, the crinkle of stiff papers turned page after page, and Homer's enraptured murmur. The blond detective enjoyed those reports as other men read the sports pages. He scrutinized each number from the blood work to the joints, whose stiffness he always noted in his spiral-bound pad. This was his part of their work together: the closer its resemblance to tangible science, the more Homer relished it; the more it depended on feelings and hunches, the more he left it to Shelly.

"Anything catch your eye?"

"Mmmmm," replied Homer. He poked his finger at a page about halfway through and scribbled another note in his pad.

"Don't tell me," said Shelly. "He choked on his champagne, right? Which went down the wrong pipe?"

Homer shook his head.

"A heart attack, then? Or a stroke? Just tell me he wasn't poisoned."

"He was poisoned, Shell. On the spot. No doubt in the coroner's mind."

"Was it the flower? He sniffed it just before the toast. Or didn't the lab boys snatch a piece?"

"They got the flower, all right, chopped it up in pieces and tested every part. Know what they found? *Shortia uniflora rosea,* untreated and naturally unpoisonous."

"So it had to be the champagne," Shelly conceded. "Did they find any trace in his glass?"

"They didn't even find the glass," said Homer, consulting a note on his pad. "You remember what happened when he fell, don't you? Everyone in sight dropped his glass. There were plenty of shards all over the floor, but which of the bits were Tanagaki's? Not so easy to tell. They haven't turned up ciguatera on any that they've tested, so far. But they haven't tested all of them very carefully yet."

"Ciguatera? Is that what did him in?"

"Right. The kind of poison you find in mackerel, perch, and sea bass at the wrong time of the year."

"So he could've died from a seafood dinner?"

"According to his aide, he hadn't eaten any."

Shelly sighed. "Then we do have to figure out how the poison was placed in Akira's glass, and in no one else's."

"Fascinating, wouldn't you say?"

They reached the Nisei warehouse near the Brooklyn docks and parked on the street in front. They banged on a garage door for two or three minutes, then tried lifting it—unlocked. Inside was a bay where a van might have parked between steel shelves of cartons stacked floor to ceiling. Some had splashy, two-color packaging in English, designed for sale in the box. Others were marked in black laundry pencil with scrawled Japanese characters. In the back was a platform and the office. Through a plastic window overlooking the loading dock, Shelly saw Michiyo Kadomatsu inside, shouting soundlessly into a telephone.

Kadomatsu was the sort of man whose decisions were always reviewed. His ancestors might have been counselors to the shogun but never soldiers themselves. He had made a habit of deference, to Akira Tanagaki and Yakura, which had become his personal style. They entered his office without knocking, their steps obscured by the beeps of computer terminals on the two littered desks. From the surprise on his face when he saw the two detectives, they might have caught him placing a bet with his bookie. He muttered two more syllables into the mouthpiece and hung up the phone, straightening to receive his guests.

"Gentlemen," he said, "you are welcome here. Please, sit down." His English was excellent—a slight accent, but fully grammatical. He was either a crackerjack student, or had been stationed in New York a long, long time. Kadomatsu rolled forward a single leather chair from below the desk on which he was sitting, leaving the two of them to work out their own accommodations.

Homer took the seat before Shelly could spin the back around, which left him no alternative but to lean casually on the corner of the desk. Kadomatsu did not sit, but opened the pencil drawer underneath the desktop and began rummaging through bills of lading and packing slips.

"I hid it in here . . . one minute, please."

Homer leaned back in the ragged chair and waited for the discovery. Shelly found the corner of the desk uncomfortable and ambled to the window, looking out on the loading bay.

"Where's your driver, today? Frank?"

Kadomatsu scowled, deepening the lines in his wrinkled

face. "Where is he? Indeed! He never came in today. Sick again . . . with twelve dozen radios due at noon! He comes in like clockwork when there's no work to be done."

Shelly strolled over to the time clock and squatted before the wall, lifting one card from its slot. "Not according to this. He hasn't punched in for two days."

Kadomatsu looked up blankly. "Who hasn't?"

"Your driver. Didn't you know? Haven't you been here recently?"

He shook his head. "Only when I need to. Even then, only when no one else can go. After yesterday . . . may the gods bless Akira! . . . we are short-handed, now. The son mourns his father and cannot be expected to pick up and deliver radios."

Shelly nodded sympathetically. "Of course. But that would mean your driver has been missing since your van was stolen. Maybe no connection; maybe, yes. Can you give us an address we can use to find him?"

"On the card," said Kadomatsu. "On the back."

Shelly flipped it over and copied down the address on Avenue U that had been lettered on the printed line by Franklin Muntz. Beneath it was a phone number which Lowenkopf called, after holding up the receiver for permission. It was a dial phone, which he preferred to the push-button type. He let the line buzz seven times before returning the receiver to its cradle.

"If he's sick," said Shelly, "he's very sick. Too sick to come to the phone. Too sick, maybe, to stay at home."

Kadomatsu didn't seem to be listening, or to care about his employee's absenteeism. He had found what he had been searching for and was engrossed in a creased sheet of paper recovered from the scraps in the drawer.

"Here . . . here. That should tell you something about the death of Akira Tanagaki."

Homer accepted the piece of paper, reading it over slowly. He held it by a corner which he gripped through his handkerchief. "Where did you find this?"

Kadomatsu shook his head. "I didn't find it. It was given to me . . . by Hitoshi Shirane. He found it among the papers

97

in Akira's briefcase. I asked him to go through them, in case there was any urgent business that needed our attention."

Homer noted something in his pad. "Where do you think we might find him now?"

"Shirane? I don't know. You might try at the apartment of Eddie Tanagaki. He is deep in grief now, mourning his father. Shirane might have gone to comfort him."

"Tell us about Eddie," said Homer, licking his pencil point. "Did he get along with his father?"

"Get along?"

"Do you think he might have harbored any bad feelings toward him? Sons do, you know."

Kadomatsu shook his head. "Not Japanese sons. Eddie is a good Japanese boy. He accepted the position with Nisei Importing to please his father and has done very well by it. His approach has been . . . original for us."

"How do you mean?"

"We are importers: we arrange for merchandise to be made overseas and bring it into this country. Most of our business in electronics, for example, is done through a few large retailers. When Eddie first joined us at his father's instructions, he tried to learn from Yakura, but could not sell his TVs the same way."

"Why not?"

Kadomatsu shrugged, but not to signify ignorance. "Japanese products are resented by Americans but bought for their company reputations. Eddie's televisions carried a new brand name, with no such advantage to trade on. But he was determined not to fail his father and tried another strategy, after the smaller outlets. No big orders, but two sets here, four there, all together plenty of sales. All of it in cash. I did not think he could succeed in such a way—perhaps that is why I will not replace Akira when our company chooses a new president."

There was an acceptance mingled with sadness in his voice that made Shelly wonder about the corporate ramifications of Akira Tanagaki's demise. Homer did not seem to notice, rereading the note. When he had finished, he offered the page to Shelly, who had no handkerchief in his pocket and was forced to take the smudged sheet by the corner, in his hand.

It was written in an unsteady hand, as if the author had struggled for control of the pen, on a sheet of cheap typing paper, without watermark—the kind sold in a stationery store in packages of five hundred for high school student essays. The message began halfway down the page, cramped at the bottom, suggesting that the author had underestimated the final length of the note. It was undated, but by the crispness of the paper at the folds, couldn't have been older than a day or two at most. It read:

> *To Nisei President—*
> *Don't think you're pulling the wool over anybody's eyes—we are onto your invasion. You people may own the ten largest banks in the world—and a third of our toy business—and CBS Records—but you'll never own the people of this city. Go back to Japan, Mr. Tanagaki! We don't need any Jap flowers in our gardens! If you know what's good for you, you'll hop on the first plane to Tokyo and tell the emperor that the Americans beat you once and they can do it again, any time they want!*
>
> *The park is ours—stay out of it.*
>
> *The Robbin' Hoods*

12

The difficulty about a terrorist threat was that you had to take it seriously no matter how long the odds against its panning out. Especially a threat with overtones of racial prejudice; if you just spit and threw the damn note in the trash, and something unfortunate actually happened, you would never hear the end of it. So when Michiyo Kadomatsu showed Shelly and Homer the letter found in Akira Tanagaki's briefcase, the two detectives did not ask themselves how genuine the threat might be. They asked what they could do to check it out. And the first person either of them wanted to see was Hitoshi Shirane, who claimed to have found the thing among his dead boss's papers. He had also, Shelly remembered, been the one to open the bottle of poisoned champagne in the gardens.

Akira Tanagaki and his colleague had taken hotel rooms in Manhattan, but the two detectives decided to accept Kadomatsu's suggestion and look for Shirane at Eddie Tanagaki's apartment. Before leaving Brooklyn, however, they would pay a fast visit to Frank Muntz, just to check out his absence. If he was really ill, they should know in no time. If he wasn't, that would be worth learning, too.

The hallway of Frank's apartment building on Avenue U was dark even in the morning. Somehow the dusty windows, tile floors, and marble steps with wooden bannisters managed to block all of the light and trap all of the heat of the summer sun. The walls seemed to be sweating as they picked their way door by door, stopping at each entrance to search out the number in the discontinuous series so common in old buildings: apartment *A*, followed by *2*, followed by *III*, as each broken number plate was replaced in the fashion of its time. When they finally found *g* in an alcove at the back, and thought they had identified his name in pencil on a matchbook cover above the doorbell, they heard through the door a muffled sneeze and a death rattle of a cough.

Shelly was willing to walk away then, but Homer was set on verification. He knocked on the door with three firm raps, waited, and knocked again. No one answered, but they heard from inside another thunderous sneeze. Shelly reached for the bell and rang it three or four times in succession, which produced a shuffling of slippers behind the door and a throaty, "Hold onna yer shirt! *Ack, ack, akrrrumphh . . .*"

When the door opened partway, still clasped by a chain, a man of twenty stood in the crack, about five-eight, one hundred forty pounds, with a pasty complexion and puffy eyes. His jaw hung loose over uneven teeth, as if the effort of keeping it shut had long before overwhelmed him. From what they could see, the room was suffused in a bright, blurry light, obscured by a window of textured glass in the kitchen behind him. Muntz blinked into the darkness of the hallway for a full minute before his eyes focused on the men at his door.

"Who're you?"

"Police," said Homer, showing his badge.

Muntz stared at it hard as if he were memorizing the number. Then, without further questioning, he undid the chain and fled into the apartment, leaving them to find their own way into a dim vestibule and his kitchen. There was a card table, a folding chair, some blue plastic milk cartons stacked face-out as a sort of cupboard, a small stove and refrigerator, and a stained sink, filled with dirty dishes.

Homer, as usual, occupied the chair. Shelly pushed back an old curtain and leaned against the windowsill. Through the wall they heard a toilet flush, followed by another round of *ack*ing. When Muntz at last dragged himself back into the room, his irises swam in a yellow sea.

"Sompen I can do for you?"

He walked directly to Homer and hovered over the folding chair like a bird over its occupied nest. Homer stood up to the pressure for about ten seconds, vacating the seat before Muntz fell headlong into his lap.

When Homer had balanced himself on the aluminum shelf, Shelly asked, "Are you Franklin Muntz? Who drives a van for the Nisei Import Company?"

"At's right," mumbled Muntz. "Pleased t'meetcha."

He did not offer his hand and Shelly felt no impulse to seek it out. "Are you aware that Akira Tanagaki was killed last night? In the Bronx Botanical Gardens?"

"No shit," said Muntz, almost opening his eyes. "The old man? Bodyguard finally sat on him, huh?"

Shelly shook his head. "Poisoned. Why weren't you there last night? Weren't you invited?"

Muntz stared at him for a minute and a half. "Sure I was invited," he said finally. "But I'm a little under the weather today. Like I was last night. Din't you notice?" He leaned forward as he spoke, and Shelly had to catch him before he fell out of his chair.

"We wanted to be sure," he said, with a quick glance at his partner.

Homer was nearly satisfied. Reaching forward, he pulled down Muntz's eyelid with his thumb and examined the red blotches on its underside. "How long has this been going on?"

"Comes and goes," said Muntz, trying to blink while Homer held open his eyes. "Third day now. Fuckin' flu . . . I've almost got it beat, and *zing!* it knocks me right back on my ass."

"Upper respiratory infection?"

Muntz shook his head violently, which wobbled on his shoulders as if it might come loose. "Stomach! Is the worst. Outta nowhere, cramps so bad I can't wait for a dump. Start to feel better, eat a chili dog and *zong!* like a knife through the gizzards."

Homer's pursed lips looked medically professional. "Maybe you should give up chili dogs."

"Naaahh," said Muntz with a weak grin. "Love 'em. What's a little suffering now and then for something you really love?"

Homer was about to respond when Muntz stood suddenly, brows gathering, as if sniffing a scent in the air. For a moment he wobbled, waiting for something to clear. Then he bolted from his folding chair, scrambling down the hall, and they heard those phlegmy noises.

"I think," said Shelly, speaking loudly to drown out the sound, "we can safely assert Muntz has been ill."

Homer hesitated, listening until the toilet flushed again. "He certainly seems so now."

Shelly did not want to be in the kitchen when Muntz finished up in his bathroom. He heard the tap squeak on and the faucet running . . . now was their chance to escape. "It was worth a visit. But since we have no reason to doubt his flu, I suggest we move on to Eddie."

Reluctantly, Homer agreed. They returned to their Reliant and crossed the Fifty-ninth Street Bridge in a mood of mutual silence—Homer mulling over what they had seen, Shelly trying to forget it. As they bumped onto the broken asphalt streets of Manhattan, the car seemed to pick up speed, relieved to be out of Brooklyn. Manhattan was neutral ground for all the outlying boroughs—Brooklyn was another country entirely.

"What's that address again?" said Shelly.

Homer found it in his pad.

Eddie Tanagaki lived in a small apartment in a building off Second Avenue in the sixties, with a glimpse of the East River from the lobby window. The doorman allowed them up at the mention of Eddie's name, without showing their shields—he would, of course, be receiving all sorts of unexpected sympathy callers and had doubtlessly left word at the door. When they reached the apartment, however, they found no one there except Eddie himself and Kayoko, the tall, butterfingered hostess from the reception at the Botanical Gardens. She opened the door, saw Shelly, and blushed, leaving them to stand in the hall for a moment before Eddie appeared beside her.

"Sergeant!" he said hoarsely. "Kind of you to come."

He drew Kayoko away from the door by the elbow to clear a space for the detectives to enter. Homer nodded to each of them, eliciting a wan smile from Eddie and a stare from the hostess, which did nothing to disturb her delicate good looks. She was dressed in a simple white dress with a scooped neck and arm holes that showed pale skin nearly to her lowest rib. Eddie wore a steel-gray and white shirt, buttoned to his neck, with a tie hanging unknotted from his collar. His face seemed to have suffered tragic surgery since they had last seen him—red lids, puffed below, streaks in his cheeks still visible from his nails. His manner was calm, composed, but every few minutes a shudder shook him, as if catching up with powerful emotions that had just roared through.

"Forgive my appearance, please," he croaked. "Kayoko was helping me."

His fingers shook as he reached toward his tie, and Kayoko resumed her position in front of him, tying the knot. She was not particularly good at it, however, snaring her thumb as she stuffed the material through a loop, and the resulting knot must have distressed Homer, who said, "Allow me."

In a flash, a neat Windsor knot fell into place at Eddie's throat, and the young man nodded unsteadily at Homer in a gesture of relief and gratitude.

"Domo. Thank you."

Shelly settled in a rattan chair and waited out the sartorial exchange. The room was decorated in an Asian mood, though not with straw mats and paper screens: lots of space and light, some interesting sticks rising overhead from a purple urn, a rattan sofa and loveseat in a floral print that matched the chair in which he sat. In the center was a glass table, its invisible top bordered in a fine plum line around the edge, on a square stand of white wood. Under the table and the three rattan pieces, a rug in soft pink and blue covered exposed pine floorboards.

Homer reached behind Eddie's neck and folded down the back of his lapel. Then he stepped back and appraised his handiwork. "That should do it. Going out?"

"Just to the consulate," said Eddie. "To sign some papers. They're handling all the documents I'll need to bring my father's body home to Japan."

Kayoko cleared a zoology text and a flowered notebook from the table and set down a bowl of pretzels in their place. Shelly tasted one: no sea salt or other Japanese variation, but a plain brown twist that broke as he bit it—stale.

Eddie's head spun around at the snap, and the sight of the pretzel in Shelly's hand seemed to increase the grief at his brow. "We weren't prepared for anything like this," he said in apology. "You don't anticipate how much entertaining you're expected to do, when someone in your family dies . . ."

The last word trailed off as he fought back a sadness that welled in his face, brimming at his eyes. Shelly said, "Of course not. If you were prepared for his death, this would be a different sort of visit we'd be paying you now."

Not the most sensitive thing he might have said, but it had the desired effect: Eddie's eyes lost their redness as the comment engaged his attention. He turned hesitantly from Shelly to Homer and back again, trying to read their sympathies. "Just . . . what sort of visit is it you're paying me, sergeant?"

"An official visit," said Shelly quietly, "but one that need not alarm you. We're looking for Hitoshi Shirane. Has he been by here today?"

"No . . ." Eddie said, thinking back with difficulty. "Which is sort of strange, now that you mention it. He's probably my father's oldest friend."

"They met . . . where?"

"Here—in the United States, when my father was our

sales rep in this country. Shirane is a *nisei,* a second generation American, whose parents were interned during the war. My father hired him as a driver, because he knew the docks and back streets, and they set up operation here. It was not so easy for Japanese in those days, and Hitoshi's size was an important asset. When my father went back to take the top job in Japan, he brought Shirane with him as a VP."

"And now that your father's gone?"

"I don't know what will happen to Hitoshi," Eddie said. "It depends on who takes over, and the deal my father made."

"You mean an arrangement for Shirane? What if he didn't have a chance to make one?"

Eddie thought about that. "Old Kadomatsu would probably keep Hitoshi around for his loyalty and Michiyo's own soft heart. But I doubt if Kadomatsu will get the job. Yakura is another story entirely."

"Hiro Yakura?"

"Would cut Shirane loose."

Homer made a note in his pad. Shelly said, "So if your father didn't make a good enough deal, Shirane had a motive to plot against him?"

"I can't imagine that," Eddie said. "Motive has nothing to do with it. They worked together too closely, too long. And their time together was dwindling in any case. My father was stepping down at the end of the year. That's why he was here in New York—to talk with the candidates most likely to replace him."

"Kadomatsu and Yakura? Not someone from the home office in Tokyo?"

"No," said Eddie. "We're an import company, you see, not a manufacturer. Our product is made in Singapore, Thailand, even Korea. Our most important market by far is the United States, so our president must understand the American consumer. That's why my father was given the presidency straight from his post here, and speculation settles on Kadomatsu as his likely successor. But my father was leaning toward Yakura, I believe, and needed to check on the likely fallout if he passed over Michiyo. He also wanted a good, hard, heart-to-heart with Hiro—to see what really makes him tick."

"How do you know all this? Did he tell you?"

"No," said Eddie, blushing, "not directly. But he asked me a lot of questions about both of them. Questions always reveal a lot. Besides, I'm not the only one: he's been asking about them wherever he could, discreetly."

Shelly wondered for a moment what the interview revealed about *him,* but shoved the doubt away.

"What sorts of questions?"

Eddie upturned both hands. "You know . . . how they handled their sales accounts, what sorts of gifts they gave. A blend of ethics and strategy. Checking them out as businessmen."

"What answers did he get?"

"From me? Nothing but praise. Whichever way the decision goes, they'll both still be my bosses. One here, the other over there—it's just a question of who's on first. Kadomatsu is a man of honor, I said, and Yakura really knows how to sell. Those things don't seem to run together too often, so it's all in what you prefer."

"Do you know what your father heard from other sources?"

"He didn't confide in me," regretted Eddie. It was a painful confession, apparently, because his brow wrinkled and the color returned to his lids, though he held his head high. "He did seem a little less cheerful as his visit wore on, more somber—almost as if he knew what was coming . . ."

Kayoko moved beside him, resting a hand on his arm. Eddie grasped her knuckles.

Shelly didn't want to see him cry again and stood, offering his hand. "Thanks. That should help. Can you tell us where Shirane might be?"

Eddie took a deep breath. "They're staying at the Saint Bernard, on Central Park South. My father's suite was 504; Hitoshi's would be nearby. He's not an expressive man and might be walking off his grief in the park. That's what my father would do."

The memory provoked him to a brief smile, a brave stab at self-possession. Shelly reached forward and shook the young man's hand. With sympathetic nods in the direction of Kayoko, the detectives found their way out.

They did not see the look of unstifled fear that followed them to the door.

13

Hitoshi Shirane was not in his room at the Saint Bernard Hotel. He did not answer his phone when they called from the lobby, or his door when they went up and knocked. The maid had found the door ajar when she first came by at ten. He had not walked out since nine o'clock when the desk clerk came on duty. Homer and Shelly had no idea where Shirane might have gone and didn't want to risk a bad guess. They sat on the carpet outside his room and waited until 11:30, when the gray-haired behemoth lumbered out of the elevator with a briefcase clutched in his hand.

His bulk seemed to shake the hall with each step, an aging sumo wrestler in a tight brown suit. When he spotted them, he stopped in his tracks, thought a minute, and resumed his trek to his door. Shelly felt an urge to show him a badge, though he certainly knew them already. When he stood between them, fitting the key into the door of 507, Shelly said, "Mr. Shirane? We'd like a word with you. If you don't mind. About the death of Akira Tanagaki."

Shirane said nothing but left the door open behind him.

Shelly and Homer followed him in and found the room empty. Shirane had passed through a connecting door that led to the adjacent bedroom, where springs groaned under his considerable weight. They waited in two identical chairs on either side of a print sofa with end tables, arranged to make a sitting area in the outer room of the suite. The ashtrays bore the hotel logo, as did the unused matchbooks in them. They heard him in his bathroom, running water and gargling loudly. He reappeared a few minutes later, shoeless, in a plum-colored kimono of flying cranes. He dropped deeply into the comfortable sofa and put up his feet. "Awright . . . let's have it. Whaddya wanna know?"

His speech came as something of a shock—pure Flatbush. A graying sumo wrestler with a Brooklyn accent. Shelly looked at Homer, who produced from inside his jacket the letter given them earlier by Kadomatsu. Shelly waved in the general direction of his partner's evidence. "Did you find that today?"

Shirane glanced at the sheet Homer held in his handkerchief. "Looks like it." He reached over for a closer inspection, but Homer refolded the note carefully and returned it to the pocket inside his jacket.

"You know what it says?" Shelly asked.

"Sure—some kinda threat from a group calling themselves the Robbin' Hoods. Never heard of 'em before I saw that thing, but wouldn't mind meeting 'em now."

"You think it's on the level, then," Shelly observed.

"Isn't it?" said Shirane.

"That's what we're trying to determine. Would you show us, please, exactly where you found it?"

Shirane tilted his head toward the briefcase he had carried down the hall. "In there—Akira's case. Kadomatsu asked me to look through the papers, for anything we needed to know . . . on the business end. I did like I was told, and there it was."

"Where?" asked Shelly.

"Inside . . . you mean, where inside? About the third or fourth sheet down. I'll show you."

He started to stand but Homer blocked his access to the case by interposing himself. The look in Shirane's eye suggested he might be weighing the blond detective in his mind.

"Explain it to me in words," said Shelly. "We don't want any more smudging than you've already done."

"Sure," said Shirane, sinking back into his cushions. "It was a few pages down from the side with the clasp. The third sheet, maybe. Or fourth."

Shelly had to determine the truth of Shirane's account, and the best way to do that was to press for tiny details. "You don't remember, exactly?"

Shirane scowled. "Not exactly. I didn't know that would matter, when I found it. Damn! There's no reason to be busting my balls about the damned thing. I thought you guys would be tickled that I found it."

Shelly nodded reassuringly. "It'll be an important clue, either way."

Shirane did not sound comforted. "Whaddya think, I planted it there or something?"

Neither detective answered.

"Well, I didn't!" Shirane insisted. "I was just doing what I was told to do—why don't you go grill Kadomatsu? He's the one who told me to look in the case in the first place. Could be he knew the letter was in there."

"We'll check on that," said Shelly, "when we're done here. But there are other things we'd like to ask you."

"About what?"

"About Akira Tanagaki. Your late boss. From what we hear, you knew him pretty well."

"Better than anybody," Shirane said—evidently a point of pride. "Here or over there. Whenever some senior veep wanted to try and get through to Akira, he'd come slinking around my desk, looking for the inside word, y'see. I gave it to 'em, all right! Then I would mention this or that to Akira later on, over a tuna roll after hours. We had our little system, believe me."

"I believe you," Shelly said.

"We trusted each other, y'see," Shirane continued. "As you can only trust the people you know from before you were top a the heap. Akira knew that I knew that I never had nothing to gain from stabbing him in the back. So I never did, and he knew that, and trusted me better for it. I hitched my wagon to his star a long time ago, and it carried me right up. So why would I wanna do anything to mess up a deal like that?"

"Nobody's saying you would," replied Shelly. "But somebody did. We're trying to figure out whose faith in Tanagaki was several notches lower than yours."

The news that he wasn't a suspect at the moment did not lead Shirane to start talking. On the contrary—he thought hard but said less than seemed to cross his mind. "Everybody I know loved him."

Shelly's experience of his fellow human beings made such a state unlikely; when a source reported this unlikely state, odds were good he was lying. Shelly could think of many reasons to lie, of course, and all of them made good clues. He said, "Let's just take them one at a time, then."

"Who?"

"Everyone you know who also knew Tanagaki. We can start with your pals at Nisei Imports. We hear he came to New York to size up two candidates as his successor: Michiyo Kadomatsu and Hiro Yakura. Any idea which one he preferred?"

Shirane grinned. "You hear things pretty good. Who do you think he preferred?"

"Yakura. At least, when he first got here."

"Righto," said Shirane. "One for your ears. His numbers, y'see, are awesome. The man was born for sales. He once sold a CD player—with a graphic equalizer—to a school for the deaf."

"But not so strong on ethics as Kadomatsu?"

"Ethics? Nobody cares about ethics in business, really. Breaking the law is one thing: you don't want your executives in jail. Or, even worse, losing lawsuits. Hiro has never crossed that line, as far as I can tell."

"How far is that? Do you know what your boss found out from all those questions he was asking?"

Shirane's mouth clamped shut like a drawbridge. Shelly

saw the slack grow taut, the guard spring up in his eyes. The big head shook slowly side to side.

"He didn't confide in you?" Shelly sounded surprised. "I guess you weren't as close as I imagined."

It was a problem for Shirane: the ignorance he hoped to maintain implied less than full confidence in him on the part of his boss. The conflict stymied him for a long minute until he said, "I never got around to asking him."

"But you could read his moods, couldn't you? An old friend like you? He came into town rather cheerfully, they tell us, but that's not the way he stayed. Did he learn something that troubled him?"

The question seemed to stir in Shirane a thought that hadn't occurred to him, and deep lines of concern crossed his brow. He looked desperately from Lowenkopf to Greeley, found no answer in either face, and raised himself uncertainly to his feet. Shelly tried to read the man's confusion to discover what he was hiding. His silence had to mean that each of the choices presented to him involved some betrayal—of Tanagaki, presumably, since no other loyalties seemed to complicate his thinking. But how could his silence benefit Tanagaki now? Akira had investigated Kadomatsu and Yakura—what secret had he discovered that was following him to the grave?

Shirane shook his head. He couldn't say what was on his mind, and wouldn't say anything else. "No comment."

Shelly leaned forward. "This isn't an interview with the press, Hitoshi. Obstruction of justice is a crime. You could go to jail."

The big man offered his wrists, almost gladly—relieved to have escaped his personal dilemma. Neither detective reached for his handcuffs. After a moment, Shirane said, "Are you gonna arrest me or what?"

Lowenkopf looked at Greeley, who looked at the carpet. They could lock this lug in the slammer for a hundred thousand years—and still learn nothing from him. Their only hope was to leave him loose and tail him day and night. Sooner or later, he'd give his secret away. Shirane saw their expressions and dropped his wrists to his sides. At that moment, there was a ring at the suite's front door, followed immediately by a knock. Shelly and Homer looked at one another, at the suspect, at the door. No one moved. The knocker knocked louder.

Shirane decided to answer it and stepped between them, his lumbering authority restored. He had called their bluff and learned they weren't ready to bust him. That knowledge set him free. Shelly considered trying to stop him from reaching the door, but imagined their attempts to counterbalance the man's massive weight with their own—not a picture he wanted for his album. He settled instead for a stern scowl and a suspicious tone. "Are you expecting somebody?"

"Lunch," Shirane shot back as he peered through the keyhole. "I've got me a date with a poison fish."

Shelly and Homer waited in their look-alike chairs while Hitoshi Shirane opened the door to his hotel room, reached in his pocket for cash, and returned with a folded takeout plate and white Styrofoam cup. He set the cup on the end table near Homer and settled into his sofa with the takeout plate in his lap. "Ahhh . . ." he said with delight, opening the lid, "now that's what I call a delicacy!"

Inside were arranged thin, white strips of raw fish, like the petals of a flower, in a semicircle around a cup of sauce. Shirane scooped up one strip, nearly translucently sheer, stuck it in the sauce and into his mouth. He chewed the resilient stuff four or five times, then said in explanation, *"Fugusashi."*

Shelly hadn't the slightest idea what the word meant, but Homer leaned forward to inspect the fish more closely. "Is that tiger puffer?"

Shirane nodded. *"Tora fugu.* From the only takeout place in New York City. They also serve a *chiri nabe* with *zosui* soup that'll knock your socks off. Wanna try some?"

Homer shook his head. Looking up, finally, into Shelly's perplexed face, he said, "Blowfish. The innards carry a deadly poison that has to be extracted by carefully trained Japanese sushi chefs. Every year, a hundred people or so bite the dust in Japan after nibbling this stuff."

Shelly looked in horror at the beautifully presented fish. "Why do they eat it, then?"

Shirane laughed. "It's delicious! Here, why don't you try some? A little bite'll do ya."

Shelly shrank back from the offered morsel as if it might leap off the plate.

Shirane laughed again. "It's the way to show you're macho in Tokyo—like Russian roulette for lunch."

"I'll pass," said Shelly, turning to his partner, who seemed to hesitate before declining.

"There's really no need to worry about it here," Homer said. "The FDA has put this stuff through a screening more intensive than it ever gets in Japan. Only ten-year chefs can cut out the entrails of the exported stuff, which is shipped frozen and inspected all over again here. And it's guaranteed for safety by the Japanese government."

"So try some," said Shirane through a mouthful.

Homer shook his head. "Some other time."

Shirane lifted the lid on the Styrofoam cup and swilled a big sip of green tea. "Are we finished here?"

"Just one more thing," said Shelly, his eyes still on the strips of fish in the open takeout plate. "Akira Tanagaki found something during his investigation of Michiyo Kadomatsu and Hiro Yakura. Don't bother to deny it. Can you at least tell us which of them it concerned?"

Shirane said, swallowing, "Damned if I know."

"Look," said Shelly, making one last try for the record. "You've certainly proved your loyalty. We'll tell it to anyone who asks. But who is your silence loyal to? The Nisei Import Company? With Tanagaki dead, they might throw you out any time now. And what about your loyalty to him? Would Akira consider you loyal for letting his murderer get away free?"

Shirane paused at that, staring into space with eyes that seemed to gaze into the nether world. He held that stare for a minute or so before Shelly began to grow uncomfortable. He didn't want to interrupt the man's dialogue with the spirit of his boss, but there was just so long they could sit still, witnessing this seance.

Homer sat forward, passing his palm before the man's face. "Mr. Shirane?"

No reaction.

Shelly reached over and lifted the hand, which hung like dead weight from the lifeless arm. Pressing his two fingers over the wrist, Shelly felt for the pulse but couldn't find it. He shifted his grip, pressing his fingers closer to the base of the thumb.

No pulse.

The two detectives leaped into action. While Shelly threw the inert body down and administered artificial respiration, Homer dialed for the paramedics, redialed, and asked for a doctor on duty at the poison center. He was told to flush the mouth with water as soon as breathing resumed and the victim regained consciousness.

Homer rushed to the bathroom while Shelly worked desperately, twisting back the victim's arms to force air into the lungs. No change. He turned the body over and blew through his own cupped hands into the victim's mouth. Homer returned with an ice bucket, filled to the brim with water—which rested, untapped, next to the head. The victim had to breathe before water could be used. But the chest took a beating and refused to rise. It took more than ten minutes of contorted emergency tactics before Shelly was ready to concede that Hitoshi Shirane was dead.

14

The report called in by the coroner to midtown Manhattan and from there to the Allerton Avenue precinct house identified the cause of Shirane's death as tetrodotoxin—blowfish poisoning. So much Shelly and Homer learned from the sergeant at the desk, who recited the message in a doubtful monotone, as if he were reading a recipe for lasagna from a diet cookbook. The homicide team in Manhattan with jurisdiction over the Saint Bernard Hotel considered the poisoning an accident of the type that was bound to happen if people insisted on eating weird foreign foods. They were seeking an injunction from an American judge, prohibiting the restaurant that provided the meal to Shirane from selling any more *fugu*, and an inquiry was filed with the Japanese government, requesting an investigation on their end. The men of Manhattan were hard-nosed realists who had heard everything, twice—they did not want to think about nuns in Ferraris, or vans donated to African kings, or businessmen gagging on their champagne toasts in the Bronx Botanical Gardens.

Shelly and Homer perfectly understood; they would have felt that way themselves if the only case they had to solve was the death of a *fugu* eater. But Shirane's demise made another loop in a tangle of unsolved cases which were growing more tightly knit and intractable by the hour. They had to close the files somehow on Felix Aguilar; the stolen Testarossa and Vanagon; the deaths of Akira Tanagaki, and now Hitoshi Shirane. And the only clue that might address them all was a death threat in the name of a punning terrorist group.

Homer looked at Shelly with an unsaid accusation. Why couldn't they have kept their vigil for Felix Aguilar at the playground? The red Ferrari had led them down this rabbit hole of a case. Who would they stumble on next—Humpty Dumpty?

When they trudged upstairs to the squad room, they found to their surprise Jimmy Twotoes, leaning back in Lowenkopf's chair. Behind him, they saw through the captain's glass panels Cesar Catalan's sleek head bobbing back and forth as he paced in front of the desk. Madagascar sat behind it, his mouth a grim line, following Catalan through half-closed eyes. When Shelly and Homer crossed his field of vision, he signaled with two fingers for them to join the lively discussion in his office.

". . . and still not arrested?" Catalan was saying, thrusting his face across the desk. He was dressed in a suit of shimmering black, despite the heat, and a collarless, gray silk shirt. "These are known criminals—receivers of stolen property—walking the streets. And you sit here like a bull chewing cud."

Madagascar stopped grinding his teeth. "What is it with you and the nuns, Catalan? You got some kind of bug up your ass about clergy?"

Catalan's face lengthened. "No bug up my ass, as you so delicately phrase it. I am not an anticleric. The church is an important institution in my father's country, with many uses. I am interested in the ones who stole my car. Since they gave it to the sisters, they must owe a debt to them. I think they will not like to see the sister punished for their crime. If the nun is incarcerated, someone will step forward.

That is what I am after. If you find me the ones who stole my Ferrari, I will have no further interest in the sisters."

The captain sat forward, leaning across the desk. "Are you offering us a deal, Catalan?"

"A deal?" said the drug dealer. "If you like. I'll trade you the nun for the identities of the thieves."

The captain seemed to be thinking it over. "And what will you do to the thieves, if we find them?"

"That is my affair."

"No," growled Madagascar. "You can take your affairs to hell with you, Catalan. We don't do the dirty work for anybody. And we don't make deals with shits like you."

Catalan did not grow enraged; instead, a pencil thin smile creased his face. "You make plenty of deals with people like me, captain. When you are fortunate enough to be able to. I have many friends at the bar, prominent attorneys and jurists. We'll see what you will and won't do." He strolled out smartly, crossing the squad room without a backward glance. Jimmy Twotoes fell in a few steps behind him, looking around on all sides at the cops who glared at them.

Madagascar turned to his detectives, pouting bitterly. "That slimy son of a bitch can force our hand in court. The clock is ticking now. How are we planning to settle this thing?"

"We were just about to file our report," said Shelly, with a glance at his partner, who nodded. "But, captain, we're not really going to find these people for him, are we? You know what will happen to them—in or out of the slammer."

Madagascar scowled. "That's a hole they dug for themselves when they ripped him off. I'd like to nail the bastard as much as anyone, but we've nothing that'll stick. It's nice to keep an eye on the law, now and then. So tell me—what've you got?"

Shelly ticked off the list on his fingers. "Two poisonings, two stolen cars, and Felix Aguilar."

"I mean just this case."

"That is just this case," Shelly said, "as best we can make it out. It's all connected, one way or another."

"Give me a name," said the captain. "Who looks good for the stolen Ferrari?"

"The Robbin' Hoods," said Shelly.

"Who?"

"It's a long story."

"All right then. Go forth and type," Madagascar commanded, pointing toward their desks. "Just get this creep off my back, will you? Before Jack's back in my lap."

An hour later, they were back in their usual seats—Shelly at his Remington, finger by finger, while his partner listened to the keys strike the page. Shelly tried to recount what they had witnessed in Shirane's room at the Saint Bernard Hotel while Homer hummed and muttered "the Robbin' Hoods" under his breath. No one in the squad had heard of them, and the card file on gang members provided no clue. Their attempts to sound out the street proved equally fruitless. The Aces denied any knowledge of the group, threatening a fierce campaign of self-defense should anyone impinge on their territory. The Creeps claimed to know of the Hoods as a subgroup of the Aces. Ten minutes after that word came in, a second report from a contact in the Aces changed their earlier story: some of the gang members did know the name—as a splinter group of the Creeps.

Shelly and Homer were not impressed with the intelligence they were hearing: no one seemed to know these guys, who claimed to have ripped off one of the meanest dealers on the scene in the middle of a drug buy and escaped in his personal vehicle. It was an embarrassment he could not forgive, which meant Catalan had to be looking for the Robbin' Hoods, too. So how was it nobody had the slightest idea who these characters were?

With the death of Hitoshi Shirane, the detectives lost their best avenue of investigation. The discovery of the threatening letter could provide valuable clues about its authors, since details of delivery often suggest opportunities for access and so on. Without Shirane, Shelly and Homer had the note itself, which they had dropped at the lab for analysis; they had the name, *the Robbin' Hoods,* which their investigation was even now spreading all over the streets; and they had the alleged "gifts" of the Hoods, the Vanagon and Testarossa, to follow up as leads. These last pointed in two directions: first, to the convent, where a link might be found between benefactors and beneficiaries—thieves and church—which might supply a clue to the gang's membership; and, second, to the Nisei Import Company, where Michiyo Kadomatsu or Hiro Yakura stood to profit most by the death attributed to the Hoods. It was hard to know exactly where to start, but Shelly and Homer were both aware that the impetus lay with them. If they hesitated, or seemed to drift, Captain Madagascar would step in and instruct them how to proceed with the investigation. The captain was competent, in his way, but it was nothing like their own. They had to move or be moved; that was the choice—and both of them wanted to make it.

"This case is confusing as hell," complained Shelly, "if it is a case, and not six or seven cases balled up. What have we actually got to connect them? Maybe Tanagaki was killed by an enemy at the Nisei Import Company, and one of the king's loyal subjects stole their Vanagon for him."

"And one of the nuns stole the Ferrari?"

Shelly had forgotten about the nuns for the moment. Homer's question reminded him suddenly of Sister Elizabeth, whom he had finally managed to drive from his consciousness. A rush of guilt followed promptly. "We'll need to question them more closely," he decided.

"I'd rather start on Yakura," said Homer, "who stood to gain his company's presidency by Tanagaki's death."

It was a reasonable suggestion, but Shelly knew he had the edge, because Madagascar would insist they pick up the trail at the convent—the loose wire he found most annoying. But what could they really learn there? Their best lead on the stolen Ferrari would have to come from Sister Elizabeth, who had been asked in front of some unknown kids to pray for a new set of wheels. Did she know the names of those kids? Would she ever be willing to tell them? Shelly still wasn't sure how to approach her—about the car or anything else. So he ceded the initiative to Homer for a while, biding his time for a more auspicious moment to return to the convent.

"All right," he said, feeling in his pocket for the keys to the Reliant. "Back to Brooklyn?"

Homer had a better idea. "We've heard that Yakura's sales practices skirt the edge of the law. Why don't we hear from a customer?"

"Nice," said Shelly. "I like it. Let's go shopping."

They drove down to Herald Square in Manhattan and entered one of the big department stores. Consulting the directory on the ground floor, they rode the escalator to the fourth floor and found the department selling "small electrics": food processors and blenders, automatic mixers, hand-held vacuums, steam irons, and every sort of handy household gizmo. There were also several items that were not electric at all: shower massagers and water devices based on hydraulic pressure for brushing your teeth or cleaning some other, vaguer, part of the human body. Prominently featured over the counter was a computer game machine, which, from the sign, the vendor seemed to feel he was giving away—for about the price of Shelly's suit.

Shelly walked over to a working demonstration model cabled to a television monitor, on which a cop in a blue uniform shot an enormous revolver at a robber in a striped shirt and burglar's mask. A boy of four stood beneath the set, expertly handling a control panel that made the robber dodge behind a steel safe, from which bullets bounced *ping! ping! ping!* and poke his head over the top, firing back at the cop. Twice, the cop ducked just in time to escape the robber's barrage; on the third time, a round caught him in the shoulder and the cop tumbled from behind a pillar, gripping his arm. As he lay back, dead, on the floor of the bank, a flower sprouted from his chest while the TV played a tinny rendition of "The Volga Boatman." Da da da dum dum . . .

"What kind of program is this?" said Shelly.

As if in answer, the screen cleared and a huge logo came on, reading *Cops And Robbers,* followed by the question,

One player or two? The four-year-old boy pressed the control button for *one,* and the image resumed with a robber in a vault, racking up points as he scarfed up cash, while an unsuspecting police officer drew near, whistling and swinging his billy club.

"You're the robber?" Shelly demanded of the boy, who nodded and drew his gun as the cop turned the corner.

Shelly's own shoulder ached sympathetically as the robber's first round hit the cop. It took him a moment to realize that Homer was tapping him.

"Shelly," said his partner, "over there."

Homer's head tipped toward a young woman in a fashionable dress with a white flower pinned to her shoulder, conferring over a clipboard with a man in his early thirties who leaned against the counter as if he owned the place. The white flower evidently marked the departmental sales manager, which made the man beside her . . .

"The buyer," Homer guessed—by his smart suit, black watch, and wrinkled, balding pate. "Just the man we've come all this way to see."

When they approached, they heard the man complaining to his sales manager, "If we have to take a bath, let's do it quickly. I can't worry about markdown dollars now. We've got to move the damn things to give me some budget to buy."

The woman said, "How?"

They hovered over and were evidently discussing a clear glass ball on the counter top, in which mysterious blue-and-pink wisps of steam wafted and curled. The buyer held his open palm an inch above the top and the smoke cleared, leaving behind a message in wavy white letters. Shelly craned his head and read: *Japanese do it on mats.*

"Now what does that mean?" the sales manager asked. "It's supposed to be a joke, isn't it?"

The buyer shook his head. "All right—they didn't quite get the idea. Let's try it again."

He touched a square on the base of the crystal ball which made the pink-and-blue smoke swirl again. Fifteen seconds later, the buyer passed his palm once again over the crown.

Richard Fliegel

The steam cleared and the message read: *Japanese do it on mats.*

"That's the only mystery it reveals," the sales manager complained. "I tried it twenty-two times."

"All right," the buyer said, turning over the globe and removing a magnetic disk. "Forget the magic. No more crystal balls. Take whatever markdowns you need to sell 'em as smoky paperweights."

The woman brought out her laundry pen as the buyer turned his back. Homer used the moment to flash his badge in the man's startled face. "Police, sir. If you don't mind. We have a few questions."

The buyer glanced furtively around his department and said, "The name's Henderson. We can talk in my office."

Shelly and Homer followed Henderson behind a display wall of computer game cartridges to a small office hidden in the back. He took his seat at a worn steel desk and waved them into vinyl swivel chairs. "What can I do you for?"

"We are conducting an investigation," Homer said, "into some people at Nisei Import and wondered what you could tell us about Hiro Yakura."

The lines of worry in Henderson's face vanished, and a broad grin lit his face. "Hiro's finally crossed the line, eh? It's about time. Sure I can tell you something about him. What do you need to know?"

Homer said, "What you think of him."

"As rarely as I can," said Henderson. "And not much, then, at that. Anything else?"

Homer turned to Shelly, who raised his glasses, rubbed his eyes, and began, "He's a vendor of yours?"

Henderson nodded.

"What do you buy from him?"

"Anything he forces me to," said Henderson, smiling more widely and stiffly. "Video games, at first. Did you see those Nintendo knockoffs on your way in here? A first-rate deal, really. You can't touch an item like that for more than double the price, and the return rate is outstanding."

"Yakura supplied them?"

124

"At a very friendly mark-on, too. He wanted to get into the stores, he said. He did that, all right."

Shelly nodded to show he was with him. "Isn't that what he's supposed to be doing?"

"Sure," agreed Henderson. "Nothing wrong with selling me those! Blew off the shelves—a hurricane. The price point was irresistible. People whose kids already owned Nintendos were picking up a second set for themselves. But they're not exactly the same, you see. Just different enough to satisfy the patent laws . . . and to require their own cassettes."

"They don't run Nintendo's games?"

"They don't run the same cartridges. The technology's just a smidgen off—for legal reasons, he said. But Yakura could provide a version of every one of the kids' favorite games that would run on his cheaper machines."

"What's wrong with that?" Shelly asked.

"Nothing—so long as he's willing to supply them. And he was, for a while. We sold those babies to everyone who set foot on this floor . . . anyone who set foot on Thirty-fourth Street. Then he changed the rules."

"Of the video games?"

"Of our game," said the buyer. "Very politely, of course. His manufacturer was having trouble making the game cartridges fast enough, he said, to meet the demand we had stimulated by selling so many machines. He had some cassettes, but *not enough to go around.*"

His voice lowered so ominously as he spoke the last words, that Shelly was obliged to say, "Trouble?"

"You have to understand—I had sold thousands of machines, promising to supply them all with cassettes at a reasonably equivalent price. I had to maintain stock on the game cartridges or all those machines would come back. We have a very liberal return policy in this store—anything returned is taken back. Do you have any idea what my weekly numbers would've looked like if all those machines were returned?"

Shelly shook his head in sympathy.

"I was trapped," the buyer said desperately. "What did my friend Yakura want to maintain my supply of cartridges for his machines? Not much—just that I should buy up whatever he needed to unload. And we are talking the flotsam of the Orient, believe me! Did you see that crystal ball on the counter just now? A sure loser—and I knew it. But I had to buy dozens of them, if I wanted to buy cassettes for those damned machines."

He covered his face with his hands.

"You should've seen what I had to buy last month—automatic bottle openers! With a special setting for twist off! I ask you: how hard is it really to twist off a bottle cap? Or even use a church key? But, no, I had to buy those, too . . ."

The memory of forced merchandising took a toll on Henderson, who gripped what hair remained to him.

"I've got to get out of this . . . you've got to help me out! Couldn't you arrest him, or something? If they would just send over somebody else, I'm sure I could get myself straight."

Homer sat motionless, unable to respond at all to the man's shameful confession. Shelly leaned over and patted his elbow. "There, now. We'll do what we can. It'll be all right." Waving at Homer to back out of the room, he followed in hasty retreat.

"What do you think will happen to him?" asked Homer as they passed the display of game cartridges.

"He'll probably lose his job," said Shelly, "one way or the other. Which is not necessarily a tragedy—for the store, or the rest of us."

They passed through a throng of customers squabbling over Yakura's cartridges. On the display monitor, the cop once again clutched his arm and fell forward; a flower sprouted and the music began. A different six-year-old boy was at the controls. He raised his thumb and forefinger to make a gun, pointed it at Shelly and said, "Pow!"

126

15

If Hiro Yakura was blackmailing his clients, Akira Tanagaki must have learned about it. If Tanagaki had threatened to use that information to keep Yakura from obtaining the presidency of Nisei Import, Yakura might have done something to prevent him. At last they had a motive in this bizarre business, something that made sense. It lent a comfortable silence to the Reliant as Shelly and Homer drove to the address supplied by Kadomatsu for Hiro Yakura.

Yakura was not at home—so they were told by a uniformed maid at his apartment in a brownstone off Central Park West. From the telephone number stitched over her frilly apron pocket, Shelly surmised she was not a live-in, but a contract maid, supplied by a service to clean the apartment on some weekly or regular basis. A woman in her fifties with unnaturally blond hair and powder-caked cheeks, she leaned against a phone table near the door and lit a cigarette as they tried to peer past her, into the apartment.

"I told you," she said, "Mr. Hiro's not home."

Shelly nodded as if the comment had been addressed to him. "I heard you. But you didn't say where he was."

"I didn't, did I?" the woman observed. She may have been angling for a fiver, but Shelly just waited, calmly, for her to risk asking for money outright.

"Don't you know?"

"Sure, I know." Her expression made it clearer she hoped for a tip, as she dragged on the filter.

"Then I think you'd better tell us," Shelly threatened quietly, "if you don't want to get caught up in this. It's not a pretty business, I'm afraid."

By the way her mouth twisted, the information might have won her a bet. "He killed her, right? I knew it. I told my mother he was going to kill her one day. Now he's gone and done it."

Shelly waited until she had finished admiring her own powers of prophesy before asking, "Killed who?"

"Who . . .?" She exhaled a mouthful of smoke, recalculating. "How should I know who?"

He smiled obligingly. "Do the words 'accomplice after the fact' mean anything to you?"

"Accomplice . . . Now wait a minute, here," she said. "I'm not a part of this. He wants to kill her, that's his business. It's got nothing to do with me."

"Kill who?"

"That girlfriend of his!" the maid spat out, disgusted with the whole encounter. "Least, that what he calls her. I wouldn't call her anything of his, if I were him. But that's none of my concern, is it?"

Homer opened his pad.

"Her name?" Shelly asked.

"Joannie," said the maid unhappily. "Something. Here." She reached past the telephone and rifled through a Rolodex file of numbers. "Valentine? Must be. If that's her family name, I'll spit up quarters."

Homer copied down the address and phone number, reading over her shoulder.

The maid watched him bitterly. "That's private information. Which shouldn't come for free, you know."

"Thanks for your generosity," Shelly said.

The address was further north, in the nineties, where the upper west side ended and Harlem began. The buildings near the park were still expensive, but the socioeconomic index plunged precipitously as one walked west. Shelly and Homer found their number between Columbus and Amsterdam and did not have to check the directory because of the plaintive voice drifting out of a second-floor window.

"Please, baby," said a male with a slight Asian accent, "don't do this to me again."

He was answered by a crash of porcelain. Shelly and Homer exchanged a glance and ran up the first flight of stairs just in time to see Hiro Yakura leap from an apartment, yanking the door shut behind him. From inside came another crash of pottery and a curse in a language Shelly couldn't identify.

Yakura saw the two detectives and shrugged. "She's not in the mood, right now."

Shelly said, "What language is that?"

Yakura listened through the door at the invectives hauled after him. "Portuguese," he said. "Brazilian style."

"Do you speak it?"

"No," said Yakura. "You?"

Homer shook his head.

"Good. I'd rather not know what she was calling me now."

There was another thud against the inside of the door and another shatter of porcelain. From the weight, Shelly guessed a plate this time—possibly a serving platter.

"Just what did you do to her?"

Yakura shrugged. "You would think she'd be pleased by it. I paid the manager fifty dollars to let me in while she slept. When she awoke, there I was at the foot of her bed, waiting for her. But she didn't see it that way."

Shelly consulted his watch: 5:15. "She was sleeping . . . now?"

"She had a rough night," Yakura said as if he wished he were part of it. "And she'll probably have another one tonight. So she needs her beauty sleep."

The door was suddenly flung open by a ravishing young woman with dark features and blazing eyes in a bare slip of a dress. Her skin glistened from the heat of the apartment, from the heat of the argument, and from an additional heat which seemed to radiate from inside her. Her accusing eyes fixed on Yakura, who melted like a popsicle before she said a word.

"Who are you talking to, out here?"

He waved toward Shelly and Homer and said, "The police."

"Then you're not listening to me."

Yakura lowered his head, already condemned. "No."

For a moment, it looked as if she might punch him—he would have offered no resistance. But she settled on an even crueler course. "I think you better go now."

Yakura didn't look up, accepting her punishment with the acquiescence of one who fully understands his responsibility for it. That acceptance did him no good, however, for she stood in her doorway, watching, while he rang for the elevator, waited for the car, and with a desperate backward giance, disappeared.

Outside, they offered him a ride, which he accepted. Shelly tossed the keys to Homer, who climbed behind the wheel. Yakura sat in the back, dropping his head against the cushion with a face as forlorn as any collar who had ever sat in that seat on his way to the lockup.

To cheer him up, Shelly said, "At least you haven't killed her, yet."

Yakura looked up, abashed, as if the cop had just read his secret thoughts. Shelly studied his face and decided, yes, this man could do a thing like that.

Yakura did not usually allow himself to be read. "Is there something you gentlemen want of me? Or were the neighbors just complaining again?"

"We're a little out of bounds for a noise complaint," said Shelly. "We're looking into a murder."

Yakura's interest deflated. "Akira's?"

"For one," Shelly agreed. "There's also Shirane's, but let's stick to one at a time. We thought you might know more than you've offered so far."

"Like what?" said Yakura. He seemed bored by the topic, distracted from his problems with the girl.

"Did Akira know how you do business? Forcing customers to buy products they don't want? Threatening to cut off supplies they really need?"

Yakura's face crinkled in unexpected lines—a smile. "Did he know? Yes, I think I can honestly say Akira Tanagaki knew how I make my business deals."

His tone troubled Shelly, who would have preferred to see some sign of worry. But, having begun, he saw no choice but to stick to his line of questioning. "That made a problem for you, didn't it?"

Yakura stroked his sideburn. "What kind of problem did you have in mind?"

It was delivered with a twinkle of levity—Shelly almost admired the performance. But he was not about to be bluffed. "You were a leading candidate for the presidency of your company, whose unethical practices were discovered by your boss. Did he confront you with what he had learned?"

Yakura couldn't contain himself—he burst out laughing. "Confront me . . . ? No, he didn't do that. He offered me the job, is what he did!"

"The presidency?" Shelly stammered. "You mean he decided to overlook—"

"Overlook? Not at all! Where do you think I learned those ideas in the first place?"

"Akira Tanagaki taught you to—?"

"Encourage my customers to buy. Yes. By whatever means I can. This was a difficult business, thirty years ago. Akira got it started—even harder! When I first arrived in this country, I told him I couldn't sell, because Americans didn't really like me. He told me that they don't like anybody except themselves . . . but they respect anyone who wins. Which means, in this country, makes money. So I did."

131

He sat back against the seat cushion, relaxing at last, and grabbed a handful of vinyl in his fist. "You know what kind of car I drive when I'm not traveling by taxi? Real leather seats! Not like these."

"All right," said Shelly, "so you're making a good living. But if you're supposed to be the next president of the company, you've got a motive again for killing Tanagaki, wouldn't you say? To speed up your ascension to the seat of power."

Yakura smiled again. "That's the funny part. I'm not the next president of my company."

Shelly leaned over the back. "I thought you just said he offered you the job."

"He did," Yakura confirmed, "but I turned him down. Taking it would have necessitated my return to Japan. I would just as soon not go back there, now."

"Why not?"

"I've developed a fondness for your country," Yakura said expansively, gesturing at the city streets flying by the windows. "I've done well here for myself. I'm an aggressive man, and this is an aggressive nation. Do you know the ideal end result of a baseball game in Tokyo? A draw. Both sides play their best and neither loses face."

At Shelly's doubtful expression, he laughed. "Not exactly the American ideal, is it? How frustrating, eh, to be unable to shine! I'll tell you something: that's the way it sounds to me too, lately. I've lost my standing as a team player. My success in this country has spoiled me . . . I've become a New York kind of guy."

Shelly was unconvinced. "The number-one spot on any team has a draw for the lonest wolf. You didn't turn down Akira's offer of the presidency—if it really came—because you'd rather not give your regards to Broadway. If you were offered a shot at the top, you'd have taken it, pal."

The cheerful gleam extinguished in Yakura's eyes, apparently at will. "I cannot leave New York now. For personal reasons."

"Such as?"

"In my culture, personal space is respected. The social sphere is open to scrutiny; the private is left alone. But my reason is all too public, I suppose." An embarrassed sadness entered his voice as he looked over his shoulder at the streets disappearing behind them.

Shelly said, "The girl?"

Yakura nodded, deeply moved by his own personal conflict. "She would never come with me. Nor would my company allow us, there, to resume what we once shared. Japan is a small island . . . smaller, sometimes, than this one."

"Well," said Shelly, "from the noises I heard, you might do worse than give her up."

Yakura stared out the window as they turned right, heading south on Central Park West. "That is how it might look," he acknowledged, "but looks are sometimes deceiving. I cannot give her up. Not yet."

Shelly watched the trees rush past on their left. From what he had seen in the hallway, and everything Yakura had said, he was finding it difficult to disbelieve the man, despite his smug demeanor. No man admitted sexual dependency to escape a little thing like a murder rap.

He ran through the logic one last time. "Then Tanagaki knew about your business deals? And had no objection? And offered you the top job? Which you turned down?"

To each question, Yakura nodded. But the pleasure had run out of the interchange for him and he seemed to wish it were over.

Shelly sighed. "Then his death will only create problems for you—since you will probably be asked again to take over now, without him to name someone else?"

Another grave nod. When he looked up, a tear clung to the inside corner of Yakura's eye.

"And you really had no reason to want him dead, did you?"

The businessman shook his head, removing a handkerchief from his jacket pocket and wiping his eyes. "You have no idea," he said, "what it is to desire someone you can

133

never have again, no matter how sweet the memory! Someone absolutely forbidden to you—" He broke into uncontrollable sobs.

But Shelly did have an idea.

It stayed with him as they dropped Yakura off at a fashionable downtown eatery and watched him disappear into the crowd. It stayed with him as they drove up the East Side Drive, over the Triboro Bridge, and across the Bruckner Expressway. As they turned north onto the Bronx River Parkway, it struck him so forcefully, he told Homer, "Turn here. Left." Homer needed no more instructions than that and soon sat at the curb outside the convent that housed the sisters of Our Lady of Regret, their academy, and their hospice.

"What are we doing here?" asked Homer.

"Wait," said Shelly. "I'll be back in a flash."

He went directly to the hospice, through the glass doors, looking purposefully through the rooms for Sister Elizabeth. But he couldn't find her. Instead, in the nursery, he found Father Charles standing over a crib. The priest's mouth was drawn in an ashen scowl as he made a cross in the air and muttered to himself in Latin. Shelly looked into the crib and saw a baby that might have been sleeping, but lay too still.

Branigan gripped the cop's arm, shaking him from his horror. "Can I do something for you, sergeant?"

Shelly tore his gaze from the crib, alighting on the priest, whose compassion was visible in his eyes. "Maybe, father. I've been struggling with a personal problem and making no progress at all. God knows I need to share it with somebody."

"God knows more than that," said the priest reassuringly. "Why don't you tell me about it?"

"I'm not a Christian," Shelly said.

Father Charles smiled wearily. "I'll forgive you for that, and we'll see Who forgives you for the rest."

The priest led him from the nursery to a pair of hard wooden chairs in a room with several small desks. It must have been a classroom, Shelly guessed, by the planets pasted overhead and the alphabetic Gumbies twisted around the walls.

"Sit down," said Branigan, turning around the second chair and dropping onto it, backwards. "Is there something disturbing your conscience?"

Shelly wavered. "You won't like it."

"I never do," said Father Charles, "but it isn't my opinion that matters."

"It's about a woman," Shelly said.

"It usually is," confirmed Branigan, "once you're out of your teens."

"This is an unusual woman," Shelly continued.

"All women are unusual," Father Charles said generously, "once you get to know them. Each is a singular instance of the complexity of creation."

He seemed to be thinking of someone in particular—a mother superior in Rome, Shelly hoped. "You don't understand. I mean a really unusual woman."

The stress in his voice must have registered on Branigan, who said, "How unusual?"

Shelly searched for a way to broach his problem to the priest. All of the details were sticky. "I'm involved with a woman I shouldn't be," he said finally.

Father Charles nodded sagely, the confessor who had heard it all. "Are you married?"

Shelly shook his head. "Divorced. I guess you people would say we're still man and wife."

"Not really," said Branigan. "The rules aren't applied to non-Catholics in the same way. You'd be surprised what the church has been willing to countenance, lately. We're quite a permissive institution, by the standards of the old days."

Encouraged by the priest's report, Shelly breathed easier. "That's good to hear."

"Now to return to your own situation: the woman in question is married?"

"Some people say so. Or you used to, at least."

"Divorced from a Catholic?"

"Married to Christ."

Father Charles blanched. Then, with a visible effort, he managed to restore a trace of color to his cheeks. "What do you mean—'involved'?"

Shelly nodded. "I've come to *know* her. In that special sense, father."

"You've . . . had carnal knowledge of a nun?"

Shelly nodded. "A sister."

The priest swallowed hard. "One of them here at Our Lady?"

Shelly looked down. "I really don't think I should say, father. To protect her, I mean."

Branigan started to nod, but changed his mind in the middle. "It's not a question of protection," he said. "Don't you think the Lord knows her fault? She must be protected, of course—but from her own impulses. How can we do that, if you won't reveal her name?"

"I'm sorry," said Shelly, "but I can't do that. I don't know if nuns have reputations, but I don't name women I've slept with. I'm not that kind of guy."

"I'm afraid I must insist," said Branigan. "How can you be absolved, if you haven't repented? Repentance begins with a full and sincere confession."

Shelly sat up. "I haven't come for absolution."

"Then what have you come to me for?"

"For help," Shelly said. "She won't even talk to me. I was hoping you might give me a clue, how I might approach her. I've never known a woman like this."

"I've never known a woman at all," said Branigan. "And I don't think I can help you. The church has many things to offer, my son, to sinners of every persuasion. But we do not usually offer advice as to how to seduce our nuns."

Shelly knew he had said something wrong, but couldn't quite figure out where. He did not have a chance to correct himself, for at that moment he heard Homer's voice in the hallway, calling his name in a whisper. "Shhhhell?"

Shelly stuck his head out the door and saw his partner tiptoeing down the hallway, as a sister in a rocking chair tried to lull an infant to sleep.

"Homer? Over here."

The blond detective spotted him with evident relief. "We've got to head out, now. A call came in from the precinct house. Jimmy Twotoes is dead."

Shelly gripped his chair. "Any idea who did it?"

Homer made a face. "You'll never guess what they wrote in blood on the floor beside him."

Shelly felt a chill tickle his spine, a premonition come to pass—the second shoe dropping. He asked the needless question. "The Robbin' Hoods?"

"You guessed it."

16

The call led them to the wreck of a building off Southern Boulevard in front of which were parked a sleek, midnight-blue Jaguar, a white station wagon, several nondescript cars in bleak colors, and an ambulance, its siren off and red light turning listlessly. As their Reliant edged between a squad car and the ambulance, Shelly gauged the progress of the investigative team upstairs. The Jag belonged to Twotoes, since no one on the ghoul squad could possibly afford the price tag. Next to arrive was probably the squad car, followed by the ambulance—the officer on the scene had called the paramedics, who had arrived too late for treatment and declared the victim dead, which meant they could not then take away the body. The coroner's office had been called next for a deputy coroner, whose station wagon showed the grave blue card of his office on its dashboard. The other cars belonged to a police photographer, fingerprint specialist, and ballistician, probably also a criminalist, who would have been called moments after the coroner's office. Each of the technical specialists would have to examine the corpse undisturbed before the deputy coroner could flip it over for inspection. Since the deputy coroner was still inside, Shelly guessed the crime lab team was still snapping and dusting and scraping the floors, which meant they hadn't arrived more than an hour before Homer and himself.

Homer was out of his door and halfway up the concrete steps before Shelly had his door locked. Then he had to unlock it again to turn off his lights, since it was not yet dark enough for him to have seen the beams from behind the wheel. It was just dark enough to remind him of his promise to Ruth, to stop by and talk to Thom before the boy went to bed. But the corpse of Twotoes on the second floor had put the whammy on that. Shelly sighed, recognizing the pattern of their life: his ex-wife home, watching the clock, while Shelly passed his time with the dead. Homer waited at the shattered front door, blocking the reflection of gray sky in its glass and peering into the lobby of the deserted building.

These were Homer's moments: among bits of inanimate matter strewn in the wake of violence. Inside, a chorus of infinitesimal signs waited to sing for a listener tuned to their minuscule frequency. Homer's ears fairly twitched with anticipation. He left to Shelly the work of sorting through lies, half-lies, and half-truths—the sloppy business of human motives, desires, and deceptions. Homer enjoyed the stillness of things, their resolute inanimateness, which never told him anything he couldn't really trust.

Shelly watched his partner stamp his feet outside the lobby, and sighed. Until Homer felt he had seen what there was to see, there would be no point in trying to talk with him. Shelly's toe touched the bottom step and Homer bolted through the door. A moment later, when Shelly followed, his partner had fused with the gloom. Inside the lobby were four or five wraiths, who drifted in and out of the light cast by a single bare bulb in a socket hung by its cord from the underside of the first flight of stairs. There were two women and two or three men, gathered under the scrutiny of a uniformed policeman, who told them over and over again to wait where he had placed them.

Upstairs, the doors had been removed from the apartments, but a white light streaming from a doorway on their left indicated the scene of the crime. Homer passed over that threshold and reemerged seconds later, examining the dust along the steps below the handrail. He passed Shelly without acknowledgment and traced the trail back into the room. Shelly followed his partner into a large, empty space, from which the walls had been removed, exposing the supporting beams. In the very center, the deputy coroner was rolling over the heavy corpse, which landed on its stomach with a thick splash of blood. The rest of the floor nearby was bare of furniture or large objects, though scattered with shreds of plaster and chips of greenish paint. Outside, night was falling; headlights from the boulevard swept the room, through windows covered only by torn panels of corrugated packing boxes. Against the far wall, under the cardboard windows, Shelly saw silhouettes which looked at first like human figures, wrapped in blankets and gathered in a circle. In the flash from a photographic strobe, he could see that it was just a pile of rags and junk, artfully assembled. As he peered at the stuff through the coagulating darkness, a bluecoat passed in front of him, a precinct cop named Sy Spinoza.

Spinoza approached Homer as the blond detective neared him, but was unable to make contact through the glaze in Homer's eyes. Spinoza turned to Shelly, who nodded once in salute and again in sympathy. At the sight of a friendly face, Spinoza sighed and wiped his broad forehead with a cotton handkerchief. Outside, the evening air had cooled, but the heat of the day was still trapped in the apartment by the sagging cardboard windows and a thick blanket of dust.

"You the first on the scene?" asked Shelly.

Spinoza drew nearer, crossing the deputy coroner's line of sight just as his Polaroid clicked. "Me and Snelling. There was a call to the precinct about a ruckus here, and we drew it over the radio. When we pull up, what do we find but old Gregory D., sitting in this lovely Jag on the curbside. Snelling cuffs him to the outside of the door and we go upstairs, just like the caller said, and what do we find? Everybody's pal Jimmy Twotoes, lying just like that in a pool of his own blood. Still warm."

"The body?"

"The blood. Somebody must've called this in real fast."

"Where's Gregory?"

"Snelling's got him downstairs, with the bums flopping in this fleabag. You wanna talk to him?"

Shelly looked at Homer, who was pacing off the distance from the doorway to the corpse, which lay face down in the middle of the floor.

"Sure."

Spinoza led the way downstairs again, to the people gathered under the staircase. An officer in a foul mood had drawn the tiresome job of keeping Gregory Dvorijak and four homeless souls from walking out of the lobby. The only way he could think of keeping track of them all was to seat them on some broken crates under the stairs, which marked the only boundary that still stood. Dvorijak sat squarely on his wooden crate, arms crossed, legs straight, but the others seemed incapable of remembering instructions and would stand uncertainly, one by one, wandering off despite Snelling's objections until blocked by his physical bulk. Their forward motion interrupted, they would cast about for another direction, find a broken crate, and sit down for a few minutes, until the next idle distraction flapped through the darkening room.

Snelling was watching the steps from below as they descended noisily. When they landed, he said, "We gonna cut some of these beauties loose?"

Lowenkopf looked at the two ragged women, who had wrapped themselves in unraveling sweaters in the shadow of the underside of the staircase. They seemed rather peaceful in there, relieved for the moment of the need to protect themselves from rapists and thieves. "We'll get to them," he said, "sooner or later. First, where's Gregory D.?"

Snelling seemed disappointed not to be rid of the women. He jabbed his thumb toward the only immobile presence and said, "The big guy in the back."

Lowenkopf stepped over the debris and pulled up an orange crate. It was filthy, so he rested his foot on it and leaned on his knee. Dvorijak's crate was cleaner by far; he sat upright, leaning on a page of yellowed newspaper between his back and a rusty oil drum. His clothes were natty, but wrinkled and stained from the day's contact with his skin. Thick lips, a large nose, heavy-lidded eyes—his face gave the impression he had just been roused from a hundred years of sleep and was looking around for the first time, hungry.

"This is a bad day for old Gregory D., wouldn't you say, Spinoza?"

Shelly's tone was conversational and his face so close to the big gorilla's that Spinoza hesitated to answer. But when Dvorijak didn't respond, and Lowenkopf didn't continue, Spinoza shook his head. "Real bad."

"How many enemies you figure he made driving for Jimmy? Who wouldn't have touched him with Twotoes around, but might take a shot at him now?"

Spinoza figured silently for a minute, but seemed to lose count. "Lots."

Dvorijak yawned in their faces.

Shelly clucked sympathetically. "Looks like he's trying to get some sleep, doesn't it? Now that he's got us watching over him. Can't blame him. How much sleep do you think he'll get when word gets out that he set up his boss for the hit?"

The driver's jaw tightened. "Who says I set him up?"

"The police think so," said Shelly, turning to Spinoza. "I think so. Don't you?"

"Yeah," said the uniform. "I'll bet he did."

"That's a bucket a shit," Dvorijak said, "and both you guys know it. I would've high-tailed it out of here, if I knew what was going down."

Shelly shook his head. "Not until you knew for sure Jimmy was really dead. Otherwise, he might've come running down and found you'd taken a powder. You're a bodyguard, right? What were you doing on the ground floor while your boss was being shot upstairs?"

"I'm a driver," said Dvorijak. "And Jimmy told me to stay with the Jag. It just come out of the shop and he didn't want to see it scratched by some punk-ass kids swinging their heels at the fender. Twotoes don't need no bodyguard wherever he goes."

"He needed one tonight," Shelly said. "Didn't he?"

The big man stewed over that for a while. Finally, he said, "How the fuck am I supposed to know he's gonna need me up there? Jimmy was in charge when they left me down here. And that kid looked so coked out he couldn't have farted without somebody holding him up."

Lowenkopf nodded as if he knew just whom the big man was talking about. "That's how the kid looks, all right— what's his name?"

A crease appeared over Dvorijak's left eyebrow and he shut his mouth. "Don't waste my time with any cop crap. I'm not telling you shit."

Shelly's impression of Dvorijak was just the opposite: the sullen bodyguard was still in shock, with a story he was just bursting to tell, to exonerate his own failure. It was a story Shelly wanted very badly to hear. The question was how to allow Dvorijak to tell what he knew. He would still be loyal to Twotoes, of course—even more so, now that there was no reason on earth for it. Shelly had to figure out a way to let Dvorijak with a clear conscience spill whatever he knew, not as a betrayal but as a final token of loyalty to his good buddy Jimmy.

Shelly scratched an eyebrow and glanced back significantly at Spinoza. "What did I tell you? The driver set him up."

"I'll call it in," said the street cop, turning toward the radio in his squad car.

Dvorijak shifted on his seat. "Don't gimme that," he said uneasily. "I never saw the kid in my life."

"Then what's his name?" said Shelly, as a test.

"How the fuck should I know?" complained Dvorijak. "I don't listen in on the back seat."

So they had driven the kid to the building, thought Shelly. He said, "Who're you trying to bullshit, Dvorijak? Jimmy must've told you his name when he sent you to pick him up."

"Yeah?" said the driver. "Listen, smart-ass . . . I didn't pick him up. Jimmy walked him out to the car while I was still busy paying our tab."

Dvorijak obviously thought they knew more than they did about what had happened to him that night. Shelly was eager to maintain that misconception, but fished around for details as they bobbed to the surface of Dvorijak's convoluted account. He risked a name. "Club Wah?"

The big man flushed. "So what? Everybody knows we hang out there. Lucky guess by the flatfoot."

Lowenkopf shook his head. "I don't know how to figure it. We've heard a whole story already that could only have come from you. You say that Jimmy Twotoes picked up a coked-out kid at the club and drove him to this rattrap. You claim to have stayed down by the car when Jimmy and the kid went upstairs. Now that sounds like you're suggesting something about Jimmy's personal preferences. Did Twotoes like 'em that way? You know something we don't know?"

Dvorijak sat forward. "I ain't suggesting nothing about Twotoes and no black kid! Where'd you get that from?"

"You just said he picked up a kid and brought him . . ."

"I dint say nothing like that! That kid come into Wah with this camel-hair on his back—a real nice coat, see? And Jimmy leans over and says, 'You ever see that coat before?' So I take a good gander and if it isn't Jimmy's own camel, ripped off a couple days before!

"See, in the nighttime, Jimmy wears that monkey wrap even in the summer—his kinda *style*, like he learned from Catalan. When this kid comes in, in a camel-hair, there ain't a lot of places he coulda picked it up. I go, 'Wanna talk to him?' and Jimmy nods his head off to the side, the way he does when he wants something done and don't wanna ask twice.

"So I invite the kid to our table, right by the stage. He is one helluva mess, and I seen plenty by now, smoking the glass dick till their lungs cave in. His hair all stuck up on one side like he's been sleeping in his own spit for a year, his chest caved in and his pants sagging around his ass like he can't be bothered hiking them up. *Where does a wreck like that get a camel-hair coat?* Is what I'm thinking, and it's what Jimmy wants to know, too.

"Because somebody ripped off his coat Tuesday night when a business deal went wrong. Know what coat that was? The same damn camel-hair. He's been looking for those son of a bitches for three days now. That's what we're doing in the club all day—waiting for someone to come sniffing around after that bonus money we're offering. Somebody's gotta know those stiffs, so somebody's gonna be willing to sell them. It's just a matter of time, Jimmy says, waiting out the news.

"And then this kid comes into the place, wearing a camel-hair coat. And I bring him over to the table. He sees Jimmy's eyes on the coat and figures maybe he's got a customer.

"He thumbs the lapel. 'You like?'

"Jimmy goes, 'Where'd you find that thing?'

"And the kid gets all suspicious. 'Why? You know somebody who lost one?'

"Jimmy smiles, in that way he has, and takes the kid by the collar. 'Feels like mine,' he says, real friendly.

"The kid looks scared but he don't wanna give up his only chance for a score, so he grabs onto the front, by the buttons and the buttonholes. 'It's mine,' he says, hanging on, 'they give it to me.'

"Now that's just what Jimmy's been listening for. He goes, 'Who give it to you?' and when the kid clams up, he takes him by the throat and lifts him off the ground. 'Who gave it to you?' he says again, meaner this time.

"The kid looks down with great big eyes but he's got one idea left in his head. 'What'll you give me if I tell you?' he asks. He's hanging in the air, scared shitless, but he's still trying to deal!

"Jimmy likes that . . . he's making mean faces but I can see he's tickled by it. He almost laughs when he says, 'All right. What do you want?'

"The kid thinks for a second and goes, 'How 'bout a Jimmy Jones Sherm?'

"Jimmy's forehead scrunches up and he says, 'You know who I am, kid?' And the kid nods. So Jimmy says, 'Didn't you know whose coat you had on?'

"The kid looks like he's gonna shit and goes, 'You think if I'd a known that, I'd a come in here?'

"It made sense to me, and it musta to Jimmy, who stares hard at the kid in his hand and says, 'No Shermans. I can let you have some water, if your information pays.'

"The kid makes like he's thinking it over, but what choice did he have? Hanging in the air by his coat? So he nods, and I can see he's sorry that he didn't get a better deal for the coat, but let me tell you, Jimmy saved his life. I mean, a joint mixed with crack and dunked in PCP? A Jones woulda finished him for sure, the state he's in. Jimmy figured he could handle some angel dust, so that's what he offered. Like a gentleman. And the kid seemed to know it, too, once Jimmy set him back on the floor.

"He told us he was staying in this flophouse, when some big motherfuckers came in and chased him out of his spot. So he goes upstairs, looking for another place to crash, and hears some loud laughing, you know? Like somebody getting off. So he creeps up for a closer look and comes on a gang who are in a mood to party. They're doing every kind of shit you can think of, which gets his attention, and when his jaw drops and they hear the clunk, they offer him a toke. He accepts, just to be sociable, and sits down next to the smallest one. They're in just the grandest old mood. When he starts coughing, they pound him on the back. And when he starts shivering, one of them throws this nice warm camel-hair coat around his shoulders. He drifts off, happy as a clam. And when he wakes up, they're gone.

"Now me and Jimmy look at each other like this guy is full of shit. But he's got the coat on his shoulders, and where can a loser like this get a thing like that, unless he's stolen it from somebody else? So we figure he's lying, of course, but if we could find out where he stole it, we'd be just as good off as if somebody really did give it to him. Jimmy tells him to show us the flophouse, and the kid's plenty scared but says O.K. What else is he gonna do?

146

"I drive where he tells us, and he points at the building, but he don't wanna go inside, see? So Jimmy tells him he'd better do whatever the fuck we say or we're gonna bust his bones into tiny pieces and pick our teeth with them. The kid agrees, and Jimmy tells me to stay with the Jag and keep kids off the hood. They go inside and that's the last thing I know until your squad car shows up right next to me.

"I mean, I hear your buddies coming up the block, but what the fuck can I do? Tear out of here? Sure, that's the first thing I thought of, but I'm not gonna leave Jimmy without a ride. That should tell you something, that I didn't just wail out the minute your sirens and lights turned the corner."

It made sense to Shelly, in its way, though he had never really doubted the driver's loyalty in the first place. Life had been good for Gregory D. since Jimmy Twotoes had chosen him as his driver and second right arm. Those good times were suddenly full of holes, taking on murky water, which Gregory had not yet fully grasped. Shelly understood that the driver would have some honest grieving to do, as much for himself as his boss.

He heard a thud on the ceiling, then another, as if someone were jumping up and down. Spinoza turned to Shelly, who said, as a third thud shook the beams overhead, "Let's see what Homer has learned." The two cops headed back to the staircase, leaving behind an unhappy Snelling, four indifferent winos, and a rapidly sinking Dvorijak.

17

When Shelly and Officer Spinoza returned to the room on the second floor in which Jimmy Twotoes lay murdered, they found Homer literally jumping up and down, trying to reach a scrap of cloth stuck between the top of a window and the frame. On the third leap he managed to grab hold of the thing, pulling down a frazzled bit of shredded material, which he examined without comment and handed to a man in a cheap gray suit, who slipped the bit of purported evidence into a specimen bag and penned a few words on the label. He seemed less than delighted with Homer's thoroughness, though he kept his thoughts to himself. The deputy coroner was giving unnecessary instructions to two men from his office as they loaded the body onto a gurney, tied two sheets over it, and rolled it from the room, clattering down the rickety staircase outside. When the body was gone, Homer squatted beside the spot where it had been examined, scratching the bloodstains from cracks between the floorboards with a Boy Scout knife and a frown.

Shelly checked his watch: almost half-past six. He had only about an hour before he had to leave for Ruth's to discuss their son's interest in a life of crime. It seemed an opportune moment to ask his partner what he had gleaned from the drying smears and omnipresent dust. Shelly squatted beside the blond detective and asked, "What'd we learn here, Homer?"

Homer shook his head. "Not much. Twotoes followed someone up here . . . somebody he mistrusted but didn't actually fear. I've been trying to learn something about the guide. There's not much to go on, but my guess would be a coked-out looking kid with more juice to him than he ought to have for the sagging of his pants. About five-ten and probably black."

Shelly blinked. "You heard that from one of the bluecoats, right? Someone who'd talked to Dvorijak?"

Homer looked surprised. "Gregory D.? Was he here?"

"Right downstairs," said Shelly, waving toward the stairs. "You didn't know that?"

Homer shook his head.

"So how'd you know about . . . ."

"The kid?" Homer rubbed his hands together, brushing dirt from his palms and preparing to launch on his lecture. The only thing he enjoyed more than scrounging for clues was explaining what he had discovered. "Couldn't be simpler. This place hasn't been swept for ages—everything's still in the dust. Where our own boys haven't trod all over it, of course."

He made a wry face at the crime lab team, who ignored him, as if some words had already passed between them.

"But there's enough by the handrail to tell a thing or two, if you know how to read it. Twotoes followed somebody up those stairs. By the size of the feet, I'd say a teenager or a midget. Now how many midgets have you seen in the Bronx lately?"

"All right," said Shelly, conceding the odds, "so a kid. But where does it say coked-out looking? And the bit about his juice?"

"Take a look at his footprints," Homer offered generously. "You can see his trouser bottoms dragging after his heels. Those pants are sagging badly! But consider the length of stride here. No shuffling gait. The height, of course, is an estimate based on stride. And the color of his skin . . . well, you see the way the second foot points sideways after each long stride? If you see a white kid bopping down the street like that, you know he's spent some time in the ghetto or the Hall."

Shelly stuck out his jaw. "And where do you get the business about not exactly trusting the kid, but not being afraid of him, either?"

"Well, look," said Homer, retracing the steps of his logic as if they were self-evident, "he fell in the middle of the room, didn't he? So no one could've slipped in behind him. He still had his gun in his hand, which means someone pulled a gun on him here—otherwise, they would've told him to drop his own weapon earlier. There are powder burns on the back of Jimmy's shirt: someone was right behind him. Now Twotoes was a suspicious sort of fellow— you have to be, in his business. So if someone was able to get close enough to pull a gun on Jimmy right behind his back, we can safely conclude Twotoes felt he had nothing to fear from that person."

"So maybe he trusted him, after all. One of his boys."

"Maybe. But that doesn't figure with the footprints on the stairs. When have you ever seen Twotoes following anybody else but Catalan? Never one of his own boys. He must've held a gun on the kid as they came up the stairs—that's why he kept a pace behind. When they entered the room, Twotoes saw something that he thought he had to worry about more than the kid who brought him here."

"Like what? The Robbin' Hoods?"

Homer shook his head. "Maybe. But my guess is that pile of rags under the window. Do you suppose they arranged themselves to look like sleeping bodies when the headlights from the street sweep this place? That's when he stepped in front of the kid. And that's when the kid plugged him with a small-caliber firearm, from behind."

Shelly could see it—the kid having finally passed the test by leading Twotoes to the thieves who stole his coat. Jimmy's guard would have dropped a second. "You don't think it was a rip-off?"

"A setup," said Homer without hesitation. "They found a camel-hair coat with a neat bullet hole, in a trashbin two blocks from here. The kid must have used the coat to muffle the shot, shooting from inside. Probably because Dvorijak was waiting for Twotoes outside. Now what kind of mugger ruins a coat like that for a chance at what's in his pockets? Only somebody who doesn't give a damn about the coat or the contents of Twotoes's pockets. Someone after the man himself."

"The Robbin' Hoods," muttered Shelly. "Catalan wanted them dead—that much he told us in the precinct house. And whatever Cesar wanted, Jimmy was happy to oblige."

"Twotoes must have been looking for them, at least," agreed Homer. "The word was out on the street. Only, before he found them, they found him."

Shelly searched the bloodstains on the floor more carefully. Finally he asked, "Where's the signature? Claiming credit for the death. You heard it over the radio at the convent."

"Here," said Homer, waving a finger at an indistinguishable part of the stain. "I think you can make out the first three letters. The deputy coroner was turning over the corpse when we walked in. Remember? He laid it right down here."

Shelly looked around the room for the deputy coroner, who seemed to have departed while they talked. "He could've waited until we saw it for ourselves."

"He should have," Homer said, "but he had another call on the far side of town. A suicide in Parkchester. The wife's been shrieking at the top of her lungs since she found the body. The neighbors had phoned the coroner five times already."

Shelly studied the floorboard under Homer's thumb, searching for letters in the bloodstains. A few smudges, maybe a stroke—nothing clear. "I can't see any of it."

"Don't worry," said Homer, "the whole thing will show up in the pictures. The photographer promised me he took half a dozen shots of the lettering. I mean, letters in blood by the victim's index finger? After six years taking pictures in this business, it looked like a clue to him."

Shelly could see how it might. It didn't make him feel any better about missing the clue, or about the prospect which lay ahead of them. "So," he said slowly, "the next thing for us to do is put out a description of this kid, and track down what comes back—especially if there's an Amerasian kid anywhere in the vicinity."

"No," said Homer, frowning. "These are transients in this building, and all along the block. By morning, news of what happened here will be all over the neighborhood, and these people will be gone. Our next move has to be to talk to whoever will answer and see what we can learn right now."

It was what Shelly expected to hear from his partner, just what he was trying to avoid. "We're not going to learn anything useful that way," he said. "These people would rather talk to the walls than to the police."

"Maybe so," said Homer, "but we're certainly not going to learn anything if we don't ask. And if we don't ask now, there's never going to be another chance."

The logic of Homer's argument was inescapable, as usual, and Shelly couldn't think of a way to complicate the question. As a result, they spent the next three hours moving from cellar to rooftop through the abandoned buildings, stirring piles of rags from which emerged hands and eyes and occasionally half a head—none of whom had seen or heard anything unusual that night, or recognized their description of the kid. When they had finished, Shelly and Homer knew nothing more than they had when they began the process, except that there was nothing more to learn there that night. It was enough for Homer, who felt satisfied by their effort; it made Shelly even angrier, who knew he had missed his time with his son for the sake of having learned that he might as well have gone on to Pelham.

By the time he dropped off Homer at the precinct house, switched to his own Volkswagen Squareback, and rumbled up to the house of his ex-wife, Shelly's watch read 10:25—more than an hour after Thom's bedtime. He knew he was too late to catch the boy awake, but wanted to give Ruth a chance to vent her rage at him before he actually managed to see them together. Clem should still have been out of town, which was some comfort to him as he ambled up the lawn that once had been his, two or three lifetimes ago.

She must have been watching through the living room blinds, because the locks inside began to unslide before he reached the doorbell. Ruth was anxious, no doubt, to confront him with this incontrovertible evidence of his disregard for her problems, or the needs of their son. The divorce had ended their marriage but not the grudges between them; this he understood full well.

But Ruth's face when she opened the door did not suggest a cat who had cornered a rat, and the lack of glee alarmed him. Was she really worried enough to forgo so choice an opportunity to demonstrate that their marital split was entirely his fault? Things must be bad indeed.

"There you are," she said, almost in a whisper. "I think he's gone to sleep." She glanced upstairs toward Thom's bedroom as if there might have been a chance to catch him up. Shelly knew his son's sleeping habits, which were very like his mother's in her ability to sink immediately into irretrievable slumber at the merest sniff of bed linen. The odds of catching Thom still awake were just longer than those of catching Tinkerbell hunting through the bureau for Peter Pan's shadow.

"I'm sorry to be so late," he said. "Our investigation . . ."

"Took a little longer than you expected—of course," said Ruth, a momentary spark of an old argument glimmering in her eye. "It doesn't matter. What matters is that you speak to the boy before we really have a problem on our hands."

Shelly nodded, not quite sure how to deal with the tolerance she was showing for his profession.

She dropped into a chair by a table near the door. "I mean, you're a cop, aren't you? That has to be useful for something, sometime. He'll have to listen to you, if you tell him about the people you live with every day. People you don't meet in Pelham too often. The kind *you* know too well."

"You want me to scare him?"

"Right down to his bones!" declared Ruth with a shiver. "Like I've been scared by this hobby of his—stealing ornaments from expensive cars. All those stories you used to tell about the kids you'd see . . . I want him to know what can happen to a boy who takes one wrong step off the daisy lane into who knows what other world! You live there. I want him to see what it's like."

So she had been listening, all those nights she pretended to be bored! Her silence had been fear—for his safety? Dozens of scenes replayed in his head. Astonished, Shelly said quietly, "I can do that."

"I'll bet you can," she told him, and the first smile crossed her face. "You look like a ghost yourself again. Have you eaten?"

He hadn't, of course, but the question conveyed more than that and he eyed his ex-wife more thoughtfully. There had been a time, toward the end of their marriage, when he would come home, they would fight, and he would fix himself something alone in the kitchen while the baby slept and Ruth thrashed out her anger on her pillow. That was how he usually remembered dinners in their home. But the tone of her question now reminded him of an earlier time, when she would rise and kiss him when he came home, and the two of them would eat macaroni and cheese with boil-in-the-bag frozen spinach at two o'clock in the morning.

"I didn't want to be later than I had to be," he said.

"Come on," she said, with a wag of her honey-colored hair. "I'll find you something in the fridge."

Her kitchen had changed less since his replacement by Clem than any other room in the house. It was her room, of course, and not her second husband's, which explained why it felt as it had when he would come stumbling down in the mornings. They sat at the small Formica table in the kitchen itself, where Ruth opened a can of grayish pâté and set it in the center of a plate, filling in the space around it with an array of inflated white crackers. Shelly broke an airy, heart-shaped one and scooped up a mound of pâté, which tasted tangier than he had expected. He tried again with the other half of his cracker and found he liked the flavor even more. As he dipped his second heart into the spread, Ruth joined him with a small piece for herself, and the two of them sat together for a delicious moment, chewing crackers in the silent kitchen.

She finished first, stood, and went for a pot of coffee already made on the sideboard. Shelly admired her moves as she turned for milk in the subzero refrigerator, reaching past him to set the plastic container on the table. She was wearing a dress, dark blue with tiny white dots and a flared waist that flattered her figure. Shelly realized that she must have put it on for his sake, since she usually hung around the house in sweat pants and a T-shirt. Just keeping in practice for Clem, no doubt, and her feet in her stockings were shoeless, but he enjoyed the fact that she had dressed for him, and wanted to make her feel good.

"Nice dress. It picks up the blue of your eyes."

She smiled—too wisely, but still a definite smile. "What's this? A compliment? You must be learning something about women, Shell. Is there a girl in your life these days? Beside meter maids and prostitutes, I mean."

The sting was just to put him on the defensive, to deflect the real interest behind the question. He was not offended. "Well, there's a nun."

"A sister of mercy? Sounds like loads of laughs."

"She's got her points," said Shelly.

"I didn't know you cared about those kinds of points."

"What kinds?"

"You know. The strictly Platonic kinds."

Shelly remembered sinewy thighs on the racquetball court. "I didn't say that," he murmured.

Ruth sat forward in her seat, reaching across the table to place a hand on his wrist. "Shelly Lowenkopf! Don't tell me . . . you've been screwing a nun?"

He wouldn't have put it that way, but she seemed to enjoy the idea. It stirred a spasm of guilt when he thought about it, but he didn't feel much like thinking just then. Ruth's eyes held his own with a fierce blend of jealousy and sexual interest he wasn't about to disturb.

"I wouldn't say I've *been screwing* her," Shelly admitted, focusing on the accuracy of her tense. "It was much more of a casual thing."

"Casual sex with a sister!" exclaimed Ruth, impressed with the progress he'd made since the end of their sexual partnership. "You naughty man! I'll have to give you a try, sometime. Just to see what you've learned since the old days."

It was the sexiest flirting they had done in a long time. She was still an attractive woman, plumper, of course, than she had once been, but round in all the right places. Shelly was tempted to push the gambit she had ventured as far as he could—the empty house seemed to offer so fine an opportunity. Clem was five or six states away; Thom was sleeping in his room upstairs; the rest of the house was silent. He knew the way to the bedroom by heart, despite the years that had passed since he had used it. But other memories occurred to him, and Shelly decided to protect the playfulness of their encounter so that he could relish it later without a final sour note of rejection.

"I ought to be going," he said.

She stared at him, trying to remember an earlier form of his face. "I suppose you should," she said.

Shelly couldn't tell if she was expecting a pass or had simply removed her contact lens. But the moment for any dramatic move had passed. He stood, clearing his throat and visions of what-might-have-been from his mind.

Ruth followed him to the door, opening the latch but pausing with her cheek pressed against the door's thickness, to listen for an imagined cry from the bedroom overhead.

For a moment they listened together, enjoying the parental silence. When it was clear their son was still sleeping, Shelly said quietly, "Why don't you have Thomas dressed and ready by seven o'clock tomorrow morning? I'll stop by on my way in and pick him up. I'm going to the funeral of a kid tomorrow, who was found dead in the playground— probably for dealing crack. That should scare him off from a life of crime, if anything will."

It was the sort of suggestion she would have scorned in the

old days, and her wavering was itself an indication of just how worried she was. "Is it safe?"

"His grandmother is a religious woman who couldn't control the kid. But nothing dangerous is about to take place at the funeral she arranged."

"All right," said Ruth, reaching over to clutch the crook of Shelly's elbow. "You won't let anything happen to him?"

"Trust me," he said.

She looked distantly into his eyes, as if reading something written in the back. "It's time again, I guess. But please . . . don't disappoint me, Shell."

"Nothing's going to happen to him," Shelly promised. He was prepared to do whatever was necessary to protect the boy from harm. Ruth sensed this determination and was reassured by his confidence. Neither one of them could have guessed how unfounded it would prove to be.

18

When Shelly rang the doorbell the next morning, Ruth looked less like a million. She had taken the trouble to brush her teeth and apply lipstick, but her hair was not fully brushed and her eyes not quite made up. She met him at the door in a silky robe over the upper two-thirds of her nightgown, showing her legs through the diaphanous hem. She held the door open, waiting for Thom, who followed sullenly in a faded pair of denim jeans and a T-shirt that read, The Worst Is Yet To Come. As he passed over the threshold, she brushed his knee and said to Shelly, "That's the best I was able to do. You should've seen the pants he tried on this morning."

Shelly wore a dark-blue suit with fur balls, a worn white shirt open at the throat, and a dangling, brown knit necktie. They were, after all, going to a funeral. Not as guests, exactly, but Shelly still felt some necessity to show respect for the dead, especially since the deceased was fourteen years old. He figured, however, that a clean pair of jeans probably counted as a show of respect from Thom, so Shelly said nothing, extending a traffic cop's arm to mark the way to the car.

In the Reliant, Homer sat in front, in the passenger seat, trying to find a classical station on the red-white-and-blue plastic transistor radio Shelly left on the dashboard. Homer wore a pin-striped suit in some shiny fabric, with pegged pants and thin lapels. When he saw Thom, he saluted, a gesture he had used with great effect when the boy was eight. "Hey, Sport. How's life in the suburbs these days?"

Thom wasn't buying it. He slunk in the back seat, sprawling on the vinyl, and put his feet up on the armrest of the opposite door. "Boring."

Shelly dropped behind the steering wheel and hit the engine, which started without complaint. He readjusted the rear-view mirror, shifted into drive, and pumped the pedal a little harder than usual. "No drive-bys in the schoolyard, huh? Well, you won't be bored this morning."

Thom didn't reply, which meant very little, really, since the boy usually said as little as possible. It came, Shelly thought, from the necessity to keep out of family fights in the strained months before the divorce and the awkward years after. Homer found his station and settled back to listen to something with lots of frenetic strings, which carried them through the silence from Pelham into the Bronx.

Shelly wasn't sure exactly what he wanted his son to see at the funeral of Felix Aguilar but knew it had something to do with the waste of a young life. The sight of the bloodless corpse in an open coffin was bound to make his point without any need for a lecture from him. If there was weeping from the family, regret among his friends, even a grieving sweetheart—so much the better for the lesson to be learned in the lower depths of the city.

Thom seemed to sense an impending idea and protected himself with indifference. His silence said to his father, *go on and show me whatever you want to. Nothing you do can change me anymore, how I feel or what I believe.*

It was a challenge Shelly would never have ignored, had it come from Thom himself. Having been called in by Ruth as the boy's father made it completely irresistible. There was a calm air of authority about him as he nosed the Reliant in and out among the trash-lined streets, which let him carry the burden of fatherhood as a comfortable, comforting weight.

Thom sat up a few inches, so his line of sight cleared the window as they bumped along the broken asphalt in the lower half of the borough. Between burnt-out buildings in a lot piled with refuse, three men slept on crumpled newspapers facing a blackened trash can. The passage of the car sent a few pages flying, which raised one of the sleepers, who sat up and hollered after them. Thom watched him through the back window, clapping when the bum raised his middle finger in a universal token of salute. Shelly felt their field trip had accomplished something before they even reached the church.

The church was Saint Augustine's, near the Dairy Queen, a gray stone edifice rising above the burned and scattered lots of the neighborhood as a thing of permanence in a transient world. Inside, the vaulted chamber swallowed all earthly noise as the darkness blinded Shelly for a moment, drawing the eye—when sight returned—down the length of the aisle toward the altar, where a closed casket rested on a flowered bier. A few people had begun to collect in the pews, which seemed gigantic for the number of mourners.

The sanctuary was dominated by an enormous crucifix suspended over a white marble altar table set in the center of the sanctuary near the rear wall. On the crucifix hung a fully realized likeness of Christ in agony, head tilted upward and to the right, where a golden cabinet with three curved doors rested on a marble stand. Across from the cabinet stood a podium, and directly below the podium, at the foot of the altar, lay the casket of Felix Aguilar. It was made of wood and particle board covered with a blue denimlike fabric, decked head and foot with yellow gladiolas, red carnations, and purplish blue irises. Beneath the casket, a white cloth overhung a wheeled cart whose steel legs wobbled in the candlelight.

In the first row, a heavy-set woman in a black dress with a lacy black veil wept into a rosary until the slender, elderly man beside her produced a white linen handkerchief. Shelly figured them for Felix's grandparents, who had taken in the boy at an early age and raised him as their own son. She sniffled, clutched the hankie in a trembling hand, and raised her gaze to the cross above the altar, from which it was drawn to the bier. When the image before her eyes fully registered, she cried out, *"Mi hijito . . . no es justicia . . . ,"* collapsing again on her husband's shoulder. His long, grave face showed nothing but pity, for his wife and the child in the box.

On the far side of the entrance, a man in his early twenties leaned against the stone arch. He wore an ash-gray jacket and charcoal slacks, an oxford shirt, and a striped college tie. His disdain ran the length of the church and fixed on the front pew. Each time the old woman's grief overwhelmed her with a wail of awful regret, the young man would stiffen, fighting back an impulse to console her, or to acknowledge a similar feeling in himself. He seemed to sense Shelly's regard, glanced up, and moved toward the front, allowing himself to be seen.

Shelly gestured for Thom and followed a discreet distance behind, preparing to eavesdrop when the young man met his family. There was still no sight of Tomas Jefferson; if he was there to pay respects to his cousin, one of the family might tip them off. The young man was evidently in from elsewhere, and might even mention some names.

When they neared the pew, the old man nudged his wife and shifted his head slightly toward the new arrival. The old woman looked up, saw the college man approaching, and opened her arms to him, calling, *"Juanito! Por qué él? Era un niño!"*

The young man said nothing, accepting her hug, his eyes remaining cool as they settled on the coffin decked with flowers. His thoughts, given expression, seemed unlikely to comfort his grandmother in her hour of grief. A troubled crease appeared between his grandfather's brows, commanding silence, as the old woman murmured, *"Era un buen niño, no era malo."*

"Sí, Abuelita," Juanito said, audibly restraining the irony in his voice, "he was a good boy."

The old woman raised herself sharply. "Do not think of him like this, Juanito! Remember instead his first day at school. *La noche anterior, planche sus pantalones y una nueva camisa blanca y los puse al pie de su cama.*"

"I remember," he said, "you did the same for me. Pressed pants and a clean white shirt on a chair at the foot of the bed."

"And the shoes," she reminded him, "with . . . *las hebillas.*"

"Buckles," said Juanito.

"Sí," said his grandmother. "Buckles on his shoes. And now this . . . *Ay Dios mío!"*

The old man offered his hand, which Juanito shook with care. "I'm glad you could come today."

Instead of answering, Juanito gazed at the coffin. "I want to see him." On his grandfather's nod, Juanito left quietly, returning moments later, leading a somber man in a funeral director's suit, who knelt beside the casket and opened the lid. Shelly edged sideways, shoving Thom into a position from which he could see the prepared body. It had been done up in a clean white shirt and pressed pants—just like his first day of school. No makeup had been applied to the face, though dyes in the embalming fluid had restored a color not far off from the living flesh. Yet the utter stillness of cheeks and mouth, which did not stir for breath, was chilling even for Shelly, a face-to-face encounter with teen-age death. He could only imagine how it might be affecting his son, who had never seen death before in any of its guises.

"Wow," said Thom in a hushed whisper. "That's outrageous. Who did that to his hair?"

"The mortician. To make him look nice for his family. Last night they prayed the rosary in here. Afterwards, everyone filed by for a good-bye glimpse in the coffin."

"What did he die of?"

"A bullet," said Shelly ominously. "He was working for a man who sold crack on the streets."

"Stupid," Thom said.

"I don't know," mused his father. "He was making good

money at it. He didn't start in that business, of course. He started small—ripping off radios and stuff from cars."

"Radios?"

"And stuff," repeated Shelly, hoping he wouldn't have to spell out h-o-o-d o-r-n-a-m-e-n-t-s to make his point.

"I don't like what they did to his hair," Thom said finally, patting down his own. "I'll bet he wouldn't have either."

Shelly loosened his collar and scratched his neck, not quite sure Thom understood. But he didn't have a chance for another stab at it, because at that moment a priest emerged from a wooden door at the end of the aisle running along the front of the sanctuary. From that discreet vantage point he looked over the altar and the podium, checking whatever preparations were necessary for the Mass to begin. Then he turned to the assembly gathering in the pews. Shelly was disappointed to see that he was not Father Branigan but a young Hispanic priest whose expression of sad expectancy seemed to mix in equal measure pity for this world and optimism for the next. He wore black robes and a narrow stole, richly embroidered with the cross and the sun, which hung down both sides of his shoulders. From somewhere beneath his robes he produced a pair of fragile gold eyeglasses, which he tilted on his nose, counting the audience in the aisles. Then he turned to the old gentleman in the first pew, whose response Shelly missed. It must have been to convey that no more mourners were reliably expected— besides Thom and the detectives, only two dozen people had collected, most of whom seemed by their ages to have come for the sake of the boy's grandparents. Juanito took a seat noisily in the second row, right behind the old man, four rows up and across the center aisle from Shelly and Thom. An adolescent male stood framed in the entrance for an instant, but did not enter the church. Shelly saw Homer near the entrance in the shadows of the vestibule, but no sign of Tomas Jefferson. When his eyes readjusted to the darkness in the church, the priest by the wooden door was gone.

There came a series of solemn chords from an organist to

the right of the sanctuary, and the faint murmuring of the crowd ceased altogether as they listened to the hymn. Then, from the entrance two altar boys began the trek down the center aisle to the altar. The one in front carried a big wooden cross; his companion, a few feet behind, carried a huge Bible. Both were dressed in white smocks over black robes which they kicked as they walked. Behind them came the priest, looking neither left nor right, gazing over their heads at the cross hanging above the altar. When he reached the front cross-aisle, he bowed to the altar and ascended some steps on the right-hand side until he reached the level of the podium. One of the altar boys heaved the Bible onto the podium with a grunt, while the other placed the cross in an alcove near the golden cabinet.

Lowenkopf suddenly felt a presence on his right and turned to meet his partner's eyes, which were twinkling significantly. "What?" said Shelly.

"Did you happen to notice the altar boy? In front, carrying the cross?"

The boy had passed by with the stem of the cross on his shoulder, blocking Shelly's view of his face. He peered through the dim light as the altar boy advanced from the rear alcove to the front edge of the sanctuary. "Is that . . .?"

Homer nodded. "Tomas Jefferson. In the flesh."

Shelly couldn't believe it. He studied the boy, who certainly looked like Tomas. There was a novice in an apse along the side wall, and Shelly decided to make sure. Mumbling to Thom to "stay right here," Shelly worked his way to the outer aisle, where the novice was replacing burned-out wicks with fresh new candles.

"Excuse me," Shelly whispered. "Those altar boys. Where do you find them?"

The novice eyed him suspiciously. "In the neighborhood."

"Are they the ones you usually use?"

The novice took out his glasses and peered through them at the altar. "Not that one—Jefferson. He used to be an altar boy here, two or three years ago."

"Then why is he doing this today?"

"He asked to," said the novice. "As a favor to the family. Besides, most of our regular boys play Saturday morning baseball. It would be a sin to turn away an alternate and yank one away from his game."

Shelly perfectly understood. They couldn't interrupt the Mass, of course, so Homer went back to his post at the entrance of the church, and Shelly to his seat. But he edged farther toward the center aisle, squeaking the wood each time he sat until the priest looked up from the podium. When quiet was restored, he addressed a few words to the congregation and began to read from the Bible. Shelly did not know enough Spanish to follow along, but the Mass was not unenjoyable, since the priest spoke with a nice sense of drama, pausing now and then for emphasis, or to wait for a response from the congregation. The language, too, was musical, round vowels rolling one into the next so that sentences rang at times like words of incantation. Ritual also played its part, incense rising through the warm air to collect under the high ceiling like the sweet breath of the congregation, who were warned, or rebuked, or summoned to praise by the priest with upraised arms. Felix Aguilar's grandmother listened to each syllable, crossing herself and moving her lips. His grandfather watched with great reserve, nodding at his wife when she looked to him for solace. Juanito scowled silently, keeping his opinions about the Catholic Church to himself.

The homily ended, and the organist played another hymn for the congregation. Then the priest cleared his throat and began to read from the Gospels. Shelly imagined all the assemblies who had listened to those pages in one language or another: medieval chapels of knights and squires, peasants and merchants, humbled kings, Roman emperors, Russian czars, German princes and English queens, whole monasteries of abbots and friars and brothers in Christ, orders and orders of silent nuns—the last made him think of Sister Elizabeth, and he turned away from the priest in shame, suddenly aware of the magnitude of their sin. It was no sorority house rule they had broken on the floor of the racquetball court.

The worshippers around him mumbled something, making the sign of the cross on their foreheads and lips, and the organist played another hymn, this time to allow the priest and altar boys time to open the golden cabinet and withdraw a golden cookie tin, about three inches in height, and an ornate chalice encrusted with precious stones, covered with a square of white cloth. Tomas brought forth a crystal decanter filled with red wine while the other altar boy bore a similar decanter of water with a linen towel over his arm. The priest poured some wine into the chalice and a few drops of water, wiping the spout of the second decanter carefully with the towel. By the care taken in redraping the towel, Shelly guessed the second decanter had to contain holy water, which was returned reverentially to its place in the cabinet.

Now the priest raised the chalice, turning to the assembly, and called out something in Spanish. The congregation responded, and as they did, Tomas rang a silver bell. The priest mumbled something under his breath and set his lips to the cup, offering it next to Tomas, who drank more briefly from it. Then the other altar boy was given a taste. Shelly felt thirsty and would have enjoyed a sip, but the chalice was covered again with the square and given to Tomas to remove. The priest then lifted the lid off the golden cookie tin and raised a big wafer. He spoke over it while the second altar boy chimed the silver bell and the assembly once again replied. The priest broke the wafer into halves, ate one, broke the second half into quarters, and handed one to each of the altar boys. Then he and Tomas moved to the front edge of the sanctuary, across from the casket, and signaled for the congregation to approach. Row by row the worshippers walked to the front, where the priest placed wafers in their open mouths with some words to which they replied, "Amen." They returned to their seats with cupped hands, where they knelt on red velvet and prayed. Juanito, Shelly, and Thom kept their seats while the rest of the people in their rows went forward to receive communion. When all had returned to their seats, Tomas and the priest returned the tin of holy wafers to its place in the cabinet, and the priest took the podium for the eulogy.

Shelly expected this second round of Spanish to bore his son completely, but Thom listened with interest, watching the faces in the pews as the priest delivered an impassioned sermon on the death of Felix Aguilar. Now came the tears and the sniffling, from older women in long black veils and young girls with white lace doilies bobby-pinned to their heads. The priest gestured sympathetically to the family in the front pew and thundered his fist in anger at the violence on the streets. *Dios*, however, was merciful and knew whom to forgive for youthful ignorance in an evil time. His words rang in the vaulted chamber, echoed by the stone. Each time he paused for breath, the church lapsed into silence as his words floated up through the arches and past the stained-glass windows. Even the coffin seemed to be listening— perhaps for the wings of the lightened soul, struggling to clear the eaves.

The priest concluded with a bowed head and signaled to the altar boys. Tomas went to the recess in back and returned with the giant cross, taking a position at Felix's head. The second altar boy brought forth a golden bucket with a ladle, which the priest used to sprinkle holy water on the casket, pronouncing a somber prayer. Then he crossed back to the podium for the closing exhortation.

The mourners made their ways into the center aisle and filed past the casket and the family. Some of the women knelt quickly, crossing themselves before the altar. When they had kissed the corpse's grandmother and shaken his grandfather's hand, extending an arm to pat Juanito's shoulder, the line of guests moved along the front aisle, which led to a curtained side door. There was a small commotion at the curtain, a back-up, no doubt, where those going on to the graveside confirmed directions to the cemetery. Suddenly a head cleared the edge of the drapery folds and ducked back again in a flash of white sleeves. Shelly looked for the priest, who was still standing at the foot of the altar with one of the two altar boys.

Señora Aguilar lowered her handkerchief, leaned forward to see around the curtain and called, *"Tomás, a dónde vas?"*

Shelly wondered the same thing: where the hell was he going, still in his altar clothes?

A muffled voice whispered back, *"Tengo un negocio, Abuelita. Horita vengo."*

Shelly glanced at Homer, who was already moving toward the crowd clogging the side door.

"Who's that?" asked Thom.

"Tomas Jefferson," Shelly said, sidling down the pew into the center aisle. "Someone we need to question. He's the last person we know who saw Felix alive."

Thom jumped to his feet. "I'll go that way."

Shelly froze, taking precious seconds from the pursuit to point a shaky finger at his son. "This is police business, you understand? I want to find you right where you are."

Thom smiled, nodding his head.

Shelly had no time to discuss it further, hurrying down the aisle toward the exit, full of uneasiness. Thom's gestures mirrored his own, in all their ambiguity. The nod alone was all right: though it might have been meant to indicate that the boy in fact understood, he preferred to interpret it as a promise of obedience.

It was the smile that troubled him.

19

Shelly pushed his way through the mourners who were blocking the center aisle, waiting for their chance to comfort the family. Felix Aguilar's grandfather was talking to another gentleman as elderly as himself, with a face as long and wrinkled and grave. "There was nothing I could offer him," the grieving grandfather sighed. "Juanito here was a star student from his first days in school, and Felix hoped to follow in his footsteps. I remember the first time he brought home a *D* on a spelling test—what do you think I could tell him? That there is no room in college for an average student from the ghetto? And when he saw them on the streets, with their fine clothing and expensive cars and ready money to spare—what could I offer him to compete with the crack business?"

The other man shook his head as Shelly nudged past, making for the side door. In the tiny vestibule just inside the exit, he had to slip between two women dipping their fingers in crystal ashtrays of holy water. Most of the mourners were already in the street. As he stepped through the portal, the heat and humidity of the day hit his skin just as the brightness of the pavement struck his eyes. Blinded again, he stood, blinking at the cars lining up behind the hearse, passenger doors slamming as women on the sidewalk readjusted their veils and found husbands or rides to the grave site.

The hearse sat in front of the church, just outside the main entrance, where the altar boys and priest had led the pallbearers pushing the wheeled bier. As the casket was loaded into the back of the funeral coach, a black Mustang with oversize tires pulled up beyond the procession of autos and triple parked, engine revving. All that Shelly could see of the driver was a pair of black hands on the steering wheel, but an Amerasian kid hung halfway out the passenger window, cradling his head in his arms. He was smiling, a taunting grin, at someone in the crowd of mourners, who ran to the Mustang and climbed into the back, shucking a bright white smock. Another boy ran behind him, but not in funeral clothing—a pair of jeans and a T-shirt.

Shelly shouted, "Hold it!"

The kid in the car stared curiously at him as the Mustang squealed away, burning rubber and raising a cloud of dust to mark its passing. When the dust settled, the kid in jeans was still standing there, scribbling something on the back of a donation envelope. He looked up, and Shelly recognized his own son, Thom, who raised the small envelope overhead and hollered, "I got the plate!"

Homer reached the spot before Shelly did, taking the slip from Thom without comment and heading directly for the Reliant to call in the license. Shelly arrived breathless and grabbed his son by both shoulders. He wanted to hug him but held him at arm's length and shook him, hard.

"What did I just tell you about where to wait?"

Thom shrugged. "I couldn't stay in the seat. Everyone else had left the church except the family and the pallbearers. They started marching up the center aisle, so I knew where Tomas would be waiting for them. I ran directly out the front door in time to catch the plate number. I thought you'd be proud."

"I am," said Shelly out of habit—at that moment, he didn't give a damn about the license plate. "But they could've fired a shot or two, just for kicks. You might've been hurt. What would I tell your mother if anything happened to you?"

"Tell her I went bravely," Thom said, placing a hand over his heart in salute. "Like they would've told us if anything happened to you."

Shelly reexperienced an ancient guilt for the widow and orphan he would have left behind had anything happened to him when Thom was young. But Ruth was quite comfortably set now, and Thom . . . he wasn't sure about his son. The best he could think to reply was, "Don't make jokes like that," though both of them knew it hadn't been one.

When the two Lowenkopfs returned to the Reliant, Homer was sitting behind the wheel with the microphone still in his hand. The radio sputtered with static, but Shelly could make out enough from outside the car to know that something more was going down than a check on a license plate.

"That's right," a scratchy female voice was confirming for Homer. "A warrant. You know what those are, dontcha?"

"Copy," said Homer, nodding his head.

There was no reason to nod for the sake of the dispatcher, so the gesture had to be a comment on some irony of the universe. Shelly shut the back-seat door after his son, then opened the driver's door, waiting for his partner to scoot over. "We can't do anything risky until we get Thom home."

Shelly was senior and usually had his way, but Homer failed to reassure him. "Nothing risky about it. We've got orders to stop by the convent and pick up Sister Margaret. She should come quietly, don't you think?"

"Sister Margaret? I thought the captain was cutting us some slack on that, as a gesture of goodwill for his old army buddy."

"Our slack just went taut," said Homer, "by order of Judge Wilbur Reese of the state superior court. Cesar Catalan has a lawyer with a friend in the D.A.'s office, who filed charges on one Margaret Mary Findlay, who admitted to the police that she did in fact receive stolen property. The judge may not have been told how she earns her living. Or Catalan may also have a friend on the bench."

"We've got to pick her up now?"

"Before eleven, according to the court's instructions. Or somebody else from our precinct could. It doesn't have to be us, if you're afraid."

Shelly didn't like the sound of that. "Thom can handle the convent—wouldn't you say, son?"

The boy in the back nodded, *sure.*

"Shove over," said Shelly, taking charge again. The main thing was to teach Thom respect for the law. "If the judge says 'bust her,' that's what we'll do."

As he drove to the convent, Shelly tried to remember how they had tangled themselves in this business, and decided it was all a result of chasing the damned Ferrari—their original sin. The discovery of his stolen car gave Catalan the right to force them to do his digging for him. What else did the case include? Felix Aguilar was dead, true, but another gang killing in the crack wars would hardly have kept them long. The two Japanese poisonings had fallen into their laps, but would otherwise have fallen someplace else. Midtown Manhattan had already written off the death of Hitoshi Shirane to poison blowfish; Akira Tanagaki's death would probably have been handled by robbery homicide, if the medical examiner's report suggested it warranted that much attention. Most poisonings were self-inflicted or negligent, by vendors or shippers or restauranteurs—no reason for homicide cops on the case.

Except the note, from the Robbin' Hoods, who might have stolen the car. And a van, though no evidence had yet turned up linking the two grand larcenies. Donations of vehicles are not everyday occurrences, but would hardly serve to convince a judge to issue a warrant.

But Cesar Catalan was looking for some kids who had ripped off his crew during a drug buy. And the blood-red Testarossa gave him just the leverage he needed to put them to work on his behalf. So Thom was going to get to see more than they had bargained for. The boy would see an actual arrest—would see his father in action. The fact that the collar was a nun and the victim a crack dealer made the logic of the bust a bit confusing. But it made the seating arrangements in the car more convenient. Thom could be seated in the front with him and Homer in the back, if they needed to transport a dangerous suspect, but Shelly felt confident that Sister Margaret could be trusted to ride to the precinct house sitting in the back with Thom. That way, the boy could experience vicariously what a perp felt like on the way to the lockup.

Imagine how pleased Ruth would be.

When they reached the convent, Shelly did not like the look of the street in front, where two men, overdressed for the heat in windbreakers, argued over something at the gutter. The idea of leaving Thom alone in the car troubled him, so the three of them went together to the dormitory lobby to ask for Sister Margaret. It was just after lunch, a busy time for the sisters, when all of the children in the hospice—some more patiently than others—waited to be fed. Several were too weak to support bottles or utensils, and needed to be spoon-fed. The nun at the reception desk was sure they understood. What was it exactly they required of Margaret? Perhaps someone else could do as well? Shelly shook his head, and the three of them trooped across the brown lawn to the laundry where Sister Margaret was reported to be working.

They found her standing on a washing machine, turning the blades of an overhead fan. The machine under her feet was going, however, rumbling now and again and coughing spurts of hot water into a deep sink. The water passed through a rubber tube running from the back of the washer, and spewed out the other end with a smell of rubber, laundry powder, and stewed socks.

Sister Margaret made one final adjustment to a screw holding down the screen over the blades and clicked on the fan by a switch halfway down its electrical cord. The blades cranked and started rotating with a soft *whirr*, which became a horrible *clang* as they picked up speed, banging into one of the wires supporting the screen. The sister reached in between the wires and pulled the screen away from the blades, reducing the clang to a clatter before she switched off the power and reached for a pair of pliers on the back of the sink.

"Hand me those, will you? That's a good boy."

She used the pliers to bend back the edge of the screen, waiting for the blades to stop. Then she reached in and moved one manually back and forth past the bent screen wires, checking the clearance.

"The thing is," she explained to no one in particular, "when the power goes on, the blades slide forward along this shaft and smack up against the screen. When it's off, they slide back down again and there's no accurate way to judge the space they're going to need."

Shelly took back the pliers he had handed her and replaced them between the taps of the sink. She switched on the fan again and screwed up her face to listen, but it sounded like she had finally gauged the necessary distance, since the blades swept by the screen with a comforting hum.

"Hmmm," he said, bending his head to allow the breeze on his neck. "That's a luxury."

Sister Margaret scowled, climbing down and brushing the dust from her skirt. "Not a luxury, please—a necessity. We spent quite a lot of time discussing that. We voted against disposable diapers on ecological grounds, but the cloth ones keep this room in a constant cloud of steam. These machines are old, given to overheating, and beyond my skills to repair. If we want to avoid befouling the earth, we've got to keep them cool."

"All right," said Shelly, "something you had to do. There are jobs like that for nuns . . . and for policemen, too."

She looked up sharply at the note of regret in his voice, glancing shrewdly from Shelly to Homer to Thom. "Are you here to arrest me again?"

The question seemed directed at Thom, who looked to his father for help. Shelly said, "We have a warrant instructing us to do so. A necessity. I'm sorry. Officer Greeley will read you your rights."

"He read them to me last time—when you busted us,

brought us to your precinct house, took our fingerprints and photographs, and released us. Any chance you'll be doing that again?"

"Not much," said Homer, drawing her hands gently behind her back and snapping on cuffs. Thom watched her fingers wriggle, testing the give of the bracelets.

Shelly said, "Why don't you listen to what Homer has to say now? I'll be back in a couple of minutes."

Thom nodded, propping himself against the sink while Greeley began reciting Miranda. Shelly left the laundry and crossed to the front of the hospice, where he pushed through the glass door and moved quickly through the rooms. He found Sister Elizabeth in the playroom, a small room lined with cubbies of rag dolls and plastic blocks, puzzles and games, and a toy stove on which real aluminum pots and pans cooked. The room was warm and bright with a haze of dust particles floating in the sunshine that streaked through clean scrubbed windows. Taped to the walls were sheets of rough paper on which young hands had been traced in crayon, or pictures of houses drawn. It struck him that these children, who had lived all their lives in apartments, still drew a home as a single-family structure with a triangular roof and a chimney—an image rooted so early in the recesses of their minds.

Sister Elizabeth was sitting in the middle of the floor on an oval rug while six children under five years of age ran circles around her, now and then pausing to roll an inflated ball at her back or tug on the hem of her gown. Each time one bumped into her shoulder, or threw himself in her lap, she would blink at the impact, recover, and stroke the child's head. One boy in particular, with cherubic cheeks and a halo of soft brown hair, sat near the window erecting a tower of blocks. Each time he set one piece upon another, fitting them securely together, he called for and received her earnest attention and silent applause. When she heard Lowenkopf's footstep enter the room, she turned and looked up expectantly.

Though she uttered no words, the question was clear in her eyes. Why was he there? What did he want from her?

The answer was vaguer in Shelly's mind, though fully formed in his heart. He had come to ask her to speak to him. But what did he hope she might say? The names of the boys cleaning erasers that day—but much more than that. What had they done? They had shared a special moment two days before—or did she often do that stuff? She didn't strike him as the kind of woman who slept around, though their intimacy on the racquetball court hadn't required much of an interview.

"I was hoping we could talk," he said.

She touched her lips, smiled, and waved her hand to offer a seat on the rug. He crossed his legs and sat beside her, just in time to catch a whiffle ball on the elbow. He picked it up as the tot responsible ran up to reclaim her toy. He handed it over and received for his trouble a grateful, untroubled smile.

"Nice work, if you can get it."

Sister Elizabeth nodded, shaking the train of her veil. It was a different one than she had worn the day before: instead of a long black veil over a white coif wrapped around her face and neck, she was wearing a single head-piece, black over white, which seemed clipped to her head. Her skirt, too, was shorter, falling around the knee, less of a habit than the black dress a widow might wear on the street.

She noticed his glance at her knees and tucked them farther under her. The boy near the window called her and she looked at his tower, pursing her lips—impressed.

"We are here to arrest Sister Margaret," Shelly told her, "for receiving that stolen Ferrari. I know she had nothing to do with that—don't bother objecting. But the man whose car it is has another idea. He wants to see her behind bars—he thinks her benefactors might step forward to protect her. I cannot stall any longer, now. She'll have to go to jail. Unless you save her that indignity."

Sister Elizabeth touched her fingers modestly to her breast and raised her eyebrows.

"Yes," said Shelly, "you. She asked you to help her pray for a car, didn't she? When your old Rambler groaned its last. She said some boys were nearby, banging erasers against the bricks, when she asked you for your prayers. Tell me who they were."

Sister Elizabeth held his eyes for a long minute as she thought over his request. He tried to imagine how the nun might conceive of her conflict. To him, the choice was obvious: she would have to break her vow of silence, but what was that next to Margaret's freedom? And once it was broken, for a good cause, Shelly had a question or two of his own he was aching to put to her.

She seemed to read those thoughts, too, before he could push them into the back of his mind. She stared down at the rug on which they both sat and tucked a stray yarn into its stitches. It looked like a handmade job, knit by one of the nuns, maybe, or one of the neighborhood women, interweaving cheery yellow with remnants of red and blue and green. Something to brighten the nursery room where dying orphans played. The little boy who had been building with blocks left his plastic tower and came up behind Sister Elizabeth, softly tapping her shoulder. She didn't seem to feel it, engrossed in the choice before her: to speak or remain silent. She looked up at Shelly and shook her head.

He couldn't believe it. "No? You're going to make us take her away in handcuffs?"

Sister Elizabeth nodded, pointing to her habit.

"Sure, she's a nun," said Shelly. "But that doesn't mean she's prepared for what's involved. You have no idea what a cell can be like until you've slept in one of ours."

She shrugged apologetically, touching her lips, raising her palm toward heaven. The boy behind her tugged at her sleeve.

Shelly said, "I know, you've made a promise. But your God is a god of forgiveness, isn't he? Can't you break your vow even to save another nun?"

Sister Elizabeth's features drew together in the most compassionate expression Shelly had ever seen—full of sympathy for the suffering of human beings bound by the will of God. Her heart seemed to go out to Sister Margaret in her steel bracelets, as it did to all of the children running around the room. Their obliviousness to their illness for those few noisy minutes was worth all the pain that she would share with them in the days and months ahead. Shelly did not want to imagine them then but knew that Sister Elizabeth offered each one the same loving patience in their hours of need that she gave now, in their moments of joy. Her life was dedicated to easing the suffering of those who least deserved and were least prepared to handle it—and her strength, all the courage that she shared, rested in turn on the faith she renewed through her own silent devotions. In the world she daily frequented, the problems of Sister Margaret seemed a trifling inconvenience, nothing to distract her from her work in the playroom of the hospice.

Until the little boy behind her, in a third bid for her attention, tugged at the back of her veil, which slid from the combs in her hidden hair and came loose in his hand.

"Jesus, Mary, and Joseph!" cried Elizabeth more in surprise than anger, as she felt her head suddenly bare. No sooner were the words formed than she covered her mouth with a hand in a vain attempt to restrain them—alas, too late. They sounded, and her vow of silence was broken.

Her hair slipped down around her shoulders, combs falling free after the veil. She looked disheveled, her silence and air of grace vanishing together. Shelly knew she would answer his questions, then, had he recovered his will to ask. But he couldn't open his mouth. She threw herself onto the rug, burying her face against his leg. Her hair tumbled forward over her face, covering forehead and hands and mouth and chin, halfway down his knee. The little boy stared at her, dumbfounded, aghast at the veil in his hand.

She did not cry; Shelly did not hear another sound. But he wouldn't have heard one anyway, lost as he was in contemplating her mass of rich red hair.

20

It had been blond on the racquetball court—blond and short, shoulder length, in his hand. He could imagine a nun coloring her hair, even styling it. But lengthening? Was that possible? But how else to explain . . . could Sister Elizabeth wear a wig under her veil? The sister sat up as if she heard his thought, though she turned not to Shelly but the child, whose incomprehension at her collapse had become fear.

"Ah, well, Angelo. It's not your fault."

She smiled warmly, took him in her lap and cuddled him, tapping the end of his nose and her own. He laughed in her embrace, his guilt dispelled, and reached for her warm red hair, which she let him feel a moment before sweeping it back under her veil.

Shelly reached forward just before her hair disappeared completely. His hand touched her cheek and pulled back with a start. The touch of her skin was electric. She looked up in surprise.

"Didn't you . . . weren't you a blonde?" he managed to stammer, embarrassed by the question and yet unwilling to allow the evidence to be tucked away forever.

For the first time, she gave him a personal smile—not of

sympathy, or charity, but of plain good humor. He must have said something funny, he thought, though he couldn't imagine what.

"Is that why, Sergeant Lowenkopf, you watch me like a ghost? Someone you've seen in another life?"

That was it exactly, Shelly felt. Another life.

She grinned again, plainly enjoying herself. "You've seen me before, haven't you?"

He nodded—now he was the mute. Of course he'd seen her before, if that's what she wanted to call it. They'd seen each other buck naked. Didn't she remember?

"I should have known," she mused. "Sister Sylvia."

Who was Sylvia? His mind reeled. Was there . . . could there be yet another nun who had lain with him on the racquetball court? Impossible. Those features—there couldn't be two. And yet, the strangeness of her face . . .

Sister Elizabeth stood and carried the boy to his plastic tower, *ooh*ing and *aah*ing over it. Then she set him down gently and returned to Shelly on the rug. He was staring at her unabashedly. She said, "You want to know who those boys were? Banging erasers on the bricks?"

He sat forward. The case—he had nearly forgotten about Catalan's stolen Ferrari, Sister Margaret in cuffs. Elizabeth knew something about that too.

"Go ask Father Charles," she said. "He teaches here, a class for boys who have nowhere else to go but juvenile hall, and then prison. Those boys cleaning erasers were in his class. There were two of them: one Hispanic and one Amerasian. I only heard the name of the former. He was called—"

"Tomas," Shelly said.

"—Tomas. That's right. It sounds like you might be onto something, after all."

The smile she gave him was a different one now: knowing, tolerant, forgiving. Still not the smile of a sister in Christ, but another he recognized: the smile of a woman with a man she rather liked because of his interest in another woman. Not that she wanted him for herself, he understood, but a woman looking out for another of her kind, amused by his distress and generous with her sympathy.

He said, "Sylvia?"

She shook her head. "First things first: Father Charles. His class should be meeting at the convent school in twenty minutes or so. Why don't you find a way to take those handcuffs off Margaret?"

"I can't tell you how much I'd like to."

"I'm sure you would," said Elizabeth kindly, "as would we all. But Sergeant Lowenkopf—if doing so would increase any risk to those boys, I'm sure she'd rather keep them on."

Shelly nodded, certain that she was right. That knowledge created a problem. There was a risk to the boys, once they had been identified as the thieves of Catalan's Ferrari. Elizabeth's information had come with a responsibility to respect the trust the nuns had established with the children of the streets. So it was with an uncertain mind that he presented the new information to Homer. They didn't quite have the boys—yet. They could bring Sister Margaret to the precinct house and process her arrest. Or they could stall, waiting for a chat with Father Charles, who might know something about his students that would save her from a harrowing ordeal. Homer felt a strong obligation to the warrant requiring them to take Margaret Findlay into custody. But, Shelly argued, so long as they had her handcuffed between them, no one could deny she was in custody. It was just the sort of point that appealed to Homer's mind—technical, specific, faithful to the letter (if not the spirit) of their instructions.

They headed over to the school, with Margaret leading the way, a watchful Homer beside her, and Thom close on their heels. Shelly watched his son from the rear, wondering what he thought about his day with the law. The boy did not seem to sympathize with the nun as a prisoner, but felt curious about the prisoner as a nun. He would not, of course, have had occasion to spend much time with a sister, and her vocation would have a certain exotic appeal. Thom had eyed her outfit with a scrutiny he might have shown an exhibit of twelfth-century armor, or the dress of a medieval princess. For her part, the nun would turn now and then to glance or even to wink at Thom, drawing what conclusions she could about the senior detective on her case.

They arrived at the classroom, an odd party of four: two cops, a boy, and a nun in chains. Father Charles was already at the board, copying from a sheaf of paper: *The three P's of a Job Interview: 1) Punctuality. 2) Politeness. 3) Preparation.* The chalk squeaked as he printed each word, stopping to erase a letter that slipped out of alignment. Not a frequent teacher, Shelly surmised, but apparently an earnest one. In the corner of the blackboard was a box in blue chalk, in which was inscribed: *Today's reminder: Thou shalt not steal.* Branigan glanced up, saw them enter, and turned his back immediately, extracting from a paper bag another crumpled sheet of blue-lined paper.

"Father Charles?" said Shelly. "If you don't mind, we'd like a word with you."

Branigan's head turned slowly, as if he saw no alternative. He looked from the cop to Margaret, drawing his own conclusions about their personal relations. His interview with Shelly had evidently left him wondering which of the nuns had partnered him in sin, and his eyes darted from Margaret to Shelly as if he had figured it out. Her handcuffs seemed to reinforce the idea, as if her legal transgression were no more than a substitute for the higher moral violation. The cleric fixed his eyes on Shelly in an effort to avert them from the sister, who showed no remorse or shame. "Hello, sergeant. Are you here to arrest us again?"

"Not you, this time," said Margaret. "Only me."

"That's what we're trying to avoid," Shelly said. The last thing he needed was a nun conducting his interview. "We'd like to close this case without incarcerating any more clergy than are absolutely necessary."

"Please," said Branigan, "have a seat." He waved his arm magnanimously as if offering them their preferences, but all the seats were student desks, fixed to slanted surfaces for writing. Margaret plopped into one, Thom slipped into another, and the two detectives remained on their feet. For himself, Branigan drew a straight-backed chair from behind the desk and set it in front of the others. He placed the paper bag on his knees and began rummaging through it again.

"All I can offer is a stick of gum," he said apologetically. "It's in here somewhere. I took it away from a boy who popped his bubbles."

"That's all right," Shelly said, "we'll skip the gum for now. Your class should be here any minute, and we'd like a few words before then. We're on duty."

Homer squared his shoulders, looking every inch the officer. He took his clues from Lowenkopf: if Shelly was going to scare the priest, he could play the tough guy.

Sister Margaret cleared her throat. "I don't mind a stick of gum, father, if you don't mind."

Branigan dug an old silver-wrapped stick from his bag and offered it to the nun, who was unable to accept it with her hands behind her back.

Homer reached behind her and opened one side of the cuffs; before he could fit his key in the other, the nun reached for the gum and undid the wrapper.

"Thanks," she said, popping it in her mouth with a clank from the bracelet at her wrist.

The priest nodded, trying not to mention her handcuffs as a matter of politeness. Instead, he turned to Thom, who shook his head at the offered stick.

"Tell us about your class," said Shelly, hoping to jar what information he could before a sense of discretion set in. People were usually willing to share the most in the first few minutes of talking—after that, they started thinking of all the reasons for keeping quiet.

Branigan was obviously thinking already. "What class?"

"Your creative child class," said Sister Margaret. "The one you run here at the convent every Saturday afternoon. With all of the criminal boys."

"They're not criminals yet," Father Charles said, recovering himself in defense of his students. "Which is the point, as I'm sure you're well aware, sister. They're troubled young men—that much is true. But with a bit of good advice and a chance to speak their minds . . ."

"They steal cars and donate them to the church."

"What?"

"Sister Margaret," said Shelly, "if you don't mind, I'll handle the questioning from here."

"I was just trying to get him started," she said.

"I appreciate that. But I'd rather take a whack at it myself. How would you feel if I started tinkering with your washing machine?"

"It would never recover."

"Exactly."

She shrugged. "Go ahead."

Shelly turned to Father Charles with a sigh. Where was he, now? Trying to start the priest talking about his students. Anything he said might prove useful later on, and the main thing was to make him enjoy talking. He began with an easy one. "How many kids do you teach in this class?"

"Anywhere from eight to twelve on a given day. They're ordered to attend by a judge, who can send them away if they don't, so most of them show up every week. I may not be Berle, but I'm better than a reformatory, and the kids can tell I'm trying to help."

"What do you teach? Math and reading?"

The priest shook his head. "Life skills: how to get by in the world outside of the prison system. If they need to learn to read, I'll hook them up with a tutor, too. But that's not what we're here for." He pointed toward the blackboard, with its list of job interview skills. "We're here to talk about how to stay alive in a world that has no place for these kids—except a jail. They don't know things that you and I take for granted, that are fed to your children with their mother's milk."

"Nobody taught me how to get a job," Thom said.

"Didn't they?" asked the priest. "Tell me—were there any magnets on your refrigerator in the shapes of the ABC's? Or letters on the wall above your crib?"

Shelly thought of the alphabet of toy soldiers parading around Thom's bedroom at the walls, and the trouble he had hanging them.

The boy shrugged. "I don't remember any."

"You don't have to," said Branigan. "Because you were white and middle-class, which means you were saturated with that stuff. In everything they modeled and punished or rewarded, your parents taught you to sit and stand and walk and talk the way a white, middle-class person is supposed to act—the way an applicant for a job is expected to act. When you bring your chair up to the desk and clear your throat to speak, you're relying on years of interview training. Not these kids."

He glanced at the door to make sure no one had arrived who might overhear what he was about to say.

"These kids are not trained from birth for job interviews. They have to learn, and remember, every little gesture that comes naturally to you. When to make eye contact. When to look down. When to reply. When to be silent. What sort of grammar and diction are called for. Nobody speaks at home the way they do in an interview—you have to learn different words and ways of putting them together. Your parents learn to speak like that in their middle-class jobs. But nobody speaks like that in the ghetto at all."

"And that's what you teach them?" Shelly asked. "The rules of the game in the employment market?"

"Some of that," said Branigan. "First I have to teach most of them that it's worth bothering to try. These kids do not have what psychologists call healthy self-esteem. They have to learn that they're worth the trouble before they're going to try to make something more of themselves. That's the first thing I try to help them learn here. That the things they feel are real things, that they deserve more than the miserable lives they've had handed to them so far. That's another lesson I'll bet your boy didn't have to learn."

Shelly looked at Thom and hoped the priest was right. The boy said nothing. But Shelly had to make sure Branigan kept talking. "Sometimes they slip back, don't they? And do something they used to do?"

Father Charles said, "Everybody slips, sergeant. Let him who is without sin throw the first stone. Everybody needs to feel competent at something, sometime."

"But if they do slip into old habits," Shelly said, "they

might do something differently. Isn't that your hope? That what they've learned here will make a difference?"

"I suppose . . ." It was hard for the priest to disagree with the words, but unclear where they were heading.

"For example," Shelly went on, "a kid who used to steal things—cars, say—might steal a car, but give it away, now, to somebody he thinks needs it?"

"Someone like the convent?" Branigan said, finally catching the drift. "What makes you think one of my boys did that?"

"Two of your students overheard Margaret asking Elizabeth to help her pray for a new set of wheels."

He turned to Margaret. "Who?"

"She didn't know their names," said Shelly, cutting off the nun before she could reply. "But Sister Elizabeth did—whose vow of silence ended just now, in the hospice. They were out in the yard, cleaning your erasers. One was Tomas Jefferson."

"And the other Vinny Nguyen," Branigan muttered, filling out a scenario he knew too well. "Our blackboard monitors."

"What was that name?" asked Homer, pad in hand. *"Win?"*

"That's how it's pronounced," said the priest, "though it's spelled N-g-u-y-e-n. The first name's V-i-n-h. An Amerasian kid who smuggled himself to America, looking for his father."

"Illegal alien?"

"Not if he finds his father," said Branigan. "Though there's not much chance of that." He stared at the empty desks where those boys might sit, sagging into a blue funk.

"You must get this all the time," Shelly said, "working with these kids."

"We do better than you'd think," Father Charles insisted. "Usually you can tell who's vulnerable. But Tomas and Vinny . . ." He shook his head ruefully, keeping the rest of his thoughts to himself. "Tell me about the car. The Ferrari. Who owns it?"

"A crack dealer," replied Shelly. "Who else can afford a car like that?"

"An insider trader," the priest said.

"We don't see a lot of stockbrokers in the Bronx."

"No," said Father Charles. "And that's the way it is for these boys. All the honest men they see are unemployed, or unable to earn a decent wage. So a murderous hoodlum with a few pounds of crack becomes a man to respect."

"Or rob," Shelly said. "Cesar Catalan wasn't proud exactly, when they gave his car to the sisters."

Branigan looked up slowly. "The man who owns the Ferrari is named Cesar?"

"That's right. Does it matter?"

"It could," said the priest. "Tell me: how many toes does he have?"

21

Father Branigan's question set Lowenkopf's scalp tingling with the peculiar sensation he felt just before a case opened up. It was a matter of staying with him now, staying on top of the details of the investigation and the witness's own, sometimes rather eccentric, point of view.

Shelly said, "Cesar Catalan has ten toes, like an ordinary man—like the rest of us. But his lieutenant has only two on his left foot. He was killed yesterday under strange circumstances. How did you know about that?"

Branigan thought for a full minute before answering, and when he did, he chose his words carefully. "There is a young man in this class you should talk to. Who has been . . . obsessed . . . to find the individual who introduced his mother to crack. She died a year ago from AIDS, which she passed to her daughter in utero. Her son is a very bright, very determined individual. He doesn't know much about the man he's after, but he remembers his mother cursing her connection, someone she called Twotoes. I told him that Twotoes was *not* the man he wanted. That held him off for a while—or at least I thought it did."

"Just a second," said Shelly. "You told him? How do you know who he was after?"

Father Charles bit his lip. "I'm a priest," he said softly. "His mother used to come to me for confession. She told me—as her confessor—about a man she was forced to sin for, a man named Cesar. I could not and would not tell that name to her son, of course. But I was willing to reveal enough to prevent him from killing the wrong man."

"What would you have done if he had asked you about the right one?"

"I've given that lots of thought," said Branigan, "and I'm still not sure. I would have urged him to forgiveness, first, if possible. I read to him from Ecclesiastes: 'To every thing, there is a season. A time to be born and a time to die. A time to kill and a time to heal. A time to throw stones and a time to gather stones together.'"

Shelly thought the Byrds had composed those lines. "And if he could not be dissuaded?"

"I don't know if I would have lied. To save the man's life and the young man's. I think he sensed my doubt, and it encouraged him—at least to stick around. I knew what he was aching to learn, and the closeness of that information was difficult to resist. Sometimes comforting, sometimes frustrating, but always a temptation."

Shelly wasn't sure whose temptation was greater—the son's, to pry the name from the priest, or the priest's, to reveal it to him. And there was another name he hoped to learn from Branigan before his professional discretion reasserted itself.

"That must have been hard on you, father, keeping his trust and your own. And it must've been rough on . . . what's his name?" Shelly asked as if he'd forgotten.

"I haven't said," the priest reminded him.

"Don't you think you should?" demanded Sister Margaret, unexpectedly joining the debate. "For God's sake, Charles, the boy's life is at stake. If by your silence something awful happens to him, it won't be your responsibility alone, you know. All of us here at the convent will have to share in it."

189

"And what if my speaking isn't enough?" Branigan asked her. "Enough to spare his life?"

"We don't have to do everything," Margaret responded. "The Almighty is watching, too. But that's no reason for us to shuck our parts—to do less than we need to do."

"It's not the work," said Branigan, "but the responsibility. You want to help these kids, but there's so little you can really do. They need everything. It's difficult even to start. They can't afford to make it easy for you. I've made promises to them and they watch me like hawks. Everyone breaks promises to them—that's what they've learned to expect from us. Can you imagine how my conscience would torment me if I betrayed what trust they have mustered?"

"We haven't time for your conscience, Charles," the nun said sharply. "If you're having a rough time of it, go see your confessor. There are lives riding on your information. Now tell these gentlemen what they need to know!"

Branigan regarded her thoughtfully, sizing up her theology. Her conviction derived from no training in the fine points of spiritual thought, but flowed instead from her own feelings about the goodness of her Lord. It was a passion the priest seemed to envy. The resolve in her firm lips left no room for wavering faith. He said, "You're looking for Robbie Delaud."

Shelly paled. "You mean the kid I met the other day with a sister in the hospice?"

"How do you think she got there, now? Her mother gave her AIDS in the womb. She acquired that horror doing what she had to, to get high—at the rock house, going down on her knees and drinking in sickness for a bowlful of smoke. It was this Cesar, whoever he is, who started her on crack. That's all Robbie remembers now, and all he wants to remember. God help you find him before it's too late."

He studied Lowenkopf's face, turning away only when the sound of wheels and ball bearings echoed in the hallway. It was Branigan's first student, skateboarding his way to the classroom. He was a slender kid with long, curly blond hair, a surfing dinosaur on his T-shirt, and baggy black-and-white shorts to his knees. He stopped just at the door frame, kicking the heel of the skateboard as he dismounted so that it somersaulted through the air and landed in the crook of his arm. By the baked red tan at his eyelids and neck, he had been living on the streets for a while.

"Hey," he said, raising the palm of his free hand as he passed between them on his way into the room.

Branigan's hand closed on the offered palm, twisting the anticipated slap into a handshake. "Welcome back, Razi. Take a load off your feet."

The kid found a seat in the last row, disturbing three desks before settling into one and putting up his sneakers on another. The rubber edges around his soles had been decorated with the ace of spades, the totem of a local gang.

The priest said nothing about the noise, so Shelly ignored it too. "Will he be in class today? Robbie?"

Father Charles picked up the stump of his chalk and returned to the blackboard, enclosing his lesson in a squeaky square of lines. The kid in the last row watched between half-closed lids, picking up clues fast. Branigan seemed conscious of his scrutiny, and the fragile trust he needed to maintain.

"Why don't we wait and see?"

It didn't take long to establish that some of the creative children had made other plans for the afternoon. Tomas Jefferson and Vinnie Nguyen did not appear, and, by the anxious looks the priest cast down the hall, neither did the kid determined to kill Cesar Catalan. Fifteen minutes later, six students had gathered with Father Charles for their weekly dose of self-esteem and tips on the world beyond the ghetto.

Between them, they represented a junior league of most of the major gangs in the area. Their ages ran from ten to twelve, a couple of years too young for acceptance but old enough to aspire to membership in their local gangs. In some cases, their crimes represented attempts to prove their toughness and heart. A year or two in juvenile hall would complete the transition from ghetto kid to gangster—a finishing school teaching the finer points of drive-by shootings, including the use of automatic weapons and sawed-off shotguns, awarding street names, colors, and tattoos on graduation day. To keep these kids out of the youth correctional facility and the gangs recruiting there, some judges ordered impressionable adolescents to attend the creative child program at the convent high school, taught by Father Branigan. Shelly had visited the Hall on more than one occasion, and had no illusions about the draw of the class—a prison was probably the only place that made school look good to these kids.

The collection of faces ranged before them represented a fair cross section of the ethnicity of the Bronx: two blacks, one from the Carolinas, the other a third-generation New Yorker; one Puerto Rican kid; one from Hong Kong; a young Mafia aspirant; and the sunburned blond with a skateboard. They wore baseball caps and golf caps with the brims folded up, a red "mocha rag" tied in back, T-shirts, V-necks, sleeveless undershirts, baggy shorts and denim "counties." Their feet were clad in athletic shoes of every possible color and fastener type: laced, snapped, and Velcroed. Some had notebooks or scraps of paper on the desks in front of them. Others had ragged red folders with the stamp of Saint Augustine's embossed on the cover. All lounged in various contortions of disrespect, united in the face of a common enemy, having collectively identified Shelly and Homer as *po-lice*, hot on the trail of some unfortunate felon.

"Look," said Shelly when the murmuring grew audible and the glares increasingly direct, "we're not out to bust anybody, here. We're trying to understand who's doing what on the streets, so that nobody gets the credit for somebody else's *boo-yah*. We hear the baddest crew in the Bronx today are some homeboys called the Robbin' Hoods. The ones who offed Jimmy Twotoes. Anybody got another idea?"

There was a silence, as each of the kids waited for another to speak first. Finally, the third-generation ghetto kid said, "You ever seen one of them motherfuckers?"

"Maybe," said Shelly. "But if we did, we can't confirm it. That's our problem, exactly."

"You know why, man?" said the Puerto Rican kid. "You

know why you never seen one? 'Cause they ain't no Robbin' Hoods, man. If there was, you'd see their *placas* up on a wall or something, their logo and writing somewhere. They got no turf, see? No home ground. Nobody ever fought with them, neither. So how come you looking for them?"

The others grumbled general agreement. Shelly shook his head, insisting, "They exist, all right. Or somebody does, using their name. Somebody scratched that name in blood on the ground near Jimmy Twotoes. Somebody signed that name on a threat to a murdered Japanese businessman. And somebody stole a Ferrari from Cesar Catalan."

The students exchanged conspiratorial silences, and Shelly felt sure they knew which of their classmates had committed at least one of the three crimes. Their gazes did not gather on anyone present, confirming his earlier suspicion—Father Charles's suspect was not present. So where was he?

The question took a back burner when Tomas Jefferson entered the room, dressed for a funeral in baggy black pants, sharply creased, and a dark-gray shirt, buttoned to the throat without a tie. "Sorry, father," he said, standing on the threshold of the room. "I had to bury my cousin." His eyes slid from Branigan, surveyed the class, and fell on Shelly and Homer.

That was when he bolted.

Homer was after him in a flash of summer cotton, his pale blue tie streaming back over his shoulder as he disappeared into the hall. Shelly was up and after them a moment later, making his way through an aisle of legs that shot out from under desks, slowing his pursuit. Peripherally he saw Sister Margaret rising too, and a blur of movement to his right where Thom had been.

"Everyone stay put!" he shouted, though it was not clear that anyone else had moved. Shelly did not have time to explain to whom his order should apply. He hoped Thom would take it to heart as a loving request from his father, but if his son was the principal audience, he might have made his command more explicit than *everyone*. He did not, however, have longer to reconsider his diction than the three bounds from his seat to the door. Once in the hallway, Shelly hesitated as two pairs of leather soles slapped a hasty retreat on the tile. He saw Homer crash through a staircase door at the far right end of the corridor, and ran for the stairs to his left—complementing his partner's effort, covering ground, coordinating as a field team.

When he reached the ground floor, his strategy paid off: Tomas Jefferson fled from Homer through the building, directly into his arms. Shelly almost felt sorry for him—a street-smart kid should've known better. As the fugitive came flying down the hall, looking back at Homer on his heels, Shelly went for his legs, sending them both sprawling in a heap below the lockers on the wall. Jefferson banged into the dull green metal with a sickly crunch and lay on his side, tumbled against the dented aluminum, not bothering to rise. Shelly stood over him, looking for signs of damage. Homer caught up with them, whipped out his cuffs and read the kid his rights under the law.

"What is this shit?" Jefferson said. "I ain't done nothing to nobody."

Shelly helped the shaken kid to his feet. "Maybe," he said, "but a lot of people on the street are saying you killed Jimmy Twotoes."

Tomas's face registered a grim, inevitable misery that meant *things always work out like this, don't they?* "I don't know nothing about that," he said flatly.

"No? Then why don't you tell us where your buddy Robbie is today? He's supposed to be here, isn't he?"

"How the fuck should I know? I've been at a funeral all morning. Even out to the graveside."

Shelly was about to say something nasty and disparaging when Sister Margaret emerged from the staircase, having followed him from the class. She knelt beside Tomas and looked into his eyes severely.

"Tomas," said the sister, "now is not the time for lies and half-truths! Your friends may be in trouble right now, praying for you to help them."

"Yeah, and how is telling these chumps anything going to help my boys?"

"Not telling them could prove fatal to your friends. You don't want that on your shoulders, do you?"

With a sure touch, the nun had shown him his obligation to the tiny part of humanity he cared about. Tomas sat up against the locker and tried to draw a deep breath, but the closest his lungs would allow was a muffled gurgle, halfway between a cough and a sneeze.

"I gotta go back to the father's class, according to the law," he said.

"If these gentlemen allow you to attend the class," Margaret asked, "would you be willing to help them?"

"Help them do what?"

Shelly motioned to Homer to fit the key in the handcuffs on Jefferson's wrists. "We're trying to find the asshole who gave Robbie's mother her first taste of crack."

Tomas hesitated a moment, studying the detectives with a wry smile that meant *at least you know what you ought to say, man*. As each wrist came free, he rotated his hand, rubbing away marks from the bracelets. "We wasn't even in the room, man, when Jimmy Twotoes got popped."

"Good," said Shelly. "That makes it easier. Now help us save your friends."

"And all you need to do this is . . .?"

"To know where Robbie is now." Shelly said it with a clear brow and untroubled determination, supported by Homer's nod and Sister Margaret's silence.

Jefferson raised his ragged sleeve and consulted a big gold Rolex. "I'll tell you . . . because it's too late to do anything to stop them. Robbie, Vinnie—and me too. I was supposed to go with them today, but I had to bury Felix."

Tomas turned to the sister for verification, who crossed herself and nodded.

"Go where with them?" Shelly asked.

Tomas Jefferson scowled at him. "Don't you know nothing about shit, man? A little pay back to settle the case you're working on. Robbie's had that man's ticket for more than a year now. They're off to dust Cesar Catalan."

22

The logic was plain enough: Robbie was out to kill the man responsible for his mother's illness and the impending death of his sister Julie, as well. If the kid stood half a chance of succeeding, Lowenkopf might have sat with Sister Margaret through Branigan's class, waiting for word that all their troubles were over. But Robbie and his pals stood no chance at all against the drug dealer, whose territory had been consolidated by violent confrontation with some very nasty rivals. Catalan now had an arrangement with the street gangs whose turfs he crossed—for a small piece of his net receipts, his trade went unimpeded. Catalan's own sales force in the streets and rock houses had been carefully selected early in the game for their ruthlessness and loyalty, among the first to score big in the traffic. His organization was well armed and rumored to be protected politically and in the courts. Whether those rumors were true or the man was cagey, his people rarely spent much time in prison, and the fringe benefits came plentifully and often.

Two or three adolescents intent on taking down Cesar Catalan would only succeed in following Felix Aguilar to the graveyard. Someone needed to stop them from whatever they hoped to try, and when Shelly looked around, the only ones who could do that were Homer and himself. But they had to act without hesitation. Thom was easy enough: they could leave him with Branigan's class, or with the sisters after class. A convent was safe as any place. But what could they do with Margaret? She was formally in their custody; a court had ordered them to arrest her. But if they brought her down to the precinct house and did the necessary paperwork, Catalan would blow Uzi holes through Robbie and his Hoods.

Margaret decided the conflict by refusing to be left behind. "I'm coming with you," she said resolutely, "whatever it costs me to get there. If you need a scene in your precinct house, I can deliver one. If your captain wants to hear from the bishop, I'll arrange that too. Whatever you'd hate to see a sister do, that's what you'll get if you leave me behind."

Shelly was not about to be blackmailed by a nun. "Once we drop you off, you're somebody else's headache. Feel free to bang your coffee mug against the bars! If you want your picture in the paper, go ahead. Somebody'll be there to shoot it. But we can't endanger a civilian."

"So you'll endanger younger civilians," Margaret replied, "whose lives are just beginning."

"That's who we're trying to save," insisted Shelly.

"Then take me along!" cried Margaret. "You saw how well I spoke to Tomas just now—he told you what you never would've learned on your own. What are you planning to do if you manage to find Robbie? Identify yourselves and command him to drop his firearm? You know what he'll do: he'll draw it. Adolescents think they're Superman, every blessed one. None of your bullets can hurt him. He'll raise his gun and one of you will shoot the boy, dead through the heart. You'll be square according to law, and maybe even your conscience. But you'd have done better to bring the nun along."

In the end, it was not quite clear what had persuaded them, but they packed her into the back seat and drove to Catalan's duplex. It had been only forty-eight hours since their earlier visit to the willowy Riverdale building over-looking the Hudson, but the place wore an altogether less casual air. Their mission lent new significance to the doorman's suspiciousness, the careful lobby security, and video camera watching over Catalan's front door. As they waited for a response to their ring, Shelly noticed that the apartment right across the hall showed no name over the bell—a bastion of Catalan's muscle, no doubt.

"Hello, sergeant," mused the Mediterranean woman, sounding genuinely delighted to see them again. She wore a gown of sheer, supple gold which, by the way it clung to her curves, might have been painted on. In her ears were plain flat hoops, carefully detailed, and her long throat was graced by a golden chain dangling into her décolletage.

"Please come in."

Catalan was sitting on the couch almost exactly where they had left him, though his suit had changed to a breezy green silk that floated from his shoulders. His shirt was crisp white, as though it had come directly from a press, and was soon to return. Shelly again felt shabbily dressed and overheated, which gave a special twist to the creases between stains on his six-year-old suit.

The drug dealer looked up from a copy of *Forbes* and removed a golden pair of bifocals from his nose. Though he recognized the two detectives, his guard was up until he saw Sister Margaret enter behind them.

"Ah, sergeant." He addressed himself to Shelly. "There was no need to bring the nun here. You were bound to do your duty, however unpleasant. I have distasteful responsibilities as well. The court has ordered her imprisonment; I was confident she'd be imprisoned. We all have predictable roles to play."

"Sister Margaret, this is the man we were talking about. Cesar Catalan."

"Charmed," said Catalan, offering his palm. The nun didn't accept it, but the hand kept moving until it came to rest rubbing his left elbow as if that had been its trajectory all along. "The man whose car you stole," he reminded her. "I hope you enjoyed it, while it was yours."

Sister Margaret grunted. Catalan had pressed just the right button—it pained her not to talk about the Ferrari, having found at last a fellow enthusiast. But she pressed her lips together firmly and managed to hold in everything except a slight shudder, which might have registered disgust with the owner or a fierce pleasure in his car.

"I'm glad," said Catalan, settling his own interpretation. "But now I think it's time that you were jailed."

"That's not why we're here," Lowenkopf said, cutting off whatever reply was on the tip of Margaret's tongue. "The sister's arrest is a charade—you know it as well as anybody. We wouldn't have wasted everyone's time by bringing her here to show you what you damn well know."

"Then what are you doing here, Lowenkopf? Come for the view of the river?"

"I came to warn you, Catalan."

The drug dealer crossed his legs. "A threat, sergeant? Are you leaning on me?"

Shelly flushed with anger—deliberately provoked—and bit it back. He wasn't about to play the asshole's game. "You've made some enemies in your business, Catalan. More than you can keep track of. And one of them is about to catch up with you—a kid you won't remember, whose mother you destroyed."

"A kid?" Catalan asked. "Is that whom you're warning me against? I thank you for your concern, sergeant, but I suspect I can protect myself."

"You don't understand," Shelly said. "I'm not concerned about your safety at all. If I thought the kid could dust you, I'd wish him well. But I agree with you on that: you probably can protect yourself—only too well. That's why I've come to warn you: if anything happens to that kid, I'm not even going to try to build a case against you. I'm going to stop by one night and blow your miserable head off."

Catalan listened politely to Shelly's recitation, raising his eyebrows at the ultimate line. When it was clear Shelly had nothing to add, the drug dealer said, "Is that all? Very good. We should understand one another. Which is why I must tell you: if that kid—or anyone—comes gunning for me, I will certainly dispatch him with all deliberate speed. If you can find a judge to arraign me, please go ahead. But if you decide to settle the matter personally, I will see to it that you are sent to your own just reward as quickly as this kid goes to his."

Sister Margaret could apparently stand to hear no more from him and burst out, "You horrible, sinful man! Standing there, cool as the devil, declaring your intention of shooting a young man to death! How do you live with yourself, Mr. Catalan? How do you sleep at night? Our boys are troubled but they're good boys, each and every one of them. Suffering from the fate you shaped for him! And now that your own influence returns to haunt you, you plan to shoot it down on your doorstep? Have you no shame? Or compassion? Are you nothing but a mockery of a human being, created by God in His own image?"

Catalan waited, stone-faced. "Do I understand that you have something to do with this? You and your sisters at the convent school?"

The nun faltered. "I didn't say anything about the school."

"Of course you didn't," Catalan said, reaching to press a white button beside the base of a lamp on a side table near the couch. It did not ring, or buzz, and effected no appreciable change until a moment later when two burly hoodlums entered from the apartment across the hall, looking at Catalan and then his guests. Both men were over six foot two, with long, muscular arms. The first one had fists the size of softballs, and the second carried an iron poker.

Shelly brought out his firearm and trained it on the man in back, who sat in a chair, lowering the iron rod. His partner hesitated, and Shelly turned the gun on Catalan. "No need to show us out—we're on our way. Don't forget what I said about the kid."

Catalan showed ragged teeth. "I will forget nothing I learned here today. Thank you for coming, sergeant. It has been most instructive."

As Shelly and the others rode the elevator back to the lobby, he had an uncomfortable feeling that their visit had cost them more than it had gained. Catalan had learned that a kid was coming to kill him; he had learned also that the nuns were more involved with the thieves who stole his car than he had suspected. What had they learned from the visit? Only that Catalan's defenses were as formidable as they expected. The confrontation between them hadn't gone too well, either: the tougher Shelly talked, the more civilly Catalan behaved. It gave the drug dealer an edge which sharpened as Shelly tried to blunt it with each empty threat. What, after all, could he do if Catalan killed Robbie as an act of self-defense? Shoot the bastard in cold blood and spend the next ten years in prison? Was Robbie really that important to him? He didn't believe it himself, which made it difficult to fault Catalan for doubting him too.

"What now?" asked Homer once they were back in the Reliant. "Any more excuses for not running her in?"

He tipped his head toward Sister Margaret, who sat forward indignantly. "You can't just drive off now!" she said, shaking a disciplinarian's head. "The boy will certainly show up here. If we don't stop him at the curb, that butcher will cut him to pieces."

Homer rolled his eyes. "We can't undertake a stakeout here, with no more reason to believe there'll be trouble than the word of a suspicious homeboy."

Shelly cranked the engine.

Margaret said, "If Tomas said Robbie and Vinh are coming for Mr. Catalan, then they will be here. He might have lied about you or me, but he wouldn't lie about them."

"It's not what you lie *about* that counts, it's whom you're lying *to,*" muttered Homer. "Jefferson would've told us anything he thought that we'd believe, no matter how unlikely it might actually have been. And we did believe it—I can't imagine why. Two twelve-year-olds gunning for Cesar Catalan! Just listen how it sounds. He must be laughing up his sleeve at us right now."

"Catalan's not laughing," said Shelly as he slipped the gear into drive.

Homer snorted. "You think he had a bad case of gas?"

"I mean he's not laughing now," Shelly said, as an

ink-black Porsche Ruf Twin Turbo pulled out of an underground garage, its mirrored window rising. Catalan, at the wheel, twisted toward the back, where the mass of two thugs filled the window.

Shelly eased the Reliant into traffic three cars behind and one lane over from the Porsche. "Let's see where they're going," he said. Sister Margaret could hardly complain: Robbie would show where Catalan was, sooner or later. Homer was less agreeable.

"Now we're going to follow him to the club?"

"Look at it this way," Shelly suggested. "Twotoes was his bagman, right? Only the two of them knew the entire route—all the street-corner operations and crack houses, the face of every pitcher. Now Twotoes is gone, so what's Catalan's problem?"

A gleam entered Homer's eyes. "His money."

"Right. His crews are out there, raking it in, with nobody to bring it home to papa. He can't leave the daily bundle in the hands of his crews on the streets. All that cash burning pocket holes is sure to give somebody an idea about how nice it would be to keep it every day. Catalan can't afford that kind of thinking—it's no good for morale, however the shotguns blow."

Homer grinned. "So Catalan collects, today."

"At least until he trains somebody to take over for Jimmy Twotoes—showing them where and who to see. Why don't we just go along for the ride and pick up what we can?"

They trailed Catalan's Porsche over the Henry Hudson Bridge, off the highway at Dyckman Street, and up Nagle Avenue to Tenth Street. Shelly did not risk following the Porsche down the side streets to Ninth, which were usually deserted around the power station, but waited instead at 207th Street at the foot of the University Heights Bridge. The Porsche would either head there or double back to the Harlem River Drive, and the bridge made a better bet, given the turn at Nagle. When the Porsche reappeared at 207th Street and crossed back into the Bronx, the Reliant was behind it, a knight's jump away. They followed Fordham Road and turned right on Third Avenue. Shelly lagged a block then two blocks behind, letting the Porsche pass from sight rather than risk being seen.

Catalan turned a corner into an alley, and Shelly saw a kid go running ahead of him. That would be the *lookout,* going to warn his pitcher that their boss was heading his way. They were close to a street-corner operation. Shelly hit the gas and turned after Catalan before the lookout could resume his station. They came up short behind the Porsche, drawing seven pairs of eyes from the sidewalk. The lookout was already returning to his post—the newest face in the crowd. Shelly recognized most of the team, having crossed their paths before. The *hawker,* whose job was to approach potential customers, was a street rapper named Merlin; he reached for a golf cap on his head and snapped down the brim over his eyes. Behind him, the *steerer,* who frisked and questioned interested buyers, was a bald ex-con named Cueball, whose parole had been violated just by standing there. Leaning into the window of Catalan's Porsche were the *pitcher,* a man called Doctor Snow who actually sold the rocks of crack in five or ten dollar vials, and the *bang-bang,* a mug called Boo-yah after the sound of a fired shotgun, who stared back at Shelly with brutal, empty eyes. Disappearing beyond the far corner of the block were a *runner,* nine years old, starting on a delivery, and a woman pushing an old baby carriage—the *stasher,* whose storage box on wheels allowed the sales force to reduce the crack in their pockets to less than felonious amounts. Homer opened his door to go after her, but Boo-yah stepped forward to block his progress and Shelly touched his sleeve at the elbow. The carriageload of vials would be gone before he reached the corner, and Shelly wanted to be able to take off after the Porsche if Catalan's foot hit the gas. He couldn't leave Homer on that street.

The crew on the pavement looked at each other, then at Doctor Snow, wondering whether to run. Snow ducked his head into the car and exchanged a mumble with Catalan.

The Porsche didn't budge.

Shelly pulled up the Reliant alongside the driver's dark window and gestured to Homer, who rapped on the expensive glass with the nose of his Beretta. "Open up, Catalan. We know you're in there."

As the window descended, Homer's reflection was replaced by Catalan's expression of patience worn thin. "What is it you want now?"

"Whatever's in his pockets," said Shelly, pointing his own firearm at Doctor Snow. Homer turned the Beretta on Boo-yah, just in case.

Catalan said, "Empty your pockets."

The Doctor looked at Lowenkopf. "Wanna frisk?"

Shelly knew better than to turn his back on any of them, which left two choices: to lean them all against the wall and frisk each one while Homer watched the others; or to keep himself and his partner in the car. Rousting street-corner gangs was a job for uniforms, and the Doctor's question suggested he was not about to shoot them. "Go ahead," Shelly said, and to Boo-yah, "You don't move, or he's gonna blow your fucking head off."

Homer nodded.

Slowly and carefully, the Doctor emptied his pockets. Keys, change, a roll of bills fat enough to choke a cow—but no vials of crack or other drugs. From the back pockets came a wallet, a comb, and an address book. He unbuttoned his shirt, took it off, and raised his arms, showing his sleeveless undershirt, without bulges. Then, unbidden, he unhooked his belt and dropped his cranberry pants around his Converse. No sign of hidden firearms or secreted vials. He circled around and began to dress again.

"There was no need for that," Shelly said.

"Just wanted you to be sure," said the Doctor.

Shelly looked at the others, who avoided his gaze. One of them must have been carrying a rock or two at least, but the message from Catalan was clear: if trouble had been taken to keep his pitcher clean, there would be nothing to indict him in the Porsche. They didn't really even have probable cause: a Porsche stopped at the curb with someone leaning into it didn't have to mean a drug transaction. They knew it was a transaction because they knew the driver dealt, but that wouldn't hold up in court. Catalan understood this and drummed his fingers on the wheel of the Porsche as if he were waiting for a ticket from a motorcycle cop which he'd rather pay than discuss.

Shelly leaned over and said, "We're not in your living room now, Catalan. Jimmy's gone—there's no one to keep your nails clean. Somehow or other, you have to deliver in the mornings and collect at night. And whenever you try to do either one, you'll find us right on your ass."

Catalan looked over, bored. "Maybe you'll find something else to keep you occupied."

Shelly was about to reply when the call came over the radio: a drive-by shooting, blowing out two classrooms.

Classrooms?

Classrooms. Our Lady of Regret Convent School. The captain said they'd know where it was.

23

When Cesar Catalan's black Porsche pulled up curbside near the Doctor, Cueball, Merlin, and Boo-yah, two slim figures took up positions in a window over the bodega. Robbie Delaud and Vinh Nguyen had been waiting nearly three hours for the drug boss to appear. Among the IOU chits and betting slips in Jimmy Twotoes's back pockets they had found a sleek black book that laid out the route of his daily deliveries and collections. Most of the names they could match to crews working rock houses and street corners in the neighborhood. The book gave no clue as to order; they had no idea where Catalan would go first, or when he would make a particular stop on his rounds. But the apartment over the bodega on the Doctor's block was empty, which meant they could hide out there and wait for their man as long as was necessary. Sooner or later he would have to claim the bankroll collected for him—and when he came, they would be ready. One clear shot was all they needed.

But they never got that one clear shot, since Catalan, when he finally arrived just after 4:30, kept cloistered in his car. The Porsche had evidently been chosen for its discreet anonymity. They could see movement through the tinted windows, but nothing more certain than that. Two men sat in the back seat and one in the front, their vague shadows moving across the glass. One of the pair in the back was probably the drug boss. But which one? It was impossible to tell from their vantage point over the ground-floor bodega. A shotgun blast right down the middle might take out both men in the back—or tear up the cushion between them. Pressed against the window frame, holding their breath, the two adolescents waited for a sign: a lowered window, a nod of respect, something to tell them apart. But no clue appeared. Robbie angled the barrel of the shotgun toward the Porsche's back windshield, shifting his aim from one mass of shoulders to the other, until Doctor Snow and Boo-yah blocked his line of sight. His finger resettled uneasily on the trigger. But no shot was worth the reaction it would stir unless it stood at least a fair chance of reaching the brain of its target.

Doctor Snow leaned half his body into the Porsche's window, having a word with the driver; as he came out, Robbie heard him say, ". . . That ain't gonna last through the morning, if you don't. These people have *respect* for your merchandise, my man."

And then the Reliant rounded the corner, and the situation changed. Vinnie's face screwed up, acknowledging the difference. A shotgun blast at a drug lord would make them targets for half the guns on the street. Let a cop near the cross hairs, and the other half would be on them, too. This was just too much risk, as both of them knew. Their chance of taking down Cesar Catalan vanished in the exhaust from the unmarked police car. As they watched the stasher's baby carriage slip around the corner, Vinh Nguyen stretched his legs as if to declare it was time, perhaps, he too was moving along.

He sat back on his haunches, shaking his head, and murmured, "No luck, Bro. Your lollipop's picked up a fuzz ball. Time for us to blow."

"Chill out, man, will you?" said Robbie, peering over the barrel of a sawed-off shotgun propped on the peeling wooden windowsill. "Give me a second to think here."

"Take all the time you need," the Amerasian said. "Just remember what time we're looking at now. We're late for class, again, man."

Robbie nodded his head, still staring out the window. On the street below, Catalan's head clung like a turtle's to the inside of his tinted car.

"You hear what I'm telling you?" asked Vinnie, laying long fingers across the sight of the shotgun. "The son of a bitch slipped away. It's time we made the convent now. Old Charlie'll be wondering."

Robbie stared down the barrel as if the fingers were unable to block his line of sight. Vinh knew what that blankness was all about. Having come so close to his target, he was unwilling to move on without firing a shot. Yet there was nothing in the street below he could reasonably blow to bits.

He looked up at Vinh finally as if considering whether to blow *him* to smithereens. "You go."

"Alone?"

"Tomas'll be there by now."

"I meant, without you, man? That don't seem right. We're in this together, you and me. You got some other business, maybe I better come too."

Robbie shook his head. "The next move's a solo, homeboy," he said, forcing a smile. "You done your duty in the trenches already. I got to become invisible now. You're a good soldier, with a steady heart, but you don't exactly fade in around here. Go to class. You like it more'n I do."

"Just the stories," said Vinh defensively. "The shit about how to get along in this world—I sure can live without that. But you know, I've always been a sucker for stories."

"That's cool," Robbie said, propping a hand on his shoulder and pushing his friend toward the door. "I just want to do this one thing. Go hear your stories, man. I'll be fine by myself now."

Vinh looked uncertainly at his companion, who had

settled against the wall beneath the windowsill, resting the shotgun across his knees. Vinh wavered, wondering just how much bullshit his pal had passed off. What did Robbie have in his mind? He decided it didn't matter: Robbie's thoughts, like his own, were a tangle of mixed emotions that could not be shared in their full complexity with a soul in another skin. Robbie's life was a mystery he carried alone—there was no way to protect him from his destiny. Vinh smacked his own thighs, shaking the dust from his skintight Levis. "Take it light, Robbie, man. No Rambo chances, hear?"

Robbie nodded, turning his attention back to the window as the Amerasian kid tramped out of the apartment in steel-toed leather boots.

In the street below, a drama played itself out. Boo-yah had stepped between the car and the carriage as if one of the cops might go after it. But no one came out of the battered old Plymouth, which rolled up next to the Porsche. A nine-millimeter weapon emerged from the passenger window and tapped on the mirrored glass, which opened—wrong side. Robbie still couldn't clear a shot.

Then Doctor Snow, at the curbside, emptied his pockets onto the roof of the Porsche, starting with a bankroll of fives and tens thick as a baseball. Then he removed his white satin shirt, and began to undo his pants. And still neither Catalan nor the cops risked a toe outside their cars. Everyone playing it safe, Robbie thought with a frown, leaving no targets for the other side. Which meant no targets for him either. He straightened, stretching his joints, watching the Doctor's striped boxer shorts flutter in a breeze which did not reach his second-floor window. Then he cracked open the weapon in his hands. Withdrawing both shells, he slid the shotgun down the leg of his camouflage pants and pulled his yellow bowling shirt over the stock. The cool barrel pressed against his thigh. Catalan had other stops to make. Robbie could catch him later. And he thought he knew how to locate that rendezvous site.

Vinh Nguyen meanwhile wasted no time on the surface streets, but headed over to the convent by way of the rooftops. Vinnie loved the landscape of chimneys and peeling tar that floated over the city like the tops of jungle trees. In parts of Vietnam there were animals that never set foot on the ground, his mother had told him, moving from one branch to the next, living in the sky. That was how Vinh would have lived, if anyone ever asked him his preference. No one had ever asked, so his life had been spent instead among the garbage in the gutter—of Saigon or New York or anywhere in between, the differences never mattered. There were people who walked on the pavement: men in business shoes, women in heels or slippers, families whose children's feet told everything about them. And there was garbage, a shifting mix of paper and glass and cans and food, reflecting the tastes and appetites and resources of the people who emptied it into giant bins or tossed it into the gutter. Yet, at the same time, it retained its essential character, despite the abundance of bok choy or frozen french-bread pizza. Each kind was different, and all kinds the same.

He could remember days and nights on the open sea when he would have done anything for some rotten vegetables, or the rind of an orange. On the passage from Mui Bai Bung to Songkhla in southern Thailand—a taste of salt that lined the nose and throat until every breath was a cry for water. So that the camp seemed a deliverance at first, before a prison, where again he had fed himself on a diet of other people's refuse. In his escape, crossing to Georgetown and Kuala Lampur, where he first crept onto the freighter, the one constant on which he could reliably depend, no matter where the ship loaded, was garbage.

No, he told himself, dropping from a rusty fire escape onto the pavement, *that was not all.* There had been two other things, compasses, by which he guided his progress. Both had come from his mother, and Vinh felt an obligation to remember his personal history as a testament to her. She had given him the photograph and told him that *Gas Car comes from the Bronx.* So when at last the freighter docked in the New York Harbor he had taken a dive over the side and found his way to the Bronx.

It was a big place, too, bigger than he had hoped, and no one had heard of his father. Which meant he would have to find a way to feed himself until he could learn where he was. No one was offering any kind of job to an underage illegal immigrant with no papers or schooling or relevant skills. And there at his feet was an answer, the river that had nourished him in every corner of the globe since he had left Saigon.

So after all that had passed in between, he found himself once again rooting through the garbage in the gutter for his meals. Different foods, of course, different tastes: a crust of Big Mac smothered in vinegary ketchup, the slushy remains of a lump of purple ice staining a soggy paper cup. He had learned to read this foreign menu, to spot what was edible and devour it, quickly enough, before it could be stolen by a bigger appetite. He had an eye for it, a talent for garbage, that allowed him to survive his first American winter on heels of ground meat and tomato sauce and the last sip in a crushed can of sweetened, colored, carbonated water. In the gutter, he had come home to Saigon. It was a specialty for which he felt confidently trained, a portable skill. Garbage was garbage, and he'd seen enough of it to last a lifetime.

And a lifetime on the streets had taught him to watch how a vehicle moved and didn't move, an intuitive radar which served him well as he slept and scavenged and holed up, deciding where to place his eyes and what to allow them to see. The particular type of nonmovement he spotted in a green T-bird, with two men in a plush front seat doing nothing much of anything, would have touched off his warning system, had the car been idling halfway down any other neighborhood block. The convent had its own rules, he was grateful to acknowledge—it was the thing he liked best about the place, beside the stories. He didn't have to watch his back so closely all the time. And it wasn't that some other eyes kept watch instead of his own. The nuns didn't even lock their doors, a statement of defiance of the logic of the streets: other rules applied. His hours in the classroom with Father Charles, under the protection of the sisters, were his happiest of the week.

He ascended the wide, flat steps leading to the entrance of the school and set his weight to the blue-painted metal door, which gave way before him. Unlocked. He was allowed to enter, they were waiting for him to come inside. To Vinh, it was a strange but pleasant feeling, like a cop who winked and passed. It reminded him of something he used to know, from before the day they had come to take his mother to the camp in the country, for retraining. She had tried to hold him, as the soldiers pulled her away . . . but that was not a memory he felt like recalling just then. He stood in the doorway a few seconds, savoring the joy of welcome, before disappearing into the hall's fragrant, musty dimness.

As soon as he had gone inside, the engine of the T-bird was suddenly ignited and slipped into low gear. The two men in the front seat wore grim, expectant faces as their vehicle rolled silently over the garbage in the street.

When the call came in over the radio about the drive-by shooting at the convent, Shelly's first thought was not for his son. He had momentarily forgotten that they had left Thom in Father Charles's classroom, and remembered instead only the young men in the class who were likely to have provoked this sort of gang violence. He felt a certain irritation that the gangsters in the class had brought the street war onto the convent grounds, where Father Charles or even Sister Elizabeth might be endangered by stray gunfire. Then he remembered, and the thought of Thom among the schoolroom debris—bleeding, lifeless—gave a dramatic urgency to the call. His horror as he imagined the unconscious form of his son worked a metamorphosis in Shelly: his foot turned to lead on the gas pedal, and his Adam's apple to stone in his throat.

When they reached the convent grounds, they could see where a classroom along the ground floor had been pummeled by a shotgun and perhaps even an Uzi. A great black powder stain marked much of the white exterior wall. The lower half of the windows had been completely blown out, glass and wood, while the panes of the upper half had collapsed in sympathy, or thunderous vibrations, leaving gaping wooden holes like torn-out teeth. Inside, the shadows of adults moved among the wreckage, responding to teenage groans. An ambulance blinked silently in front as a pair of paramedics hauled a stretcher over the lawn.

The Reliant leaped up on the pavement halfway to the gaping classroom. Shelly was out before the engine was still, helping a Hispanic paramedic load a wounded figure through the ambulance doors. The patient was resisting, fighting him off, trying to climb from the stretcher.

"In Christ's name, leave me alone!" the patient hollered. His voice rattled like an echo whistling through a drainpipe. "There are boys inside who need your help and mine. When they're taken care of, you can tend to me!"

It was Branigan, struggling to rise. By his arms he lifted himself vertically, lifting a hand to poke at his rescuer and tumbling down again. But his left leg never stirred, and a grimace of pain gripped the cleric's face as he twisted against its angle. In the moment it took him to recover his breath, Shelly said, "Branigan! Have you seen my son?"

Father Charles tried to lift himself again and flopped back, his face gray as gravel. "I didn't see anything—not in time. There was a flash of light like a flare outside and then everything went to pieces."

"There was nothing you could have done."

The priest shuddered, remembering the moment. "I thought, 'Nearer, my Lord, to Thee,' and then thought of all the children. I couldn't help them at all."

The confession seemed to ease his mind, and he stopped resisting passage into the bay of the ambulance. Shelly felt a surge of relief, at once undone. Where was Thom? The priest hadn't seen him call for help. Was that because the boy had walked away unharmed? Or failed to rise from the floor?

The strapping paramedic did not interfere as Shelly peered into the bay, looking for a smaller version of his own features. Only when he was sure that Thom was not already among the wounded did he enter the classroom, searching through the smoke for his son.

He found Thom sitting against the front of Branigan's desk, drinking water from a plastic cup. His forehead was bandaged with some white gauze and adhesive tape that reached around the corner of his temple over his ear. His nose was scratched and one of his eyes looked like it might be purpling. But altogether he was fine, anyone could see, by the regularity of his breathing and the pleasure he seemed to be drawing from drinking the lukewarm water.

Shelly watched a moment as the boy's hardly articulated Adam's apple bobbed greedily, taking in the liquid as quickly as possible, pumping it through his limbs. To Shelly, the movement was beautiful, demonstrating the resilience of all the muscles, nerves, and bones that must function competently to perform the simple action of drinking. When he had drained the cup, Thom looked up to a sister to pour him another from a crystal decanter in her hand. She was busy filling a cup for another thirsty boy, and so Thom had a moment to look past her and focus on the grave face of his father.

"Dad!" he called with genuine delight, raising himself into a crouch and finally to his feet. Shelly tried to read whether the shift in position was painful, but couldn't tell—from the big grin spreading over Thom's shaky jaw, the boy seemed to have forgotten the recent risk to his life and limb.

"Are you all right?" asked Shelly, enormously guilty for having left his son exposed to grievous harm.

"You should've seen it!" said Thom, ignoring the question with the unmistakable thrill of true adventure. "We were just sitting here, you know? Talking about cutting your fingernails, when all of a sudden there was this crackling sound outside. Some of these kids know a lot about this stuff and hit the floor as soon as they heard that sound. I had no idea what was going on, but decided to follow their lead, and the next minute the air was full of fire! Like the room had burst into flame. I shoved my head against a desk leg and stayed there, while the glass in the windows just fell in, smashing on all sides—loud first, then quieter, until only the tinkling was left. It was eerie, like a rain. I had a sliver that long in the leg of my pants but I just yanked the fucker out."

Shelly nodded, still in shock. Thom made the shooting

sound like Coney Island, while behind him the paramedics scooped up a kid from the glistening floor and slid him onto a stretcher. The wounded boy moaned; they murmured some words of encouragement and exchanged brisk observations. Four nuns had crossed the grounds from the convent and were ministering to the lesser casualties as best they could.

"Can you help?" asked one of Shelly, turning to face him suddenly. It was Sister Margaret, who had come from the Reliant with Homer and made herself useful at once. The problem was a large wooden cabinet, which had stood against a wall between the windows. The wall was now a yawning hole where a shotgun shell had blasted through it. What remained of the cabinet was now lying face down on the ground. From beneath it came a whimper, and Shelly realized that someone was trapped below. He moved immediately into place, squatting beside Homer, lifting from his thighs, until, with a shared grunt they managed to raise the cabinet just as the two paramedics returned to the room to assist them.

"Holy shit," said the smaller one.

The Hispanic nodded, confirming the diagnosis.

There on the floor, lying face down, was Vinh Nguyen, head resting at an angle to his shoulders that made him look like a doll. No human neck should have bent so far. His arm, too, was folded back unnaturally high. There was some blood, not much, that all seemed to flow from his head. The big paramedic knelt at once, feeling for a pulse at his throat.

"He's alive."

It didn't seem possible. But they touched him tenderly, easing him onto the stretcher, carrying him out like a baby. Shelly heard the bay doors slam and the ambulance siren whine, like the announcer at a track, calling the race for Vinnie's life. The floor where he had lain was strewn with books and unsharpened pencils, a ruler, some gray-and-gray erasers—the contents of the cabinet that had stood by the window. Still wrapped in cellophane were sets of attendance cards, index cards, a yellow pad, two binders, sheets of lined loose-leaf paper, some black construction paper, and a scissor. And a stained, glossy rectangle that had once been white.

Shelly knelt and flipped it over. A photograph. He knew it at once: a serviceman with a thin mustache, standing in front of a private house some fifteen years before. The house Vinh had tried to find along the bus routes of the borough, looking for the man he called his father.

Shelly studied the face carefully as an odd familiarity grew. The mustache was of a type that had gone out of style: low on the lip and carefully, narrowly trimmed, as if it had been drawn by hand with an eyebrow pencil. Shelly's uncle had worn a mustache like that, twenty years before—which must have been what made the face so familiar. But a tingle at the back of his scalp warned him to look closer. He noticed the set of the mouth, drooping at the edges, and the unyielding clinch of the jaw. He knew exactly how that mouth would work, gnawing at something unpleasant before spitting it out. The eyes were just the eyes that always surmounted that jaw, looking down at the desk in front of him, or off through the glass-paneled walls.

Whenever Shelly sat in the captain's office.

24

Y ou mean you still haven't picked up that goddamned nun?" Madagascar roared when Shelly and Homer returned to the precinct house with only Tomas Jefferson in tow. Thom was with them too, but he had stopped on the way into the squad room to check out his wounds in the men's room mirror.

Shelly preferred to face the captain in Thom's temporary absence. Madagascar was prone to swings of mood and opinion, which were sometimes hard to anticipate. Saving face was easier one on one. "They couldn't spare her just now, sir. They had a little problem with their physical facility today, and Sister Margaret's the one in charge of that."

The captain shook his head in mock sympathy. "They're gonna have to spare her, aren't they? When the woman goes to jail?"

"You asked us to try to prevent that, sir."

"That was before there was a warrant out for her, sergeant. You remember that little thing, don't you? And the judge who issued it? We can't exactly ignore him, now can we?"

"No, sir. But what about the bishop?"

"We can only do so much. The law, after all, is the law. Vietnam was a long time ago."

Which brought up a topic Shelly was loath to broach— though it had to be raised. Since he didn't know when another chance would come. "Not that long ago. What is it now? Ten years?"

"Almost thirteen for me."

A pregnancy and twelve—just the right number. Madagascar had left just when the boy's father did. Shelly steadied his nerve, cleared his throat and said, "Do you ever feel, sir, that you left something of yourself behind?"

"You mean my youth—some shit like that?"

"Not exactly," said Shelly, trying for a casual tone. He didn't know why he thought his tone should be casual, but it seemed somehow the safest way to sound. No moral judgments here. Just a word about the son you left behind.

The captain found the question odd but intriguing, a stimulant to his memories.

"I left behind a lot of stuff I thought I'd want to take: V.C. weaponry and hats and that sort of junk. But when it came right down to packing my bags, I didn't want to take any of it. Didn't want to remember it all, I guess. Wrapped it up in brown paper and left it for a gift. For a woman I was seeing, like, over there."

Lowenkopf took a breath and asked, "She didn't call you 'Gas Car' by any chance, did she?"

Madagascar stared at the sergeant as if he'd never seen him before—as if he'd never seen any of his kind before. "Now how the fuck did you learn something like that?"

"She did?"

"Who told you? The bishop? No, I never told him about her. He wouldn't approve of our liaison. A hotshot MP like me with Loan Thi Nguyen, a local Saigon girl. I called her 'Little Lo' and she called me 'Mad Gas Car.' Now are you gonna tell me where you heard that name or aren't you?"

Shelly nodded. There was nothing else to say. "I heard it from your son."

"My . . . what?" The captain's stare made the last one

look like a wink from a pal. He sat down heavily on the desk behind him, which was Homer's, scattering papers.

Homer recovered his papers with a glance at Shelly but no word of remonstrance or sympathy. He had learned the difficult trick of keeping his mouth shut and used it to advantage. The captain glared at Lowenkopf alone.

"Your son," Shelly repeated. "Or a boy who thinks he is. He's been looking all over the Bronx for his father—a man called 'Gas Car,' according to his mother. The photograph he uses is something you should see."

Shelly drew the frayed snapshot of the serviceman from his pocket and held it up for the captain's scrutiny. Madagascar took it from him, eyeing the shot like a friend he hadn't seen for years.

"Sweet Jesus," said Madagascar with a strange grimace that stretched his mouth from its usual configuration. "My father took that shot the day I enlisted. I haven't seen it in . . . you know how many years?"

"Thirteen?"

"That's right, almost thirteen years. The day I left Saigon, I gave it to a woman I knew there. Something to remember me by. And now you say she's given it to . . .?"

"A boy who says he's your son. Only he doesn't know where to find you, yet."

Madagascar's brow furrowed. "You mean he's not sure I'm really his dad?"

"He doesn't know you're you, sir. He's been looking for 'Gas Car,' someone he hasn't been able to locate yet. He doesn't doubt that 'Gas Car' is his father."

"Well I'll be," said the captain, uncertain how to respond. He tried to smile, felt uncomfortable, and scowled. "So, uh, is there some place I can look in on him? Just to check him out? To see if he might be who he says?"

It was then that Shelly remembered how much the captain did not know about the drive-by shooting at the convent. The targets might have been Robbie and his friends, or any of the other gang affiliates. Their best chance for a break in the case would be a disgruntled informant, or a suspect caught red-handed in another incident willing to trade for his charges. But those sorts of breaks were catch as catch can; they could not be systematically produced. While the casualties from this drive-by would elicit predictable calls for action. A priest hurt; a convent school desecrated; innocent children wounded. Not to mention the twisted kid under the school supply cabinet.

"He was hurt, sir. Badly. In the drive-by. The paramedics didn't look hopeful."

"My son?" said Madagascar incredulously, gripping Shelly by both arms. "Do you mean to tell me, Sergeant Lowenkopf, that you have discovered a son I did not know I had—by a woman who was practically my wife—and, that same day, some miserable scum with an Uzi and a shotgun blew him to smithereens? Is that basically your report?"

"More or less, sir. He's not smithereens, yet. And there is one other thing you should know about him, just to know the whole story so far."

"So far?"

Lowenkopf unhooked the captain's fingers from his arms. "He's probably involved in the stolen Ferrari. Maybe even with Jimmy Twotoes or Akira Tanagaki."

If the captain had missed twelve years of aggravation in the life of his son, he recaptured most of them then, as fierce desires to meet, embrace, cherish, and demolish the boy fought themselves out in his chest. He leaned back again on Homer's desk, crushing a Styrofoam cup with a dried brown tea bag at its bottom. When at last he raised weary eyes and demanded where the paramedics had driven the casualties, Shelly recognized the mantle of fatherhood in all its complexity yoking another pair of shoulders.

Madagascar left at once for the hospital, abandoning in his glass office a deskful of requests and strident complaints from the public he had sworn to serve.

Shelly sank into his own chair, across from which Homer sat with a black folder on his knee and a peculiar look of satisfaction on his face. He turned a page and lifted an eyebrow, glancing up at his partner with a composure bordering on indifference. Shelly could feel the difference in Homer's attitude: the tension of the unsolved case had been broken for him, as if only the mopping up remained. Homer knew something, or he felt he did, with dramatic implications.

Shelly tried an off-hand casual tone. "What's up?"

"Report came in on Twotoes."

"Anything in it?"

"In the text?" said Homer. "Not much. Nothing we haven't already surmised."

So not in the text. Then where? "Any diagrams?"

Homer shook his head. "Not one."

"Evidence?"

"Nothing interesting."

Not the text, no diagrams, not the evidence bags—what had Homer hit upon? Shelly thought about the information due from the lab. The blood specimens would be reported in the text and the ballistical conclusion as well. So where the hell was the big breakthrough? In the cover of the report?

"I think you should look through the photographs, Shell," said Homer with satisfaction. "The ones you bawled out the shutterbug for, in front of the deputy coroner."

He had bawled out the police photographer? Of course, when the d.c. flipped over the corpse, right onto the bloody floor. Before they had a chance to read . . .

THE ROBIN HOODS.

He reread the words in the photograph twice, then confirmed them against another angle. There was no doubt about it. They stood out from the floorboards, a shiny brownish red against the dull, scuffed matte of the wood. The photo of the corpse's left index finger was covered in blood—but dipped, probably, since the upper arm development exposed in the autopsy confirmed that Twotoes was right-handed. So the signature had been scrawled not by the victim but the murderer, after the fact.

THE ROBIN HOODS.

Shelly turned to Homer. "Misspelled?"

Homer shook his head, deeply gratified. "No it's not. It's quite correct, historically. That's what's so odd about it. The name is spelled exactly as it should be—as it always is spelled, in fact. In every case but one."

"The first murder."

Homer nodded like a teacher with a pupil who is finally catching on. "So what do you make of that?"

"Well," said Shelly, trying to retrace a deduction he was sure had already been made, "I'd say that the letter found by Shirane was written by somebody other than the person who wrote this here."

"Two different members of the gang?"

Shelly shook his head. "These gangs are very important to their members—their whole sense of belonging is tied up in them. And they see their names all the time, on every space big enough to invite a graffiti writer. Some members might not know how to spell the names of their congressmen, or even of their parole officers, but you can be damn sure they know how to spell the name of their gang."

"That's what I think," Homer said quietly. "No misspelling. So you conclude . . . ?"

"That the note to Tanagaki and the name on the floorboards were written by one gang member and somebody else who was not a member of the gang."

"Very good," said Homer, "sticking close to the facts—a difference in writing, at first. And what does that difference imply?"

Shelly did not enjoy reinforcing Homer's pedagogical impulse. But long experience had convinced him it was the quickest way to find out what Homer had uncovered. With a sigh, he recited the catechism. "That whoever killed Twotoes was not the same person who murdered Akira Tanagaki."

"And so?"

"A copycat killer?"

Homer nodded again, with a twinkle in his deep green eyes—always greener at times like this.

"But do you notice anything strange about the sequence of the spellings? Unusual for a copycat killing?"

Strange? The whole fucking case was a trip to the fun house. A businessman is poisoned in the Botanical Gardens and a note found in his briefcase. A crack dealer is knifed in an abandoned building and his assailants named in blood. Is that unusual or not? Just the run of the mill on an average day in the Bronx? But Homer had something particular in mind—Shelly was sure about that. So why didn't he just lay it out on the desktop, instead of making them both sweat it out? Shelly's patience for this game of wits never held up long enough. He would have loved to rattle off Homer's own deductions, but could never stand the question-and-answer period.

"Just spit it out, Homer, will you?"

The blond detective shrugged as if to concede there was no point in hoping Shelly might figure it out for himself. Then he settled into his seat, propping his feet on his desk with a gracious wave of his palm.

"From what Tomas told us, we can surmise that the Robbin' Hoods probably comprise Tomas himself, his friends Robbie, Vinh, and possibly one or two others. Not too many others, of course, or somebody else on the street would doubtlessly have heard of them."

"Right," said Shelly, sticking close, looking for a flaw in the reasoning. It was his turn now.

"But we have just learned from the signature in these photographs that the killer in the gardens is probably not the same as the killer in the abandoned building."

"Agreed," Shelly said, not quite sure why his partner had prefaced the observation with a *but.*

Homer smiled. "Now think about our suspects. Which do you think they might actually have murdered: Akira Tanagaki or Jimmy Twotoes?"

Shelly thought about the three adolescents. From what Father Charles had said about Robbie Delaud, their true target was Cesar Catalan—which made Twotoes their likeliest victim.

"Jimmy."

"That would be my guess," Homer mused softly, "and that is what I find strange. You see, Twotoes was killed *after* Tanagaki, according to these reports. You see the problem?"

Shelly felt it as an uneasiness before it fell into words he could articulate, even to himself. It was all about copycats, and when they did their copying. The whole point was to lead the police to conclude that someone else was responsible for their crime, because of its similarity to an earlier one. For that to happen, there had to be an earlier crime—at least one—whose pattern is duplicated by the copycat criminal. If someone were copying the Robbin' Hoods, they would have to do it after an actual crime by Tomas and his friends. Otherwise, how could they be sure another crime had been committed?

But if that were true, the real Robbin' Hoods would have had to kill Tanagaki and not Twotoes—completely inconsistent with everything Father Charles had revealed to them. If they had only killed one of the two victims, it had to be Twotoes. Which made the copycat killer act first.

"Are you telling me, Homer," Shelly said slowly, "that we've got a copycat killing *in advance?*"

"Appears that way, doesn't it?" Homer said. "I thought it was a little unusual."

"All right, already," said Shelly, excited by the unmistakable potential for a case-busting question he couldn't wait to ask. He sat forward sharply, eliciting a groan from his chair springs. "Where's Tomas?"

"Showing your son around the precinct house."

They caught up with the boys at the holding cells downstairs. Thom was bent over a match in Tomas's cupped hand, lighting an unfiltered cigarette. While Thom puffed, Tomas said, "They keep you here, see, for a few hours, till they get their shit together to nail you with the judge. If it takes them longer than that, or they feel like busting your balls, they can hold you a coupla days. A bus comes and rounds you up and drops you off in prison for the night."

Thom nodded, drawing deeply with two fingers on his Lucky. "They send you to prison even before you're indicted of any crime?"

"Before you even seen a judge," said Tomas seriously.

Thom shook his head. "That sucks."

The tone of the exchange troubled Shelly in some inner recess of his fatherhood. Thom's cigarette made him queasy. But he was not about to act on that now. "Tomas," he said, calling from the stairs before they had actually entered, "tell me something."

As soon as he heard his name pronounced by an officer of the law, the kid's whole demeanor shifted perceptibly. His eyes, which had been moving around the room, sunk to floor level and emptied of readable content, emotional or otherwise.

Shelly saw the transformation and said, "I'm not looking for secrets. I'm looking for a way to get a handle on the shooters who sent Vinny Nguyen to the hospital."

"Now who coulda done that?" Tomas wondered.

"Catalan?" Shelly proposed the name as if there was still some doubt in his mind. "If that's what you think, you're going to have to help me see it. Tell me something new."

"Like what?"

"Like where you and your crew first heard the name, *the Robbin' Hoods?*"

Tomas was offended. "How do you know we didn't think it up ourselves?"

"Did you?"

His hangdog reserve broke in a wolflike grin. "No, man— it was you. You starting calling us 'the Robin Hoods' and Catalan picked it up and soon it was all over the street. Robbie kind of liked it, you know? So he said, 'Let's use it,' and that's what we did."

"On Jimmy Twotoes?"

"I thought this was a friendly conversation," said Tomas. "I don't know nothing about that."

"All right," said Shelly, "a friendly conversation. Doing your part for the neighborhood. Just tell me this: if you guys weren't the Robbin' Hoods, why were you giving away cars?"

"We couldn't keep them, could we? We could've trashed them. But there's a lot of people who need a car or a television set."

"Television sets?"

"Yeah. Didn't you come across any of those? We gave away about ten of those, too."

"But why?" Shelly asked. "Catalan's car I understand—you picked it up as a bonus when you ripped him off the other night. But why take the risk of stealing all those other things when you didn't plan to keep or even sell them?"

"It was the same as the Ferrari, man."

"No it wasn't. Each theft was a separate occasion, another chance to be caught."

"Who told you that shit?"

"Who told us . . . ? You mean they weren't stolen at different times?"

"You think we're crazy?"

"Then the television sets . . . and the van . . . came into your possession the same night you took the Ferrari?"

Tomas said nothing to contradict his surmise—which was all that Shelly needed. He reached over, snatched the cigarette from the mouth of his son, and threw it, sparking, to the ground.

"Wait here," he told Thom, with a glance at Tomas. "I'll be back soon to drive you home. We've got to run down to Manhattan right now, and no, you can't come along."

Thom looked up, hearing the excitement behind his father's words. "Where are you going?"

"To arrest a murderer," Shelly said—not to impress his son with the importance of his job, or for any premeditated purpose. In his mind was one thought only: he knew.

He *knew*.

25

As the gray sky over the housing authority projects cooled into darkness, Robbie Delaud crouched at the edge of a walkway, rubbing an ice cream stick against the rough concrete until the tip was smooth and sharp. Behind his head, a drooping chain marked the border of a patch of grass in the narrow space between buildings. It was just after supper and people were starting to stir again from their apartments, riding the elevators, moving through the stair-wells, meeting one another on the green benches facing the grass where the walkway widened near a drinking fountain.

Robbie bent his head to the task at hand and began on the round side of the ice cream stick, keeping one eye and all of his mind on a side door of the building at the end of the walkway. Each building had one: green steel, without peep-hole or number, planned as a custodial apartment in the architect's original design. But things never worked as planned in the world Robbie knew. The custodian lived in a third-floor apartment and had rented out the basement to Kalie, when she had come down in the world so low there was no place lower to go.

Robbie raised his eyes, not his head, as a thin man in a dirty army shirt rapped on the door, waited barely a minute and rapped again. The door opened slowly, though it shut very quickly, closing off the world without from the darkened sanctuary within. Robbie remembered every inch of the interior—three steps down, not as steep now as they once had seemed, to a sagging sitting room where an old green couch and two brown chairs did their best impression of a social space. The dim light issued from a porcelain lamp with a gilded, fringed shade. There was another room, to the right, with a TV set for the kids, and a kitchen to the left, where he did not go. It was the shade he remembered best, vaguely Arabian. Staring at it would take him to some other place while his mother sucked the glass dick with Kalie in the kitchen.

He had not been back to Kalie's place since his mother had come down sick. Once she did, and the word got around, she could no longer work a twist, and had nothing else to trade for crack. And soon after, had no need for anything. He hadn't even thought about the place, as a matter of fact, and would just as soon have wiped it from his memory. Except now, when he needed to know what no one but Kalie could tell him.

Robbie caught himself staring at the green steel door and quickly resumed work on the ice cream stick, until a few pairs of Converse had passed him. As he scraped, he repeated to himself the words he had heard from the bodega: *That ain't gonna last through the morning, if you don't. These people have respect for your merchandise, my man.* Doctor Snow had muttered them into Catalan's car, before the two cops pulled up.

The Doctor was asking for crack, of course, which Catalan supplied. The Doctor was short of merchandise, because they had robbed Catalan in the middle of a buy. The Doctor was feeling the pinch—his crack would be gone tomorrow morning . . . *if you don't.* If Catalan didn't do what? Deliver more? But Catalan was right there, then—if he had any backup supply, he would've delivered it on the spot. So

Catalan was out of stock and needed to score more. *If you don't* probably meant *if you don't score tonight.*

This presented Robbie with a rare opportunity. Catalan was impervious so long as he hid behind surrogates—Jimmy Twotoes, or whoever would take his place. But Catalan had no chance to train a replacement, yet. He wouldn't want to trust more than one of those at a time. If he needed to score, now that Jimmy was dead, he would have to do it himself. He would take great care in the choice of a site, especially after the rip-off earlier in the week. But he would be out there himself, personally vulnerable to the violent risks of the trade.

If Robbie could learn where the deal would go down. Felix had told them that Catalan's supplier refused to meet indoors. He wouldn't trust Catalan on the dealer's home ground or allow him into his own. And Catalan could not use the same place they had jumped Jimmy Twotoes. It was known—that would be enough to drive him away to another, safer location. But where? Catalan had probably not arranged a transaction personally for some time. Where would he go if he needed a place? Somewhere he had used in the old days, when he had to do everything himself.

Father Charles at the convent thought Robbie didn't remember who had screwed his mother. But he remembered. Enough to find the place Catalan would go for a fast, dirty moment of personal vulnerability.

Somewhere Kalie would know. She and Catalan had something going when he first hit upon crack. She helped him make a go of it, using her apartment as a place for people to come and check out the new thrill. That's where his mother had first gone, the apartment near the roof. Kalie had been pretty strung out, even in those days. But the crash came when he pulled out, setting up house uptown. Kalie had fallen through the floor, straight down, landing flat on her back in the basement. And she hadn't stopped falling still.

It was possible that Kalie would help him, just to get even with Catalan. But Robbie didn't believe it. She was afraid of

Cesar, more afraid than angry or resentful or humiliated by his desertion. Her fear would keep her quiet—Catalan made sure that nothing loomed more significantly in her thoughts or imagination. Except one thing.

Robbie felt in his pocket for the four vials taken from Jimmy's camel-hair coat. He held them in his palm, halfway out of his pocket. Inside each cylinder, a small, dull rock gleamed through the plastic. Crack. His ticket through the green steel door—and maybe further. The thing Kalie cared most about in all the world.

He waited for a moment when no one was in sight and crossed the stretch of walkway to her door. He felt the old upsurge in his gut, involuntary revulsion at what he would find inside—but also a peculiar expectancy that he knew was groundless and yet insisted on feeling like hope. Every time he had come to this door, his mother had been inside, and he couldn't shake the sense that her ghost would be there still, propped in the arms of the smelly brown chair, smiling as he crossed the threshold.

He raised his arm and banged on the steel, three short bangs, which rang heavier than he remembered. He had no idea whether the knock had changed, or if Kalie had forgotten him. He waited what seemed like a long time, and then banged again, three times. The door opened, and Kalie was behind it—more emaciated than he remembered her, which was thin as a broom. She wore a loose robe in a woolen plaid that was pinned at her waist, the loops sagging without a belt. Her hair had been pulled back and gathered with a ribbon, which had come undone, trailing down her back. Above all were her eyes, swollen globes in a shrunken face, twitching with pleading and confusion. At first they did not seem to recognize him. But her lids tensed for a second and she looked past him, and Robbie knew she was looking for his mother—whom she couldn't find, of course, and her eyes returned to his face with an accusation in them.

"Robbie? What are you doing here?"

Disappointment, but not for the loss of a friend. Another sort of frustration, more desperate . . . he reached deep and pulled out a vial from his pocket.

When her eyes fell on it, they gleamed more brightly than the plastic. Her mouth lost its pinch and tugged into a crooked smile. "Oh, that's a reason to come here. Indeed. Let me just help you with one of those, now."

She took one vial with a five-dollar rock and stepped aside, admitting him into the crack house. Inside, a damp, musty smell overwhelmed even the darkness, stinging his eyes. He didn't need them to negotiate the three concrete steps down into the room he thought he had fled forever.

The couch was still green and the armchairs brown. One of them was empty; in the other, the man in the work shirt dozed. But the lamp on the end table was no longer porcelain. A cheap plastic lamp with a fixed plastic shade had replaced the Arabian wonder, an exchange that seemed to him for the worse. "What happened to the lamp?"

"Huh?"

"The lamp you used to have there. What happened to it?"

Kalie looked at the spot where the cheap plastic thing gave off a negligible glow. She didn't seem to remember the other one. "Broke, I guess."

Robbie felt an inexplicable outrage over the missing gilded fringes. His anchor into his childhood in this place had been cut loose, and he looked around as if for the first time. There was a framed painting over the couch, a red-coated English horseman on a fox hunt. He remembered it at once, though he had forgotten it completely. How out of place that picture seemed to him now!

"You wanna do some a that?" Kalie said, looking at the pocket from which he had taken the vial. She held a bowl with two stems in her hands, which were shaking with anxiety and the weight of the glass. "I can show you how to burn your shit to squeeze out every hit."

He glanced toward the kitchen, where this woman used to go with his mother. "In there?"

She shrugged. "Anyplace you want."

There was nothing in the inner room to suggest a kitchen except a sink and a table with a glazed pink top and spindly aluminum legs. The places where a stove and refrigerator must have stood were now empty, though no attempt had

been made to restore the floor and wall even to the dilapidated condition of the rest of the room. There were cabinets
over the sink, with ill-fitting doors, behind which no plates
or cans or boxes could be seen. Three chairs were arranged
around the table, with stuffed vinyl seats and backs, and
Kalie now dropped into one, leaving Robbie his choice of
the others.

He sat as she arranged the pipe in front of her, opening
her palm for a rock. He had given her one vial for herself as
his price of admission, but she clearly preferred to use his
instead for her lesson in the fine points. He fished out a
second vial and handed it over. She opened it and examined
the frog inside, rubbing it tenderly between her fingers.

"All right," she said. "Let's get off."

The pipe was an empty bottle with two glass tubes
extending from it. The longer, skinnier tube stood up from
the top of the bottle, running down about halfway into the
center. The shorter, fatter tube stuck out from the side of the
base, where it was secured with aluminum foil. About an
inch from the top of the upright tube, a wire mesh screen
had been jammed. Kalie now dropped the rock from
Robbie's vial onto this screen, rotating the bottle until it sat
directly in the center. From a cabinet under the sink, she
produced a blowtorch, which she lit with a kitchen match,
and applied to the upright stem, brushing the glass around
the wire screen with bright blue acetylene flames. The crack
melted into a thick brown goo, bubbling slightly, as Kalie
nodded with approval.

"Just like this."

She set her mouth to the lower stem, drawing hard. The
bottle filled with white smoke, from the neck to the base and
up the lower stem. When she felt the hit, she sat back and
closed her giant eyes.

Robbie took the pipe from her and noisily slurped a hit,
then returned it to Kalie for another. She sucked at it,
nodding. "You see? You see?"

He nodded back and she sucked a little harder.

When she opened her eyes, he handed back the bottle for

her to take a hit. She didn't seem to mind how often it came her way, or how long the five-dollar rock seemed to last them. When it was done, frying off the wire screen with a final sizzling sputter, she shoved the pipe back at him. There was nothing left in the screen, of course, but he might feel like opening another vial sometime.

He drew the pipe closer and reached into his pocket . . . and hesitated as if something had occurred to him. "You know, Kalie, you could help me out."

"Well, sure, honey," she said. "Your mama was a friend a mine, you know. We always helping one another. Anything I can do, you just tell me now."

"I was thinking of Cesar," he said, "in the old days. You and him and my mom."

"Don't let them stories bother you none," Kalie said, but looked away, as he knew she would. "There wasn't nothing between him and her. She was my friend, your mama, and Cesar was my man, don't you know?"

"I know that," he said softly. "You must've known more about that man than anybody, then."

"I know more about him than anybody, ever," she said. "Not even his old mother knows more about him than me. I did anything for that man, everything he needed. There was nothing he could keep from me."

"That's what my mama told me," Robbie said, "but I never believed her. A man like Catalan has got to keep some secrets. From everybody."

She shook her head. "Not from me. I know where he cooked his coke and where he stashed his stash. Where he hid his money, and his bodies, and his piece. I know where he went when he had to hide his ass—I brought his food there, and soup when he was hurt. There ain't nothing I don't know about Cesar Catalan that anybody's gonna know in this world."

It was the only vehemence that could have worked through her constant hunger for crack. For a moment, her eyes settled on Robbie with a calm satisfaction. Then it passed and they resumed their restless searching.

Robbie tried a bluff. "You remember, one time, Cesar had to score from that bastard who shot him?" Someone had to, some time.

"Ricardo," she muttered. "With that wormy little hand."

"Right," said Robbie, "only one of the gangs was looking for him and he didn't want to show his face?"

"Oh yeah."

"My mama was worried that night. But you said not to worry, Cesar had a place they could meet. You remember?"

She stared past him, evidently recalling more than Robbie had asked for. After a long silence, she said, "Not that night. But enough like it, that it don't matter."

He took out a vial of crack and held it in his palm. "You do remember the place, then?"

She eyed the vial in his hand. "Shit, I remember all them places. Like I remember your mama. She was a good friend to me, Robbie. Just like you." She reached for the vial with its soft white rock, but Robbie pulled it back.

"Where did Cesar meet with Ricardo that night?"

"Oh, no," she said, shaking her head. "I can't tell you that. He'll kill me."

Robbie stood up the vial on the table, holding it at the top with his finger. "He'll never know. And if he knew, he'd thank you. I'm not going to hurt him, Kalie, you know that. How could someone like me do anything to a man like Catalan? I've just got a little business to discuss and want to make sure we've got a good place to talk."

She licked a bead of sweat from her thin upper lip. She knew he was lying, but didn't care. It was just the fear. And the lure of the crack was overwhelming that. "You won't say nothing about where you learned it?"

He shook his head. "If you won't say nothing about my asking. We'll have a little deal, you and me. And you know, in every deal you're entitled to a taste."

He popped open the vial and dropped the crack in the pipe's upper tube, where it landed on the screen. She started to pull the pipe toward her, but he grabbed it by the neck of the bottle.

"Where?"

234

She swallowed hard, visibly at her throat. "You know the playground by Waring Avenue? If you go left at them big rocks there, where the old men play cards?"

"At the entrance on Bronx Park East."

"Go past there, past the playground. You ever see this old white circle out back? Used to be like a gazebo or something, only now it's all crumbling to shit?"

Robbie said, "No."

She gripped the pipe by the base and lower stem, afraid he would withdraw it. "It's there! Go and look. You can climb through a hole in the playground fence, back behind them swings."

"Is that the way Cesar comes?"

Kalie shook her head. "He comes by car. That's the trick, you see. The old ring, it used to be just in the park, somewhere nice and leafy. Then they put in the highway right next to it. Cesar just bumps off the roadway there, onto the grass, and wham! he's right at the ring. He tells somebody to meet him there and they leave their car on the street outside the park. So he's got his car and they don't have theirs, and if things go bum, nobody can catch him."

Robbie released the bottleneck, and she snatched the pipe toward her. Unwilling to set it aside, she gripped the blowtorch in her knees below the table, lit it, and brought it to bear on the upper stem. Again the crack dissolved into a sizzling brown puddle as the bottle filled with white smoke and Kalie relaxed. She looked at him, tilted her head as if to offer him a hit, but never eased the grip of her arms on the pipe.

He shook his head. She sucked again at the lower stem, a long, violent draught. He stood, leaving it to her, but as he did she placed her hand on the wrist near his pocket.

"I couldn't help noticing," she said, pausing to gasp for a breath, "you got another one a these in your pants there. You gonna use that? Or maybe you wanna work a twist with me for the last frog?"

She tilted her head coquettishly, to tempt him into the bargain, leaning forward to allow him to look down her robe. He caught a glimpse of her collarbone and desiccated

235

breasts over the soiled lace edge of a nightgown. She was about his mother's age in years, but hardly more than a skeleton. His mother had died sooner than that. Her hand caught a wisp of hair and tucked it deftly back into the bun held by a rubber band. Her eyes were less hungry now, softened by the smoke. He touched her cheek with his fingertips, and took her hand in his. When he let go, the vial was in her palm.

"Why don't you just take it?"

For a second she looked offended, but closed her hand on the vial and thought better of it. She smiled weakly, her lips no longer able to stretch across her teeth.

"That's real nice of you, Robbie. Giving it to me like that. I guess that's why they been calling you boys the Robbin' Hoods, huh?"

He looked at her sharply, but her eyes were closed, enjoying her joke and the fine white smoke, laughing to herself in silence.

26

Kayoko Wasabe was alone when Shelly and Homer buzzed from the lobby of Eddie Tanagaki's apartment building, and hesitant to let them up. "Eddie not home," she repeated, in reply to their questions about his whereabouts and the anticipated time of his return.

After the second time, Lowenkopf said, "Miss Wasabe, excuse me but wasn't that zoology book in your arms last time an English-language edition? It would be hard to read one of those with no more English than you seem to be capable of now. Either hit that button or get on the phone and ring up your attorney."

At the sound of the word *attorney*, the intercom went dead and the lobby door buzzed loudly. Lowenkopf caught the handle and held it for Greeley, who stepped through, surveying the scene. There was one elevator and an interior staircase, with another probably emptying into the street on the side of the building. To the right of the elevator, past a cigarette machine, was the corridor to the rear exit. Homer took up a post outside that door, from which he could see the side staircase. With all the likely escape routes covered, Shelly was ready to approach the apartment.

He rang briskly, three times, announcing his arrival with a maximum of noise. If Eddie was hiding anywhere nearby, Shelly wanted him to believe there was a division of police downstairs. But Eddie was not on the premises, or so it appeared when Kayoko opened the door.

"Yes?"

She was dressed in a man's sleeveless undershirt and tight denim shorts. The blue was faded nearly to white on her rear, and a soft fringe of cotton brushed her thighs where the trouser legs had been cut off. The shirt was stained under her arms and over her breasts near the nipples, which showed darkly through the thin fabric. She wore dirty tennis shoes with a hole at one toe, and her knees were filthy with dust. Behind her, a trunk sat open in the middle of the floor, surrounded by a few orange crates and stacks of cardboard cartons.

"Going somewhere?" asked Shelly.

She shook her head and looked over the evidence. "Not me. Eddie. He has to bring his father's body back to Tokyo tonight. I'm doing his packing for him."

"Nice of you," said Shelly, forcing a smile.

Kayoko didn't return it. "Just part of my loyalty to the company."

Shelly nodded. "Nisei Imports certainly get their wages' worth from you."

She laughed. "You don't know the half of it! This . . . is a little vacation."

She tried to kick an orange crate from the front of the couch, but it was too crammed with ledgers to be budged. Shelly squatted beside it, lifting from his thighs, and set it down with a grunt alongside the trunk.

"Do they ask for more strenuous work than this?"

"More strenuous?" She thought about it for a second while she waited for him to seat himself on the newly accessible couch. When he did, she sat at the opposite end and said, "Not more strenuous. More straining work, yes."

Shelly picked up the distinction as a way to keep her talking. "There are lots of different kinds of strain in a job like yours, aren't there? Some seem directly to help make sales. Others seem to help less."

She was sensitive to the implications of his observation and knelt at the foot of the couch to repack a perfectly packed carton. "It is the boss who decides what the company needs," she said, reciting an article of faith.

"But which boss?" wondered Shelly. "The big boss in Tokyo, thousands of miles away? The titular boss of your local sales office? Or another boss, closer to home?"

"My personal boss, whoever he is."

"I'll bet he's plenty personal. Ms. Wasabe, what is your principal responsibility to the company right now?"

Her eyes rose sharply to meet his, with a streak of outrage in them. "I was hired by Mr. Kadomatsu, to help with the billing last summer. He was pleased with my work and promoted me to an executive assistant in the television department."

"Where you met Eddie Tanagaki?"

"That's right."

"Who fell for you immediately. I can see why. So he told you about his connections in the upper reaches of Nisei."

"He didn't have to tell me. Everybody knows. Eddie's going to be an important man in this firm one day."

"He certainly had a head start! A bloodline to the top. All he had to do was sell a few TV sets to the Americans, and make his father proud of him. Only they didn't exactly jump into the stores, did they?"

"He's doing all right, for a new man on the job."

"Is he? That's what I've been wondering. You know, my own set's getting old now, and the picture's not so good. A lot of snow and static, just when I want to watch. I've been keeping an eye out for a new one and you know what? I haven't seen a Nisei in any of the stores."

Kayoko nodded vigorously, as if to imply the explanation was perfectly obvious. "Eddie doesn't sell to any department stores. He targets the local retailer. That was his marketing innovation when he first figured out this territory."

"That's what Kadomatsu said. But I don't like department stores for this sort of item. Too much overhead. So I've been looking myself in some smaller, local stores."

"The wrong ones, it sounds like."

"Are there small retailers in other neighborhoods who carry Eddie's brand? Why don't you give me some names, then, because I'd like to check them out."

Kayoko crossed to the trunk in the center of the room, pulled out a neatly folded sweater by the sleeve, and began to refold it. "Why don't you call Kadomatsu for that kind of information? Names of retailers and so on. I don't know enough about it."

"Really? In the television department? I expect Kadomatsu would refer me to you."

For a moment she was silent, shaking loose the sweater she had folded twice, and folding it again.

"What does he do with them?" Shelly asked gently.

The quietness of his voice made her look up, slowly, almost against her will. "Hnh?"

"Eddie. What does he do with the television sets he can't sell? Not the ones in the warehouse. I mean the others—the ones he reports he sells."

"I don't know what you mean. Some are stolen, of course, or broken, in shipping and deliveries . . ."

"I'm not talking about the stolen ones, like the sets you lost in the van when the Robbin' Hoods took it. I'm interested in business as usual for Eddie Tanagaki. A shipment comes in, assembled in Taiwan. Eddie and Frank go meet it at the docks and drive back the sets in the van. What happens next? What does Eddie do with the sets? Do most go over a cliff somewhere? Except, of course, for that special one with snow in the tube instead of a picture. That's how he pays for the sets he can't sell—with cash from smuggled cocaine."

Kayoko's lips had turned pale as he spoke but she maintained her composure. Her voice, however, cracked a bit when she said, "Why do you ask me these things? If you are right, Frankie Muntz would know everything. Go ask him! I'm sure you can frighten him as effectively as you do a woman."

Lowenkopf shook his head, sidestepping her assault on his manliness. "I don't think Muntz knows a thing about it. That's where you came in."

She looked down at the sweater.

"Your interest in zoology—it wouldn't focus, by any chance, on ichthyology, would it?"

She shook her head violently.

"We can check with your school," he said. "Because if you've shown a particular interest in fish—that would explain a whole lot of things."

"Explain . . . ?"

"Fish poisons, for one. Let's imagine Eddie had a reason to want Frankie out sick. Let's say he needs the van, for example, to dump a few television sets. So he convinces a friend with access to a lab to lift a smidgen of ciguatera, which he slips into Frankie's lunch. Just enough for an awful bellyache—enough to send him home. Now let's say Eddie's father, in checking out Yakura as a potential successor, learns something curious about his son's business. Or starts to suspect something fishy and begins to make inquiries. Eddie, we'll say, adores the old bastard, and can't stand to fail in his eyes. So what does junior do? He arranges to send papa home to Japan a little ahead of schedule. By slipping him some of the stuff that gives Frank Muntz those belly-aches. Only Eddie doesn't realize that the same poison is a lot more lethal when it's injected than when it's swallowed in a chili dog."

Kayoko stood warily, backing away.

Shelly grabbed her wrist. "The red carnation—the only one in a field of white flowers. You jabbed him through the shirt front with a specially dipped stickpin when you fixed it to his lapel. Then, in case anyone remembered your stab-bing Akira, you jabbed pins into a few other guests—including me—so he wouldn't be the only one. We were looking for slivers of poisoned champagne glass, but all the alcohol did was speed the poison faster through his system.

241

"How did Eddie feel when he realized he killed his father? That was never part of the plan, I'll bet—just to send him home ill before he learned the truth about his son's sales campaign for the Nisei Import Company. But Shirane figured it out, didn't he? He must've known Akira was making inquiries about his son. So Eddie had to kill him too, before he talked to me. Shirane's taste for *fugu* made it easy. Midtown was convinced . . . we would've been too, if it hadn't been for some teenage kids with a grudge against a coke dealer.

"You see, Eddie was robbed this week, just as he was selling his Thai coke to a man named Cesar Catalan. The thieves grabbed the money, the coke, a camel-hair coat, and two vehicles: Nisei's delivery van and a red Ferrari Testarossa belonging to Catalan. Eddie would've written the van off and let Frankie take the blame for its disappearance, but this man Catalan is another sort of character. He wanted to know who had ripped him off. So he reported his car as a larceny and insisted we investigate—which turned up some nuns and an African king, given the vehicles anonymously. Eddie heard about that from us at the greenhouse and invented the Robbin' Hoods. He wrote a xenophobic note from a terrorist gang and dropped it in daddy's briefcase, in a desperate attempt to distract our attention before we hit on his smuggling. Shirane didn't buy it—he knew Akira was worried about his son. So Eddie begged you to fetch him some blowfish poison from your school's zoology lab.

"Which leaves you, Miss Wasabe, in a very delicate position. You actually administered the fatal dose of poison to Akira Tanagaki—at his son's instructions, no doubt, but that doesn't help your case much from a legal standpoint. And you provided the blowfish toxin Eddie used to kill Shirane—which makes you an accessory before the fact. These are two very serious charges. I'm afraid I'm going to have to inform you of your rights under the law."

Reciting Miranda, Shelly brought out his handcuffs from the back of his belt. Kayoko threw herself on the couch and buried her face in her hands. She looked as if she were weeping, but no sound accompanied the contortions of her face and shuddering of her limbs. He knelt beside the couch near her shoulder and said, "There, there," as he snapped the first bracelet around her pale, thin wrist.

She sat up, staring at the dull steel as if she had seen it there in a nightmare. The shame of accusation gave way to the reality of likely imprisonment, and he saw her mind working furiously as her mouth twisted right and left, until finally she said, "Eddie Tanagaki can go fuck himself. So many promises, and this is how he delivers on them! I can tell you all about him—whatever you need to know."

"Unfortunately," said Shelly, snaring her free wrist and fastening the second cuff, "there's not a lot we don't know already."

"You want to know where he is now, I'll bet," Kayoko said, stretching the length of chain between bracelets.

"We'll find him," said Shelly.

"But not right now," she insisted, "not while he's in the middle of a sale to Cesar Catalan! You could catch them in the act—wouldn't that be nice for you! And worth a lot to your district attorney, too."

Shelly couldn't deny the appeal of her offer. "They're making a deal right now? I could talk to the district attorney, if your information's good. Maybe get him to reduce the charges against you."

She shook her head. "No reducing! No charges at all."

"Can't do that," said Shelly. "I'd have to reach someone, to cut you loose on a plea bargain."

"No time to bargain," Kayoko said, "or you'll miss them—too late! We have to go now to catch them in the park."

Shelly looked at the lovely zoology student and felt sure that the district attorney would rather bust Cesar Catalan. On the other hand, Shelly would shy away from the gefilte fish if Kayoko was his waitress in a deli. He picked up the phone and dialed the captain, who was out—at the hospital, the desk sergeant said. He tried the district attorney's office, which was closed for the evening. Kayoko stood behind him, watching him dial. When he hung up the second time, she raised her manacled wrists and rattled the chain.

"Now or never."

He took the key from his pants pocket and opened the cuffs. "All right," he said, "no charges. If this works out the way you promised and we catch them making a buy. Otherwise, we'll both have a lot of explaining to do."

"Domo arigato," said Kayoko, twisting her freed wrists. "You got a car downstairs?"

They picked up Homer at the back of the building and hurried off into the Reliant. The blond detective saw his partner hold open the front door for Kayoko to sit between them, and frowned over the roof of the car. "She isn't under arrest?"

Shelly shook his head. "I made a deal."

Homer frowned. "Don't we bust anybody anymore?"

"We will," Shelly promised, "sooner or later. We're going to nab Catalan."

"Where?"

"Someplace in the park."

"I thought we had a murder rap in hand here. You've traded it away for a coke dealer in the bush?"

"This is the best shot at Catalan we're ever going to get. You want to keep looking for the kids who stole his car? While he blows away the suspects one by one?"

Homer climbed in the passenger door after Kayoko. "I hate it when you go upstairs alone to make a collar."

Shelly cranked the engine, loosened the brake, and gripped the steering wheel in two hands. "Where?"

Kayoko studied both directions down the street. "That way, I think. No, the other way . . . behind us."

Homer looked away, gazing out his window. Shelly fit the gear in drive, pulling away from the curb. He put the bubble on top, turned on the light but hesitated with the siren. At the corner she said, "Left. Is that uptown? Left!"

27

Eddie Tanagaki parked the silver Volkswagen van at the curb outside the Waring Avenue entrance to Bronx Park and locked the passenger door. He rolled up the window on the driver's side and twisted the handle a bit farther, just to be sure. He climbed out, tried the door behind him, then checked to make sure the rear door was also secure. He was taking no chances, tonight, that the van might be stolen in the course of his business. One theft and recovery was difficult enough to explain, to the police as well as Kadomatsu. A second would certainly give him away. He caught himself sighing at the thought of it, an expression of the guilt and shame he felt over the whole business, a longing for relief and punishment. But he had done too much to protect himself already. Caving in now would be just what you'd expect from a typical Japanese son— something he refused to be.

He had made mistakes, of course. That much he saw clearly. The dosage he had given his father was intended to send him home. How was he supposed to know the difference an injection would make? Kayoko should have known something about that—why she had settled on zoology instead of medicine was a mystery to him. Why study fish in America? That kind of thing made sense in Japan, where people cared about fish. The only thing that counted here was money, and making enough of it. Hadn't his father told him that often enough when he was growing up?

He had taken that lesson to heart, as his father had hoped he would, and it had proved the death of old Akira. There was a certain satisfaction in that. Otherwise, there was only the shame he would feel before his mother, when she knew. He meant to say *if she knew,* but couldn't shake the feeling she would get it out of him, once he arrived at Tokyo airport. Her tears he could countenance, but the look of dread in her eyes . . . it was the old way of thinking, he knew, that a widow was half-dead herself. He hated that part of her, but had never figured out how to stand up to it. He would glare at her fiercely; her face would buckle in agony as she threw herself on the coffin; then—then what could he do?

He put it out of his mind, as he had put so many things over the last few days. The sales report he had sent to the home office in Tokyo would lead them to expect nearly forty thousand dollars next month. The only way to supply that much money was to make up for what had been stolen. He had only half of the shipment from Thailand still on hand, but it could cover the bill if he added his personal reserve. It almost made him laugh—the only drug importer in America who never earned a penny for his labors and risks! But personal income was never his real motive for arranging the Thai connection.

Protected from the light of the street lamp overhead by the deep black shadow of the van, he withdrew the pistol from the waistband of his pants, squeezed it by the grip, and replaced it. He shook his briefcase, testing the weight. Everything seemed in order, as it had each time, including the night they had been robbed. He didn't want to think about that just then, either, so he pushed it from his consciousness into a vague compartment that included his father's murder, his mother's anguish, his personal sense of family honor—all of the things that had driven him into this awful business. For a moment he didn't distinguish between Nisei Imports and the cocaine trade. Then he stepped out from the shadow of the van and disappeared into the park.

The lawn where old men played cards during the day was empty now, as Catalan had said it would be. There was a paved tar path through some leafy trees. That would lead to a playground on the right, and beyond, to their assignation site at the white circle. In general, he trusted Catalan with these sorts of things—not to meet indoors, on his own ground, of course, but with directions to secluded public places. After all, Catalan needed to buy the coke as much as he needed to sell it, didn't he? He would hardly risk an entire import route for a briefcase worth a few thousand dollars. Jimmy had always shown up on time, just where they had arranged.

But you couldn't be absolutely sure with these people. You couldn't rely on the constancy of their motives, or their ability to see where their true interests lay. What if Catalan ran short and thought of Eddie as his chance to find his feet? Or if Jimmy decided to stiff his boss and go into business for himself? How better to start than with a free shipment, stolen from a Jap who couldn't report it or complain? The idea sent a chill through Eddie's bones, which seemed to be rattling inside—as usual, at this point in a sale. He could not see through the trees to the playground, and that made him nervous, too.

And then he saw it: the short path to the playground gate and the swings and seesaw inside. In the headlights from the highway on the far side, he saw figures of people moving inside. What were they doing in there? Drugs, probably. And wrecking the place. Couldn't they even manage to keep out vandals overnight? Chain-link fences were susceptible to wire cutters, of course, and kids could always climb over. Still, a little fear of being caught inside would go a long way toward keeping them clear. So he and Catalan could meet in the back without fear of being seen.

247

He passed the gate and at the end of the fence left the path, cutting right across the grass. It did not take him long to find the dilapidated white circle, about as high as his hips, tucked between the back of the playground and some trees lining the highway. Catalan was not yet there—as he expected. He had come a few minutes early, just to take the lay of the land, in case he needed to know it. He checked the far extension of the path, beyond the spot, where it dipped through a grassy area past a green wooden bench and climbed toward a farther breach in the stone park wall. He could run that way, if he had to, escape to Bronx Park East and double back to the van. Or, in a desperate emergency, he could run out onto the highway in sight of passing cars. He liked this place: there were multiple exits, too many to be covered by Catalan or the police. He lay down his case sideways at the foot of a tree about ten yards from the ring of white stone and peered through the links of the playground fence. A couple necked on a dark bench between the moon and the monkey bars; a kid in a yellow shirt rocked on a swing.

Eddie sat there for about thirty minutes, waiting for Jimmy Twotoes. This was longer than he usually waited— what was keeping Twotoes? Had something unexpected gone wrong again? His fingers closed on his briefcase grip and he almost fled. But he needed this sale, needed the cash, and decided to wait out the delay. Maybe Jimmy had been held up by his boss. These things happen in any business. Their last encounter would make him more cautious; Eddie could understand that. Maybe they were checking *him* out, wondering if he had something to do with the robbery. That made him more nervous, but he didn't really believe it. Catalan must know a hundred men more likely to rob him than Eddie—no dealer with any self-respect would tolerate such a suspicion. So where was he? Eddie waited another ten minutes, nearly despaired, then jumped up as a long headlight beam swept the ring from a car turning off the highway.

A black Porsche. It had to be Jimmy, arriving at their

meeting by car. Eddie felt cheated, almost. Hadn't they agreed to meet on foot? It had been he, of course, who wanted to do so: no more chances with the van. But Catalan had agreed. Did they actually stipulate that *both of them* should arrive on foot? He couldn't remember. And it didn't really matter now, in any case. They were together; they would make the necessary adjustments. Jimmy would climb out of the Porsche as he had climbed from the Ferrari, with a grin on his face and a fist in his pocket. They would exchange no greeting, swap the briefcase for a bankroll, and go their separate ways. A business like any other—cleaner than most, cash on the barrelhead. A straight-forward exchange of goods for capital with no bullshit about it.

But it was not Jimmy who stepped out of the Porsche.

It was somebody as big as Twotoes, who did not head toward Eddie, or even toward the stone ring, but back behind the car, where he took up a position behind the trunk. Then another door opened, and again it wasn't Jimmy. Another big man climbed out and edged along the front of the car, crouching beside the right headlight with an automatic weapon in his hand. He scoured the scene in front of the car, scrutinizing the oncoming traffic and the empty tar path through the park. Then he raised an arm and signaled toward the cab, a wave that might have meant *attack!* The car opened a third time and a figure emerged from the front seat with the sharp silhouette of a stylish suit and the creak of expensive leather. In his hand was a slim pouch, like a big wallet or woman's purse. He headed straight for the circle and slapped the pouch on the worn flat stone.

"Come, Eddie," said a voice. "Let's trade."

It was chilling, that sound in the soft night air. But also irresistible. Eddie recognized it at once as the voice of a man he had never hoped to meet—civil, collected, and cruel. Eddie stood, raising the case to his chest like a shield as he moved toward the man in the center of the ring, his heart beating audibly in his chest.

"Señor Catalan? I didn't expect—I mean, you didn't say you would be . . ."

The man reached out a gloved hand. Involuntarily Eddie drew back, fearful of what it might contain. It was empty; he was reaching for the briefcase. Eddie handed it over, hesitating to pick up the pouch of money until Catalan approved the purchase. But Catalan did not open the briefcase. He lifted the pouch from the top of the ring and tossed it to Eddie.

"Do you count it?"

"With Jimmy? Usually, yes. But there's no need for that tonight, with you . . ."

"Count it."

Eddie opened the pouch and counted the bills. Thirty-two thousand. All in hundreds.

"It's fine."

"Good," said Catalan. "Everything as usual. We don't want anything different."

Eddie shook his head in agreement.

Without taking his eyes off Eddie, or turning his head, Catalan held out the briefcase behind him and called distinctly, "Vincenzo."

The man who had disappeared behind the Porsche was now to reappear and take the briefcase from his hand. Catalan stood confidently, for a full minute, holding the case extended while he continued to stare at Eddie. But the man did not reappear. Eddie watched with horror as another figure appeared instead to take the case from Catalan—a young black man in a yellow shirt and camouflage pants, with a shotgun in his hands and a stocking pulled over his head.

"Thanks, Cesar. Thanks again."

Catalan turned, took in the gun and stocking together, and said with grim satisfaction, "You are the same one who robbed me earlier this week?"

It was an observation rather than a question, which the kid couldn't help but confirm. "That's twice now. Don't it make you feel like a fool?"

Catalan said nothing, sizing up the robber without regret,

as if their face-to-face encounter were worth the price of a second interrupted transaction. "That was a messy thing you did to my friend Twotoes."

The shotgun wavered for an instant but relocated its mark on Catalan's smooth forehead. "Jimmy was just a distraction, man. He came after us, so we had to do something about him. The real target has always been you."

"Me?" said Catalan with a note of mock surprise, as if the kid had just declared him Mr. America. "But not a business matter. Something personal."

There was a long pause in which the kid seemed to struggle with his memories. "A bit of both, to you. My mother."

"Yes," said Catalan, "I think I remember her. Your mouth has a familiar purse."

His eyes flickered toward the back of the Porsche and the kid laughed. "Don't go looking for your muscleman there. He's not coming back no more. And if your man in the bushes by the highway so much as stirs a finger, I'll blast your fucking head to kingdom come."

Catalan glanced sharply toward his second bodyguard, who stood with his weapon in his hand. As he started to raise it, Catalan said, "Please lower the gun, Willie."

The kid watched it descend with one eye on the coke dealer. "Have him toss it."

Willie did not seem to like the sound of that at all, but on Catalan's nod, threw his weapon, a black Walther automatic that glinted once in the headlights before disappearing into the weeds under the Porsche.

"Smart man," said the kid.

"Not at all," Catalan insisted. "You got me."

Eddie didn't trust the sound of that at all. But he didn't want to call attention to himself, either. If they were being robbed, he hoped the robber might overlook the wad in the pouch under his arm. He tried standing perfectly still, as if he might disappear into the landscape as a tall, skinny blade of grass. The kid looked ready to run.

"What now?" asked Catalan, making no effort to keep the impatience out of his voice.

"Now?" the kid replied. "Time to die, Cesar."

Catalan winced. "That will make a big noise. Don't you want the money first?"

The kid was plenty suspicious. He wouldn't take his eyes from the dealer long enough to pick up a pile of money.

Catalan turned to Eddie. "Hand it over."

Eddie couldn't believe he had been betrayed by Catalan— was there no longer even honor among thieves? Catalan's life was certainly forfeit—did he have to surrender Eddie's cash as well? He didn't move, but Catalan tugged the pouch from under his arm and offered it to their assailant.

"There should be thirty-two thousand dollars there. If our Asian friend hasn't lifted any."

Eddie almost shook his head in protest, but thought better of it. His discretion was soon rewarded—the kid didn't reach for the pouch. And, to his relief, Catalan handed it back again.

"No? Enough cash, eh? How about the Porsche, then? You have a taste for foreign cars."

Catalan flicked his wrist and a silver key flew through the air, lit by the headlights of a passing car. The glare caught the kid's eye, which flickered for an instant from the person of the dealer.

Kabloom! That was when the blast came from under Catalan's coat. The expression on his face did not change at all: the same thin smile that had held all along. But the expression on the face of the kid changed dramatically, even through the stocking over his head, as if he had suddenly remembered something he had forgotten to do, a horribly disturbing thought. And then he crumpled, gripping his stomach, where a black hole had opened up, already filling with darkness. In an unexpected spurt from deep inside him, an artery suddenly pumped. Soon blood was everywhere, making mud of the ground below their feet, staining the cuffs of their trousers. A moan arose from the earth below their feet, which lasted forever and died. Eddie felt sick to his stomach but choked it back in his throat. Catalan held his eyes throughout the episode, sizing up the likelihood of his silence. His hand came out of his pocket with a piece of metal in it, a shotgun with a ragged stump of a barrel. Just a yawning mouth—which rose through the stinking air like a black moth, settling on Eddie.

"I'm sorry, Eddie," Catalan said. "I don't like to do business this way."

That was the last Eddie remembered before the noise and lights—a whine that sprang from nowhere to fill his head as the highway suddenly turned its brightness on him. He was filled with a sudden resentment. Unwilling to fail at his father's business, he had done what was necessary to succeed, and it led him . . . here? *Is this where it ends—in the grass at the side of a highway?* His chest throbbed with a terrible rage that burst from his mouth in a mournful wail—the wail his mother would have loosed. Eddie felt his knees give way as he tumbled down, the grass racing up to assault his face with a sweet, sticky stench of blood.

28

Shelly and Homer approached the scene from the highway, as Kayoko instructed. She had suggested the same to Eddie, after studying the assigned rendezvous point on Hagstrom's map of the Bronx; but Eddie had been unwilling to risk the van again, and chose to approach as Catalan directed, on foot through the park. It was lucky for her boyfriend that the two detectives made no such veto of her directions, because when they neared the ring of white stone, they saw Catalan threatening a shivering Eddie with a slim form fallen at his feet.

Then they saw Eddie faint dead away, confronting Catalan's sawed-off. That was more than enough to kick in the siren and go bumping off the highway onto the grass, blocking the Porsche's escape. Their headlights caught Eddie and Catalan, as the dealer grabbed a briefcase, wheeled on his expensive shoes, and fled toward the playground. His bodyguard dove for cover, producing from inside his coat a second, backup weapon, which spat a choking round at the police. Shelly pushed Kayoko's head under the dash, while Homer returned fire. Slamming on the

Reliant's brakes, cutting the engine, Shelly leaped from his door and took off after Catalan.

Behind him, he heard Homer curse as he shouldered his way through the passenger door, rolling to the ground and firing into the bushes at the edge of the highway. There was a staccato burst of return fire and Homer's single, nine-millimeter reply. Kayoko followed Shelly out the driver's side, raising her hands and shrieking as she ran across the grass perpendicular to his line of progress. She was after Eddie, of course; she must have seen him go down. But Shelly did not have time to think about it, because at that moment Catalan appeared inside the playground fence, raised his hand, and *Kabloom!* the earth exploded at Lowenkopf's feet.

Shelly leaped over the smoking ground, tumbled to earth and smashed his shoulder into the concrete base of the fence. The thick, gray wire doubled back at the bottom of the lowest links, catching the fabric and tearing his sleeve as he started to rise. But it also pulled at the weave of the fence, exposing the rent where the fence parted at an opening in the rear wall. Shelly ducked his head and went through, holding back the gray wire that ached for a second taste of his jacket. This was how the kids went in, he realized, after the main gate had been locked for the night. Catalan had evidently arrived by Porsche, so he might not have known the gate ahead was chained. It was all a matter of who moved, when. If he kept between the fugitive and the hole in the fence, Shelly thought, he should have the crack dealer trapped at last.

There was a *clang* from the main gate, which sounded like Catalan had discovered his mistake. Shelly knelt and trained his gun, but the shadow at the gate merged into the darkness behind it, heading for the far side of the brick restroom house. In the penumbra of a street light over the basketball court, he thought he saw a movement on a bench near the monkey bars. Shelly sidled over carefully, keeping the street light from shining on or behind him, since a silhouette made as clean a target as an illuminated police-man.

As he neared the bench, he was certain that he saw movement behind it. What was Catalan doing back there? He approached cautiously, a step at a time, holding his Beretta in both hands in front of him. Catalan's face did not appear at the side or top of the bench, and no telltale glint of metal gave his weapon away. Shelly crouched three benches down the line, two benches, one—there was no further cover. He checked a last time for the mouth of a shotgun, said a quick prayer, and dashed across the last bench, squatting behind it and poking his gun at a twisted figure writhing on the ground.

"Don't move a muscle," Shelly hissed. "Not one."

The twisting stopped immediately on his whispered command. In the dark shadow of the bench, Shelly could not at once make out which side was Catalan's head and shoulders, and which side was his feet. There seemed to be too many limbs. He waved the barrel from one end to the other, keeping it aimed somewhere toward the middle.

"All right," he said, breathing again, "now, on your feet. Slowly."

Then he was really confused, because the twisted figure on the ground separated into two, with two heads rising in different places. As they cleared the top of the bench and moved into the light from the basketball court, Shelly realized that neither of the heads actually belonged to Cesar Catalan, but to a boy and girl in their early teens, with flushed faces and rumpled shirts pulled up under their armpits. Their jeans were unbuttoned and unzipped, halfway down their hips, and their shoes were off, abandoned where they had landed under the bench. The two lovers didn't know what to say—their eyes shifted back and forth between each other and their stockinged feet, looking almost as embarrassed as Lowenkopf felt.

He moved away his gun. "Police," he said. "You shouldn't be doing that here."

The boy nodded, glancing at his partner. "We had no idea you fellows felt so strongly about it."

There was another *clang* from the far side of the playground, duller than the sound at the gate, and Shelly saw a blur of darkness scaling the far fence. He braced himself to fire his gun and called out, "Stop! Police!"

The climber paid no attention, jangling his way through the linked diamonds to the top of the fence.

Shelly squeezed the trigger. The gun exploded in a loud flash that blinded him for a moment. He listened and heard the climber drop with a thud on the far side of the fence—and pad off through the rustling grass.

"You don't fool around!" said the girl. "It's a good thing we froze when we did."

Her boyfriend covered her hand on his arm and rubbed her gripping fingers.

Shelly had no time to explain, but pulled them along to the base of the fence and ordered the boy to kneel.

"Here?" He looked doubtfully at his girlfriend.

"Do it," she said. "Before he gets mad."

The boyfriend knelt, and Shelly stepped on his back, jumping for the top of the fence. He didn't quite make it but stuck his shoe in a diamond of the links and hoisted himself over. He fell on the far side heavily, flat on the soles of his feet, with a sore ankle and thirty yards between him and the fugitive—who was not heading back toward the entrance, but climbing a low hill deeper into the park. Shelly knew that incline. It led to an overpass crossing the highway and, on the other side of the road, a rear turnstile of the Botanical Gardens, blocked by a row of metal bars and padlocked for the night.

If Catalan scrambled over that, he would disappear into the gardens. But if Shelly could catch him before the top, there was nowhere else to run—on each side of the overpass was a ten-foot drop to the speeding traffic below.

Shelly raced up the hillside path, expecting to find Catalan on the turnstile at its end. What he found instead surprised him. Catalan had not hurried to the back gate of the gardens but stood halfway down the overpass, leaning over a parapet. Shelly crouched immediately, thrusting forth his weapon, searching for a glint of Catalan's.

"Drop it!" Shelly commanded.

Catalan did just that—dropping the briefcase over the side, showing his empty hands.

"It's dropped," he said. "Don't shoot. I'm unarmed."

Shelly watched over the low wall as the briefcase landed in the back of a pickup and roared off into the traffic. The car behind it blocked the license plate, which he could hardly have read in any case, given the distance and angle. It was too dark for Shelly to note anything else before the truck disappeared among red taillights in three twinkling lanes.

"What happened to the weapon?"

"What weapon?" said Catalan. "I don't have a weapon." He glanced toward the edge of the overpass. "Maybe one of them has a weapon, too."

"With your left hand," Shelly ordered, "open up your jacket. Slowly. Keep your fingers where I can see them."

Catalan did exactly as instructed, careful not to give cause for Shelly to overreact. With a show of great care, he undid a button, exposing the tailored lining. No holster was strapped to his shoulder, or any other weapon to his torso. His shirt was still incredibly crisp. He let the jacket fall smartly back and, unbidden, raised his arms high above his head.

Shelly recited Miranda and motioned with his Beretta for Catalan to move away from the edge. "Let's go."

Catalan strolled toward him, keeping his arms clearly in sight, wrists together in front of him. "Where?"

Shelly cuffed him. "You're going to jail." He pushed him against the wall and frisked him carefully, searching for the gun, which was nowhere on his person.

Catalan nodded stoically. "Perhaps."

Back at the playground, Homer had moved quickly, calling for backup, ambulance, and a lab team. In addition to the Reliant, two squad cars were parked on the lawn, their red lights blinking silently through the dark trees. There was another car, too, a station wagon, with no lights but the spare look of an official vehicle. Now and then the night was interrupted by a bright flash, as a photographer from the crime scene unit began the first step of the ritual, snapping shots of everything in sight. In the playground, figures were moving. Under the street light by the basketball court, Shelly saw his partner giving instructions to a ballistician and a criminalist, each of whom gripped a lab kit tightly under an arm. Strangest of all, there seemed to be two kids on the seesaw, bouncing each other up and down with abandon. Something about them made him think of . . . Tomas and Thom. Now what were they doing here? Shelly felt a sudden urge to chase his son away.

"C'mon," he said to Catalan, who hung a step behind. His face was composed attentively, but his eyes darted from side to side, surveying the landscape. Shelly gripped his arm.

Passing under the sycamore trees, they followed the fence around to the front and tried the gate, which gave way, unlocked. Homer had seen to it, no doubt, bless his irritating efficiency. Shelly held the cold metal pole with one hand and dragged Catalan with the other, shoving him toward the center of the playground, where Homer leaned against the small brick house. Mounted on an outside wall was a public telephone, into which he was speaking unhappily, grimacing as he nodded with the receiver at his chin. He looked up distractedly when Shelly approached, the handcuffed coke dealer in tow.

"All right, we'll hold everyone here. I said I understood. Until he comes."

He hung up, banging the receiver.

"Look what I found, Homer."

The blond detective glanced at Catalan as if they'd had him all along. "Where's the briefcase?"

Shelly shook his head. "Over the edge of the overpass."

"And the shotgun?"

"He says the same place. Who knows?"

"We'll have some of the boys look around for it. Just in case," said Homer. "We've got to kill some time here, anyway. Speaking of which, your son's out back."

"Thom?"

"Have you another? He and Tomas hitched a ride from the station when I called for a photographer at the scene. They're never called until the shooting's done, so he drove the boys along. Thought he'd save you a trip to the precinct house after all this was over."

Shelly looked around the corner of the restroom house and saw Thom bumping Tomas off his seat. Tomas leaped heavily onto the back of the seesaw, and Thom's side shot into the air.

"Who're we waiting for?"

Homer scowled at the phone on its hook. "Madagascar."

"The captain? Coming here?"

"They informed him of the situation when I called in for backup. He said he wanted to view the scene."

"He drove out from the precinct house? To see a shooting in the park?"

"He wasn't at the precinct house. They had to beep him."

"Where?"

"At the hospital. Visiting some kid."

"What do we do with *him* in the meantime?" asked Shelly with a sidelong glance at his prisoner.

Homer shrugged. "Take him out back, I guess. With the rest of the garbage."

Shelly led Catalan back through the hole in the rear fence, near the rendezvous point by the highway. As they passed the ring of white stone, the criminalist emerged through the fence and squatted in the grass, collecting samples of Robbie's blood. The body lay nearby, staring at the sky with unseeing eyes. A deputy coroner crouched over it, daubing a yellow stain on the gash he had made to insert a thermometer into the liver. Robbie Delaud was already gone, his body turned to evidence. In the still features Shelly saw a trace of the soul who had never shaved and never been a boy. Following his mother into the night—sister Julie would join them soon, clearing her bed in the hospice. Shelly hoped like hell there was a place their family could come together in peace.

29

Catalan stood over the corpse of Robbie Delaud and shook his head in a show of regret. "His homeboys should have taught him always to shoot first."

Shelly didn't bother responding. He looked around the scene for a site to stash the dealer until they took him to the precinct house. He saw Catalan's bodyguard Willie in the back of a squad car, slumped against the seat. Eddie Tanagaki and Kayoko sat in the back of the other. In front of Kayoko was a plainclothes cop, scribbling on a pad as Eddie talked.

"Looks like Eddie's got something to tell us," Shelly said. "Your ears ringing?"

"He can blather whatever he likes about me," said Catalan. "It's a free country. Everyone is allowed to invent the story he tells about himself."

"You're going to have to do some pretty fancy inventing to squirm your way out of this," Shelly said. "We saw you turn a gun on nervous Eddie."

"Who fainted," Catalan reminded him. "He doesn't look too badly hurt to me."

"Sure," said Shelly, "because we got here in time for him. Robbie Delaud wasn't so lucky."

"Self-defense entirely," Catalan said. "Even Eddie will confirm it—not exactly a friendly witness, as you have pointed out. Should the case eventually come to court."

"It'll come," Lowenkopf promised. "We've got you dead to rights, Catalan."

"Do you? We'll see what the lawyers say. In my experience, they throw out charges like this, unless you can find the weapon. Which looks doubtful at the moment."

Shelly remembered the pickup disappearing into taillights on the highway. What were the odds its driver would find the money, or that someone else would find the gun and step forward? "Not for murder, then. For possession."

"Without the coke?"

"For sale. You almost shot Eddie in cold blood. Do you think he'll forget about that?"

"No—that he'll remember," Catalan said. "But I don't think he'll send us both to jail. You have nothing else incriminating him."

"But we do," said Shelly. "We've got him neat as a pin—for killing his father with a red carnation. A nice, fat, murder rap which ought to make him anxious for a deal. Now who do you think he'll trade away? That almost slipped by us, but we couldn't let it drop . . . thanks to you and your Ferrari."

The irony of his situation was lost on Catalan but not the consequences, and a new desperation showed in the crack dealer's eyes. Shelly handed him over to a uniformed officer, who led him back to the Porsche to wait for the captain. Catalan stumbled trying to climb into the rear, landing on the ground next to the tire. He raised himself with difficulty, a pained look on his face, but when the officer bent to lend him a hand, Catalan blew a hole in his chest.

Shelly turned at the sound of the blast, and what he saw amazed him. From somewhere under the parked Porsche, Catalan had drawn a big black Walther P-38, nine millimeters, which he held in his handcuffed grip, pointing it at anyone who moved a muscle toward him. Shelly froze, unwilling to make himself a target, trying to guess just what Catalan thought his next move would be. Behind him, cars zoomed by on the Bronx River Parkway, cutting off any retreat. Around him, in a semicircle, were half a dozen policemen, with twice that number blocking his route through the park to the street. There was a big gun in his hands now—no one would argue with that. What good he could make of that remained to be seen.

The uniformed officer slid along the Porsche, sitting in the grass beside the tire. He left a dark stain on the car door behind him. Shelly's hand ached for his Beretta, and he felt a similar impulse in the cops all around him. Catalan was already a corpse himself, though nothing had yet happened to him—as he must have known he would be before he fired. So what on earth did the son of a bitch have in mind?

The Walther wavered from face to face and settled at last on Shelly, passing and returning to his direction. Catalan peered into the blackness, gauging the yards between them. Was that it? Did he just want to take one of them along? And who better than Shelly, after all? Lowenkopf heard his heart pound. The silence between them hung for a hundred years. Then a flash lit up the darkness as something *zinged* into his ear, rushing toward him with incredible purpose and velocity.

For a moment Shelly couldn't see. Then he realized he had heard the sound diminish, passing his ear. Catalan had missed him. He clapped a hand over his ear, grateful to whatever power decided these things. He blinked as his irises adjusted to the double shock—the flash of powder in the dim night and the darkness that closed in behind it. When he saw again, an amazing sight confronted him.

Catalan had made his break—into the river of headlights behind him. He crouched on the broken line beyond the first lane of traffic, firing the Walther over the hoods of the cars. Two officers knelt at the grassy edge of the parkway, weapons propped in front of them, unable to return fire and unwilling to pursue the fugitive into the speeding traffic.

Homer crossed the playground in a few strides and swung through the hole in the fence. "Are you all right?"

"Fine," said Shelly, pounding his ear to stop the ringing echo. "There's an officer down by the Porsche."

The coroner and ambulance driver were already by the victim, crawling over him, trying to stop the bleeding. His eyes glazed, senseless and empty.

Homer's jaw gripped. "Catalan?"

"Playing in the traffic."

Blam-Blam-Blam! With a noisy round, the coke dealer lunged another lane through the highway. He was almost to the median now, where he would have a much easier time, running along the open grass while they tried to keep up on their side of the road, which was tangled with trees and brush. If they stopped him, it would have to be now, before he crossed the last lane. But which of them was willing to run into traffic while a big Walther took aim at him?

"Let me through here," said Greeley.

Shelly couldn't let his partner tackle Catalan alone, though he wished Homer would reconsider. They crouched at the side of the highway, extending their service revolvers but unwilling to fire into the cars.

"I've got to try it," said Homer. He leaned forward, ready to run. But there was no break in the traffic.

"He's going for it," said Shelly.

Catalan had turned, relying on his crouch to defend his back. They couldn't risk shooting at the level of the tires, no matter how much they wanted him dead. Catalan waited, watching the cars, ready to spring.

"Officer Greeley?"

It was the ambulance driver, a young man with a pale face, who crouched on the grass behind them. "There's a chance we can save your man if we take him now."

"Then take him," said Homer, "for God's sake!"

"Yes, sir!"

Homer looked after the ambulance as it pulled out with a cry of the siren, and that's when it came—a momentary lapse in the first lane of traffic. When Homer wasn't watching.

Shelly didn't really have time to think about it. "Here we go!" he hollered and jumped onto the macadam, throwing his body at the broken white line, which rose to meet him just as a Buick came roaring through behind him. To his left, glowing headlights like an army of fireflies advanced on him, roaring by and turning at once to red. In front of his nose, a 280Z screamed past, and there was Catalan, crouched one lane farther, the Walther pointed back at him.

Blam-Blam-Blam-Blam-Blam! Shelly pressed his face into the highway as the rounds passed overhead and wondered why he had been so anxious to reach that particular spot. Headlight beams rolled over him like tank treads. He couldn't stay down, since the traffic couldn't see him and some happy motorist would grind him into the asphalt. But if he raised himself, Catalan would blow his brains out.

He looked back at the edge of the park, where Homer and Thom waited, horrified. In front of him, Catalan crouched —ready to run, glancing back, waving the Walther. Cars barreled between them, with enough horsepower in each grille to bounce Shelly from this vale of tears. *Zoom*—a Toyota! A Nissan! A BMW! Death rumbled by in every model and year. Shelly clutched his Beretta, his own killing machine, until, unable to do nothing any longer, he fired it twice into the air.

Catalan glanced back, a new desperation in his eyes. The noise must have increased his incentive, because the next moment he dived into the flood of cars. He seemed to move in slow motion, timing his steps to the opportunity he must have thought he saw. A Lincoln passed in front of him, and then he leaped across the middle of the lane. Floating over the black tar, his body craned forward, his back arched, his arms reaching ahead, every muscle straining in the last lap of the race, nearing the yellow finish line at the far edge of the road.

It was then that the Volkswagen caught him.

It was an old bug—light blue, missing the front bumper. It came chugging down in the exhaust of the Lincoln, hidden from their view until the bigger car had passed. Shelly saw the moment in Catalan's eyes when he realized his mistake, an instant before the bug knocked him onto the green median and drove over him for good measure. It attacked

265

with a vengeance, as if the driver of the Volkswagen knew just what he was doing. So it was less of a surprise a moment later when the door of the bug opened and Captain Madagascar climbed out.

He moved to the front of his vehicle and glanced at the body beneath it, then squatted down, inspecting the damage to his fender. Catalan had put a big dent there, splattering the hood of the trunk as well. One headlight, smeared with gore, shone a murky beam on the grass. The captain scowled, glancing over at Shelly, still trapped between the lanes.

"Do you mind telling me what you're doing, sergeant, in the middle of the highway?"

Shelly waved his arms at the oncoming cars, trying to clear a path. "Directing traffic, sir."

Madagascar considered the tracks of his own tires on the greensward and the bloody remains under the front of his vehicle. "It's not your strong suit, is it?"

The sight of the death at the roadside eased the traffic a bit, as motorists slowed to see what had happened. Shelly made use of the morbid interest to cross to the captain, whose show of indifference was slipping now at the edges. His eyes were dark and ringed, and not for Catalan.

Shelly asked, "How is he, sir? Vinnie Nguyen?"

"He'll live," the captain reported. "That's what they say. There's a question of damage to the brain."

"I'm sorry."

On the far side of the road, Thom stood, waiting beside Homer. When he noticed his father look over, he waved. Shelly waved back.

"Yeah. Listen, Lowenkopf . . . why don't you get your own son the hell out of here?"

It seemed to Shelly like a wonderful idea. They took the Reliant—joining the traffic on the highway, driving slower and more carefully than usual. Thom insisted on dropping off Tomas, so it was after eleven o'clock when they arrived at the house the boy shared with his mother and her second husband, Clem. Clem's car was in the driveway. Clem was home from Houston. Shelly felt him at once as they neared the house.

But Clem was not waiting downstairs with Ruth when they rang the bell. She was dressed again in a bathrobe, terry this time, with her hair unbrushed and makeup smudged— probably from sleep. Shelly glanced at the armchair nearest the door and saw her afghan and a book, face down, open to the first or second page. Her face was weary with more than fatigue, and she glared without mercy from the father to the son. She rubbed at Thom's forehead and the scratch on his nose; Shelly offered a prayer of thanks that the eye had not purpled. She did not bother to ask if Thom had eaten, but led him directly into the kitchen, where a cold piece of chicken and a limp salad waited at his place.

The boy tried to meet her silent anger with a noisy display of enthusiasm. "You shoulda seen it, mom. We were every-where today. At the funeral of a dead kid—you shoulda seen his face! Like a baby Frankenstein. Dad let me help him chase down this gangster—who turned out to be fantastic! I mean, we spent the whole night together, him and me. Practically by ourselves. That was after the bombing, of course. We were almost killed in that. These guys drove by and *bang! bang! bang!* blowed the windows in. It was the most bitchin', gnarliest day I ever spent in my life!"

Ruth listened to his recitation without comment, then tugged at Shelly's sleeve. "Would you mind if I had a word with you?"

"Sure," he said uneasily.

"In the other room, please."

She didn't wait for his answer, but led the way from the kitchen. He followed her into the living room like a man going to the gallows—not quite certain what she planned to say, but strongly suspecting she was right.

"Do you mind reminding me," she said before he had quite entered the room, "why you took our son to work with you today?"

"To put the fear of God into him," Shelly replied. "So he wouldn't steal again."

"And is that what you think you did?"

"Well," he said slowly, feeling his way along treacherous terrain, "he did get to see what happens to criminals in the end. What happens to people who break the law."

"I sent him out for you to scare him—and you took him for a walk on the wild side. Did you hear how he reported your day? Bombings! Gang members! That's what he saw today."

"Ruth," he said, "you don't understand . . ."

"I understand plenty," she said. "I understand you. And I understand how your son must feel, after watching you in action. Can't you see how much he enjoyed it? Tell me, what happened out there tonight? Just before you brought him home?"

"We . . . arrested a major crack dealer. And another guy, who murdered his own father."

She groaned. "You broke a case? Just great."

At that moment, Thom stuck his head in the room and his parents broke off their talk. "Mom?"

"What is it, Thom?"

"Can I have a friend over here? A kid I met today?"

"We'll see."

"His name is Tomas. He's got a great sense of humor. I'd go over to his place, only he doesn't have any."

"I said we'll see. Finish your dinner."

Thom ducked back in the kitchen, and Ruth returned to her theme. "You see what you've done? You see? He'll be asking to join a gang next, to make a few bucks dealing drugs."

"Ruth," said Shelly, "calm yourself. He's not about to become a gangster."

"No," she agreed. "Even worse. He'll want to be a cop."

30

Shelly woke up early the next morning, heading down to the precinct house before eight. It was Sunday, a weekend, and their case had been closed—no reason to work on a day off. But there was one task he wanted to do that wouldn't hold until Monday. So he drove in, testing the steering of his Volkswagen Squareback, timing the hesitation as it pulled away from a light, gunning the four cylinders to feel the engine sputter. The play in the wheel, the squeakiness of the brakes, the lightness of the car as it cornered—each of these heightened his sense of anticipation as he pulled up at the garage in back of the precinct.

The mechanic on duty was a man named Norton who everyone liked to call Ralph. He was sitting in a folding chair in front of a black-and-white TV, watching "Sesame Street" as he slurped a burrito, holding it out from his overalls. Shelly sauntered by and watched over the man's shoulder until Oscar disappeared into his trash can. When the mechanic looked up, Shelly said, "The keys to the Ferrari, please."

Ralph glanced over at the sleek red car, gleaming in the

morning sun. It had rained overnight, breaking the heat and leaving pearly droplets on the hood. Ralph swallowed a mouthful of burrito and said, "Hot date? Or just going for a spin?"

Lowenkopf shrugged. "Case closed—no prosecution pending. I'm supposed to return this vehicle where it belongs."

Ralph eyed him sourly but pointed to a rack of keys in the office behind him. "There's a horse on the key chain. Easy does it. A scratch is worth more than your salary."

Shelly found the key, which slid into the lock, fit snugly, and slipped the tumblers. He had to crouch a bit to climb under the roof, falling into the seat. But what a seat: soft leather, well upholstered, surrounded by controls. The dashboard showed plain round dials with orange numbers and needles. Additional buttons on the console behind the gearshift lever controlled the heater and air conditioner, which he flicked on. It took him a moment to find the radio, an Alpine stereo, hidden behind a hinged panel under the dash. The gearshift did not come easily out of first, but he managed it, and sliding the key into the ignition, cranked the engine.

He expected a loud rumbling but heard instead a fairly even growl. The exhaust, too, was surprisingly muted. He adjusted the rear-view mirror, noticed that visibility out the back window (or through the windshield, for that matter) was not too good, and shoved the gearshift into first. The Ferrari rolled forward. He eased past Ralph at his TV set, passed his squareback in the parking lot, and exited through the garage gate, bumping off the curb half a foot past the driveway. He was on the road.

The first sensation of driving was not so much interior as exterior, the sense of *being* a sensation as every male under thirty cast an envious eye his way. The females didn't sneer, either. He could have crossed the Bronx on surface streets, but decided instead to take the long way around, to see what the Testarossa could do on an open highway. He climbed onto the parkway, heading south past the scene of the night before, and gave it some gas when the traffic let up. No sooner had his foot depressed the gas pedal than the car leaped forward, smoothly and powerfully responsive. The steering felt fine, snug in his hands, though the handling was spry enough to require his attention. He slipped through the traffic, in and out, hugging the road. Only a chance glance at the speedometer warned him he was doing better than ninety.

He slowed and toured the borough from the Cross Bronx Expressway. The abandoned buildings and wrecks at the side of the road took on a different aspect in the morning light. Rows of sedans and station wagons crawling over the hills seemed like sheep to his shepherd, an ambling flock through which he could move with the quickness of a wolf. When he crossed into and over the northern tip of Manhattan, turning up the Henry Hudson for the last leg of his joy ride, he couldn't forestall a sense of imminent loss. As he decelerated on approach to the exit ramp, descending into Riverdale, he thought he knew how the astronauts felt on final approach to the earth, touching down a magnificent craft they might never again command.

The streets of Riverdale seemed to sympathize, tall grass sighing on the lawns as he passed. When he arrived at Catalan's building, he did not pull into one of the visitor parking spots, but left the car in the red zone adjacent to the side entrance. A ticket, of course, he could deal with, though he suspected that no one was likely to disturb the car.

Catalan's apartment door was answered by the Mediterranean woman—Esperanza Catalan, his beautiful, grave daughter. She was clad in a simple black dress, knee length with spaghetti straps, and wore a short lace veil bobby-pinned in her hair. She seemed to be alone, though the size of the apartment echoing behind her prevented any certainty. She recognized him at once, without recrimination.

"Sergeant Lowenkopf. How nice of you to come."

"I'm sorry," he said, "for your loss." He meant it, too: not sorry for the death as it affected the rest of the world, but sorry at that moment for the grieving daughter.

She seemed to understand that subtle distinction. "Thank you. My father was not a man whose contribution will be missed. But still"—she paused, dabbing a hanky at the corner of her eye—"I miss him."

"Of course," he said. "May I come in?"

"I'm sorry. I was just about to go out. You may ride with me in the elevator, if you like."

That suited him fine, since the Ferrari was in the street. He held the elevator door for her and she locked her own behind her.

Their ride together was silent. The elevator, which might have suggested intimacy, a man and woman alone, instead enforced a peculiar estrangement, as if any sound might intrude on the private space of the other. When they reached the bright lobby, she started for the front door, but he touched her shoulder gently on the strap. "Follow me."

She hesitated for a moment, and acquiesced. He led her through the side door, beyond which the red Ferrari waited at the curb.

"This is your father's car," he said.

She nodded, biting her lip. "The Testarossa. He wanted one desperately—until he had it."

"I drove it here for you," Shelly explained. "It was being held as evidence. But there's no need for that anymore. You might as well have it now as later."

He held out the keys for her to take them. But she stared past them, at the sensual sweep of the fender over the tire. "I hate this car."

"Pardon?"

"I hate it," she repeated. "This is what my father gave his life for. A powerful machine, costing plenty of money. That is why they buy these things, sergeant. Did you know that? To show how much money they can spend."

Shelly remembered his drive from the precinct house. "There may be other reasons, too, miss."

"No good reasons," she said. "These things are insidious. You buy one, and it makes you feel you need to buy another. You need the strictures of an abbess to resist its sly seduction. Look at it! Sleeping in the sun. Flawlessly styled and shaped and painted. The color of blood—my father's blood, I see in it. I'm sure you see others."

Shelly remembered Robbie Delaud and Felix Aguilar. Their blood was on it, too. Akira Tanagaki and Hitoshi Shirane, more or less directly. And who knew how many others? Jimmy Twotoes, and Robbie's mother, and some day soon, his sister.

"I don't want it," Esperanza said.

Shelly understood her revulsion, but the moment would pass. "It's worth a lot of money."

"I know what it costs," she said. "I know what it cost me. I have plenty of money, now. I don't need this."

"Well," he said, "if you mean that, I can think of some people who do."

She looked at him. "Not you, Sergeant Lowenkopf? No, not for you."

"It was given to some nuns, when it was stolen. They needed a car. They still do."

"Fine," said Esperanza grimly. "That would be more than fitting! Just what the car needs. If the sisters will take it, ask them to pray for him, will you?"

Sister Margaret was more than happy to pray for the soul of their benefactor when the Testarossa arrived for the second time at the curbside of the convent. She had already forgiven the man in the moment of his death, she said. The gift worked a change in her, her faith in divinity restored. She accepted the keys in her cupped palms, mumbling a prayer of thanks as she moved off serenely to check the clutch.

A thought occurred to Shelly: Branigan would certainly hear of the gift—what would he think of them then? He remembered the priest's unspoken suspicions when they had entered his classroom together. That stirred another idea that had been lurking all along in Shelly's mind. He called after Margaret, "Do you mind if I use the facilities in the basement one more time?"

273

"Be our guest," she said. "There are many rooms. This is the house of the Lord."

Shelly had not come prepared to play racquetball. And he knew Father Charles had not yet recuperated sufficiently to come back to the court. But he had composed his mind in an attitude of faith and was determined to see it through.

He entered the high school and made his way down the stairs to the basement. The locker rooms were empty, as he had expected they would be. He found the steps to the racquetball courts and took them two by two, listening for a *thwoom-thwoom* that never in fact rang. He stood at the door of the first court, looking in. Empty. Of course—no sound, so no one was playing. But he could think of no reason not to check the other courts, since he was there. It was only after he had done so, and found each of them empty, that he realized his existential dilemma.

He could walk upstairs, call a cab, and disappear forever from this place. No more anguish over tempted nuns, or fears for their disgrace. His earlier encounter on the racquetball court would soon become a memory, exciting for its spontaneity and its taste of forbidden fruit.

Or he could . . . what? March to the convent and demand to see Sister Sylvia? Who had, in fact, abandoned him after their single moment of lovemaking on the hard wooden floor. What would he say, exactly, to the nun at the door? *The sister and I have a special sort of relationship . . .* That would never do. But there was nowhere else on earth he had seen her, and she was nowhere in sight. He sat down again on the polished floor, resting against the front wall, letting his head fall back. Closing his eyes for a second, he thought, *Where on Earth can she be?*

When he opened them again, he knew without checking that more than a second had passed. There was a stillness in the room and a heat that implied the late afternoon had arrived. Before him, the court was silent and empty—but the rear door now stood open. And beside him, from above, he heard a voice call:

"There you are. I've been waiting to see you again."

He looked up—Sylvia towered over him, once again dressed in sweats. In one hand was a racquet; in the other, a can of balls. The band on her forehead, unstained. Spilling over the sides of the band, a plenitude of blond curls.

"Sister Sylvia?"

She shook her head.

"Not Sylvia?"

"Not 'Sister.' Where did you get that idea?"

It made no sense to him. "Sister Elizabeth called you that. Unless I shouldn't use that title for her, either."

She laughed. "That's all right. Liz is a nun."

He sat up, a great warmth spreading through his chest—from motion or revelation, he didn't care which. "And you're not? Then why did Elizabeth call you . . .?"

"Sister Sylvia? Because Elizabeth, you see, is my mother's elder daughter. Which makes her my personal sister."

It took him a moment to work out the logic—he couldn't believe his luck. "Then you're . . . available?"

"For dinner tonight—yes. For more than that—we'll have to see. I had a good time here the other day, but I'm not usually that kind of girl."

She was just the kind of girl he'd been praying for—a lay sister, he thought they were called, though the term made him uneasy. Sylvia was watching him with bright, untroubled eyes. He accepted the hand she offered him, rising from his seat at the intersection of floor and racquetball wall. As he stood, his knees cracked from long disuse, and his back seemed to straighten vertebra by vertebra. She grinned at the noise.

"You've been sitting here waiting for me for some time, now, haven't you? That's quite an impressive vigil. A romantic soul in there." She poked him in the chest.

He shrugged, trying to tell if she was teasing or approving of him. "Whatever on earth that means."

"A promising sign, I'd say."

She winked, and the gesture carried all of his hopes along. He knew then that his good works on behalf of the convent, and the children served by it, would be richly rewarded one day—and that day might be upon him. As he watched, she pulled the band free from her head and shook out her short blond hair.

"I don't have my car," he said.

"I do. Sitting right at the curbside."

A troubling image seized him. "What make?"

"A Chevy."

He sighed. "Thank God."